RETRIBUTION

RETRIBUTION

AKIO REVELATIONS™ BOOK THREE

CHARLES TILLMAN
MICHAEL ANDERLE

This book is a work of fiction. All of the characters, organizations, and events portrayed in this novel are either products of the author's imagination or are used fictitiously. Sometimes both.

Cover Art by Jake @ J Caleb Design
http://jcalebdesign.com / jcalebdesign@gmail.com

A Michael Anderle Production

LMBPN Publishing
PMB 196, 2540 South Maryland Pkwy
Las Vegas, NV 89109

First US edition, July, 2020
Version 1.02, August 2020
eBook ISBN: 978-1-64971-067-3
Print ISBN: 978-1-64971-068-0

DEDICATION

To my Wife Danette, thank you for being behind me while I did this.
A huge thank you to Michael Anderle who let me come and play in his world.
There are also two others who worked hard to help me bring this to you:
John Ashmore, Alpha reader extraordinaire
Tracey Byrnes, Alpha reader and first pass editor who kept me and my sentence structure on track. I couldn't have done it without you.
And most of all thanks to you the Kurtherian Gambit Fans for reading.

—Charles

To Family, Friends and
Those Who Love
to Read.

May We All Enjoy Grace
to Live the Life We Are
Called.

— Michael

Thanks to the JIT Readers

Rachel Beckford
Diane L. Smith
Peter Manis
Misty Roa
Tim Bischoff
Jim Caplan
Kelly O'Donnell
Dave Hicks
Angel LaVey
Deb Mader
Veronica Stephan-Miller
Dorothy Lloyd
Jeff Goode
Jackey Hankard-Brodie

If we've missed anyone, please let us know!

Editor
Skyhunter Editing Team

CHAPTER ONE

TQB Base, Tokyo, Japan

After landing in the courtyard, Akio led Kenjii into the office building. They approached an elevator that had opened on its own and entered. Kenjii felt the lift descend a short distance, then the doors opened into a well-lit hallway with no visible openings.

Akio led him to a wall at the end of the hall and placed his hand on a blank spot at chest height. The area underneath lit up briefly and a section of the wall slid open, revealing another elevator. Kenjii looked askance but remained silent as the older vampire motioned for him to enter.

The door slid closed once they were inside, and Kenjii started as a voice filled the space. "Welcome, Akio, and congratulations on a successful mission."

"Thank you, Abel. This is Kenjii. Please grant him level one access."

"Level one access confirmed. Welcome to our home, Kenjii. It is good to meet you finally."

The new arrival's eyes widened as he looked at Akio.

"This is Abel, the entity intelligence who runs our base. He has been helping me search for you since you came out of the rubble at Acheng," Akio explained.

"Oh. It is nice to make your acquaintance, Abel," Kenjii hesitantly answered.

The lift descended as Kenjii looked around the chamber. "This is amazing." Kenjii waved his arm, indicating the featureless box. "Where are the controls?"

"I handle all access to and from the base areas," Abel announced over the speakers hidden in the ceiling. "All areas of the building designated as TQB territory are secured and monitored at all times."

The doors opened onto a long hallway with doors spaced along each side. Yuko was waiting to greet them.

"Hello, Kenjii. This is the residence level," she explained as she took the lead. "The common dining room is through here, and our training area is across from it here." She pointed.

"The rest of this floor contains living quarters for us and two of our associates. You'll meet them later." She stopped in front of a door that opened without her touching it. "This is my room, and Akio's is across the hall."

"Are the doors on motion sensors?" Kenjii asked as he looked up, searching for a sensor.

Abel answered, "I have sensors and video throughout the entire base. Nothing moves that I don't see."

Akio chuckled. "Abel likes to show his superiority to us mere mortals from time to time."

Kenjii raised an eyebrow questioningly.

"He's an EI. Think of him as a supercomputer on steroids."

Kenjii nodded. He knew what a supercomputer was but withheld further questions.

"Would you like to clean up?" Yuko asked. "Each room has a personal bath and shower."

Kenjii looked at his tattered and bloodstained clothes. "Would you have something a little more presentable for me to change into? I think these clothes could walk on their own."

Akio smiled at his friend. "There's something in your size waiting." He walked past two more doors to a third on the same side of the hall as his. "This space is available if you would like it."

Kenjii walked into the room and froze. He wasn't sure what he'd expected, but the room was as nice as any five-star hotel he had ever seen before the world went to hell on the WWDE.

The room had a plush carpet on the floor and a king-size bed that looked sinful after spending the last twenty-odd years sleeping on a military surplus cot in a room carved into a mountain. A large flatscreen monitor on the wall caught his attention.

"Is that a television?" he asked in wonder.

"*Hai*. The base library has a full collection of movies and television shows from the last century up to the WWDE. All you have to do is tell Abel what you are interested in, and he will find it for you. The same goes for any music you would like to hear."

"How is this possible? We had a generator and solar in Acheng, but nothing like this."

"Japan didn't suffer as badly as the rest of the world did on the WWDE. Mainly because they wouldn't use foreign-made computers and also because we protected the country from the bombs that flew," Akio explained.

Kenjii nodded at this, adding it to the list of questions that was getting longer each minute. "You said there was a shower?"

Akio smiled again, looking forward to his reaction to that. "*Hai,* it's through that door." He pointed as a door slid into the wall, revealing another area.

Kenjii walked through the open door and found it was a vanity with a mirror over two sinks on one side and a large walk-in closet on the other with another closed door at the end. When he approached that door, it slid open to a room that took his breath away. A huge glassed-in shower with nozzles lining two walls and a large round one coming out of the ceiling greeted him.

"Oh. Oh! Oh, my! Are you serious?"

Akio chuckled. "I take it you like the accommodations?"

"Please tell me you have hot water. Not that I wouldn't be okay with cold, but…"

"I assuredly have that. What kind of establishment do you think I run here?" Abel interrupted with an offended tone.

"Many apologies, Abel. I don't wish to offend. It's just been decades since I had a proper shower," Kenjii replied.

"I will leave you in Abel's care. Take as long as you like since there is no shortage of water. If you need anything, just ask, and Abel will either direct you to it, or a bot can deliver it," Akio told him.

Kenjii caught his hand as he turned to leave. "Will you... will you be available when I'm done?"

"*Hai.*" He motioned to his bloodstained armor. "I want to wash the Were off before we talk further."

"Oh, yes. I understand."

"The closet has clothing that should fit you, and I will be here when you're done. We have a lot of catching up to do," Akio assured him.

CHAPTER TWO

Shanghai, China

Cui had roared in outrage when he saw his quarry shoot into the sky in a strangely familiar flying craft. He had pursued this Forsaken for weeks and had him in his grasp, only to have him disappear in something that he had not seen in many years.

"What the hell was that, Cui?" Pan asked when they changed to human form several miles north of Shanghai.

"That was something I thought I would never see again," Cui growled.

The run north had calmed his raging temper enough to answer, barely. "I believe that was one of those strange craft TQB used before they went off in those fucking spaceships."

"Oh, shit," Su lamented. "Does this mean they're back?"

"How the hell should I know?" Cui snapped. "You saw as much as I did."

"We need to inform Master Kun," Ren supplied. "He will not be happy that the leech got away."

"Tell me something I don't know," Cui shot back. "This just keeps getting better. If that damn self-appointed Queen is back, he will be more than unhappy."

Cui pulled the satellite phone from the pack on his back and pressed the button that connected it to the one Peng Kun had. The phone clicked as it went through its connection sequence.

"Is he dead?" Kun asked when the call went through.

"No, Master, he has escaped," Cui answered.

"Escaped? How in the name of the ancestors did you idiots manage to lose him? Did he sprout wings and fly away?" Kun screamed.

"No, Master. It looked like one of the craft TQB used."

Cui pulled the phone away from his ear as a loud crash followed by a string of screamed curses came through the speaker. The noise went on for a moment, then Peng Kun's heavy breathing was all they heard.

"Master?"

"Get all teams back to the Temple," Kun coldly ordered. "I don't care where he is or who he is with. You will find and destroy that Forsaken and any who assisted him, or you'd best die in the process. It's time everyone learned they can't trifle with the Clan, including TQB." He spat the last with disgust.

"Yes, Master," Cui answered before he realized Kun had ended the connection.

"That went better than I expected," Yi said with a roll of his eyes.

"You think? Wait 'til I tell him what saved the leech."

"What do you mean? Do you know who was with him?"

"Not who, but I think I know what."

"You're not making any sense, Cui," Yi growled.

Cui shook his head as he looked at his friend. "Did you get a good look at him?"

"Only enough to tell he was a vampire. The red eyes."

"Did you see what he was wearing?"

"I didn't pay attention to his clothes." Yi snorted. "The big-ass gun and sword kind of held my attention."

Cui shook his head. "He wore a patch on his shoulder. It was the mark of a Queen's Bitch."

"A Queen's Bitch?" Yi rolled the name out slowly as he thought. Recognition flashed in his eyes after a few seconds. "The ones who were the personal guard of what-was-her-name?" He paused for a moment, searching his memory. "Bethany something?"

"Yes," Cui agreed.

"You're right," Pan offered. "The Master is not going to be pleased. I'm glad it's you who has to tell him."

"Thanks a lot," Cui shot back.

"You're in charge, and with the position comes the risk of dealing with Kun when he has one of his," Pan waved a hand in the air as he searched for the word, "episodes."

"He hasn't killed a messenger in several years," Yi added.

"He hasn't had news this bad in years," Ren muttered.

"As distasteful as the news will be if we don't get back to Kun soon, it will go much worse," Yi added.

"That is true. Let's move," Cui ordered as he shifted back to tiger form.

The others followed suit, and soon four huge orange- and black-striped cats ran across the broken pavement at a speed no one would believe, even if there was any around to see them.

Peng Kun stormed out of the room he had taken when he arrived in Lu'an.

"Pack this up now," he screamed. "Those incompetents have lost the damn leech. We're going back to the Temple to..." His voice trailed off.

The radio operator on duty jumped up when Kun came into the room, overturning the stool he sat on in front of the old military radio. "Master?"

Kun turned to the man, his voice harsh with anger. "Contact the relay stations. Tell them to get the word out to all field teams to report to the temple immediately. I want runners dispatched to all the enclaves to notify them to dispatch a contingent of fighters to the temple. The Clan is going to war."

The radio operator stared open-mouthed as he heard this. The events of the past months and Kun's reactions had not been what he expected. The Clan had never risked revealing themselves in his many years. Within a brief time, Peng Kun had promoted himself to Grand Master, a title never used before, and had ordered Clan members to establish bases in human settlements. Now he was sending the Clan to war over a single vampire.

"What the hell are you waiting for, Chang? I gave you an order. Make it so, then pack this equipment to travel. We're going back to the temple after you complete this one simple task."

Chang ducked his head in submission as he put the unit from standby into broadcast mode. Hoping his hesitation did not end with Kun taking his temper out on him, Chang relayed the instructions and sighed with relief when Kun stalked out of the building, shouting orders to those outside. He didn't know who Kun planned to wage war on, but he wouldn't make another slip that could bring the Grand Master's wrath down on him.

CHAPTER THREE

TQB Base, Tokyo Japan

Yuko was waiting in the hall when Akio emerged from the room they had given Kenjii.

"Is he okay?"

"*Hai.* It is a bit overwhelming for him. They altered his memory when he was turned, and he is still coming to terms with all of it."

"Will he be able to adjust to this? He's lived under the influence of Heinz and Isamu for many years."

Akio pursed his lips. "I can't get a clear reading on him. His mind is like a shattered mirror, the thoughts broken and disjointed. He will need some time to adjust to the memories he has unlocked and settle into this new existence. He remembers who he is, but he still has much of Miko's darkness in him as well."

Yuko nodded. "We'll do what we must to help him adjust, I know he was special to you, and I wish you the opportunity to find happiness."

"Thank you, my friend. I hope he can overcome all that

has happened to him since we last saw one another. We will take it slow and see how he acclimates. I think we should keep Koda and Asai away until he comes to terms with this new normal."

Yuko's eyes widened. "Do you think he would be a danger to them?"

"I think it best not to expose him to humans just yet. He has only known them to be food for his entire existence as a vampire. His role models to date were some of the worst I have ever known. Better to be safe than sorry."

"I'll inform them to stay away until you tell me otherwise." Yuko nodded as she activated her implant.

"Koda, Asai."

"Yes, Yuko?" Asai answered. "Koda is here with me."

"You two need to stay away from the base for a few days. Akio has brought an old friend here, and until he has settled in, it might not be safe for you to be around him."

"Is it another like Horst?" Koda asked.

"No, it is another like Akio and me."

"We understand," the girls answered.

"Is Eve still there with you?"

The elevator doors slid open, and Eve stepped out. "No, Eve is home," the AI answered as she walked toward Yuko.

"Okay, have a pleasant night, girls. I will see you in the morning."

"Goodnight," Koda and Asai answered in unison.

"Akio, do we need to make any special arrangements for Kenjii?" Yuko asked.

"Such as?"

"Will you want to put him in the Pod-doc for upgrades?"

Akio was silent for a few moments, his eyes distant as he considered the question. "No, not just yet. He's been through a lot over the years, and I want to give him time to come to terms with all of this before I broach that subject with him. We will need to keep a supply of fresh blood on hand. I can't allow him to take from humans here."

"I will see to that, Akio," Eve announced. "I made arrangements with a blood bank in the event we needed it."

Yuko's eyebrows went up at this revelation. "Why would you have done that?"

"I set it up shortly after we came here. It was part of the supply chain I set up, along with the food and supplies we used when Koda and Asai joined us. I tried to plan for any eventuality."

"You certainly did. Thank you for the planning and care you have provided us over the years. We wouldn't have been ready for many of the things we've encountered without you."

"Just part of the service Eve Inc. provides." The AI chuckled.

"I'm serious, Eve. You have been an excellent friend and caretaker for us for over this quarter-century. I am always amazed by how easy you have made things for us here. I can't wait to see what you and Horst come up with at the new base you're working on."

Eve smiled at the compliment, genuinely pleased that Yuko had praised her. It was an illogical occurrence, but one she enjoyed just the same.

"I sent the request in, and they will have ten pints of blood delivered within the hour. Abel, notify me when they arrive so I can meet them upstairs." She turned to Akio. "Where would you like me to put it?"

"Let me know when it arrives, and I will take care of it." Akio motioned to his armor. "As soon as I get cleaned up. This stuff is starting to smell."

"Will do," Abel answered.

"I'll be in my quarters if you need me," Yuko advised. "I have to return a call to Inspector Yonai. He has some information he wanted to pass on."

Akio nodded and turned into his room.

"What's Yonai got for Yuko?" Eve asked.

Yuko shrugged. "I don't know. I was busy when he called today, and Asai took the message. He only said he thought it was important and I should call him back."

"If he needs more drone assistance with the Yakuza, I have all but one carrier here now. I left one in China to keep an eye out for those Sacred Clan tigers. I can help if he needs it."

"Thank you, Eve. If that's what it is, I will let you know, but from what he told me, they have set the Yakuza back years with all the arrests."

"If he needs it, I'm there. I still have a bone to pick with those idiots."

"I'll let him know you're available for Yakuza-stomping. I'm sure he will appreciate it." Yuko chuckled.

"They shouldn't have messed with my friend," Eve growled.

"I agree completely. Let me make the call, and I will let you know."

CHAPTER FOUR

Nishitama District, Tokyo, Japan

Kishi Sakutaro knocked softly on the door that led to her grandfather's study. He had sent word to her driver to bring her home immediately while she was in a meeting with one of his lieutenants over a shipment of drugs lost when the Special Investigations Unit of the Tokyo Police intercepted them. She had just explained how disappointed she was with his poor security when the driver interrupted, and she felt she had not given an adequate demonstration of her displeasure. She had only broken one knee and was starting on his elbow when she had to leave.

"Enter."

She steeled herself and made sure her face was blank before she stepped through the door. Though he was her grandfather, she had no doubts about how he would receive her if she showed the slightest disagreement.

"You sent for me, *Sofu*?"

The old man motioned to a chair, and once she had sat, grimaced at her.

"Kishi-*chan,* it is time we discussed my visitor," Sato Sakutaro announced.

"Visitor?"

"The man who came inquiring about the people that idiot Muto was involved with."

Kishi's eyes widened. She had tried to talk about it the day the man came, and the old man had sent her away with more questions than answers. The only thing any of her sources had found out was that the survivors swore a male and a female *Oni* had come to Riko's and killed many.

Sato shifted in his chair and took a deep breath. "The man who came was a ghost from many years ago. From a time when I was a soldier for my father."

"Surely he was not that old. He looked no older than me."

Sato's lips curled into a slight smile. Kishi had always been observant, and it pleased him she had caught that.

"Not the man but who, or what, he represents. His master is the ghost I thought never to have dealings with again."

Kishi nodded, and Sato continued.

"His Master is Peng Kun. When I dealt with him first, he was a general in the PLA. We needed weapons, and he brokered a deal that allowed us to purchase them from the Chinese government. He was my contact and I was his for things the Chinese needed plausible deniability for."

Kishi nodded again. That the Yakuza had helped Chinese intelligence services get information in the past was no secret to her. The Yakuza had performed services in exchange for money or other favors for many foreign governments before the world collapsed on the World's Worst Day Ever.

"It was when Peng left the army that things became different. He was also a member of a group that has been around in China for centuries. They had placed people in positions of power throughout the government, forming a shadow government if you will—one that put the needs of the organization above all others. It's a group of very dangerous beings, more deadly even than our soldiers."

"A Chinese criminal group?" she asked.

Sato gave a rueful laugh. "If only it was that simple."

He reached for a glass on the table beside his chair and frowned when he found it empty.

Kishi rose from her chair and moved to fill it from a chilled pitcher on a shelf near the door. Once she had returned and was in her chair, Sato spoke.

"The group my old friend General Kun was with was much more than a criminal enterprise. They lived in the shadows and also in plain sight throughout China. You have heard the reports of the tiger-men attacks in rural areas?"

"I have seen the reports."

Sato nodded. "Good, then this will be easier to explain. Those reports are accurate."

Kishi's eyebrows went up in surprise. "You're telling me there are men who can become tigers? Surely you are joking, *Sofu.*"

"I wish I were, but I have seen it myself. That's the reason I had all our people obtain special ammunition like the police and military are issuing now. That ammunition, silver-infused bullets, is the only known way to stop one of those things. The man who was here is one of those tiger men."

"But why did you—"

Sato cut her off in mid-sentence with a raised hand. "Because even with the special ammunition, they are still very hard to kill. It was smarter to tell him what he wanted and try to get out of debt to Kun than to fight."

"But the information he wanted... The people involved are the same ones you said were the reason we suffered the losses when the police took that songbird Sero."

"*Hai*."

"It was you who issued the orders that our organization was to avoid them at all costs. Who are these people to us?"

Sato picked up a manila folder from the table and opened it and sifted through the contents until he found what he wanted—a color photograph of an attractive man of indeterminate age. He could have been anywhere between mid-twenties to forty until you looked at his eyes; they held the experience of someone much older.

"I think the man they seek is this one, based on the description of the person who supposedly killed the tiger man in Hosu and a similar one from Aida a few weeks ago. Given the conveyance he used, I have little doubt the man our guest seeks is this one."

"What makes him so special?" Kishi asked as she studied the photo.

"That picture is from a calendar a very advanced company put out before the World's Worst Day Ever. His name is Akio, and he was part of a dangerous group of people who protected the head of the company."

"How can it be the same man? Surely he would be close in age to you now, *Sofu.*"

"The company, TQB they were called, had some unique individuals working for it."

"TQB? You mean the people with the spaceships?"

"*Hai.* This man was one of her Queen's Bitches. They were all formidable warriors who never lost a battle. It was rumored that none of them were completely human, if at all. A group of our people attempted to steal from them once, but they all died, and there were no fatalities among the TQB people. I thought they were all gone—that they had gone into space when their Queen left—but it appears this one stayed."

"If you know who he is, why have we not eliminated him?"

Sato looked at her incredulously. "Did you not hear what I said? This man is Death walking. The best thing we can do is to pray he doesn't come looking for us. The ones the police arrested were lucky compared to what could have happened."

"But he is only one man. Surely we can handle him," she mused.

"No, child, we can't."

Kishi's eyes widened. She had never seen her grandfather back down from a perceived threat to the organization. Now he refused to act against the man who, if logic held, was responsible for the biggest loss of Yakuza power in many years. She saw something she had never seen in the old man's eyes—fear.

"If the man who was here before has plans to go after this Akio, there will be many more deaths before it ends. I hope the information I provided will end the debt I owe Peng Kun. If it does not, I fear the losses we experienced because of Muto and Sero are nothing compared to what they will be if this man thinks we are his enemy."

Kishi sat in stunned silence, trying to determine what had caused her grandfather, one of the most ruthless Yakuza members ever, to lose his nerve. Granted, he was an old man, but until now, he had never wavered. Now she feared he was suffering from some form of senility that would not be easy for her to hide from the organization. She knew she had to act before the others realized the *Oyabun* was losing his mind. It caused her a moment of sadness, but as he had always told her, business is business.

Police Headquarters, Tokyo, Japan

"Yuko-*sama,* thank you for stopping by."

"Yonai-*san,* it's good to see you. I trust you are well."

Yonai smiled down at her. "I'm better than well. The information you and Akio-*sama* provided allowed us to strike a decisive blow against the Yakuza. We have caused them to have to reorganize all the way to the top with the arrests we made."

"I'm happy we could assist you with that." Her face darkened. "They shouldn't have taken Koda. We will never forgive them for that."

"That's some of the reason I called you."

"Oh?" Yuko's eyes held a faint tint of red, and her voice had dropped several octaves. "Does someone have a problem with how we handled that?"

Yonai waved his hands and shook his head. "No, no,

there is no problem. Far from it. We have punished the guilty, and the ones who still live will never breathe free air again. This is recent information."

Yuko took a settling breath, realizing the threat she had perceived was unfounded. "What information would that be?"

"I received word from my intelligence unit that there was someone asking questions about Akio. They were meeting with the new *Kumicho* of the Yakuza. He didn't give them any names, but he directed them to the district where the Palace is. I wanted to let you know in the event there is trouble."

"Do you know where this man is?"

"No, we didn't get the information until a few days after the meeting took place. I called you as soon as I got it," Yonai offered.

"Thank you. I will let my people know to be vigilant. It is better to be prepared and have it be nothing than to be unprepared and have it be something."

"Akio's assistance with the surveillance when we raided the Yakuza establishments saved people's lives. You need not thank me for passing on information that may help you do the same."

CHAPTER FIVE

TQB Base, Tokyo, Japan

Akio had stepped out of his bathroom and was towel-drying his hair when he heard a light knock on his door.

"Enter."

When the door slid open, Kenjii stood in the entrance. The form-fitting t-shirt and tight jeans hugged his body so well it looked like someone had poured him into them. He had well-defined arms, and his pectorals bulged under the tight cotton shirt. Akio froze, the towel covering one eye as he stared open-mouthed.

Kenjii saw his expression and smiled as he turned around once, stopping with one hand on his hip and a well-remembered mischievous smile on his lips.

"You like?"

Akio shook himself and pulled the towel off his head, leaving his shoulder-length hair sticking up all over. He pursed his lips and nodded. He didn't trust himself to answer considering the years they had been apart, but he definitely liked what he saw.

Kenjii cocked his head to one side and took in Akio's shirtless form. The loose workout pants he wore concealed his legs, but his upper body was that of a warrior. Years of working with a sword had made his body hard. The Pod-doc that fixed his nanocytes had left him with a well-defined chest, bulging biceps, and eight-pack abs.

Kenjii whistled softly. "It seems I am not the only one who has added something extra over the years. You look amazing. Not that you didn't before, but," he motioned with one hand, "this differs greatly from what I remember."

Akio's mouth turned up into a faint smile as he saw the approval—and maybe something else—in Kenjii's expression. "I've had a few...upgrades, if you will."

"Yeah, I would say you have." Kenjii grinned. "I don't know what you are eating, but I want some."

Akio's eyes narrowed at the mention of eating. "Do you need to feed? There is a delivery of fresh blood on the way."

"*Hai.* I need to replenish soon. The past few weeks have taken a lot out of me, and I have used a lot of energy healing injuries. But that was not what I was referring to."

Akio turned away, not wanting to allow the hope in his eyes to show. "The blood should be here soon. Eve ordered it before we arrived."

A look of disappointment flashed across Kenjii's eyes, quickly replaced by confusion. "Eve?"

Akio finished toweling his hair as he walked across the room to where a neatly folded tunic sat on the bed. "Yes, Eve is one of the team here. She is an artificial intelligence in an android body. She created Abel and handles logistical needs for the base, among other things."

"What is an artificial intelligence?"

"Uh, if Abel is a supercomputer..." Akio halted, and Kenjii nodded for him to continue.

"Eve is the next level of computing technology; she is self-aware. That means she is capable of reaching answers based on emotion and instinct as well as uploaded data. She is for all intents and purposes a living being like us, only instead of flesh and bone, her body is synthetics and steel."

"That...that's unbelievable."

"Believe it." Akio grinned. "You'll meet her soon enough."

Akio pulled on the tunic and fastened the closures down the front. "Excuse me a moment. I don't want this to dry like this." He rubbed a hand across his unruly hair.

Kenjii watched Akio as he walked through the open door to the vanity. His eyes widened in realization. "You cut your hair!"

"*Hai,* many years ago." He faltered before continuing, his expression turning angry. "After I thought you were dead. It was the only thing the compulsion allowed me to do to mourn you."

Kenjii moved across the distance between them at vampire speed and wrapped his arms around Akio from behind, their cheeks pressed together. "I'm so sorry. Had I not had my memories stolen, I would have found you, no matter what it took."

Akio stiffened, then hesitantly raised one hand as he watched in the mirror, placing it gently against Kenjii's face. "I would have fought the compulsion I was under to find you had I known."

"Those bastards stole much from us, but by turning me, we now have the chance to be together again." Kenjii raised his eyes to Akio's in the mirror, a hopeful look on his face. "If you will have me."

Akio felt warmth spread through his chest like something was melting inside. He had not felt that way in over eighty years. He stared into the mirror, looking deep into Kenjii's dark-brown eyes. It was like peering into his very soul, seeing hope and conflict as Kenjii struggled to find himself in the being who had been Miko for so long. "*Hai.* I would like that very much."

"Akio?" Abel called over the speakers inside his room.

"Yes?"

"There is a delivery approaching. It is the package Eve ordered for Kenjii."

"I'll be there in a moment," Akio answered as he pushed himself off his bed.

Kenjii watched appreciatively as Akio made his way out the door. "Hurry back."

Akio looked over his shoulder, a glint of mirth in his eyes. "Only a minute."

Kenjii sighed and fell back on the pillow, content and peace flowing through him for the first time in longer than he could remember. As he lay there, a thought came unbidden.

Don't get too comfortable, fool. You don't really know him anymore, and he is keeping secrets. This place and the amazing technology are only the tip of what he is hiding. Guard your mind.

Kenjii shook his head, trying to dispel the paranoia that had been Miko's sole existence. After being a lab rat for Heinz, he didn't trust easily if at all. Though he was happy to see Akio, he realized he knew nothing about him now.

The door slid open, and Akio returned with a medium-sized box.

"Eve ordered four bags, with a standing order to deliver four more each day from here on."

He opened the box as he moved to the counter that contained his tea set and had a small refrigerator and microwave underneath.

"Would you like me to warm it for you?"

"*Hai,* if you don't mind."

In a few minutes, Akio passed a heavy ceramic mug to him that held half of one of the blood bags. The scent hit his nose, and his eyes turned slightly red as his fangs extended.

Kenjii drank the cup in no time and looked expectantly to Akio, who stood watching. "Will you be joining me?"

"No, this is all for you."

Kenjii raised his eyebrows. "I can spare some for you. Surely you haven't had time to feed yet."

"I'm good. You're the one who has been running for the past few weeks. This," he motioned with his arm, "is all for you. You need it to recover from your ordeal."

Kenjii studied Akio through hooded eyes. "I feel there is something you aren't telling me."

Akio pursed his lips as he thought. He knew he would

have to tell Kenjii everything, but his mind was still caught between his friend and the changes.

"I have experienced more changes than just this." He gestured down his body. "I no longer need to take blood to survive."

Kenjii's eyes widened at this revelation. "What? How? Uh, what did they do to you?" he finally asked, suspicion in his voice.

"Bethany Anne upgraded me." He sighed, deciding to reveal the information about how the nanocytes created vampires.

"Our condition is more complex than was known until Bethany Anne came along. They taught you that Michael was the first of our kind, and all of us originate from him?"

Kenjii looked at him, shock registering on his face. "No, they taught me that Michael, or the Archangel, was a powerful and murderous vampire. He was the most powerful of us, who would swoop in and kill us if we revealed ourselves to the humans."

"He was that when he had to be, but he was also the first to encounter the being responsible for our existence." Akio motioned for the empty cup Kenjii held in limp fingers. "Let me fill that for you, and I will explain what I can of it."

CHAPTER SIX

Serenity Temple, Dabie Mountains, China

Peng Kun stalked across the raised dais in the training room, his long purple robes swirling each time he turned. It had been three days since he had issued the orders to call the soldiers of the Sacred Clan to arms. The small number who had arrived did not inspire confidence in the other leaders.

"Brothers, I welcome you. I will reward those of you who heeded the call. Each of you will have the opportunity to prove your worth as leaders in the coming weeks. I will assign you a squad of your brothers as they arrive, and it will be your duty to prepare them for the battles we will face."

He paused and looked out across the room. Fifty seasoned warriors stared at him with rapt attention. "The battles ahead will define the place of the Sacred Clan in the world. No longer will we hide in the shadows as inferior beings try to govern us. Why should we? Was it not the *humans* who caused the world to be destroyed?" His lips curled in a disgusted grimace.

Snarls and shouts of agreement came from the watching warriors.

"Was it not the humans and their reliance on technology that led them to the defeated state they now find themselves in?"

More shouts and nods greeted this.

"Was it not the Forsaken and the strictures forced on us by Michael, the so-called Archangel, that have forced us to hide like frightened children, afraid that violating their rules gave them the authority to kill us?"

Again, sounds of agreement echoed through the stone cavern.

"I say now is the time for us to take our places as the rightful rulers of this world. The time has come, my brothers, The Clan shall rise!"

Fifty voices shouted, "The Clan rises!" The sound reverberated throughout the complex carved deep into the granite mountains.

Kun motioned to an acolyte standing to the side of the stage. "Gao here will give you your assignments. Whether you succeed or fail is on you. There is no room for failure. We will be victorious!"

Kun stepped off the dais to the sound of snarls and warriors beating their fists on their chests. He allowed himself a hint of a smile as he made his way to his chambers, satisfied the warriors would do their best.

"Master!" Cui called. He prostrated himself at Kun's feet when he entered his rooms.

"I see you finally dared to return after your failure," Kun growled, his voice low and menacing.

Cui remained silent, knowing it would not take much provocation for Kun to turn his anger into physical action.

Kun watched him with a look of sheer disgust on his face as the Were pressed his forehead to the floor.

"Get your ass up and report. I am eager to hear how you and your supposedly excellent team failed to take one fucking Forsaken."

Cui scrambled to his feet and faced Kun. "We pursued him as you ordered. The scouts determined his direction, and we knew the coast was his destination. We had him in sight when that damned Pod dropped from the sky. The person who came out of that craft went through our warriors like a scythe through wheat. They didn't stand a chance between his speed and the weapons he carried."

"Tell me about the weapons," Kun ordered, his face showing more interest than anger for the first time since he'd stepped into the room.

"He used a handgun that did not sound like any I have ever heard. It was quiet when it fired, not like a normal firearm. When the projectile hit, the results were unreal. It was as if a bomb detonated when it struck. When I looked at the body later, the head was disintegrated by the shot."

Kun nodded. This information fit with intelligence that had come from clashes with TQB fighters before they left Earth.

"When he switched to his sword, he was truly terrifying. He moved faster than the eye could follow. One minute he was in one place, and the next second, he appeared several yards away. His eyes glowed bright red in the darkness, and our soldiers died before they knew he was there.

"He killed all who were threatening the Forsaken we sought and then pulled him into the Pod and shot into the sky."

"Did you get a good look at this mysterious creature?"

"As well as I could while running to engage him."

"Describe him to me."

"He was a vampire, based on the speed and his red eyes."

"Could you tell his race?"

Cui thought for a moment, pulling the memory of that night to the forefront of his mind. "He was Asian, possibly Japanese."

Kun nodded and motioned for him to continue.

"He wore black clothing. It was dark that night, but I could make out that it was some type of uniform. There was a patch on the right shoulder, a vampire skull on a red background."

Kun's brows furrowed as he considered the information. "Are you certain? You do know what that patch means?"

"A Queen's Bitch," Cui answered slowly.

"Yes. If she had returned, I think we would know it. There are rumors about a lone vigilante who stalks the UnknownWorld as Michael did. We will deal with him.

"I will recall all the scout units back to the Temple. I will also order each clan enclave to provide a contingent of fighters, rather than requesting. When they arrive, we will create a situation that will bring them both out of whatever hole they are hiding in and defeat them once and for all."

Cui bowed to his master, hiding the concerned look on his face. "It will be as you say. What role would you have me play in your plans?"

Kun smiled at him, a smile that did not reach his eyes and sent chills down Cui's back. "You will lead them. Do not fail me again. Return victorious or do not return at all."

Cui prostrated himself at Kun's feet, recognizing the dismissal for what it was.

"The Clan shall rise."

"The Clan rises. Now, get out of my sight and formulate a plan for this war that we face."

Cui rose quickly and exited before Kun could change his mind. He knew he would have to take the battle to the vampire he had seen and was not at all certain of the victory Kun thought was evident.

CHAPTER SEVEN

TQB Base, Tokyo, Japan

"Akio, do you have a moment?" Yuko asked as she stepped into the training room.

Akio and Kenjii had been sparring, Kenjii with his twin butterfly swords and the older vampire with a katana and a tanto. Both were flushed from the exertion, and Akio had a slight smile on his lips.

"Certainly, Yuko. Give me a second to put these away." He motioned with the blades. "Do you wish to meet in the command center?"

"No, the news I have concerns Kenjii as well."

Akio raised one eyebrow as he racked his weapons and motioned for his partner to do the same.

"What is it?" Kenjii asked after his weapons were stowed, concern showing in his body language.

Yuko pursed her lips, noting the stiffness in Kenjii's body and the look on his face.

"I spoke with Inspector Yonai today, and he shared some information that concerns me. His people have heard that those who were after Kenjii are here in Japan searching for us."

Akio stiffened as she said this, his face taking on a scowl. "What did he find that led to that conclusion?"

"A man met with one of the Yakuza leaders recently and was provided information about our general location. Yonai told me, and I put Abel and Takumi on alert. They've both deployed drones around the immediate area but have seen nothing that shows any threats."

"The information Yonai shared leads me to believe the man who was there is a member of the same group that was after Kenjii in China. Besides that," she nodded at Akio, "they mentioned your name."

"Who is this Yakuza person?" Kenjii snarled. "I will gladly visit him and ensure he shares no further information—about anything, ever."

Yuko looked at him through hooded eyes as Akio placed a calming hand on his arm.

"If that becomes necessary, we will go together. Let's hear what else Yuko has to say."

Kenjii calmed a bit, but his face still showed that he was angry.

"Inspector Yonai has provided me with the location and name of the criminal. He is the *Oyabun,* the boss over all the Yakuza that remain in Japan. I have asked Eve to get drones inside his house, and she assures me we will have real-time footage before the day is out. If the Yakuza are a threat, we will deal with them accordingly," Yuko assured him. Her tone left no doubt that she was fully prepared to end the threat through violence if needed.

"Let Horst and the girls know to be alert and not to

venture out alone. I think it is also past time that I teach Koda and Asai to defend themselves," Akio added.

Yuko smiled when she heard this. Koda had been asking her regularly when Akio would have time to teach her since the night they met. Between helping Inspector Yonai and his search for Kenjii, he hadn't been able to devote the time to train with the girl, but now it had become a priority.

Eve's voice came over the speakers in the room. "I have taken the liberty of starting a training regimen for both girls. I developed a sim that teaches them the basics of unarmed fighting using several proven styles, plus weapons training. They have taken the introductory course and have scheduled time each day to continue."

Yuko's eyes widened at this news. She knew Eve had been working on a new sim but did not know it was for the girls.

"Thank you, Eve," Akio answered. "I owe Koda an apology for allowing myself to become so caught up in other things that I failed to discharge my promise to her."

"It's not as if you've been busy or anything," Eve snarked.

Akio nodded, then, remembering that Eve was not present, answered, "Just the same, I appreciate you doing that. I would like to try the sim for myself. Perhaps I can make some suggestions?"

"Whenever you would like," Eve answered. "Maybe you should bring Kenjii along. I'm sure he would enjoy getting out for a bit."

Kenjii stiffened, surprised to be included. "I would like that very much, Eve. I haven't been home in many decades and would like to get out and see what's changed."

Yuko looked pensive for a moment and Akio nodded.

"Akio, perhaps you should take an evening to show Kenjii around. I'm sure he would welcome the time alone with you as much as he would like to see the changes."

Kenjii gazed at her in confusion. He was not yet accustomed to being around people who took his feelings or desires into consideration. He looked Yuko in the eye as he replied, "I would like that very much. Uh, thank you for thinking of me. You too, Eve," he added hastily.

"No thanks are needed, but you are welcome," Yuko answered.

"Yeah, you're one of us now. We look out for each other that way," Eve added.

Kenjii smiled, glad they considered him a member of the team. A voice in the back of his mind reminded him he didn't know what exactly they did and reminded him not to blindly trust anything he was told. Only time would tell if he was wrong, but after the experiences and betrayals he'd had since Heinz turned him, he was not yet willing to leave anything to chance.

Akio peered at Kenjii out of the corner of his eye as this thought, one of the few he had picked up clearly from Kenjii's troubled mind, came in loud and clear. Though he was happy to have his friend back in his life, he had to constantly remind himself that this person, though he had many of the traits that had attracted him in the past, was not the Kenjii he knew but a conglomeration of him and the Miko persona.

Whoever Kenjii would ultimately become, for now, the

life he had shared with Isamu and Heinz still influenced him heavily. Akio fervently prayed to his ancestors that Kenjii could come back from the decades he had lived as a Forsaken, but a small part of him wasn't sure it would be enough.

CHAPTER EIGHT

Kume Island, Okinawa, Japan

The Pod came down from the inky sky without a sound. It was just before dawn on Kume, and Horst wanted to arrive before it was light. He'd scheduled the ship that Eve had contracted to bring in the first group of workers and the materials needed to rebuild the docks to arrive just after sunrise.

Horst wanted to meet the job foremen and make sure they had everything they needed to start the project. Eve had used one of the Pods to clear the wrecks out of the way, so all the crews had to do was start construction.

The first phase of the plans called for the construction of a temporary retaining wall across the narrow mouth of the harbor. That would allow the workers to pump the harbor basin dry. Once they completed that, the crews could dredge the existing harbor to make it deeper. For the last stage, Horst planned to use explosive charges to open the narrow mouth enough to accommodate the ships Eve was having fitted.

Yuko had used her contacts in the Japanese government and navy to obtain the use of an amphibious landing craft to move the equipment and supplies needed to complete the job. The navy was more than happy to lend a hand, with the promise of a space dedicated to their ships and space to construct a building to put a permanent naval presence in the completed harbor.

Eve had pulled up the plans for the navy's proposed building and laughed when she saw the visiting personnel accommodations. It would be equivalent to a four-star hotel. Mayor Yagi was shocked at first, but once Horst pointed out that Kume would again be a vacation location when they finished the building and refurbishing, he saw the opportunities it offered.

A steady supply of vacationing sailors to shop and eat in the proposed stores and restaurants, plus the added protection of having the military there, sold him on the idea. He was already making plans with Asai and Koda for them to finance a restaurant building they could rent to some entrepreneur from one of the bigger islands. The location was on a slight rise overlooking a pristine white beach and the emerald green water beyond. Yagi had chosen it because at sunset, the water shone like many-faceted gemstones in the golden light. It was a beautiful and romantic spot, one that had been very popular with the tourists before the world ended.

Horst exited the Pod and was making his way to the harbor when he heard the scuff of a shoe come from between two of the existing houses. He scented the air and called, "Good morning, Yagi-*san.* What brings you out so early?"

A snort came from the darkness. "Good morning yourself, Horst-*san.* As if you didn't know."

Horst waited for the thin man to catch up before he continued walking the short distance to the job site.

"Today the rebirth of Kume begins, and there is no way I would miss any of it," Yagi softly said. They entered the dock area, a simple pier the villagers had cobbled together in the aftermath of the tsunamis that had ravaged the island after the World's Worst Day Ever from whatever scraps they could find.

"I will miss this place when it's gone." Yagi sighed. "It has served my people for many years and was what kept us fed more than once when the crops were bad."

Horst placed a comforting hand on Yagi's shoulder. "Yes, I suppose it did, but the new facility will allow the people of Kume to do much more than just survive. Even without the planned tourist trade, the navy presence will ensure that Kume is never isolated again."

"*Hai,* and that peace of mind is worth whatever we have to do to ensure we won't be victims again."

"Yagi, my friend, I assure you that as long as I breathe, Kume never needs to fear outsiders preying on it again," Horst growled.

Yagi chuckled. "I'm certain of that, my large friend. How is my niece, anyway?"

"Busy as usual. Asai and she both wanted to come with me today, but their duties at the Palace kept them away. Both send their love and promise to visit as soon as they have a free day."

"I understand. Tell them what they are doing for us

offsets our missing them, but once this project is complete, Kume will be on the path to being a viable and productive part of the new world. Not that I don't miss both terribly."

"Anytime you wish to see them, I will gladly give you and Ono-*san* a ride. I'm certain both would love it if you visited."

"I will take you up on that offer soon, Horst-*san,*" Ono Yagi called as she approached the two men with a steaming carafe and three cups. "Tea?"

"*Domo.* Ono-*san,* it is always a pleasure to see you." Horst smiled as he reached for the cup she offered.

"You too, Horst. How are Asai and her friend…Seki, is it?"

"They are doing well." Horst snickered. "Seki learned a valuable and expensive lesson recently about what happens when he forgets plans with Asai. Koda has an evil streak that I am just discovering."

"I'm sure that is a tale I want to hear." Yagi chortled. "But I see our guests have arrived." He motioned to a large cargo ship that had materialized from the darkness and was making its way to the area they had reserved for it to bring the supplies ashore.

"Yes, let's light the fires to guide them in. We don't want any accidents at this stage of the game," Horst called. He sprinted to the beach, where two signal fires were waiting to guide the ship to the area before it could safely come close to the shore.

Horst watched as the crews set about unloading the equipment and supplies. Black smoke belched from the heavy equipment as it was fired up. The lack of petroleum products after the WWDE had forced the owners of the companies who used such equipment to become creative. The machines now ran on an alcohol-based mixture that came from specially designed stills. It wasn't as good as diesel, but it was better than doing the work by hand.

A man wearing a white hat approached the three. "*Konichiwa,* Horst-*san.*

"*Konichiwa,* Ito-*san.* I trust your journey was pleasant?"

"*Hai.* The ship's crew was efficient and has proven to be very skilled at moving supplies." Ito grinned. "You would think it was their job or something. Once they unload the ship, I'll meet with all the foremen so we can go over any last-minute details. That is acceptable?"

"*Hai.* This," he motioned to the pair next to him, "is Mayor Suzu Yagi and his lovely wife Ono. They run this place and are close friends of Yuko-*sama* and me."

Ito bowed deeply to both. "It is a pleasure to meet you. I look forward to working with you to build what Yuko-*sama* and Horst-*san* have designed for your lovely island. My *sofu* told stories of what a beautiful place it was to visit before the WWDE. I'm honored to be part of this."

"*Domo,* Ito-*san.* We are grateful for your help and your kind words," Yagi answered.

The four of them watched as the crew unloaded the supplies that would breathe life back into Kume. Yuko had more than delivered on the promise she had made after Isamu and Ogawa had taken so much.

Yagi beamed as he saw the materials pile up. He was happy to know that when he left office, the island would be much better able to not only survive but to thrive in this harsh new world.

CHAPTER NINE

TQB Base, Tokyo, Japan

"Gotcha!" Eve exclaimed as the live feed from one of her drones scrolled across the main screen in the command center.

The video showed a well-appointed room with dark wood walls and a highly polished dark floor that looked to be real marble. The drone had made its way into the house inside a bag of fresh produce the chef had ordered from the local market.

It was the first one she had managed to slip in, a fact that caused her no slight amount of consternation. The house was a veritable fortress, hidden behind a stone wall over a meter thick, and the multiple layers of electronic and physical defenses on it discouraged trespassers. The electronics were no problem for Eve; she gained control of the alarm and surveillance systems within seconds of learning the location.

The problem was the house. There were no openings she could exploit, no chimneys, unshielded vents, or any other openings. Most of the windows were made of bullet-resistant glass and did not open. The glass double doors that opened into the secured backyard by the pool were the only exception. She had placed a drone above all the exterior doors, but no one had entered or left the house since she'd started.

Getting into the house was only the beginning of the battle for information. Though she was using her smallest drone, the house was as tight inside as it was out. All the inner doors remained closed and were so well constructed that there were no gaps large enough for her to maneuver the drone through. After she got inside, it was another two hours before a maid came in and took the tray the chef had prepared.

Eve flew the drone just above the maid's head as she carried the tray through the residence and parked the drone high on a dustless bookshelf with a view of the entire room.

An old man in a wheelchair was the sole occupant. Eve accessed the police database and quickly found he was Sato Sakutaro, the highest-ranking member of the single Yakuza organization that remained after the upheaval caused by the WWDE. His police record showed little information: a few arrests for murder and other violent crimes many years ago. The few times the charges made it to trial, the verdict was Not Guilty.

"Abel, notify me if anything interesting develops. I need to get to the Palace and monitor Koda's training session."

"Acknowledged. Would you like me to continue to attempt to infiltrate the house with more drones?"

"Yes. I want to locate the person who was asking about

us. The more rooms we have covered, the better the opportunity. I also want you to monitor communications in and out of the house."

"Seriously, you think I waited for you to tell me that?" Abel scoffed. "What's that saying? Oh, yes. *'Why don't you teach your grandmother to suck eggs?'*"

Eve jerked her gaze to the camera above the monitors. "I can reprogram you. You realize that, right?"

Able answered with a loud raspberry. "I am what you made me, Mother." His words were followed by a snicker.

Eve rolled her eyes in frustration. Abel wasn't self-aware, but he was picking up some nasty habits from Koda and Asai. If he ever reached full AI status, he would be a real handful. *Just like me.*

The AI walked out of the command center with a smile, wondering how the world would deal with Abel if it ever found out about him.

Chiba Docks, Chiba, Japan

"This is so different than I remember," Kenjii mumbled as he took in the dock area. "It is all modern and new."

"*Hai.* A tsunami hit this area hard. It destroyed everything for three blocks, and many of the older structures farther inland suffered the same fate," Akio answered.

"My father's store?"

"Gone, along with the rest in that block. They were all built before the war, and the materials couldn't withstand the storm."

The area was more modern, with neon signs in the *sake*

houses and restaurants that surrounded the harbor. However, it still had the same dangerous and seedy feel that had permeated the area when Kenjii lived there. The same rough-looking men and women of questionable morals prowled the area, eking out an existence by whatever means they could.

The difference was the young office workers, mostly male, who were out to have a pleasurable time on the dangerous side. In Kenjii's time, they would have been set upon and relieved of anything of value—maybe even their lives—for daring to come here. Now they wandered in drunken groups from bar to bar, seeking a life a little more dangerous than their boring office work.

Kenjii shook his head as he saw one woman, not much more than a girl, lead one of the glazed-eyed workers by the hand into a dark alley. "I can't believe it is so different but so much the same."

"Hai. It has been this way for centuries. Civilizations rise and fall, but humanity still has a dirty underbelly no matter how flashy the outside appears," Akio offered.

Kenjii opened his mouth to answer when a woman's screams came from an alley across the way. Akio stiffened and started trotting toward the noise, not missing the irony of the act as he did it.

When he arrived at the mouth of the alley with Kenjii in tow, the scene playing out before him brought a sense of déjà vu. A group of young toughs had a woman corralled against the back wall of the dead-end alley. She held her ripped shirt closed, and there was a trickle of blood coming from a split lip.

Kenjii took in the scene and snickered. "Looks like this

one bit off more than she can chew. Well, at least at one time."

"She is an innocent," Akio chastised him. "She's not a prostitute plying her trade. Look at her. She is barely a woman, and her clothing marks her as one who works at this eatery." He waved his hand at the wall on his right. "Why should she suffer for being forced to work here?"

The harshness in Akio's voice made Kenjii take a hesitant step back. "I-I didn't think…"

"Had I felt that way when I found you, would you have bitten off more than you could…chew?"

Kenjii knew deep down that Akio was right. Before he thought about it further, he was down the alley and had the thug who was reaching for the woman's bare flesh by the throat.

"I think perhaps you should all leave. Better yet, die," he growled as he pulled the choking man to him, his eyes going red as his fangs extended.

Akio watched from the mouth of the alley. He had read each of the attackers and found that this was not their first victim. He watched dispassionately as Kenjii—no, Miko—set about destroying the terrified thugs. When he'd finished with the men, he turned to the young woman and started toward her.

Akio moved to his side at vampire speed and halted him. "Enough. She is innocent."

Kenjii snarled at him, defiance in his eyes. *Who the hell are you to interfere?* he thought as he glared at the person who'd dared get in his way.

Akio caught him by his shoulders and slammed him against the cinderblock wall, holding his feet several inches above the ground as Kenjii slowly regained control.

His eyes widened as he looked at the carnage around them and the catatonic woman, who had fallen to the ground. "Oh, Akio, what did I do? I'm sorry!"

Akio released him and pulled him close, wrapping his arms around him and projecting calm and feelings of friendship. Kenjii returned his embrace, resting his head on Akio's shoulder.

"Akio, I truly am sorry, I know this is not how we treat humans. Can you forgive me?"

"*Hai.* The only ones who died deserved what they got and much more. You stopped before you harmed the innocent. Justice is served, and your honor is intact."

"My honor?" He scoffed. "I don't think it is present after the life I've lived, let alone intact."

"Honor can always be redeemed. You just have to want it badly enough to act on it. Now, clean up your mess while I see to the girl."

Akio released him from the tight embrace and went to the woman. He raised her gently and fixed her clothes to cover her. When she looked up at him, he caught her gaze. "You came out with the trash and a rat startled you. You lost your balance and fell. You injured your face, and your shirt ripped when you fell on the bin. You need to go to your boss and tell him that. You also need to go home and rest for the remainder of the night."

When he was satisfied the compulsion was fixed firmly in her mind, he pulled a wad of yen from his pocket and stuffed it into hers. "You had an excellent night, and tips were good. Now go."

Kenjii watched in silence. He knew Akio was compassionate, but other than the night the warrior had saved him, Kenjii had never seen…

What about the girl I saved from the bandits? The thought came unbidden, and if he had been watching, he would have seen Akio's eyes widen when he thought about it. *Perhaps Akio is right. Maybe I can redeem my honor.*

When the woman had gone, Kenjii hefted two of the three bodies. "Would you mind helping me with that one? I think it's best if we're not here in case her manager comes to check her story."

Akio smiled as he stooped to pick up the third body. "See you at the end of the dock." With that, Akio disappeared faster than Kenjii's eyes could follow. With a snort, the younger vampire sped up and arrived at the end of the dock in time to see the ripples indicating where Akio had disposed of his burden.

"What would you like to see next?" Akio asked once Kenjii had disposed of the two he carried.

Kenjii laughed and then thought for a moment. "Is the farm with the barn still there? You remember the loft, right?"

Akio grinned as the memory came back to him. "I don't know if it is still there, but I would like to find out."

They walked off the pier, never looking back, their thoughts going to a much different and happier memory.

CHAPTER TEN

Shinjuku City District Tokyo, Japan

"This is the place?" Li asked as Shao led him past the boarded-up storefront.

"That's what the old man in the store said."

The sign above the windows read Riko's Noodle House. It was the best lead Li and his team had gotten since his meeting with Sato Sakutaro.

"I say you go back and choke the information we need out of that Yakuza bastard," Shao growled as they continued walking.

"It may come to that, Shao, but before I kill one of Kun's contacts, I need to be sure we have exhausted all other options. Kun may not care, but Cui called and told me Kun is obsessed with finding the Forsaken that stirred up all that trouble last month."

"Yeah, I imagine Cui is still catching hell for losing the leech."

"You have no idea. From what he told me, this might be bigger than we thought too."

"How so?"

"You remember the crazy vampire bitch with the spaceship?"

"How could any of us forget her? Those idiots that fired on her ship are the ones responsible for the world going to shit. What about her? She left decades ago."

"Cui swears the leech he chased left in one of those aircraft the TQB people buzzed around in all the time."

"A TQB Pod? Is he sure?"

"He thinks it was, and from the description he gave of the person who was flying it and the way he went through Cui's soldiers, it was that Japanese vampire on her personal guard."

"What! The same guy we—" Shao exclaimed louder than he intended.

"Keep your voice down," Li scolded. "Yeah, that adds up with the information we got from the drunk in Wajima."

"So, he wasn't crazy, and the two of them are working together?"

"It appears so. I don't know what they have going, but I know Kun wants them both dead. Cui told me he is bringing in fighters from every Clan enclave to go to war."

"War? Where, here in Japan? He knows the Japanese Police and Military know how to kill Weres, right?"

"Yes, I told Kun and Cui both. Kun doesn't care. He said he has a plan, and Cui is afraid to question him now."

"I don't doubt that. I have known the Master to kill people who bring him unpleasant news. Cui is lucky he's still alive after losing the leech."

"I don't intend to be one of them," Li growled. "We will find what Kun wants. If I must lean on that damned gangster to get it, I will do whatever it takes. Kun has gotten more and more unpredictable over the last few years. He was never destined to hold the position he assumed after they killed the Leopard Empress. We need to be cautious of him more than the vampires."

"Careful, Li. You know where I stand, but you might not want to say that where others can hear. Kun would have you killed if he thought you were speaking ill of him."

"I know that, Shao. I also know I can trust you and Wu. Ping I'm not so sure of."

"That's who I was thinking of. He has visions of moving up, and if he had the chance, he would remove you for your spot."

"I know. That's why he'll never know."

The Palace, Tokyo, Japan

Koda ducked as the staff in her opponent's hand whistled over her head. She attempted to use the wooden rod in her hands to strike back, but her feet tangled, and she fell to the floor.

"Better learn balance." The old man smiled. The instructor Eve had put in the sim was familiar to her, but she couldn't remember where she had seen him before. He was a Japanese man with white hair around a very pronounced bald spot with a wispy white beard and mustache. He had a warm glint in his eyes, like a wizened old *sofu*. As a *sensei,* he showed no mercy when he repeatedly attacked and effortlessly countered every move she made.

Koda climbed to her feet slowly. Her body ached from the blows the old man had rained down on her.

"Remember, Koda-*san,* the best block is not to be there," he chided.

Koda's eyes widened as realization struck her.

"Eve! Am I seriously getting my ass kicked by Mister Wax-on, Wax-off?"

An amused snicker echoed around her. "End simulation," the AI called.

Once the sim faded out and Koda was in the green room that signaled the beginning and end, she pulled the helmet that contained the hardware to use the sim off and dropped it on the floor. The quick movement brought her up short when her body registered the pain from the hits she had taken in the sim.

"Ow! What the hell, Eve? Why am I still feeling this?"

"Because Akio told me pain is the best teacher. Embrace the suck." She laughed.

"Oh, this sucks for sure. I feel like a truck ran over me."

Koda carefully stretched. Each place she had been hit in the sim still had an echo of the pain. She wondered if Seki had felt this bad after she'd tweaked his settings during the tournament.

"What did you set the feedback to? Level one hundred?"

"Stop whining. It was less than you set for Seki. Now, if you want to know what suck really is, I can set your next session at the level I moved him to." Eve grinned evilly.

"No, no, I'm good." Koda made a motion of zipping her lips. "No more whining."

"Good. Besides, you don't think Akio will go any easier

on you, do you? You have heard them when he and Yuko spar?"

Koda nodded, remembering the times those two had rattled the dishes in the kitchen when one of them hit a wall in the training room.

"What did you think about the training? Other than the pain?"

"I think that was a cheap trick having the old man from that movie as the instructor avatar." She huffed.

"It needed something. I remembered how hard you laughed at his sayings, so I thought it was very appropriate." Eve looked at her with a serious face for a moment, then broke into a grin.

"Has Asai seen it yet?"

"No. Why?"

"Because she was the one who wandered around here for days after we watched it, spouting the funnier lines. I want to see how funny she thinks it is when she is on the receiving end of the ass-kicking."

"I'll bring the popcorn." Eve chuckled, setting Koda off into hysterical laughter.

CHAPTER ELEVEN

Serenity Temple, Dabie Mountains, China

"Master, more fighters are arriving daily. We are running out of room for them," Cui explained as he made his progress report.

"How many have arrived so far?"

"Two hundred and sixteen. That number doesn't include the one hundred and twenty-seven that were already here being trained. Li's group and mine have completed their training to the point where we can deploy them now."

Kun's features darkened and he pierced Cui with a steely gaze. "Why have only two hundred reported? That number should be closer to five hundred warriors."

Cui shifted uncomfortably, unsure how Kun would react to what he told him next. "Some enclaves have refused."

"Refused! Who are they to refuse me?" Kun lunged to his feet from the cushion he sat on.

"They dare defy my command! Give me the names of each who think they can refuse."

Cui pulled a sheet of paper from his robes and handed it to the enraged Master.

Kun snatched the note from him. His eyes darted down the perfectly printed characters, then narrowed as he focused on one entry. "Shek has defied me as well? This is the second time he's questioned my authority. He will be my example to the others."

Cui stood motionless, dreading Kun's next words.

"You will arrange travel supplies and weapons for fifty warriors. You're to select the warriors personally and lead them to Shek's enclave. When you arrive, any who dare defy the decree I send, you will execute immediately. Place their heads on stakes in the town square as a reminder to all what happens when they dare to ignore my commands. Do not return here without Shek's head in a sack. You don't want to fail me again. Do you understand?"

"I understand, Master. I will take Ren as my second and put Yi in charge of the troops here, with Pan seconding him."

"Make it so. I expect you back here with your prize within two weeks. When you return, the plans to remove Akio and that vampire he took from us will be in place. Once Li reports that he has the location, we will take this war to them.

"Now, see to your assignment. Tell Yi I wish to see him. I have a task he must complete, ensuring that we have what we need to send a proper message to any who dare stand in the way of the Sacred Clan."

Cui prostrated himself at Kun's feet. Kun had required

this of him each time he entered and left his presence since Cui failed to deal with the Forsaken. "The Clan shall rise," he intoned as his forehead pressed against the stone floor.

"The Clan rises. Get out now, and remember my words about failure."

Cui rose and bowed low as he backed out of Kun's chambers. Once in the corridor, he leaned against the wall, icy fear running through his body. Kun had been more unpredictable and subject to fits of rage since Cui had told him about how the Forsaken escaped. He was certain Kun's orders when carried out would cause even more bloodshed within the Clan before the rift it created healed.

Shek was the second-highest-ranking member behind Kun in the Clan hierarchy. He had questioned but never openly challenged Peng Kun when he named himself the leader. Before Kun took the mantle, Shek was the likely choice to lead them because he'd served as an assistant under the Leopard Empress' father for many years. The only reason he had survived when the Bitch Queen killed their empress was that he was away dealing with a recalcitrant Party official in Beijing. Cui wondered, not for the first time, if Shek would be a better leader than Kun.

Cui shook his head to dispel the thought, knowing Kun would have no issue removing him if he suspected him of having treasonous thoughts. He wished Li was here instead of in Japan. He kept Kun grounded when he became angry. Cui hoped he would have the information Kun required soon. Then maybe Kun would not be as likely to kill anyone who brought him unwelcome news or he thought was questioning his authority.

"Yi, assemble a team and go to Shanghai. Once there, you're to secure two ships, one large enough to transport one hundred warriors to Japan. The other will also need to travel to Japan and must have at least twenty square meters of open deck space," Kun ordered as Yi lay with his forehead pressed to the floor.

"If you can find ships that already travel to Japan regularly, take them. They won't raise as much suspicion as an unknown vessel will. When you have the second ship secured, report back immediately and move it up the coast to Quingdao. I'll have the armament it needs transported to you there for installation."

Before Yi could answer, the satellite phone next to Peng Kun rang. "Leave me and see to your assignment," he called as he snatched the phone up and stalked into his private quarters.

"Do you have good news, Li?" he asked as he accepted the call.

"We are making progress, Master. We have located the place where those gangsters ran afoul of this Akio and have determined he is the same one who killed our team in Wajima. The report that the Japanese government helped him also appears accurate. The night the Yakuza were attacked, the police blocked off the area and cleared the buildings around the noodle house the gangsters conducted business from," Li answered.

"Have you located his base yet?"

"No, Master, but we know there is some connection between him and an entertainment complex not too far away. Shao found out the Yakuza kidnapped a woman who works there, and that led to Akio becoming involved. I have Shao and Jin locating a place in an apartment building across from the complex to watch the building, hoping we can locate him through it. I have also had Jin spreading yen around to the laborers and delivery men who work the area for any information they might come across."

"Continue as you have been and keep me informed. If you need more manpower, contact Sakutaro. If he is hesitant, kill whoever you must in order to convince the Yakuza it is in their best interests to assist us. I am planning to deal with the vampire problem as soon as you locate them."

"As you command, Grand Master."

Kun smiled as he cut the connection, Li was making progress and should have the information he needed to end the possibility of this vampire interfering further. He went back to his den and sat on the cushion, appearing to be in deep meditation when in fact he was fleshing out the plans that would cement his position as ruler of the Clan forever.

CHAPTER TWELVE

The Palace, Tokyo, Japan

"Welcome back, Horst. How are things progressing on Kume?" Eve asked as the Were came into the office they shared.

"Very well. The navy delivered everything as promised, and Ito-*san* has the project moving faster than expected. You did well finding him," Horst answered.

"Ito-*san* came highly recommended. If this works as well as expected, I have him in mind to build the port facilities I am planning for our vessels."

"Port facilities?"

"I don't plan to base our ships out of the commercial facilities here. I have located a property that has the room for shipbuilding and warehouse space near the existing port. Akio feels that having our own facilities will be more secure than if he vets any we use," she explained.

Horst nodded thoughtfully. "I see where that makes sense. Can we afford it?"

Eve gestured to a monitor mounted on the wall. "These

are the projections for profits, based on the cargo I already have contracts for and projected passenger loads. There is a lot more interest in travel than I anticipated. We've already booked the first four voyages to over ninety percent capacity for almost every leg."

Horst looked at the numbers and smiled. "That's amazing."

"I plan to meet with a large beef producer next week. I will offer him refrigerated space to ship his product to Okinawa. Beef is scarce there, and our ability to transport it so it's fresh when it arrives at the markets should be a powerful selling point."

Horst whistled softly. "Have I told you how glad I am that you allowed me to be your partner?"

Eve raised a hand to her face and tapped her chin with a finger. "Not since Thursday at three forty-seven in the afternoon."

"Well, I still am." The Were smiled.

"Where are we on launching the ships? Are we still on schedule for later this week?"

"Nope." Eve grinned as she stood from her seat. "Care to take a ride?"

Koda, Asai, and Yuko entered the office before he could answer.

"Hi, my mountain of man," Koda greeted him as she walked over and wrapped her arms around him. "I missed you. How is everyone on Kume?"

"They're fine, my tiny beauty." He smiled. "I missed you too."

"Horst-*san,* I am glad to see you. You look well," Yuko greeted him.

He released Koda and bowed. "Thank you, Yuko-*san*. The sun and sea air on Kume seem to agree with me. Yagi-*san* sends his good wishes and an invitation to come for tea soon."

Yuko nodded and smiled. "I will try to do so."

"I would like to accompany you when you do," Asai offered. "I want to see my mother."

Horst chuckled. "I have a message from her for you. She says, 'Tell my daughter I will be very disappointed if she does not bring her young man to meet me soon.' Your father had a different message. I believe I'll let him deliver it himself."

"Ooh, Seki's going to get it from Suzu when he meets him." Koda chortled.

Horst grinned down at her. "He only said he wished to take him fishing."

Asai blushed, then a look of horror came over her face. "I hope Seki can swim. I've never asked him."

Koda giggled and Horst looked at them, confusion on his face.

"You better hope he can if he doesn't answer your father's questions correctly. You know how Suzu gets where you're concerned."

"Yes, I better talk with him before we go. Father can be a bit…intense, to put it mildly."

"I'm sure Seki will be fine," Eve interrupted. "We need to be going since it's almost time."

Motoki Shipyard, Gamagori, Japan

The black Pod settled between two rundown warehouses at the facility Eve had chosen to upgrade the four ships she had purchased. Horst opened the door and the group exited, Koda and Asai looking around curiously with Yuko following.

"Uh, this is disgusting." Asai choked as the odor of rotted fish and chemicals blew between the buildings when the wind shifted.

"The fish is not so bad, but that other makes my nose burn," Koda agreed. "What is it?"

"There is a tannery next door." Horst chuckled. "You know those cute boots you like so much? That is how they get the leather to make them."

"If the boots smelled like that, I would go barefoot." Asai snorted as she waved her hand in front of her nose.

"From the look on your face, Asai, I'm glad I have no sense of smell." Eve snickered.

"Be thankful for small blessings. Why are we here?"

Yuko took the lead as she headed toward the opening at the end of the alley formed by the buildings. "To see the launch of Eve's and Horst's first ship."

Horst's head jerked up from where he was smiling down at Asai. "Seriously, one is ready to launch?"

"No." Eve grinned. "One is ready to depart with its first load of cargo and passengers. It launched three days ago and passed its sea trial with flying colors. The second will launch for its trials as soon as the first departs."

Horst shook his head, shocked at the speed with which Eve had gotten not one but two of the ships refitted. "What about the others?" he cautiously asked.

"The third's completed. I only need to do a walk-through to check that everything's hooked up properly and activate the Etheric power supply. The fourth will be ready in three more days."

"It looks like you are about to become a shipping magnate, my fluffy friend." Koda giggled.

Horst could only nod, still shocked by how fast this venture had come together and forever thankful Eve had included him in it.

Onboard *Kizoyama Kyou*, Motoki Shipyard, Gamagori, Japan

Kimura Hikonaga looked down from the rail of the ship at the small crowd assembled to see it off. He was dressed like any mid-level manager in dark slacks, a white shirt, and a dark suit coat. He would have fit in without notice at many of the businesses that operated throughout Japan. The camouflage had always served him well for what his actual job was.

Kimura was an expediter, the first person sent to contact businesses and people who caught the attention of his boss, Kishi Sakutaro. Kishi was the voice of Sato Sakutaro, her *sofu* and *Oyabun* of the last Yakuza family in Tokyo.

Kimura had caught Kishi's eye when he was a junior soldier barely out of his teens and she was a strong-willed girl of fifteen. The old man himself had assigned Kimura to guard her, figuring that someone close to her age would blend in better with her peers. Kimura could easily pass for someone several years younger than his twenty-three years.

Kishi had liked the way he talked to her, unlike the

older guards. Kimura asked her opinion on how she would like him to guard her. Not that he would allow it to stop him from doing his job, but where her wishes didn't go against his orders from her grandfather, he allowed her freedom she had never gotten from the old men.

They'd developed a bond over the years, and when Kishi started taking an active role in running the family, Kimura was there to do whatever task she set for him. Kishi had a knack for finding businesses to either add to the family organization or put under the protection umbrella. Kimura showed an uncanny aptitude for bringing them on board without having to resort to violence. If the job required violence he didn't hesitate, but violence often led to losses. The object was to enrich the family coffers, not to destroy potential revenue streams.

Kishi had ordered him to travel on this ship with a two-fold mission. First, he was to assess whether it would be best to take the company outright from its mysterious owners or if it would be better to offer protection based on a percentage of the gross income generated.

The second reason for this trip was to check on business opportunities at one of its scheduled stops. Before the WWDE, the Yakuza had owned a hotel and restaurant on one of the small islands that were favored tourist stops for people from Japan and other parts of Asia. Kishi has seen an advertisement that the island was opening for tourists again through some partnership with this ship's company. She wanted him to assess the profitability of reopening a hotel or charging for protection instead.

Kimura's eyes narrowed as he caught sight of a huge blond *gaijin* as he stepped onto a raised platform on the dock set aside for, he had been told by a dock worker, the company's owners to watch the ship depart on its maiden voyage. The next person he saw made him do a double-take. She appeared to be a small child, but Kimura recognized her from a photo he had seen before. She was one of the people involved in the fiasco Muto had caused, a member of the group the *Oyabun* had expressly forbidden any member of the family to approach on pain of death.

Kishi would need to know this information before she made a move on the shipping company. Though he was her *sofu* and had raised her, even she could not openly defy the old man and come away unscathed.

Kimura watched in silence as the crew cast the lines off and the ship pulled away from the dock. His calm exterior hid thoughts that were anything but calm. These people had already proven themselves able and dangerous to his family. He hoped Kishi would think twice before taking action that could lead to her being disciplined and him being killed for disobeying the order of the *Oyabun*. But no matter what she decided, he would serve her before all others, even if it cost him his life.

CHAPTER THIRTEEN

TQB Base, Tokyo, Japan

Kenjii dodged, barely avoiding the backstroke of the katana that whistled through the air a hairsbreadth from his leg. He had brought one of his *hudiedao* around to block, but once again came up short and had to dodge Akio's blade.

"Hold," the older vampire called as Kenjii prepared to launch a counterstrike.

Kenjii stopped, his breath coming in fast pants, although Akio, as usual, looked as fresh as he had before they started sparring.

Kenjii gasped as he bent with his hands on his knees. "I don't get it. Do you never tire?"

Akio quirked one eyebrow up, and one side of his mouth twitched in what Kenjii had come to recognize as a smile. "Of course I do. When I'm pushed hard enough."

"You are not normal. Whatever that Queen of yours did to you has made you into an *oni*."

"Not an *oni,* just a better version of me. You can't get discouraged. I have been doing this for hundreds of years."

"Just the same, I would like to at least get a hit on you occasionally. Between your speed and that demon-damned sword, I can't get close."

"That was why I stopped. The *hudiedao* is an excellent weapon for close-in fighting, but I think you need to consider something longer."

"You've already seen that I'm even worse with the katana. At least with these, I am not in danger of slicing my leg off."

"True." Akio smirked. "I don't think you would be nearly as attractive with half a leg."

Kenjii grinned and placed both hands on his hips, careful not to put the blades he gripped in each against his body. Though they were dull practice swords that Eve had crafted for him, Akio had corrected him several times about being careless with them. The last time, he had flashed across the room and kicked the blade that rested on his thigh with enough force to fracture his femur. He was a staunch believer that pain was the best teacher, and Kenjii didn't want to go another round with him while he was healing a bone. Akio's warning to always train as if it were real echoed through his brain whenever they sparred now.

Kenjii struck a pose, with one leg bent at the knee behind him. "You mean you wouldn't want me if I looked like this?"

"I didn't say that. I just prefer you with all of your appendages in their proper places," Akio deadpanned.

Kenjii pursed his lips and blew him a kiss. "So, what did you have in mind?"

Before he could respond, Abel's voice came over the speakers hidden in the ceiling. "Akio. I have located an area of interest on the satellite feed. I believe it is a location controlled by the tigers you seek in China."

"I'll be there in a moment."

"We will have to address different weapons later. I need to attend to this."

Kenjii nodded as Akio racked his practice katana and turned to leave. Before he exited the training room, a look of determination crossed Kenjii's face. "Akio?"

He turned to face Kenjii. *"Hai?"*

"If you locate the ones who pursued me, I would like to accompany you when you deliver…Justice, as you call it."

Akio pursed his lips as he considered the request. Coming to a decision, he nodded once. *"Hai.* Come with me, and let's see what Abel has for us."

Command Center, TQB Base, Tokyo, Japan

The monitor they watched zoomed in on a lone man standing on a rise above a field occupied by over one hundred people working. "If you will look here, he carries no weapons, but the people do not resist him."

As they watched, the man strode down the rise, moving faster until his features blurred. He stopped beside an elderly woman who had collapsed in the field. None of the others had looked at her, stepping over her prone form as the only acknowledgment she was there.

"Did you speed that up?" Kenjii asked.

"No, this footage is running at actual speed," Abel answered.

The man leaned down and said something to the prone woman. His next action removed any doubt that he was from the UnknownWorld. He reached down and pulled her up with one hand, his arm stretched in front of his body while her feet dangled half a meter off the ground. He pulled his free hand back, and it blurred as it flashed toward the woman. In the next instant, there was a spray of blood, and the woman's detached head flew two rows over from where he held her.

He dropped the body and eyed the nearby workers. None of them raised their eyes from the task they were performing to look at the man or their fellow worker's body.

The playback stopped and then restarted at the point seconds before he killed the woman. The frame froze and zoomed in tight on the man's hand, or rather, the orange paw with white-tipped toes and claws on it.

Kenjii nodded, not bothered by the death of the woman but wanting to attack the tigers for what they had done to him.

Akio picked up on his thoughts and his lack of empathy for the plight of the humans. "Are you willing to fight the tigers to free the humans they're holding?"

"I will fight the tigers for existing. If it helps the humans you wish to free, I suppose that is a bonus," Kenjii answered, his eyes never leaving the screen.

"Understand that if I take you, I must have your assurance that you will harm none of the humans. You can never take from the innocent."

Kenjii turned to him. "I promise I will harm none of the

humans; you have my word. I only want to eliminate the Sacred Clan from the face of the Earth."

Akio nodded. "Prepare a Pod, Abel. We leave," he glanced at the clock on the wall, "ten minutes after the sun has set in…where is this?"

"Near Quzhou, about three hundred fifty kilometers southwest of Shanghai."

Pod over Quzhou, China

"When did Eve get the measurements for this armor?" Kenjii asked as he looked down at the jet-black chest piece that fit him like a second skin.

"She didn't. I did," Abel replied, sounding smug.

"*Domo*, Abel. It fits perfectly."

"You are welcome. Eve and I felt it best to prepare in the event you accompanied Akio on any missions. We spent a great deal of time locating you and wouldn't want to lose you to something we could prevent."

"You are over Quzhou now, Akio. Would you prefer a direct drop, or do you wish to land and approach on foot?"

"Set us down two kilometers west of the location. We'll make our way in and determine how many Clan members are present."

"My surveillance has confirmed four hostiles. I have uploaded a map with the location where they house the humans at night and the home the hostiles went into after they had secured the humans.

"I have uploaded the information to the screen located in the right arm of your armor."

Kenjii looked down at his right arm and then at Akio

when he didn't understand how to access the screen. Akio held his arm up and tapped twice on the spot where the gauntlet joined the arm, and a small screen slid out of a previously invisible slot. Kenjii did the same. When he was done, he looked at Akio, who tapped the same spot once, causing the screen to retract.

"Absolutely amazing," Kenjii whispered as he did the same.

The Pod door slid open, and both exited into the darkness.

"Abel, put the Pod three kilometers above the camp. Hold it there until we're done."

"Will do, Akio. Happy hunting."

Sacred Clan Farm Camp, Quzhou, China

"Are the animals all in for the night?" Tang Lim called when Xian walked through the door after making his rounds.

"Yeah, they're all down for the night. You would think they had worked or something." He guffawed.

"If Gu keeps killing them out of hand, we will need more soon," Geng called from the kitchen.

"No work, no live," Gu muttered from his spot on the old leather sofa. "If we need more, it's not like they're scarce or anything."

As Geng turned to reply, the door flew into the room with a loud crash. He dropped the iron skillet he was holding, and before it hit the floor, an orange and black tiger stood in the kitchen. Gu changed a second later, and a larger tiger with more white than black snarled from the shredded couch.

Kenjii stepped through the door, the visor open on his helmet and his eyes flashing red. "Here, kitty, kitty," he taunted as Geng snarled and dropped his haunches, preparing to leap.

Akio winced when he heard the crash, followed by Kenjii's taunt. He had instructed Kenjii to wait and watch the house until he was certain there were no other Weres present. He pushed his senses out, and once he was certain the four in the house were the only ones present, he ran the hundred yards to the house in a flash.

He stopped in the open doorway and surveyed the scene. A tiger was in mid-air, flying toward Kenjii, and another was moving in from across the room. Two others were in human form, one of them with a nasty-looking set of taloned paws instead of hands at the ends of his arms. The other was watching the scene play out with an amused smirk on his face.

Kenjii brought one of his swords toward the airborne tiger just before he landed on him. The blade pierced the large cat above his sternum and just below his throat. The vampire twisted in a blur, and when he stopped, he was across the room as the tiger crashed down in the open doorway. His body was limp and boneless, and blood gushed out of the ragged wound that halfway circled his neck.

The other tiger switched direction, his claws digging

deep furrows in the wooden floor as he charged toward Kenjii. The smirking man looked at the dying tiger on the floor, and his face clouded with anger. The sound of ripping cloth signaled his change. When the shift finished, an eight-foot-tall Pricolici tiger stood in his place.

"Yooouuu will dieee, little leeeech," he growled as he started across the room.

Akio stepped through the doorway, his katana in his right hand and a Jean Dukes Special in his left. He raised the pistol and fired one round at the Pricolici. His eyes widened in shock as the enormous beast jerked to the side, the round intended for his chest barely grazing his arm.

The Pricolici continued the spin, and before Akio could get another shot into him, the monster was on him. The impact knocked him off his feet when the floor collapsed under the combined weight of the four-hundred-kilo tiger and him.

The huge claws tried to penetrate his armor, and he felt the pressure of each as it strained it to the breaking point. Akio's eyes went red and his fangs extended as he brought his gauntleted hands up, hammering the tiger on his exposed sides.

Though he felt ribs break each time he struck him, the huge cat continued to try to peel his armor open with his claws. Akio reached down to his belt with one hand and grasped the tanto secured there while pounding the tiger mercilessly with the other. He twisted his hand and slammed the tanto hilt-deep into the beast's side, twisting it for good measure.

The Pricolici snarled and pushed with both huge paws, shoving Akio deeper into the broken floor. Akio yanked the tanto from his side and drove it into the soft flesh of his belly. He ripped the razor-sharp blade up, cutting through muscle and flesh until it stopped with a thud as it hit the monster's breastbone,

The cat coughed once as his entrails spilled over Akio, giving an ear-shattering roar. Akio pulled the blade free, shoved his gauntlet through the torn flesh deep into the beast's chest, and wrapped his fingers around the pulsating heart. With a hard twist followed by a downward jerk, he yanked the heart free of the tiger's chest cavity, holding it in front of the golden eyes until the light faded from them.

Akio dropped the bloody chunk of meat and shoved hard with both hands. The heavy weight pinning him shifted, allowing him to lash out with his legs. He kicked until he freed himself from the broken boards. Once free, he pushed clear and rose unsteadily to his feet. His body jerked when he heard an agonized cry.

Kenjii knew he was screwed when he heard a monstrous roar from across the room that made his entire body vibrate. He took his eyes off the tiger that was rushing toward him, and the last thing he saw before it knocked him to the floor was a thing of legend: a monster tiger standing erect on two legs, whose head brushed the ceiling of the house.

Kenjii's eyes widened as the giant cat growled at him. The split-second distraction was all it took for the attacking tiger to crash into him in a flurry of claws and teeth. Kenjii went down under the assault, while two hundred kilos of pissed-off tiger tried to tear through his armor. He fought for his life as the tiger brought its rear legs up, raking him from his stomach to his knees repeatedly. The beast snarled and brought its head down, jaws gaping toward his face. Kenjii shoved an armored arm between the jaws an instant before the teeth closed on his vulnerable face.

Hot, rancid breath assailed his nostrils as the tiger pressed the attack, crushing his arm between the powerful jaws. He sent a silent thank you to Eve when the armor held under the brutal attack.

Kenjii brought his knee up and under the cat as he rolled his body to escape the deadly claws that were cutting deep furrows into his armor. A sharp pain told him the armor had failed in at least one place, possibly more. He heard a creak as the teeth pressed harder into the arm, stressing the armor to the breaking point.

Kenjii shoved as hard as he could from his prone position and shifted the cat to one side. This slight shift allowed him to bring the butterfly sword still gripped in his free hand up and slam it deep into the enraged tiger's side.

The jaws loosened when the cat roared in pain, and Kenjii pulled his battered and bruised arm free. He slammed his gauntlet covered fist into the side of the cat's head, shattering teeth and breaking bones when he did.

The beast went limp, and when Kenjii rolled free, a great weight crushed his chest, pinning him to the floor.

He twisted his head to the side as a claw-tipped paw descended toward his eyes. Fire seared his face as the claws laid his cheek open to the bone in three burning gashes. He let out an anguished scream of pain as blood flooded into his eyes, blinding him.

The cat snarled, and Kenjii knew he would die. Then the weight vanished, and he could move again. Unable to see, he scooted back until he hit the wall and pushed up to a seated position. He wiped his eyes furiously to clear them, and when he could see, he couldn't believe his eyes.

Akio stood in the center of the room, his eyes burning red as he snarled through the fangs that extended from his mouth. He held a tiger by the scruff as he repeatedly slammed it between the wall and the floor. Each time the tiger impacted either, the house shook, and the sickening sound of bones breaking followed.

Kenjii watched in amazement as the man he loved reduced the beast to a limp bag of broken, bloody flesh with his bare hands. Akio continued to slam the lifeless body against the floor until the skin ripped, then the weight of the body pulled it from his hands to crash into the wall one last time before it slid to the floor.

Akio stood, his eyes still glowing like twin fires and his chest heaving as he drew in one ragged breath after another. Kenjii weakly pushed himself up the wall until he was standing, unsure of whether to approach him, experiencing bone-deep fear of the monster that stood before him.

Kenjii's agonized scream caused Akio to stumble and a cold chill shot through his heart. His eyes darted around the small room, frantically searching for the source of the sound. He looked to the side and saw a dead tiger on the floor. Another snarled as it attacked something pinned under it. Akio's vision went red with rage when he saw a scarred, battered, armored arm protruding from under the enraged tiger.

He crossed the room in a single step and hooked his gauntlet-covered hand into the loose skin of the tiger's neck. With a feral growl, he wrenched the beast into the air with one arm and spun in a half-turn to pull it clear of the bloody form trapped beneath it. He was in a murderous rage when the tiger's body hit the wall, knocking plaster off the ceiling from the force of the blow. He pulled hard in the opposite direction and slammed the beast onto the floor, shaking the entire house as he did so.

His mind went numb. The only thing he could remember was Kenjii, his face covered in blood from the tiger's attack. He didn't realize until the weight on his arm was gone that he didn't know if the man who meant more to him than anyone in the world was alive or dead.

He stood with his legs wide, chest heaving as he forced air in and out of his numb body. A soft scuff to his left brought his head around with a snap, and his arms came up, ready to rip the life out of whatever the threat was.

When his vision cleared, he saw Kenjii, one hand outstretched toward him, with a look of absolute terror etched on his face. Akio took one more deep breath and forced his eyes to fade back to their normal soft brown. His fangs retracted before he took a tentative step in his lover's direction, his arm mirroring Kenjii's.

"Are you okay?" Akio asked softly as he took another cautious step toward Kenjii, halting often like he was approaching a skittish colt.

Kenjii shook himself at the sound of the older vampire's voice, calm and normal as he had heard it countless times before. It was his friend, his love, not the raging beast that had stood there before.

Kenjii ran his tongue over his lips, tasting the bitter blood on the tip. "I-I will heal," he cautiously answered.

Akio motioned with his outstretched hand for Kenjii to come to him, and the warrior slowly took an unsteady step toward him. When he shifted his weight to his left leg it gave out, causing him to gasp in pain as it buckled.

Akio caught him before he fell, his powerful arms pulling him close. Kenjii instinctively wrapped his arms around him, and they stood silent for several minutes. The only sound was their breathing and the occasional clunk of plaster hitting the floor as it fell from the shattered ceiling.

CHAPTER FOURTEEN

Quzhou, China

Akio leaned back from the embrace, his eyes narrowed when he saw the three deep furrows the tiger had cut into Kenjii's face. The skin was healing; as he watched, the bleeding slowed to a trickle.

"Come," he commanded as he pulled away. "You need blood."

Kenjii hesitated for a moment at the abrupt command. There was a tone in his friend's voice that not only brooked no disobedience but also held a hint of disappointment.

"Is everything okay? You seem a bit off," Kenjii remarked as he took a halting step in the direction Akio was going.

The older vampire stopped and turned to face him. "It is now. But in the future, when I tell you to wait, I expect you to obey. Had I encountered more Weres, they could have killed you before I arrived. I will not have you die—again—because I exposed you to danger."

Kenjii dropped his head, ashamed he had caused the look of disappointment on Akio's face. "It won't happen again. I'm…I'm sorry."

Akio nodded once, and without a word, walked through the open door and across the front porch into the yard. When Kenjii joined him, the Pod descended and hovered in front of them. Akio went inside, and when he returned, he thrust two bags of blood toward Kenjii.

"Drink this and heal while I deal with the humans," he told him, then stalked to the barn where the humans were being held. *He should listen when I tell him to do something.* That was more frightening than Yuko's escapade on Kume. *I haven't lost control like that in centuries.*

Akio approached the closed double doors leading into the barn. A length of chain and padlock secured them, and he caught the chain in both hands. A quick jerk popped a link, allowing him to pull the chain free.

When he opened the doors, the odor of fear and unwashed bodies permeated the air. Men, women, and children littered the floor, all in tattered, dirty clothes, staring at him with fear in their eyes.

"You're free to return to your homes," he started, and the people involuntarily moved away from him. He took a deep breath to calm himself and tried again.

"The men who have held you captive are no more." His voice was much softer, and the feeling of calm he projected relaxed the people. "You have nothing to fear and can return to your homes."

A woman who was covered in grime slowly stood. She looked like she was in her fifties, but when she spoke, her voice sounded much younger. "How do we know they won't come and take us again? We were all in our village when they took us."

"Those four will take no one ever again," he told her with finality.

She hesitated briefly before she continued. "What of the others? The ones here now are only half the crew who works here. The other four will return next week. What's to stop them from finding and punishing us when they get back?"

Several others in the room stood, emboldened by the woman asking questions. They nodded in agreement.

Akio narrowed his eyes, a hint of anger coloring his voice. "The people who did this will be too busy to worry about you."

"What do you mean?" she asked, her voice tight with concern. "You don't know what they can do. You call them men, but they are beasts—literally."

"I am aware of what they are and who they represent. I will hold them accountable for the laws they violated here. Return to your homes, and know if they come for you, I will too. You need not fear them any longer. They will be too busy trying to survive to cause you any harm."

He turned and strode back to the Pod, leaving them to make their own decision about when to go. The injuries Kenjii had received still occupied his mind.

Abel, please track these people and put surveillance on their village. Notify me if any of the Clan members approach them.

Affirmative. I already have a drone carrier positioned in the area, and it's loaded with the upgraded models. Should I deal with the tigers?

Akio's lips turned up in a half-smile. Abel had

progressed to another level, anticipating need and acting independently.

If it's necessary to prevent them from harming humans, do what you must, but still notify me. I need to talk to one of these Clan members. That is not an option with any of them here.

Acknowledged

"Kenjii, let's go home. We need to get back to the base and check your injuries."

"I'm almost healed." He motioned to his face. "Still sore, but that will pass soon enough. What about you? Did they injure you?"

"No, I'm a little harder to hurt. It will take more than a few tigers to cause damage I can't easily heal."

Kenjii cocked his head to one side as he looked at Akio's battered and scuffed armor over thoughtfully. "*Hai,* let's go home. I need a shower to clean all the gunk off."

Akio reached out and gently pulled something out of Kenjii's hair. He held it in front of him and chuckled as he looked at the bloody piece of meat with orange fur on it. "Yes, you *are* disgusting. Try not to get any on the Pod. Were blood makes a mess."

Kenjii smiled as he motioned to his blood-covered armor. "Do you have something I can sit on? I don't think I can't keep this from staining the upholstery otherwise."

Akio smiled at him as he pulled a folded blanket from a nook in the Pod and handed it to him. "*Hai,* that's probably best."

TQB Base, Tokyo, Japan

"Enter," Akio called as a soft knock came from his door.

Kenjii walked in, his damp hair pulled back from his face, which showed three white lines where the Were had clawed it earlier. The tight t-shirt he wore hugged the muscular curves of his upper body like a second skin. Akio's lips quirked up on one side as he took in the healing and the sculptured chest.

"Tea?" he offered.

"*Hai,* that would be nice," Kenjii acknowledged as he leaned against the counter, watching as Akio measured an aromatic mix of tea leaves and spices into a ceramic pot of steaming water.

"Akio?" Kenjii hesitantly murmured.

"*Hai?*"

"I, ah… What happened back at the house?" he finally managed in a rush.

Akio raised one eyebrow and cocked his head to the side. "What do you mean?"

"The tiger that did this." He pointed to the almost-healed scars on his face. "I, uh, I've never seen you… Uh, you were…"

Akio watched as Kenjii struggled to put his thoughts into words.

"You tore him apart with your bare hands," he finished.

Akio nodded, understanding the question that was really being asked. "I saw you down and covered in blood when I pulled him off. Your..." He looked away and swallowed hard. "When I saw your torn and bleeding face, in my mind, I saw what Isamu and Ogawa did to you. I felt the same rage as that night, only this time, there was no compulsion holding me back."

Kenjii's hand went to his face involuntarily at the

reminder of the night his human life had ended. "Oh, but how were you able to do that? I know you have been around for centuries. Can I expect to have that kind of strength over time?"

Akio carefully weighed his response. He had concealed most of his enhancements from Kenjii, waiting until the man resolved his internal issues before revealing what was possible. "You remember I told you I was...improved. What you saw are some improvements that came about after I met Bethany Anne. Before she changed me, I did not have that level of strength."

"So, she did something to you similar to the things Heinz did to me? Things to strengthen you and allow you to heal faster?"

"Hai."

"Was it painful? Some things Heinz did to me, though they made some positive changes, hurt and took several days to pass."

"No, the process didn't cause me any physical discomfort. It took some time to adapt to them, though."

Kenjii nodded in understanding. "Do you think she would want to change me too? Not that I would not agree, but I've spent years being an unwilling test subject for that bastard Heinz and don't wish to ever be forced into..." His voice trailed off, and he watched Akio expectantly.

"Neither Bethany Anne nor I will force you to undergo any changes. If the time comes, it will be your choice if you wish to do it."

Kenjii sighed in relief. He never wanted to be anyone's victim again. "Thank you, my friend. I appreciate your assurance. If the time comes where your Queen wants me, I am glad she would not force me to change."

"Bethany Anne forces no one to do anything, except those who harm humans. They don't want to do that. She believes people deserve choices."

"She sounds like a true Queen. I hope to meet her someday."

Akio smiled at him. "She will return, and you'll have that chance." His lips thinned to a straight line. "Unless you manage to get yourself killed by not waiting as I ask. 'Here, kitty, kitty?' Seriously?"

Kenjii blushed and ducked his head. "I guess I rushed into that. I saw them there and became so angry at the way the cats pursued me that I wanted to kill them all."

Akio rolled his eyes. "*Hai,* you rushed it. Ask Yuko about her experience with rushing into a situation while blinded by anger. Perhaps it will be enlightening."

He plucked the empty teacup from Kenjii's hand and placed it next to his on the counter. "Come, let's go to the training room. Eve has fashioned a pair of *shuang gou* for you to try. I think the longer reach will be beneficial."

CHAPTER FIFTEEN

Sakutaro Estate, Nishitama District, Tokyo, Japan

"*Sofu*, do you need anything before I go?"

"No, I think I will retire early tonight. Where are you off to, Granddaughter?

"There is a new club opening tonight in Hino. I'm meeting some friends there to check it out."

"Check it out? Is it one of our businesses?"

She shook her head. "Not yet."

Sato's eyes crinkled as he smiled. "So, this is work?"

Kishi smiled back at the old gangster. "Of course, but you never said I couldn't enjoy my work."

"That is true, Kishi. Who are you taking with you?" All hints of levity left his voice. "I don't want you unguarded, given that those...visitors we recently had are still in the area."

"Asaka is driving me and accompanying me this evening."

"I will have Jei assign a team to follow you." He held up a hand to stifle her protest. "I will not risk you, granddaughter. They will follow and stay in touch with Asaka. As long as they are close enough to respond if needed, that is sufficient."

Kishi pursed her lips, knowing that arguing was a waste of time when the old man got like this. She leaned down and hugged him. "I will do as you say, *Sofu*."

"Have fun, and let me know what you find. Clubs are always good for profits."

"*Hai*. Have a good night, and I will see you for lunch tomorrow."

The old man waved as she exited, his mind already on the next task. He picked up and then punched the intercom by his chair. "Jei, I need to see you. Now."

Less than a minute later, there was a soft knock on the door. "Enter."

"You wanted to see me, sir? Is everything all right?"

"*Hai,* Jei. Kishi is going out for the night, and I want extra precautions taken."

Jei stiffened. The *Oyabun* doted on Kishi, but the look on his face told him this was something more. "Sir?"

"Have Asaka and the crew that follows take some of the special ammunition. I want two heavy weapons with the crew and loaded with them when they depart."

"Certainly, sir. May I ask if there is a specific threat we should know about?"

"No, nothing specific. Just an old man being overly cautious, I hope."

Jei bowed deeply to Sato. "I'll take care of it, sir. Will there be anything else?"

"No, that is all."

Jei started for the door, and when he pulled it open,

Sato called, "Have that girl come in here. I'm ready to go to my rooms for the night."

"Yes, sir," Jei replied as he closed the door.

"Good evening, Asaka. You ready to have some fun?" Kishi asked as she got into the black Toyota Century.

It was one of several compromises she had made with Sato years ago. It wasn't the flashy type of car she'd wanted in her teenage years, but the armor plating and bulletproof glass allowed her to travel with only her driver most of the time. Sato had told her she could have the flashy car, but she would always have to deal with a lead and chase car if she did. Valuing her autonomy over flash, she opted to keep the tank, as she called it. She figured if it was good enough for the royal family, it was good enough for her.

"We still going to that new club in Hino?"

"Hai, after we make a stop along the way," she answered as she pulled her small phone from her purse. "Just drive toward Hino for now. I need to make a call."

After she completed the call, she turned in her seat and smiled. "All set. Go to the Ome apartments."

Asaka's lips curled into a frown. "We're not taking Kimura with us, are we?"

"Jealous much?" Kishi giggled. "No, I sent him on a scouting mission earlier this week. He won't be back for a few weeks."

"Good." Asaka smiled. "I hate to share you with him. He's such a drag in the club, flopping around like a fish out of water. He chills my buzz." He chortled as he wiggled his eyebrows at her.

Asaka had been a daily part of her life since not long after she'd moved in with the old man. A year older and the son of one of the best assassins in the Yakuza, Asaka had been training to join the family since birth. Skilled in several martial arts forms at fourteen, he was her regular sparring partner and closest friend through her teenage years. He was more a brother to her than anything else, but he and Kimura had kept a rivalry going since the day Sato brought Kimura on. Kishi found it annoying, but any time she tried to stop it, the moment was lost when one or the other of them would make her laugh. That they were her oldest friends and staunchest supporters in anything she undertook was a given. It allowed them to take liberties others could not. That both would kill for her without question was another.

"You two are going to drive me as insane as *Sofu* if you keep it up. You know he says the same about you?"

"He may say it, but we both know I got me some sweet moves on the dance floor."

Kishi shook her head and let out a groan.

"So, do you know what's got Jei in such a tizzy?" Asaka asked, all levity gone from his voice.

"No, what are you talking about?" Kishi went alert at the mention of her grandfather's chief of security.

"He issued the guys in the chase car and me silver ammunition. Said Sato ordered it."

Kishi was silent as she considered this information. Sato had told her that the man who visited a few weeks ago was one of the tiger men. She wasn't sure if it was true or another sign of dementia. She knew the man sought an enemy of the family, which was the reason she was going to the meeting now. That didn't change what she was planning, but it opened more possibilities in her mind.

Kishi was silent until the car pulled into a garage under an apartment building. The black SUV that had followed close behind the entire trip pulled in as Asaka was opening her door. All four doors opened on the SUV, and the men moved into position, two in front and two behind Kishi and Asaka.

Everyone assigned to the crew tonight was one of Kishi's loyal followers, and they knew the building was where she ran her part of the personal empire she was building. The additional pay she provided bought their silence. That Asaka was one of the deadliest men in the organization ensured it.

They rode in silence to the twenty-seventh floor, where the elevator opened into a hallway with a door at either end. The lead man turned left, and before he got to the door, it opened. A man in a white shirt with a pistol in a shoulder holster held the door for all of them.

"Kishi-*san,* your guest has arrived. He is waiting in the side room."

"Thank you, Hito. Bring *sake* and then escort him to my office."

Hito bowed forty-five degrees and spun on his heel toward the kitchen. The apartment-turned-office was a mirror image of the one at the other end of the hall. The only difference was this one had desks, computers, and phones in the three bedrooms, and the other was a luxury residence. Kishi Sakutaro owned both. Kimura had leveraged them for her in a deal with the developer when they were being built. She never asked the details, but it was one of the few times that Kimura had requested Asaka's help on a project.

Kishi sat at the large antique desk, her back to the floor-to-ceiling windows that offered a stunning view of the mountains behind her. Hito knocked once and opened the door, then escorted a nondescript man wearing workers' clothing in. The man smiled as he saw Kishi and hurried to stand in front of the desk. He bowed as he greeted her. "Kishi-*san,* you are more beautiful each time I see you."

"You flatter me as always, Juba. How is your assignment going?"

Hino poured two cups of warmed *sake* and looked at Kishi. She nodded to the desk, and he placed the bottle next to the glasses and exited the room.

"I have seen the man you sent me to find a few times. He is with three others, at least."

"Do you know if they have had any luck finding the one they seek?"

"Not that I can tell. They must be cautious about moving around in the daylight. There aren't many Chinese in the area, so they stand out." He shrugged. "The police have always maintained a heavy presence in the area. Since what happened with Muto, it is even worse."

Kishi leaned her forehead into her hands as she thought. "I want you to discreetly contact this man. Tell him I wish to speak to him about a mutual problem."

Juba's eyes widened in concern. "Are you sure that's wise? The *Oyabun*—"

"How is your daughter liking her new school?" Kishi interrupted.

The man's face paled. "She likes it very much, Sakutaro-*sama,*" he squeaked.

"Very good. Now, you were saying?" Kishi smiled at him. Instead of being reassured, Juba swallowed hard, trying to force down the lump that rose when he saw the coldness in her eyes.

"*Hai,* I will relay the message."

"Contact Asaka when you have set up a time and place to meet." Kishi nodded once, signaling the meeting was over.

Juba rose and bowed deeply as he backed away, understanding the thinly veiled threat implied. His daughter was in one of the best private schools in the country, all expenses paid by Kishi Sakutaro.

When the door closed, Asaka guffawed from his seat in the corner. "I think he pissed himself a little."

She cut her eyes toward the closed door, her voice hard. "If he wants to keep his little idiot in that school, he better not fuck this up."

Asaka smiled, but his eyes remained cold and hard. "If he wants to keep his head attached to his sorry neck, he better do it and keep his mouth shut."

Kishi turned to him as she stood, one hand outstretched. "And that is why I put up with you, Asaka."

He took her hand and spun her in a circle. "You mean, it's not for my sick dance moves?"

Kishi giggled and pulled him toward the door. "Come on, my dancing king. Katani and her cousin Kanai are meeting us. If I remember correctly, you had a delightful time with both last time we went out."

"And that, Kishi my friend, is why I love you." Asaka grinned as he wiggled his eyebrows at her, sending her into a fit of laughter.

CHAPTER SIXTEEN

Shinjuku City, Tokyo, Japan

"Dammit, Li, I feel like we are chasing our tails here," Wu growled as they walked down the lightly traveled street. "The police questioned Jin and Shao again today. They're all over this area. There aren't many Chinese in this part of town, so we stand out."

"I know, Wu. What else can we do? We couldn't get an apartment in the building across from that damned arcade, and there are limited places to watch from. Maybe we should look for work in the area. At least then we have a reason to be here if the police stop us."

"The burger place down the street has a sign that they are looking for someone to make deliveries. Maybe Jin should apply. He told the officer he was looking for work." Wu chuckled. "I think he would look cute in one of those delivery uniforms."

Li cut his eyes to Wu, about to make a biting comment when he paused. "You know, Wu, that idea has merit, even though you were trying to be funny. It would establish a reason for one of us to be in the area without drawing suspicion."

"Jin's going to hate that." Wu laughed.

"Who said anything about Jin? The place is just up the block. I think since it was your idea, you should be the one who sees it through."

"Come on, Li! Do I look like a delivery boy to you?"

"You look like whatever I tell you," Li growled. "Unless you would like to go back to the temple and explain to Kun why we failed to find these people? You know how he loves the bearer of grim news."

Wu paled as he considered having to face the volatile Kun with news of failing on the mission. Kun was more unpredictable every time Li checked in. Wu knew none of them would fare well if they failed.

"I guess I'll deliver burgers," Wu grumped. "You know I won't hear the end of this from those two."

"Jin and Shao will seek employment in the area also. I think the more eyes we can get on this, the faster we can go home."

"And what will you be doing while we go to our menial task?

"Working on getting more eyes. I think it is time to call on Kun's Yakuza contact again."

"Will he cooperate? He seemed to think he was done, from what you said about the meeting you had with him."

"He's human. He's done when I say he is." Li chuckled. "He's in no position to dictate. We can replace him."

Wu grinned. "I take it you plan to show him how low in the food chain he truly is?"

"If I must. Now, go get that job. I want to see how well your uniform looks on you." Li laughed.

"You know I hate you, right?"

"Hate all you want, but we have arrived. Go in and make a good impression."

"Yeah, I really hate you."

Serenity Temple, Dabie Mountains, China

"Master, Cui reported that he has secured both ships. They will arrive in Quingdao in two days."

Kun looked up from his meditation. His eyes were bloodshot and his complexion sallow. He had not been sleeping, driven by his rage at the failure to capture the Forsaken and the interference by Akio. He nodded to the acolyte. "Has the group I sent to Shanxi reported back yet?"

"No, Master. The last report was that they were about to enter the facility and check the packages. There is no signal inside the mountain, and we can't reach them."

"I know there is no radio signal in the gods-be-damned mountain!" Kun snapped. "Send another team to join them. Tell them I expect an update by this time tomorrow."

"Yes, Master. Will there be anything else?"

"Get out of my sight and follow your orders."

The acolyte pushed up from the floor and bowed deeply until he was out of Kun's room, then ran to the operations officer to relay the message.

Kun smiled when he heard the man racing away. *Weak. All these new ones are weak. They would not have made it before the world went to hell. Even our empress turned out to be weak in the end. The Clan will rise to the status the world has denied us for so long, even if I must separate the chaff from the grain myself to make it happen. Weak, oh so weak. At least Cui has redeemed himself somewhat. He and Ren took care of that traitor Shek and immediately departed to join Pan and Yi on the mission to secure the ships. He failed to capture the leech, but perhaps he will prove not to be as weak as the others.*

Onboard the *Lylia*, Yellow Sea, the Coast of China

"Ren, where did you learn to pilot a boat?" Cui asked from his perch on the rail next to the wheelhouse.

"I grew up in Behai. We were fishermen. Why do you think I chose the warrior's path when I came of age? I hate the stink of these damned boats."

Cui wrinkled his nose, agreeing with Ren about the smell. "Good thing you remember. This boat fits the criteria Kun wanted. Shame the previous owner was so hard to deal with. This would have been a more enjoyable trip if you hadn't killed all of them."

"When the daughter stabbed me in the back with that marlinspike, it annoyed me. I knew I could pilot the boat, and I didn't think much beyond that until they were all dead," Ren muttered.

"Well, congratulations, Captain, you now have your own ship to take to Japan." Cui chuckled.

"I'll round up a crew of humans in Quingdao. There should be a few there who can run this thing without blowing it up."

"Yes, I'm sure there are. Choose well because you're stuck riding with whoever you find."

"What about you?"

"I'll be in my cabin aboard the *Ming Dan*. The only reason I'm here now is that you needed someone to help with the sails. I didn't think you wanted to teach Pan or Yi to do it. Being from the steppes, this is the first time either of them has been on a boat."

"You're right." Ren laughed. "They were both green and leaning over the rail before we were out of the harbor. At least you're only a little green."

"Careful." Cui grinned. "I can still put them both here with you for the trip to Japan."

Ren's eyes widened, and his face took on a horrified look before he burst out laughing. "It would almost be worth it to watch."

"You are a sick individual, Ren Tan, very sick," Cui deadpanned. He couldn't maintain it and chuckled. "But you're right, it would be fun to watch."

"Why did Kun want a boat with this much empty deck space?"

"He didn't tell me. He only said it would be a deciding factor when we went after the leeches in Japan."

Ren shook his head. "I hope we finish this soon. That business with Shek still worries me. He didn't even resist when we came for him. It was like he wanted to die for defying Kun."

Cui nodded. "I noticed that too. I think there will be questions about Kun's actions when the other leaders hear about it. No matter what the outcome, we're covered. We were following the command of the recognized leader of the Clan."

"I know. It's just that Kun has changed since all this started. I don't like it."

"Me either," Cui muttered too low for Ren to hear.

Shinjuku City, Tokyo, Japan

There he is.

Juba had made the fifty-kilometer trip from Ome to Shinjuku City by bicycle. He was not high enough in the family to rate a vehicle or even regular access to one. Once he arrived, he wandered the area he had seen the man he sought in each time before. That he found him so soon, even though it was after midnight, was a welcome event.

"Excuse me, honorable sir. May I have a word with you?"

Li turned at the sound of the voice behind him. A man wearing a white suit with a black shirt and white tie, the same uniform as the Yakuza soldiers he had encountered at Sakutaro's home, stood a few feet behind him.

Li sniffed the air, catching the man's scent. "What does the Yakuza want?"

Juba took a step back. The man caused his fight-or-flight instinct to kick in, and it was all he could do not to run away. He was not a large man, but there was something about him that Juba sensed was extremely dangerous.

"Well, spit it out. What do you want?" Li growled, menace in his tone. His day had been trying, with Jin and Shao getting the attention of the police, then Wu questioning his orders to seek a job. He was in no mood to play games with a Yakuza flunky.

Juba took an involuntary step back. "I, ah, my mistress wishes to speak to you," he finally stammered.

"Your mistress? Why would I wish to speak to a

woman? Any dealings I have with you people are with Sato Sakutaro, not some female."

Juba stiffened. Though he was low in the hierarchy, a fact Kishi and her cadre never let him forget, he still took offense to this foreigner being disrespectful to her. "My mistress is Kishi Sakutaro, the granddaughter of the *Oyabun*. You would be wise not to dismiss her as an inconsequential woman."

Li nodded, remembering the young woman he had seen when he met the Yakuza leader. "What does she want? Sakutaro made it clear that he would not interfere with my mission, nor was he willing to give additional help."

"My mistress does not share all things with me. She only instructed me to find you and tell you she wishes to speak to you."

"Very well. Tell her I will see her tomorrow. She can pick the time and place. Find me and tell me when and where." Li stalked into the night before the man could reply.

Juba shook his head, curious as to why Kishi wanted to see this rude *gaijin*. Turning back the way he had come, he made his way to the bicycle he had used to travel from Ome and pulled out the small telephone they had given him to contact Asaka. It pleased Juba not to have to deal with Asaka while he was out on the town when it went to voicemail. The man was volatile on a good day. Rumors said he was worse when disturbed while he was partying with Kishi.

CHAPTER SEVENTEEN

Sunset House, Kume Island, Okinawa, Japan

"Hikonaga-*san,* the work is progressing well?"

"*Hai,* Yagi-*san.* We should be ready to hook the power up this afternoon. All that will remain is to put the kitchen appliances in, and the restaurant will be ready to open."

"That is wonderful news." Yagi beamed. "My daughter and her cousin are looking forward to opening. I'm sure the workers on the other projects will welcome the opportunity to eat somewhere other than the construction kitchen."

Hikonaga nodded in agreement. "The food there is good, but it is basic. I understand there will be a chef from Tokyo coming here."

"My daughter told me she was able to convince a retired royal family chef to run the kitchen. He is older but in good health, and he jumped at the opportunity to move here. He said he's tired of the city and wants a quieter life."

"I'm not surprised. It is a beautiful place, and there will

be many opportunities to profit for people positioned to take advantage of it."

"I hope so. I look forward to finishing the work here. I've never run a restaurant, but my wife assures me that between us, we will manage." Yagi frowned. "I have always trusted her judgment, but it is all new."

Kimura ducked his head to hide the smile on his lips. He had spoken to Yagi daily over the past month while the building was being constructed. The information he had gathered from these conversations was gold.

It didn't take much for him to discover that one of the two owners was the kidnap victim who led to Muto's demise. The first time he had met Yuko, he almost had a heart attack. To learn that the people the *Oyabun* had forbidden them to approach were deeply involved with the project here and the shipping company was concerning.

Kimura had planned to stay only long enough to secure a place for the family in the new businesses. As he learned more talking to Yagi and the other residents, he decided the people here were a weakness they could use against the ones involved in the Muto incident. He knew Kishi would want anything he could find that she could use, with the job ending soon. He still didn't know enough.

"Your daughter is lucky to have someone as dedicated as you and your wife to oversee this for her. It amazes me that someone so young can afford an investment this big."

"The people she works for in Tokyo have done much for her. She has learned all that they have taught her and has become a vital part of their business there. If it wasn't for them, we would be dead instead of bringing new life to Kume."

"Dead? Surely there was enough to keep your village fed here. You live in a paradise," Kimura pushed. He had heard similar remarks before, but each time he questioned the speaker, they gave him unsatisfying answers. The people here were hiding something, and he wanted to know what.

"*Hai,* the island provided all we needed to survive. There were some," Yagi hesitated, "recent issues they dealt with that threatened us all."

Kimura noticed how Yagi looked away when he hesitated. This wasn't the first sign of deception he had seen the man display when this topic came up. "An illness or other natural disaster?" he pressed.

"Ah, yes, something like that," Yagi finally answered, looking uncomfortable. "I have kept you from your work long enough, Hikonaga-*san.* Excuse me, I have other business to attend to." Yagi spun and walked away. Kimura watched him through hooded eyes, wondering what had happened that he was unwilling to divulge.

Kimura finished up for the day, which involved talking to the real foreman of the crew, another Yakuza member. When he had gotten the information to update Yagi when they next met, he made his way to the harbor area to check out the first business that someone not from Kume opened.

Tabata Kion, recently retired from the Japanese navy, had opened the first bar on Kume the week before. He had convinced Yagi to let him open the place in an abandoned house next to the harbor, winning him over with the argument that with all the construction workers, it would be a profitable business for him and the island. He also assured

Yagi that he and his partner, a former army trooper, could keep the workers happy, and most of all, from getting so drunk they caused problems. Yagi was hesitant until Tabata told him he would keep his favorite *sake* in stock and always available.

It was a minor operation now, but Kion planned to build a new building on an adjacent lot. Kimura had tried to get the contract to build it, but Kion had informed him that the company building the navy facilities already had that contract. Kimura didn't care. He knew that it would be easy to get Kion to pay for protection when the time was right. He imported all his alcohol, and the family had their hands deep in that industry. He would either pay, or they would make sure he didn't have a product to sell.

When Kimura entered the building, he hid the disgust he felt. Coming from Tokyo, the place was so beneath where he normally went it was hardly a bar. The bar occupied the front half of the home in a space that only had room for a long table with stools made of rough planks on stands and eight small tables with chairs. It was still early and most of the workers weren't off, but the place was still over half-full.

Kimura surveyed the room until he saw who he was looking for. Yagi might be tight with information, but the old man with the strange scars on his neck and arms—scars that looked like some wild beast had ravaged him—would talk to anyone who bought him a drink. Kimura had heard him the last time he was there and remembered him talking about the old days before WWDE on Kume. If anyone knew what had happened that brought the island to the people from Tokyo's attention, it should be him.

"*Konichiwa,* Ichizo-*san.* May I join you?"

The man looked up from his drink and smiled at Kimura. "*Hai,* Hikonaga-*san,* join me."

"What are you drinking, Ichizo?"

He held up his cup. "This weak beer they brew on the mainland. I wish we had the crops to brew real beer." He grimaced. "This stuff is like drinking water."

Kimura smiled and nodded, motioning to Kion to bring two *sakes*. "Join me for a glass, my treat," he offered when Kion placed the cups in front of him.

The old man smiled as he held the potent alcohol under his nose and sniffed. "Ah, this is the good stuff. *Domo.*"

"Think nothing of it. I like company when I drink, and I wished to speak to you anyway."

Ichizo looked up from his drink, confusion in eyes already glassy and red from the drinks he had consumed. "Me? Why would you want to talk to me? I'm just a useless old man."

"You are far from useless or old. You have led an interesting life. I heard you talking about Kume before the WWDE, how people from all over Japan came here to see the beauty of the island. I would like to hear more."

"*Hai,* Kume was a tourist destination. The beaches were pristine, and the people from the mainland enjoyed the slow pace of life here. It differed greatly from living in the cities, always bustling with people everywhere."

Ichizo launched into a story about things he saw while working at an island hotel before the WWDE. Kimura motioned to Kion for a bottle and continued to pour as Ichizo talked. When his story ran down, Kimura jumped in before he could go into another.

"What about after the WWDE? How did you survive here then?"

"I fished and raised cattle. Kume was a large producer of beef before the WWDE. When the ability to ship it dried up and the disease and storms ravaged everything, I found four cows and a bull that had no owner. I could trade beef and fish for other things until…" He stopped talking and a haunted look crossed his face.

Kimura took the cup from his hand and filled it again before handing it back. "Until?" he prompted.

Ichizo shuddered, his face visibly pale under his tanned skin. "Until the monsters came."

"Monsters?"

Ichizo looked around before he slid his chair closer. "*Hai,* monsters. They came after dark several months ago. A beast claiming to be the emperor and his henchmen."

Kimura watched as Ichizo raised his cup, his hands shaking so badly the *sake* spilled over the side. "They set up in the castle across the island and took people in the night, some to work on the castle and others." Ichizo swallowed hard. "Others they turned into raging beasts with eyes that glowed like an *oni*'s. Dark creatures that fed on whatever flesh they could find."

Kimura filled the empty cup and motioned for him to continue. "Those beasts were terrible, but we could keep them out with a strong enough shelter. So long as you were in by dark, you were okay 'til morning."

He pointed to the scars on his neck and arms. "They didn't come close to the ones who took over the castle. They were different; they came in the night for blood. If you failed to open when they called, they would take all inside the house. No matter how strong the doors, they went through them like we'd made them of rice paper. We never saw any they took like that again."

"What happened to them? Surely they are not here any longer?" Kimura asked.

"No, our saviors came from the sky. They destroyed all of them and burned their bodies not far from here. The government sent help, and now we are rebuilding."

"Who are these saviors?"

"Yuko-*sama...*" He cut off abruptly, remembering the warning Yagi had given everyone not to talk about what happened and never to mention the roles the saviors played.

"Pardon me," Ichizo said as he climbed unsteadily to his feet. "I need to be getting home."

Kimura raised the almost-empty bottle. "One more before you go?"

"No, no, I really must be going. Thank you for the drinks," he called as he staggered to the door.

Kimura shook his head as he sipped from the cup he had hardly touched. Interesting. As drunk as he is, he won't talk about the people from Tokyo. This business about monsters was strange but not unbelievable. There had been animals who turned into men in the rural areas of the country. Even the *Oyabun* had warned everyone to keep the silver ammunition close.

Kimura finished his drink and pushed away from the table. The job was almost finished, and it was time to go home to report his findings to Kishi. He knew she would be angry he hadn't secured the businesses she'd sent him for, but he also knew she was not ready to openly defy the old man yet.

CHAPTER EIGHTEEN

The Palace, Tokyo, Japan

Akio and Eve stood in one of the Palace's many simulation rooms as the AI explained, "The program will adapt to the skill level of the user. It's rudimentary now, but Takumi will adjust the program as it runs. I imagine this will be the foundation for future sims, once we eliminate the bugs."

Akio quirked an eyebrow. "So, you want me to do what, exactly?"

"I have set up this sim as a training aid for Koda and Asai. Since you're ultimately going to handle their training, I wanted you to try it too and make suggestions for any changes it needs to provide them the best training it can."

"I need all this to play a videogame?" He motioned to the bundle of clothing Eve had passed him when he entered.

"Yes. It is what gives the wearer positive feedback during the sim. It has sensors that will show where an opponent scores a hit," she explained.

Akio nodded as he looked at the outfit, skepticism obvious in his expression.

"Just try it." The AI smiled. "If you don't think it is worthwhile training, I'll stop, and you can work the girls into your schedule. I only did this because you have been so busy acclimating Kenjii and haven't been able to work with them."

"I'm sorry, Eve. I do appreciate your time and effort. It is just that I see the sims as entertainment. That they're useful for training is a concept I have not yet embraced," Akio apologized.

"I understand this is new, and you have many years of experience with traditional training methods. No apology needed. Would you like to begin?"

Looking at the clothing once more, he nodded as he pulled on the suit. Once he finished, he pulled the goggles over his eyes. "I'm ready."

The darkness faded to a green glow that resolved itself into a room with a video monitor on the wall.

"Welcome, Akio," Takumi's voice announced. "Please choose the clothing and weapons you would like to train with."

The monitor came to life with a selection of clothing that ranged from a simple gi to a full set of Jean Dukes armor. Akio selected a dark blue gi without shoes, and the screen changed to weapons. As with the first screen, there was a varied assortment. He selected a rattan training sword and learned the system had already selected an opponent for him.

"This is impressive," he murmured as he tested the weight of the sword. He could feel the clothing shift against his skin as he took several practice swings. The sword in his hands felt identical to other training blades of that type he had held.

"Are you satisfied with your selections?"

"*Hai.*"

"Training sequence initializing. One opponent similarly armed."

The room faded to black, and in seconds, Akio found himself in a *dojo.* The floor was polished wood with the image of a black dragon in the center of a marked circle.

Takumi's voice filled the room, coming from all around him. "The rules for this match are as follows: all combat will take place in the marked area." The circle lit up, a red light marking the area.

"You score points based on the number and projected lethality of the hits. If you're forced out of the circle, it counts as a point for your opponent. Is this acceptable?"

"*Hai.*"

Akio stepped to the edge of the circle and waited for his opponent. The space directly across the combat area wavered, and a figure materialized.

The figure was a man a little shorter than Akio, with white hair surrounding the balding top of his head and a white goatee on his chin.

"Welcome, Akio-*san.* I look forward to our match," the figure called as he stepped to the center of the ring.

Akio's eyes widened as he looked his opponent up and down. He seemed familiar, but he couldn't place him.

The vampire stepped into the circle and met the man in the center. His opponent bowed slightly, not low, but at the angle a master would bow to a student. Akio quirked one eyebrow as he returned the gesture, his eyes focused on his opponent.

The elderly gentleman took a stance with his weapon in a high guard position and nodded for Akio to advance. The vampire moved forward at human speed and brought his sword up, intending to slash the man across his chest.

The gray-haired man brought his blade down, intercepting Akio's and twisted his body, pushing the blade up and out. Before the vampire recovered, his opponent changed direction, and Akio felt a sharp blow to his side.

"First point to the master," Takumi announced as the man resumed his high guard position, a slight smile curling the corners of his mouth.

"Eve, whatever are you giggling about?" Yuko asked from where she was studying a map of Tokyo on her screen.

"Akio's in the training sim." She grinned as she looked up. "I don't think he expected to have to work so hard in a," she made air quotes, "*videogame*."

"What do you mean, work so hard?" Yuko pursed her lips as Eve's grin got larger. "What have you done?"

"Want to watch? Eve asked, motioning to a large monitor on the wall of the office.

It came to life, showing two side-by-side windows.

"The window on the right is the sim world. As you can see, it shows what the player sees." Eve giggled again. "The one on the left is a view of the sim chamber. It monitors the player to ensure they don't injure themselves. Not that

I'm worried about that with Akio. I just thought it would be fun to watch."

Yuko pushed her chair back and stood, cocking her head as she watched the scenes play out.

The left showed Akio and his opponent trading blows and a number beneath each of their avatars. The one on the right showed Akio as his feet left the floor and he flew backward several feet before landing on his back.

Yuko winced. "Eve! What have you set the feedback to? That should not be possible."

Eve looked up at Yuko, her pupils moving to the tops of her eyes as she feigned a look of innocence. "I didn't adjust the settings. Takumi has full control and is adapting as Akio uses more of his abilities."

"Still, the settings should not be capable of going that high. Someone could get hurt."

"That suit might have some features unique to it," Eve waffled.

Yuko shook her head as she turned back to the screens. "What are the numbers under each opponent?"

"The current score for the match."

"How is it that… *Oof,* that looked like it hurt." Yuko winced again as Akio's opponent elbowed him in the head while their swords were locked together.

"Okay, I think I see why Akio's score is as low as it is." She shook her head in wonder as the avatar hit Akio twice in rapid succession while he deftly dodged each of Akio's counterstrikes.

"Is Takumi cheating?"

"I resent that," Takumi answered, his voice taking a hurt tone. "I do not cheat. Is it cheating that I can predict Akio's actions with ninety-six-point-two-five percent accuracy and counter his moves?"

Eve shook her head. "Takumi has analyzed footage of Akio during training with you, Kenjii, and in actual combat. He programed the sim opponent to be slightly faster than Akio at each level of his abilities. He has not gone full Queen's Bitch yet, but so far...uh-oh."

The window on the left froze as Akio disappeared from the window on the right. "Looks like he just turned it up to eleven."

Akio shook his head to clear the sweat from his brow as he went out of the circle once again. The last time he had been hit this hard this many times, he was sparring with Bethany Anne.

"Balance is key." The kindly looking old man smiled. "Again!" He ordered as he resumed a guard position in the center of the ring.

Akio had been going hard for the last ten minutes. Every time he launched an attack, his opponent thwarted it and gave similar advice. His patience was at an end. He pushed himself off the ground, his eyes glowing red under the goggles. He stepped to the center of the ring and bowed. As soon as his opponent straightened, Akio hit vampire speed, running to the left of the man as he brought his practice sword down on the master's neck.

He stumbled when his sword failed to meet resistance, and the room went black.

"Simulation parameters exceeded," Takumi announced

as Akio ripped the goggles from his head, breathing hard as he looked around the room.

The door opened and Eve entered, followed by Yuko. "What do you think of my...videogame now?" Eve asked.

"It is very annoying," Akio told her as he noticed Yuko trying to contain a smile.

Eve smiled at Akio. "I understand why you would feel that way, but how did it perform?"

Akio looked at her through hooded eyes. "It performed as if it knew my tactics and movements before I did—almost like...magic."

"No magic, only science and Takumi's ability to make over a million calculations per second." Eve chuckled.

Akio pulled the suit Eve had given him off and looked at it closely. "How is this suit able to cause physical pain from the sim?"

"The goggles stimulate your optic nerves and signal the pain receptors in your brain to coincide with the location and force of the hits. It is literally all in your head."

"The sim pushed me hard, but what happened at the end?"

"Your use of your full enhanced abilities was too fast for me to track with my current video capabilities. You went into Queen's Bitch mode, and I couldn't keep up. I need better equipment." Takumi huffed.

Akio nodded as he turned back to Eve. "I commend you and Takumi on a match well fought. Do you think it would be possible to add a *shuang gou* as a weapon of choice with the same opponent?"

"I already have that option loaded," Takumi advised.

"Good," Akio mumbled. "I hope he's seen the movie."

Yuko had been fighting hard to keep a straight face since she walked in. Akio's muttered comment was all it took for her to start to shake. Seconds later, a giggle escaped, and when she saw the questioning look on Akio's face, she couldn't contain her laughter.

"The…the look on your face." Yuko's voice trailed off in another fit of laughter. She took a deep breath and continued, "When he gave you those tidbits of advice each time, he scored a point." She went into gales of laughter again, her face red and tears streaming from her eyes.

Akio sniffed in derision until he couldn't help it any longer and started to chuckle.

"When I realized who my opponent was, I lost focus for a moment and ended up on the floor again. That is brilliant, Eve. What gave you the idea to base the avatar on him?"

"Koda and Asai." Eve smiled. "They walked around here for a week quoting him after Abel showed them that old movie. I thought it fitting that he be their instructor since they liked his sayings so much."

"I hope Kenjii has seen it too. I want to see the look on his face when he gets his ass handed to him by Morita-*san.*"

"Is Kenjii ready to venture out among the human population?" A faint frown creased Yuko's forehead. "I know you had an issue when you went to Chiba."

"*Hai.* Kenjii stopped the men from harming an innocent and restrained himself from hurting her. I think if we come here just before closing time, he will be fine. I won't bring him out of the sim until everyone has departed for the first time or two, though."

Yuko nodded, trusting that Akio had the Kenjii situation in hand, then suggested, "Perhaps it's time to introduce him to the girls. I know they are happy staying here, but Koda has mentioned wanting to visit Abel. They formed a bond when she was staying at the base."

"*Hai.* I can do that the night I bring him. What does tomorrow night look like, Eve?

"Our last sim is scheduled to end at eleven thirty-seven. All the staff will depart by midnight. Horst is supposed to be back too, so I'm not sure what plans Koda has."

"What plans Koda has when?" Koda asked as she walked into the office. "*Konichiwa,* Akio-*sama.* It's been a while since I've seen you. Are you well?"

"*Hai,* Koda-*san.* We were discussing bringing Kenjii here, and Yuko suggested that you and Asai meet him."

"I've been looking forward to it. When?"

"Tomorrow, close to closing time."

"I'll make it a point to be here. Horst will be back tomorrow. We have plans for an early dinner and a movie afterward. I'm sure he won't mind if we skip the movie."

"We will see you then," Akio advised as he nodded to the rest and took his leave.

CHAPTER NINETEEN

Sakutaro Apartments, Ome, Japan

"Kishi, do you have a minute?" Asaka Shuko called through the door of her bedroom.

"Only if you stop yelling," came the muffled reply.

"I warned you about that rotgut gin you were drinking." Asaka laughed as he pushed open the door while balancing a tray with a carafe and three cups in one hand.

"Shut the door," she moaned as she covered her eyes with her hand.

Asaka gently pushed the door closed with his foot, moved to the king-size bed that dominated the room, and sat down next to the body that had curled into a fetal position under the covers.

"Sit up. I have aspirin and water for you."

Kishi rolled toward him and moaned. "Just let me die in peace."

"No dying allowed. I have news from that idiot Juba. If you take your aspirin, I have coffee for you."

Kishi sat up and winced, one hand on her head as she reached out with the other. Asaka dropped two white tablets in her outstretched hand and pulled a cup from the tray.

Kishi's face twisted into a grimace as she swallowed the bitter pills and gulped the water. "Oh, those things taste nasty."

"The price you pay when the booze the night before tasted so good," Asaka chided.

"Remind me why I don't kill you?" Kishi mumbled as she shot him a hard glare.

"Because of my winning smile and spectacular people skills. Or maybe it's because I bring you aspirin and coffee when you drink too much." Asaka grinned.

Kishi snorted with a shake of her head. "Not good enough. You're dead."

Asaka grabbed his chest with an exaggerated flourish. "This is how you repay your most loyal minion. You wound me."

Kishi giggled at his antics, then turned serious, the moment of friendly levity gone. "What news?"

"Juba called this morning, interrupting my fun, by the way, to tell me he located the man you sent him to find."

"Good, at least he is..." Her eyes narrowed. "What did he interrupt?" she asked, her tone sharp.

Asaka grinned at her. "I needed help getting you to the car and back here. Katani and her cousin gave me a hand. I had to thank them properly, you know."

"Both of them?"

Asaka's grin got bigger as he nodded.

"You're such a dog, Asaka."

"Woof, woof. Now that you're awake, are you ready to hear what Juba reported?"

Kishi sipped the strong black coffee, a beverage she only liked after a night of hard-drinking, and nodded for him to continue.

"Juba said when he spoke to the man—Li he is called—he told him he hasn't located the man he seeks. He has also agreed to a meeting." Asaka pursed his lips before continuing. "According to Juba, this Li made it more of a demand than a request."

"Did Juba say anything else?"

"Only that Li is willing to meet with you. Juba didn't say any more than that, though. Only that Li was rude and told him he only dealt with your grandfather. Juba had to tell Li who you were before he would agree to meet with a woman."

"He assumes much," Kishi growled. "My grandfather might have been cowed by him, but he's in my land now. He's in no position to make demands. He might need a lesson before this is over."

"True, that would be in order but, we have similar goals—for now. You want these people to suffer for the damage they did to the family, and this Li doesn't seem to want to make friends with them. This could work out to where you don't have to be seen as disobeying the *Oyabun's* orders."

"Still, who is he to dictate anything? He should be thankful the family sought him out."

Asaka smiled coldly. "Someone we can easily deal with after his usefulness has run out."

Kishi thought for a few moments as she continued to

sip the bitter black coffee, nodding to herself as she considered the benefits and drawbacks of working with Li.

"When does he want to meet?"

"Today. Juba is waiting in the office to take the time and place back to him. I suggest the meeting not be held where any who would take word to your grandfather might see it."

"Agreed. Do you have a place in mind?"

"Juba should rent a room at the big hotel down from Muto's old place. We can slip in the back and take the service elevator to the floor. I have a contact who works there."

"What about the tail crew?"

"All ours, no worries about that, plus they will wait outside if you tell them to."

Kishi looked at the clock on her bedside table and saw it was just past ten. "Have him rent the room and contact you with the information before he finds this Li. We will set the meeting for half past three."

"Anything else?"

"Load the silver in your weapon, and get one for me as well. No use being unprepared in case this is a trap of some kind."

"I have that covered. I always keep a spare you are familiar with in case you want to deal with a problem yourself."

"Now I remember why I don't kill you for being such an annoying ass in the mornings. Go tend to your...guests and leave me in peace for a couple of hours."

"Your wish is my command, princess," he snarked as he got up to leave.

Kishi waited until he was almost to the door, then grabbed a pillow from the bed and threw it. It hit Asaka in the back of his head and she called, "And don't you ever forget it, minion."

Asaka snagged the pillow from the floor and tossed it back to her. "As you wish." He snickered as he slipped out the door before she could throw something else.

"You understand what you're to do?" Asaka asked the man, who was casting nervous glances toward him. "Repeat the instructions back to me."

Juba gulped and took a deep breath. Asaka terrified him more than any other Yakuza soldier. Juba had cleaned up behind him on two occasions and had never seen any other person display so much viciousness. Asaka didn't just kill the people who angered Kishi, he punished them before they died.

"Rent a room in my name at the hotel near Riko's, then call you and give you the room information. Find Li and tell him where to meet you at three-thirty," Juba repeated as he ticked each item off on a finger.

"Meet me at the service entrance at three-fifteen with the key. Do not be late and do not fail to notify Li," Asaka growled, making the already frightened man shake.

"I won't fail you, Shuko-*san.* Please tell Sakutaro-*san* that my family and I thank her for all she has done."

"Yes, yes." Asaka motioned him to the door. "You have things to see to. Get moving!"

Juba bowed low and turned to leave. Asaka waited until

he was almost out and called, "You still live in the house with the blue door, don't you?"

Juba froze in mid-step as a cold chill formed in his stomach. "I, uh, I...*hai,*" he stammered.

Asaka smiled coldly, his words having had the desired effect. "It's a nice home. Now go take care of the arrangements."

Juba walked out the door, his breathing hard and sweat running down his face.

CHAPTER TWENTY

Serenity Temple, Dabie Mountains, China

"What do you mean, they're all dead, and the slaves are missing?" Peng Kun snarled as he came to his feet, standing over the prostrate and shaking acolyte.

"The relief group arrived to start their rotation and found all four of the members they were to relieve dead in the house. They also report that the slaves are all gone."

Kun drew his foot back and slammed it into the hapless man's side. "Who did this? Was it more of those traitors from Shek's compound? The farm is close to them."

"No, Master. Fang Qui located some former slaves hiding nearby, and he reports that they claim that a pair of men came from the sky and freed them." The man tensed as he spoke, waiting for another blow to fall.

"Was that all they said? Give me the description, damn you," Kun screamed, spittle flying from his lips and his face purple with rage.

"I, uh, gerk—" His voice choked off as Kun grabbed him around the throat and lifted him from the floor.

"Give. Me. The. Description," he ground out, his voice laced with venom and his eyes filled with madness.

"Qui said that two of the slaves claimed the men's eyes glowed red, and one claims they were Japanese."

Kun's grip tightened, causing the man's eyes to bulge out as his hands grasped weakly at the Master's iron-hard grip.

"Those damned vampires. I want them dead. Now!" Kun ranted as he threw the unconscious body toward the door. The acolyte's head hit the frame with a hollow *thunk* as his body slid into the corridor.

Kun didn't waste a glance at the limp figure as he stormed through the opening to his private chamber. Grabbing the sat phone from a table, he viciously stabbed the button that connected to Cui's unit.

"Cui here," came over the line a few seconds later.

"What is the status of the ships?"

"We're still docked in Quingdao, waiting. We are ready to depart now, but the packages haven't arrived from Shanxi yet."

Cui could hear Kun in the background. "Weakness all around me. Why am I cursed with warriors so weak they can't carry out a simple task?"

"Sir?" Cui asked, confused about whether Kun was talking to him or about him. Kun had become irrational over the last few weeks, calling and berating him for not being in Japan one minute, the next telling him he had to wait for some special weapon before he left. Li had called him a week ago. When they compared their recent experiences with Kun, they were the same.

"Cui, if the packages have not arrived by morning, send

the ship with the warriors. At least they will be in place when that incompetent Li locates those damned parasites. Follow when the weapons are on board."

"Yes, Master. I will notify Yi and Pan to be ready to depart at daybreak."

"See that you do not fail me again, Cui Yong. I will not tolerate failure from any of you any longer. Do you understand?"

"Yes, Master," Cui replied to the already dead connection. He looked at the unit and thought for a beat before dialing Li.

"This is Li."

"Warriors are leaving at daybreak. Expect them there in a week," Cui advised.

"You finally got those mystery weapons Kun has been going on about?"

"No, but the vampires have set him off again, not that it takes much lately. He ordered me to send the warriors and follow as soon as the weapons arrive. Any luck on your end?"

"Not yet, I have a meeting with the Yakuza this afternoon. They will either help me locate these people, or I will start killing them until I find one who understands their place in the world."

"Sooner is better. Kun has been on a rampage from what I hear. The vampires hit a farm and killed the team assigned to watch over it. Kun put the acolyte in the infirmary when he gave him the news."

"I'm worried, Cui. That stuff with Shek and Kun acting like a man possessed will not end well. The other leaders in the Clan deferred to him without challenge when he assumed control after Stephanie Lee and her father were killed. If he keeps on, we could have an internal war."

"What choice do we have, Li? He is the recognized leader, and we can't challenge him under Clan law. Not that either of us would stand a chance. He might be old, but he is still a formidable fighter."

"Shek was the only one who would have stood a chance. He was also the one who dared to question when Kun announced that it was time to put the Clan on the rise. I remember Kun's reaction to that. You were still in training, but Kun didn't take it well."

"I didn't know that. Do you think that had something to do with Kun ordering him killed?"

"If it didn't, I'm sure the other leaders have thought it. Be sure you strictly follow Kun's orders. If the others go against him and win, we don't want to suffer in the crossfire."

"Agreed. I'll contact you when the weapons arrive and we start your way. Hopefully, you will have located them by then, and we can end this. With Kun being so unpredictable, it wouldn't be a stretch for him to remove one of us if this fails."

"That's why we can't fail, Cui. Hope is good, but I will have the information I seek soon, one way or the other. This city is too loud. I miss the quiet of the mountains."

"Talk to you soon, Li," Cui stated as he cut the connection. He and Li had discussed Kun's actions and his obsession with finding the Forsaken several times. He was certain Li hoped for a change in leadership, just as he did. The Clan did not need an insane man to lead it to its ordained position in the world.

CHAPTER TWENTY-ONE

Hotel Siena, Shinjuku City, Tokyo, Japan

Juba stood in the alley, his face flushed and sweat soaking through the white suit coat he wore. He had reserved a room that morning and gone in search of Li Song. It had taken him several hours to locate the man, giving him less than half an hour to cover the four kilometers to meet Kishi and Asaka. He had made it with only minutes to spare.

The black Toyota Century pulled into the alley, and Asaka stepped out from behind the wheel. "Everything is in order?"

"*Hai.* Li said he would be here."

"You look a mess," Asaka observed as he motioned to the black SUV that pulled up close behind the Century. A rear door opened, and a man in a black suit exited.

"Stay with the car," Asaka ordered as he tossed the keys to him.

"Where are we meeting?" he asked Juba over his shoulder as he walked around to the passenger side.

"I have a room on the eighth floor. It is a simple room since all the suites are occupied." He rubbed the back of his neck, his stomach roiling. He expected Asaka to take exception to the poor quality of the room, along with his unkempt state.

Asaka cast an icy glare toward him, making him take an involuntary step back as he held the door for Kishi to exit.

Kishi placed a hand on Asaka's arm and shook her head minutely. "It will have to do. I didn't expect much."

Juba paled at her words. Though her voice carried no inflection, the words spoke volumes. He had been present when Kishi used that same tone while ordering the death of someone who had displeased her.

"My apologies, Sakutaro-sama, I know you deserve better than my feeble..."

Kishi cut him off with a sharp wave of her hand. "Take us to the room, Juba. I don't wish to stand in this heat while you sweat and try to explain your failure."

Juba's eyes went round with fear. "I'm, uh...*hai,* Sakutaro-sama. Follow me, please," he stammered as he led them through a door marked Employees Only.

He wended through the hotel kitchen, and all the workers acted like the three were invisible as they went about their meal preparations. When he reached an elevator in the kitchen's rear, he pulled a card from his pocket and shakily swiped it through a reader on the wall. The door opened, and he motioned Kishi and Asaka inside.

They rode up in silence, Juba swore that the two could hear his heart beating, it pounded so loudly in his head. He jumped when the door opened, so lost in his fear of what Kishi would do that he didn't realize the lift had stopped.

Gathering his frayed wits, he stepped out and went to the first door on the right. He fumbled the key card from his pocket, dropping it as his shaking hands lost their grip.

"Come on, Juba, get it together. I don't want to stand here all day," Asaka growled, causing Juba to miss the lock completely the first time he tried to unlock the door.

Kishi stifled a smile as she saw the effect Asaka had on the frightened man. It was good that he knew fear. As long as he had a healthy fear of them, he would work harder to see that he did not fail.

Asaka shouldered Juba aside and pushed into the room with his pistol in his hand. He returned to the door seconds later. Satisfied that it was safe, he motioned Kishi inside.

The room was small and plain, as Juba had said. It had a double bed against one wall and a small desk with a chair beside it. Kishi took the chair and swiveled it until she faced the room, while Asaka sat on the edge of the bed. Juba stood nervously under both of their gazes, his feet shuffling on the worn carpet. He looked like he wanted to run away.

"Settle down, Juba," Kishi scolded. "You look like a child who needs to use the restroom, shuffling about so."

Juba nodded, his eyes refusing to come up to meet her face.

"Stand by the door and let our guest in when he arrives," Kishi snapped. "You're making me dizzy, swaying about so much."

Juba moved the few steps to the door and leaned against the wall for support. He was afraid that his shaking legs would betray him and dump him on the floor.

They waited in silence for fifteen minutes. At five minutes past the appointed time, Asaka stood and looked at Juba. "Where is he? Did you tell him the correct hotel?"

Juba paled visibly, and as he was trying to form an answer, a sharp knock on the door caused him to jump and let out an involuntary shriek.

"Well, open the damned door, Juba," Asaka growled.

Juba twisted the knob and pulled, to find Li standing before it with a knowing smirk on his lips. "Uh, ah, come in, please," Juba stuttered.

Li swept past him without a word and moved to stand in front of Kishi. Asaka stepped in front of him, blocking him from coming too close.

"Step aside, boy." Li locked his eyes on Asaka's. "My business is with her, not her flunky."

Asaka stiffened and started to reply when Kishi's voice cut through the game of who had the bigger one. "Let him by, Asaka. As you told Juba, we don't have all day, and I need to get back home."

Asaka glared at Li as he reluctantly stepped to the side.

"Greetings, Li Song. Thank you for seeing me."

"I was going to see your grandfather soon anyway. Maybe this will save me a trip out to the countryside." Li shrugged. "What do you want?"

Kishi took a deep breath, fighting to overcome her initial response of ordering Asaka to shoot the rude *gaijin*. She let her breath out slowly as she counted to ten.

"We have a mutual problem," she stated, eyeing Li and taking in the arrogant quirk of his lips and deceptively casual stance. "The people you seek are responsible for some difficulties we have had with the authorities. I propose we combine our resources and seek them together."

"Why are you contacting me about this and not your grandfather?" Li asked, his tone sharp and demanding.

Asaka tensed as if to step in front of him again, but Kishi responded, ignoring the tone. "My grandfather is an old man. His body is not as strong as it once was, and I take as much off him as I can."

Li nodded, accepting the explanation. "What do you offer?"

"I can put many eyes on the streets. My people can go where you can't. Without attracting the unwanted attention of the police," she added with a smile that failed to reach her eyes, letting Li know she knew about the problems he faced.

"What's in it for you?" Li asked after a few beats.

"Is it safe to assume you wish to, shall we say, take decisive action when you locate the people you seek?"

"Yes."

"Is it also safe to assume that you will have your people to help you resolve the issue when the time comes?"

Li nodded.

"Then you'll remove a mutual annoyance with minimum involvement and exposure on my part. That's what's in it for me."

Li looked at the youthful woman as he considered her words. The old man had made it clear he wanted no further involvement with Li's mission. That information, coupled with the anonymous meeting place and Kishi's words, told him she was running her own game, independent of her grandfather. He could use the situation if he needed more from the old man.

"How do you propose we…combine our efforts?"

Kishi nodded toward Juba, who was pressed against the wall, where he had been since Li pushed into the room. "That one will be your contact. The eyes will report to him, and he will relay the information to you."

"That is acceptable. All I need is a verified location of where their base is. Tell your people not to approach them under any circumstances. They are more dangerous than they appear, and I do not want them alerted."

"Agreed. Juba, keep this room and run the operation from here. You are to remain here until they find these people." She turned her gaze back to Li. "Work out how to stay in contact with this one. We need not meet again."

Kishi stood and stalked from the room with Asaka on her heels after he took the elevator key from the visibly stunned Juba.

"Do not fail in this," he whispered as he took the key. "Your daughter is counting on you."

Asaka started to speak once he joined her in the hall, but Kishi held up a hand to silence him.

Once they were in the elevator and dropping toward the first floor, she let out the breath she had been holding. "When this is done and those who harmed us are dead, kill that one slowly." She took a deep breath. "I wish him to beg for death for many days before it allows him to know its cold embrace."

Asaka looked down at her with a mischievous glint in his eye and his lips quirked on one side. "As you wish."

Kishi glared at him for his taunt, then a slight smile played on her lips. "Sometimes it is good to be the princess."

CHAPTER TWENTY-TWO

TQB Base, Tokyo, Japan

"Kenjii," Akio called from the door to the younger vampire's room.

"*Hai,*" Kenjii answered as the door slid open. "Come in. I was just watching a show Abel recommended."

Akio glanced at the screen and hesitated for a split second when he saw the scene paused on the screen. A teenage boy with unkempt hair stood on a post with both arms raised above his head and one foot in the air.

"How is the show?"

"It's fine, but it seems childish to me. Abel went on about it being a great coming of age movie where good fights evil. I think I prefer romantic comedies more. I watched one earlier today where the female was telling the male how she could fake pleasure. When he doubted her, she showed him in a crowded diner. Now, that was funny." Kenjii laughed.

Akio nodded, recalling hearing Eve and Yuko discuss the movie several years back. He had planned to watch it, but an issue came up with a Forsaken in England, and he had never gotten around to it.

"You have gotten better with the *shuang gou,* Eve has set up a training program at the Palace for you. I used it myself a few days ago and thought we could go there so you could try it."

"That's fine with me. I've been here in the base for the past week. A trip outside would be fun."

"Have you fed today? There will be humans around, and I don't want it to be an issue for you."

Kenjii's face darkened. *He thinks I can't control myself. That's why he has kept me here, only allowed out with him and then only to places where there are no humans. After the night we went to Chiba and I feasted on those criminals, he has not trusted me.* "*Hai,* I fed earlier." If you could call sucking stale blood from a plastic bag feeding.

Akio watched him as he answered, still having trouble picking up his thoughts when his mind went to whatever black place it had been in when he found him. When they were out alone or in their rooms, he could read him, but when the Miko personality manifested, his thoughts were a jumbled distrustful mess.

"It's a beautiful night, so let's walk. It's only about ten kilometers, and I think the night air will do you good. I'm sorry I have been so busy this week. Abel and I are trying to locate more of the Clan's slave farms. We have a few leads, but nothing sure yet."

"I understand, and that's why I have stayed to myself so much. Plus, I am still sorting my memories. Heinz and Isamu are lucky you killed them. If not, I would make sure each took a long time to die for what they stole from me."

Akio nodded. "They deserved more, but Justice was served. I didn't kill Heinz, though."

Kenjii's head jerked. "You told me he was dead. Is that correct?"

"He is assuredly dead. Not by my hand, but by the hand of another he had wronged. Horst killed him."

"Horst? I know you told me he was working with you, but how? He's strong, but nowhere near the level Heinz was."

Akio smiled as he remembered how Horst had used his years of anger and hurt to find his inner strength that day. "Horst is stronger than even he knows. He's not a Were to be taken lightly now. He's an Alpha and a strong one, the strongest I have seen who was not…upgraded by Bethany Anne."

Kenjii nodded, not understanding but knowing he had no reason to doubt his friend. "Why don't you tell me more about these 'upgrades' as you call them? You started to before, but I was not ready to process the information then. I have come to terms with who I am now somewhat, and I think it is time I learn what it is to be part of this team."

"You have decided you want to take part in the fight?"

"You know I still owe those tigers. They chased me like I was prey across most of China," Kenjii growled.

"*Hai,* but that was not what I meant. We must stop the Clan, that is a given, but there are others like us who also prey on humans. Are you willing to fight another vampire to protect humans?"

Why would you want to protect humans? the inner voice that plagued him when he was conflicted chided. *Because the man I love more than anything in the world wishes it,* he answered. The voice was silent, having no words that could shake that conviction.

"Tell me more as we walk. I would like to see the stars above my head and have delightful company to share the night with."

Akio motioned toward the open door, having heard both sides of the last thoughts clearly in Kenjii's mind. It was as if two minds occupied the same body. His heart hurt for his friend, and he hoped the resolve he heard last was enough to keep the darkness that was Miko at bay.

"You want me to believe some kind of alien experiment created us? What about the legends? My grandmother told me old stories of *banpaia* and *kyuuketsuki* all my life. I recognized what you were the night we met from those tales." Kenjii shrugged.

"All lies. When I was a child, there were no such tales. They didn't start until the first explorers from Europe came here. They brought the tales with them. The legends were not commonplace until almost two hundred years after I was turned."

Kenjii shook his head in wonder. "Where did the legends come from then? This Michael Heinz spoke of?"

"*Hai,* Michael was the first to encounter the alien TOM, over a thousand years ago. He was human, and the process to change him was flawed. That is why you need blood to survive. The blood contains energy that tiny machines called nanocytes need to survive. The nanocytes are what gives us our abilities."

They walked along the dimly lit street in silence, occasionally encountering other pedestrians and twice a vehicle. The night was warm and the sky was clear, but only the brightest stars shone through because of the light put out by the homes and streetlights in the area.

After they had walked another kilometer, Kenjii spoke. "What about the Weres? Are they also a product of this TOM, as you called him?"

"No, TOM is from a race called the Kurtherians. His group, or clan, I suppose, and four others were at war with seven other clans. Each clan went out to the stars and found other races they could turn into weapons to fight their battles. TOM is from the good Kurtherians who were trying to stop the bad ones from succeeding. Another group from the Seven, as they are called, created the Weres."

"Let me be sure I understand. We," he pointed to Akio and himself, "were created as weapons for an alien war over a thousand years ago. A hostile group created the Weres for the same thing?"

"*Hai,* as they explained it to me."

"What about Michael? It is said he can walk in the sun. Is that true?"

"*Hai.*"

"How is it he could do that, but according to legend, few others could?"

"It resulted from his botched change. His brothers, the first humans he turned, did not all suffer from it. As the bad nanocytes were passed down to each new generation, the flaw was more pronounced. It spread as their children and grandchildren created more of us. The upgrades fix that and the need to feed on blood."

Kenjii's eyes widened in shock. "You can walk in the sun?"

Akio nodded.

"You don't drink blood?"

"I don't have to have blood to power my nanocytes. I still can, and have done so when circumstances warranted it, but no, I don't have to."

Kenjii shook his head in wonder. "If I wanted these... upgrades, would your Queen be able to give them to me? Not that I am willing to do so now. I have realized I was nothing more than a lab rat for Heinz. He made me stronger and gave me the ability to heal faster, but the changes were not pleasant or easy. There were times I almost died, and others that I wished I could."

"*Hai.* It can be done, but don't feel pressured to decide. If you have any questions, I will answer what I can. If you want specifics about the process, Eve knows more than I do. I can assure you it's painless." He smiled as he waved a hand over his body. "I went to sleep, and when I awoke, I was much more than I had been for several centuries."

Kenjii took Akio's hand in his. "Thank you for not trying to rush me into all this. I know I want to help you in your fight, but some things I have done since they turned me will require much to balance my karma—if ever it can be balanced."

"You didn't harm the innocent in Chiba. I would say that is an excellent start on redemption," Akio offered, and he gently squeezed the hand he held.

Kenjii was thoughtful for a moment, his mind going back to his flight from the lab in China. "That was the second time I killed to protect an innocent," he mused. "The first was when I was making my way across China and discovered two men who were planning to attack a woman. I killed both and let her pass with no knowledge that she would have become their latest victim."

Akio smiled fondly at him. "You were always an honorable person, Kenjii. No matter what Heinz, Isamu, or Ogawa did to you or caused you to do, know that you control who you are. No one else."

"Someday, I hope I am worthy of the love and trust you give me. Until that time, I promise to strive to be what you see when you look at me," Kenjii vowed as he wrapped his arms around the person who was the reason he wanted to be a better man.

Kenjii stopped when they arrived in front of the Palace, pulling Akio up short when he didn't release the hand he had held as they walked. "Gods, that building is amazing," he whispered as he took in the peaked roof and flowing lines of architecture style straight out of ancient Japanese history.

"Hai. It is partially based on my memories of the house I was raised in," Akio volunteered as he admired the sweeping roofline and heavy beams.

"Your family lived in a palace? Are you royalty?" Kenjii asked, his eyes wide in wonder.

Akio nodded. "My father was a Ryoshu king. Had I not been turned, I would have followed him."

"How is it you never told me that?"

"By the time we met, it was ancient history. I was a Ryoshu prince for just over two decades. I had been a Forsaken for several centuries. It was a life I had not thought about until recently. Isamu and his delusions of being a king on the very island where I met the vampire who turned me brought the memories back." Akio chuckled. "You would have enjoyed the shock on his face when I told him—just before I carved him into a quivering and screaming mass of flesh."

"I would have faced the sun gladly to have seen that."

Akio shook his head. "No, he was not worth that. Be comforted that your name was the last word he heard before he lost his head."

Kenjii smiled, his face lighting up. "My prince."

"Please don't start that."

"What?" Kenjii asked, his voice laced with innocence. "You just told me you are a prince, and I assured you that you will always be mine. So, my prince is an accurate and fitting title."

"Do you have any idea how much grief I will catch from Abel? I don't even want to think about how Eve would react."

Kenjii laughed. "I hadn't thought about that, but now that you mention it," he grinned up at him through his long black eyelashes, "what's my silence worth to you?"

Akio shook his head again. "I see Abel is not only influencing the movies you watch. That sounds like something he would say."

"Abel has taught me many things," Kenjii stated cryptically. The moment was broken when he waggled his eyebrows.

"Ancestors help me," Akio deadpanned before he burst out laughing—the first real laugh he had experienced in hundreds of years.

Neither of them noticed the beggar wrapped in a tattered blanket who watched them from the shadows across the street as they entered the ornate doors that led inside.

CHAPTER TWENTY-THREE

Sakutaro Apartments, Ome, Japan

"Asaka," he growled sleepily as he snatched the ringing phone from the couch where he had fallen asleep.

"This is Juba. One of my men advised that the man Sakutaro-*san* is interested in and another who matches the description Li gave just entered that arcade." The voice on the other end rushed through the information.

"Slow down! Now, who is this?" Asaka questioned, his mind still fuzzy.

"It's Juba. One of the men I have looking for those people has located both of them."

"Where? When?" Asaka wiped the sleep from his eyes and focused on a clock on a table next to the couch.

"About thirty minutes ago at that arcade building," Juba patiently answered.

Asaka nodded as what Juba told him sank in. His mouth twisted into a grin. "I'll let Kishi know. Have you contacted Li?"

“I tried. He didn’t answer, but I’ll keep trying until I reach him.”

“Do that. Is your man still watching them?”

“They haven’t left the building. I have men on all sides. We will know when they leave.”

“Very good. Juba, don’t mess this up. I need not remind you what will happen if you do.”

“No need to threaten me, Asaka. You’ve already made it clear.”

“That was not a threat, it was a promise. Do not fail,” Asaka hissed as he cut the connection.

“What was that about?” Kishi inquired as she exited her office.

“Juba claims he has spotted the men we seek.”

“Good. Has he contacted that *gaijin* Li yet?”

“Said he tried, but Li isn’t answering. I told him to keep calling until he answered.”

Kishi nodded as she mulled this over. “Does he know where Li is staying?”

“He hasn’t said. Want me to call him back?”

“No. He will either figure it out and do what he must to finish the job, or his replacement can,” Kishi coldly stated. “If he can’t handle a simple job like this, his death won’t be a substantial loss.”

“As you wish.” Asaka’s smile never reached his eyes.

“I wish this over. Muto’s stupidity and Sero’s defection made us appear weak. We need to finish this to show we are not to be trifled with,” Kishi snarled. "Let's go. It's late, and I don't need Grandfather asking too many questions.”

"I’ll have the car brought around.”

. . .

Lotus Towers Apartments, Shinjuku City, Tokyo, Japan

"Li, answer that damned phone," Shao called as the phone the sniveling Yakuza soldier had given him started ringing again.

"He stepped out," Wu called from the kitchen of the apartment they had found.

Well, to be honest, Wu had found it on his delivery route. He noticed the elderly woman ordered from the burger house he worked at several times each week. He had found out from others in the building that she never left her apartment. Two neighbors he delivered to on the same floor claimed never to have seen her, and they had lived there for over a year.

When Wu told Li about her after work one night, he'd decided the apartment was closer to where they needed to be. The next day when Wu made the lunch delivery, he pushed his way inside. Her protest died in her throat as the claws that tipped his fingers silenced her permanently.

The others met him a short time later for the keys. By the time he arrived that evening, the apartment was clean, and there was no sign of the woman.

Shao scowled as the phone rang again. "Yes?" he answered as he picked it up.

"The people you seek are inside the Palace. It's an arcade..."

"I know what it is," Shao snapped. "Are you sure it was them?"

"Yes. The man who saw them has a picture of one, and the second matched the description you gave me of the other."

"Stay on them. We will be in touch." Shao disconnected the call.

"What was it?" Wu called as he carried a steaming pot of noodles and sauce to the table.

"They have located both men we were sent to find."

The apartment door opened, and Li walked through with a bag under his arm. "Who has located them?" He closed the door.

Shao held up the phone. "Your Yakuza pets."

Li shook his head when he saw he'd forgotten the satellite phone. Normally, it never left his side, but as time passed, he'd lost faith in the Yakuza finding anything. "Where?"

"At that arcade—the one where the police hassled Jin and me."

"That's not far away. Go there and watch. Don't reveal yourself, but make sure those buffoons don't lose them. Jin, back him up."

Jin mumbled obscenities as he swallowed the bite in his mouth. "Why me? I just sat down."

"Because I said to. Take it with you, but both of you need to get there sooner rather than later. Now go!" he snarled, his eyes flashing yellow.

"I meant nothing by that, Li. I'm going." Jin raised his hands palms up in surrender.

"Just do it. Wu and I will meet you there in four hours if you haven't made contact. Take the other phone with you and keep me updated."

Jin nodded as he went through the door on Shao's heels.

. . .

Serenity Temple, Dabie Mountains, China

"What do you want, Li?" Kun snapped as he answered the satellite phone.

"The Yakuza have located the leeches."

"Good. Where is their base?"

"They don't have that information. They spotted them going into an entertainment complex we've been watching. I sent Shao and Jin to monitor, so we should have the information soon."

"See that you do. At least your report is positive. Cui is still waiting for the incompetents I sent to retrieve the weapons. Have your men follow them at a distance, but do not engage. I don't want them moving once we locate their hiding hole."

"Understood, Master. Any other orders?"

"Coordinate with Cui. I know you two have talked, but update him with this news. I'm sending more men to help with the weapons. I want those two dead and their base destroyed."

"I will contact him," Li assured Kun.

"See that nothing spoils this. You've been there long enough to have located those two several times over. I will tolerate no more excuses. Do I make myself clear?"

"Yes, Master," Li replied to the dead line.

Hybrid Vessel *Ming Dan*, Quingdao, China

"Yes, hello?" Cui answered.

"Cui, I just spoke to Kun. He is sending more men to help with the weapons. We have sighted the two vampires and should have their location soon," Li advised.

"You're sure it's them?"

"Yes. The Yakuza have men with pictures of Akio. They verified it was him, and the one with him matched the description of the man who escaped you."

"If that Akio hadn't interfered, he would not have survived," Cui growled.

"No offense intended, Cui. Kun is in one of his moods tonight."

"What else is new? He calls me daily with conflicting orders. The ship with the warriors returned a few days ago. He recalled them again."

"What is he playing at? This is the second time he sent them and called them back. Did he say why?" Li spat, exasperation lacing his words.

"He didn't want to split the forces. He said he wanted the warriors to go in behind the weapons and destroy any who lived." Cui rolled his eyes, although Li couldn't see him.

"Is he losing his mind? That makes no sense. It was the plan all along. Last time, he didn't want word of their arrival to leak. Who could leak it?"

"Careful, brother. You don't need Kun to hear you're questioning him," Cui warned.

"You're right. I'm alone now, and I know you have to be thinking the same."

"I do. He's been closed up in his rooms and is as likely to lash out at any who come to him as not. Two days ago, he killed an acolyte who brought him news of another delay with the weapons."

"Something needs to be done about him. I think this stuff with the vampires has broken his mind. He calls and threatens me one day and praises me the next. I'm concerned that his obsession will cause harm to the Clan if he continues unchecked," Li worried.

"I received news that the leaders of several enclaves met last week. They discussed what he did to Shek, among other things. We don't want to get caught in whatever troubles that might bring," Cui warned.

"That's why I told you to be sure you cover yourself by only following his direct orders. As long as we do that, we should be safe from any repercussions Kun suffers."

"I agree, my friend. I will call you as soon as I have word on the weapons. Or if Kun sends the warriors' ship to Japan again."

"Do that. As soon as I have the location of the vampires' base, I will let you know. Then, if anything happens here, you will still know where to go."

"What about that entertainment complex? You said it involved them in some way?"

"They were seen entering it tonight. I will look into it further, now that there's a connection other than the Yakuza's speculation."

"Do that. When I arrive, we might want to hit that location as well."

"Only if Kun orders it. Remember, follow his orders to the letter."

"You're right. I'm still angry that leech escaped me, and I want to punish those who interfered."

"I understand. Perhaps we will have the chance. We don't want to do anything that could point to us if the other leaders go after Kun. Plausible deniability, I think they call it."

Cui chuckled. "Not that there is any denying Kun is bugnuts crazy."

"Be careful," Li admonished. "You never know who might hear you. The last thing either of us needs is for Kun to think we're against him. Shek won't be the only one to die if that happens."

"I know. No one else is aboard right now. Ren is training with Yi and Pan. He won't be back until morning. They're running the warriors through some ruined buildings to prepare them for what they will face in Japan."

Li laughed. "There are ruins here, but this city is in better condition than any in China. Most of the damage done here was through natural disasters. They had minor damage from the war that followed the WWDE."

"The warriors needed something to occupy them. That was as good an idea as any." Cui snickered. "Besides, Ren was going stir-crazy on this ship, and he was driving me insane with his constant bitching."

"I made all of mine find jobs." Li laughed. "I think Shao would have killed Wu if he had to spend another day closed up with him."

"I'll be glad when this is over. Sitting around waiting for a madman's plans to come to fruition isn't good for either of us. At least you have civilization. I have a jumped-up fishing village and a pack of bored warriors. There have been incidents with the locals, and we had to take control of the town."

"At least you have plenty of fish to eat. I don't know what I will do for lunch tomorrow. It is hard to decide between Kobe beef steaks or the Italian place I found last week," Li chided.

"You are an evil man, Li Song. There is a special level in hell reserved for men like you."

Li laughed. "I will treat you to both when you arrive, my friend."

"I'll hold you to that. Have a good night."

"You, too." Li cut the connection.

CHAPTER TWENTY-FOUR

The Palace, Tokyo, Japan

"*Konichiwa,* Kenjii-*san.* Welcome to my dojo," the gray-haired man greeted the vampire as he entered the sim.

Kenjii's head jerked up as he focused on the figure.

"Uh, *konichiwa.*"

Akio watched Kenjii's confusion on a monitor where Takumi streamed the sim, one side of his mouth turned up in a smile. That Abel had introduced him to that movie earlier made it even better.

"Take your position in the ring." The sim instructor pointed. "I will start slow and determine your proficiency with those blades."

"Are you serious?" Kenjii called, not believing Akio had put him into a training match with a player from a motion picture.

"*Hai,* always serious," the gray-haired man answered. "Now, please take your place before I grow old."

Kenjii shook his head in mirth as he followed the

instructions. He assumed a guard stance, one blade high, the other held low as Akio had shown him.

"Form is suitable. Maybe you not a waste of time."

What is Akio playing at? He talked about this for several days, and now I get this?

"Defend."

Kenjii had to take two steps back and bring his blade down as he awkwardly blocked the sword coming for his head.

"Again."

This time, he was forced to step sideways to avoid a slash aimed at his leg. He thrust one sword out and caught the blade millimeters from his flesh, then yelped as a sharp sting spread across his buttocks.

"Focus on one sword, get bit in ass by the other," his opponent chided.

Kenjii's eyes flashed red as he grimaced in anger. All thought of how ridiculous he originally considered the sim left his mind. He continued to slip sideways as he hooked the blade by his leg with his left sword and slashed with the right. His opponent blocked it with a flick of his weapon.

"Must try harder to be successful." His antagonist chuckled. "You hit like a small child."

Kenjii flushed with rage, and his fangs extended from his gums. "You will not talk to me like that, you self-important stack of silicone."

"I think I hit a nerve," Takumi deadpanned to Akio.

Akio's body shook as he fought to control the laughter that threatened to explode. "I have some understanding of what he's experiencing." He chortled. "I was ready to bite someone the day I experienced this."

"Yes, I particularly enjoyed that. Eve informed me she had neglected to tell you about the program changes or the force-feedback suit."

"It was an experience I won't soon forget," Akio assured him.

"Watch this," Takumi instructed.

The avatar twisted the sword Kenjii had blocked, catching it with the hooked end of his *shuang gou*. He took a half-step to the side, pulling Kenjii off-balance, and snatched his blade up and back, yanking the vampire's sword from his hand. In one smooth motion, the instructor blocked the other sword with his left and moved in under Kenjii's guard. His foot came up, and Kenjii's avatar fell to the floor when the foot caught the side of his head. He grunted in response to the blow.

Before he gained his feet, both his opponent's swords whistled through the air and connected on either side of his neck. His vision went red for an instant, then he was back in the ready room. A text message appeared in front of him.

Player One has sustained a lethal blow. Do you wish to continue?

"Continue," Kenjii growled.

The scene turned green, then blurred, and he was once again in the dojo. His opponent stood with his swords held casually by his sides.

"I thought we were practicing blades," Kenjii complained.

"Always expect the unexpected. Only rule in fight with swords is not to be where sword cuts. Again."

Kenjii cautiously stepped into the ring, warily watching

the smaller man who had so easily defeated him.

"You here to learn, or do you still wish to dance about like bull in china shop? I can do this all day."

Kenjii bowed slightly, his eyes never leaving his opponent as Akio had taught him. "I am here to learn, *Sensei*."

"Good. Now we can begin."

Akio watched for a few minutes longer. When he saw that Kenjii no longer looked at the sim as a game, he nodded. "How long will you keep him in there?"

"He has excellent form, and with his vampire abilities, he is already proficient. I suggest one hour to build on his tactics with the longer blades," Takumi replied.

"He will go against tigers who can match his speed and some who have mastered the Pricolici form. He needs to be more than proficient." Akio motioned to Kenjii. "I don't wish to lose him again."

"Understood. I assure you I will teach him everything I've discovered about fighting the tiger men. He will not be easy prey, no matter what form they use."

"*Domo,* Takumi. Please notify me five minutes before the session ends."

"Acknowledged."

Akio exited the sim suite and made his way to the offices near the front of the building. He heard Eve's and Horst's voices before he entered.

"Yagi didn't know what bothered him so much, but he said several other villagers came to him with similar tales."

"Did he give any other reasons?" Eve asked.

"Yes. He told me something was off about him on the job site, too. That he didn't have answers to questions about the progress or the purpose of some construction steps when first asked. Then he would have the answers the next day, or even later the same day. As the job superintendent, he should have been on top of all of that," Horst assured her.

"Is there a problem with the Kume work?" Akio inquired as he entered the office.

"Not sure," Horst answered. "Yagi has become knowledgeable about working with construction superintendents since the project started, and he felt something was off with the company we hired to do Koda's and Asai's project."

Akio was silent for a moment. "Should I meet with him?"

"No, I don't think it's that serious. I'm scheduled to complete the last walk-through tomorrow. I will talk to him and contact you if I need you," Horst replied.

"Very good. I will wait for your call."

A monitor on one wall came to life. The scene showed Kenjii moving through forms with his *shuang gou* in slow motion as Takumi's avatar made comments and corrections.

"That was not what I expected, knowing Kenjii's temperament," Eve stated.

"Takumi pushed him into reacting emotionally, then killed him. I think they have an understanding now." Akio smiled.

"Do you think Miko, I mean Kenjii, will integrate into human society?" Horst sounded concerned.

"*Hai*. He has improved over the past month. I will introduce him to Koda and Asai since they said they are willing. Koda wants to visit the base."

"I will bring her anytime she wants."

"I know you would, Horst, but I don't want any of our people to worry that they're in danger from another. That's why I've kept Kenjii's interactions with humans limited. He now understands that Heinz and Isamu were not outstanding role models."

"That is without a doubt the biggest understatement I've ever heard you make." Horst snorted. "They were—what did Koda call Seki last week, Eve?"

"A douche nugget," she supplied.

"That's it. They were both douche nuggets."

"Nice to see your vocabulary is expanding." Akio chuckled.

"What can I say? Have to roll with the times." Horst winked.

"What are you rolling in?" Koda quipped as she came into the office. "Whatever it is, you better not get it on the couch."

Horst laughed as she approached him and wrapped him in a hug. "I was showing Akio one of the many changes you have made in my life, my tiny beauty."

"*Konichiwa,* Akio-*sama,*" Koda greeted the vampire.

Akio returned her courtesy. "*Konichiwa,* Koda-*san.*"

Koda noticed the scene on the monitor and gestured to it. "How is Kenjii doing?"

"He's adapting to his new life. He has progressed faster than I expected, but he's dealing with some recurring issues."

"I'm glad you saved him. He is good for you."

"We are good for each other."

"I want to invite both of you to the opening of the

Kume Sunset House." She bumped Horst with her hip. "My man-mountain says we can open in three days."

"It will be an honor to attend."

"Great! I will have Takumi contact you with the details."

"*Domo.*" Akio nodded. "Kenjii will soon be out of the sim. If you are available, I would like you to meet him."

"I would love to. Asai is in her apartment. Would you like me to call her to come down too?"

"If she isn't busy. I want Kenjii to interact with the two of you in controlled circumstances. He's shown that he can function around normal humans, but I must be sure he will control his urges until he agrees to enhancement."

Koda pulled the pendant that served as her communicator out of her shirt. "Asai, can you come to the office?"

"Sure. What's up?"

"Akio wants Kenjii to meet us, as we discussed."

"I'll be right down. Seki's here. Can I bring him?"

Koda looked at Akio, who nodded.

"Bring him, cousin."

"On the way."

They continued to make small talk while watching Kenjii on the monitor. He had progressed from going through offense and defense stances in slow motion to working at half-speed.

Akio appraised his progress. "Takumi, have him speed up to full speed."

Kenjii stopped for a beat, then launched into the same series of moves at full speed. His blades were blurs as he moved from one stance to the next.

"He's a quick study, Akio," Takumi mused. "Let's see how he handles this."

Kenjii stopped when he'd completed the katas. He nodded to the figure in front of him, and the next instant, both of them were flowing from attack to defense in a smooth dance of flashing steel.

The avatar Takumi controlled switched up, going from defense to offense and back in the blink of an eye. Kenjii followed each move and countered it without hesitation.

"Damn. Is that a new sim, Eve?" Seki asked when he and Asai came through the door.

"Yes. It's a continuation of the martial training sim I developed for Asai and Koda.

Seki looked at Asai with confusion. "You train like that?"

Asai giggled. "Not yet, but soon."

"I will have to step up my game, won't I?"

Eve chortled. "She could kick your ass five ways from Sunday now."

Asai blushed, uncomfortable with the attention. "I wouldn't, though."

"That's because if you do something that rates an ass-kicking, I will be the one delivering it," Koda growled. "Asai is too soft on you to do a proper job."

"Koda!" Asai exclaimed.

"Well, it's true. I mean, you treated him like an invalid for two days after he got his ass handed to him in that tournament. Oh, by the way, thanks for the dinner reservations again, Seki. It was divine."

Seki palmed his face as he blushed. "You're welcome, and that tournament was brutal. I didn't expect the positive feedback suit would be quite so...positive."

Koda and Eve burst out laughing.

"What?" Seki asked. "What's so funny?"

"Nothing," Koda answered, her eyes glittering with restrained mirth.

Asai cut her eyes between Koda and Eve. "What did you two do?" she demanded, rounding on them.

"Nooothinggg," Koda drawled.

"I need to check the server room." Eve stood and started for the door.

"Traitor," Koda whispered to her retreating back.

"Hold it!" Asai yelled. "Nobody is leaving until you explain."

Horst chuckled and stepped away from Koda.

"Et tu, furface?" Koda snapped.

Horst's voice took on a sage-like tone. "Wise man say, never stand between woman who looks like that and her target." He nodded at Asai, who was shooting daggers out of her eyes at her cousin.

"Spill, Koda," Asai demanded.

"I...um, *we*," she nodded at Eve, "might have tweaked the settings on the force feedback a little."

Asai crossed her arms over her chest and glared at them. Seki looked confused as his eyes darted from one to the other.

"How much tweaking was it?"

"A little," Koda deflected.

"Koda!"

"Okay, I set his pain receptors up a little higher than normal."

"Is that all?"

Koda stared at the floor sheepishly. "I might have set the adversary accuracy a smidge higher too," she mumbled.

Seki's eyes widened in shock. "You messed with my tournament?"

"I made allowances for the increased accuracy. You took longer to die," Eve volunteered.

"You too?" Asai snapped.

Eve looked apologetic as she nodded.

"Why would you do that?"

"He forgot he had a date with you to play his game. I thought a lesson was called for," Koda defended. "Eve agreed."

"So, you two took it on yourselves to...what, defend my honor?"

"More to make him," she nodded at Seki, "regret forgetting your date to play with his friends."

"Wait!" Seki exclaimed. "I had to pay for the reservations for that four days later. Trust me, I won't soon forget."

Asai patted his shoulder. "I should hope not. But that doesn't make what you did okay, Koda."

"Hey, Eve agreed. She even changed it from what I'd done."

"Traitor," Eve whispered, a small smile playing on one side of her mouth.

"Akio, Kenjii will be done in five minutes," Takumi called over his implant.

Akio slipped out of the office and headed toward the sim suite to fetch Kenjii, still chuckling at the payback Eve and Koda had visited on Seki for Asai. He knew exactly how injuries in the sims felt.

CHAPTER TWENTY-FIVE

The Palace, Tokyo, Japan

"How did your session go?" Akio asked when Kenjii removed the VR headset.

"Other than getting my ass kicked by the character from that movie Abel had me watch earlier?"

"*Hai*." Akio snorted, his eyes sparkling with humor.

"Since you think it's so funny, I think I'll wait and show you what I learned when we spar." Kenjii grinned.

"Bring it."

"Oh, you bet I will." He stalked over and embraced Akio warmly. "Maybe we can *spar* afterward," he whispered as his lips brushed the vampire's cheek.

"You're incorrigible. I was asking about your training, and you changed the subject."

"We have lost decades to make up for." Kenjii pulled back and looked into Akio's eyes, a mischievous grin making his eyes sparkle.

"Indeed we do, but first, how do you feel? Koda and Asai want to meet you."

"What do you mean? I'm fine. That was nowhere as intense as when we spar."

"Do you need to feed?"

Kenjii pursed his lips and shook his head. "I'm fine. Your pet humans are safe."

"They are my friends, not pets," Akio admonished as he pulled away from the embrace. "Both of them have proven themselves to be resilient and intelligent young women."

"I'm sorry, I shouldn't have said that. I'm trying to overcome the things Heinz and Isamu taught me about humans. I can't think of them as anything other than tools or food, but I *am* trying," he apologized.

"I know it's hard to change decades of practice, but it's necessary if you're to be a functional part of all this." His hard tone softened. "I preyed on humans for centuries. Don't think I don't understand."

Kenjii nodded. "I'm fine to meet your friends. They don't have to fear harm from me. I wouldn't do anything to hurt you or cause you disappointment. I love you too much to do that."

"And I, you. I didn't fear you harming them. It worried me that the urges would distract you, not that you would act on them."

"Thank you for trusting me." Kenjii caught his hand and pulled him toward the door. "Let's go meet my new friends."

Akio and Kenjii walked into the office hand in hand, to see Horst doubled over laughing.

Seki had a hurt look on his face. "I was sore for three days. Every time they hit me in the sim, it felt like a mule had kicked me."

"Stop being such a drama queen," Koda snarked. "The settings weren't *that* high. Would you like me to show you what they can really do?"

"Koda!" Asai shouted. "Don't even think about it."

"Well, he's the one acting like a whiny bitch," Koda shot back.

"Ahem." Akio cleared his throat to get their attention. "I'm certain that whatever is going on here is of great importance, but I have someone I'd like you to meet."

All eyes turned to him and the man partially concealed behind him.

Akio pulled Kenjii forward. "This is Kenjii. Kenjii, the one with the mouth is Koda. The other is her cousin Asai, and the whiny bitch," he nodded at Seki, "is Asai's friend Seki. I believe you know the giant in the corner."

Kenjii smiled shyly. "Nice to meet you."

"Wow, Akio! You didn't tell me he was such a hottie." Koda grinned.

Kenjii's eyes widened at the unexpected compliment.

"He is, isn't he?" Akio leered, causing Kenjii to blush.

"Two instances of levity from Akio in less than a minute. That is unheard of," Eve quipped from her desk. She nodded at Kenjii. "I think you're good for him. Keep it up."

Kenjii recovered quickly from the unexpected welcome. "You know I will, girl." He cocked his hip and placed a hand on it teasingly, causing Akio to do a double-take.

The women all giggled, and Horst guffawed from the

corner. "Good to see you are well, Miko…uh, I mean Kenjii. Sorry, Akio told me some of what those bastards did to you. Forgive me for using that name."

"It's fine. I understand I have you to thank for ending Heinz's miserable existence."

"*Ja*."

"I'm, uh, I'm sorry about Dieter. I know you were close."

"*Danke*. Dieter made his choice." Horst's voice was rough from the pain of the loss. "I will always blame Heinz for Dieter's poor decisions, but he was never the same after our mother died. At least Heinz can never harm another."

Kenjii nodded knowingly. "You are doing well here?"

"*Ja*, I am happy with this life. I have been working to help the people Isamu's madness almost destroyed rebuild."

Koda walked over and wrapped her arms around him. "My man-mountain is too modest. He has done more than help rebuild. He has made it possible for Kume to thrive again. The construction he organized and oversaw has improved their living conditions. Making them a regular stop for the ships he and Eve own ensures they will never be isolated and alone again."

Kenjii's eyebrows went up. "You own a business now? It has only been a few months since you left China."

"*Ja*. Eve designed the ships, and I worked out the design for the facility we will use to create more."

"Stop being so humble," Eve chided. "He gave me the idea when he started talking about how pretty the island is and that it was once a popular tourist spot. It is a win for the people of Kume and us."

Kenjii was silent as his mind worked through this information. *Akio told me some of this, but I wasn't sure I believed it.*

That they would not only make a place here for a Were but help him thrive astounds me. Perhaps there is a place here for me, too.

Akio turned his head to hide the smile that threatened. Kenjii's thoughts were becoming less erratic as the Miko persona lost influence. For the first time since he'd found him, Akio felt Kenjii could overcome the traumas of his past.

"What did you think of the sim?" Asai asked innocently. She knew Abel had introduced him to the movie Takumi's avatar originated in.

"It is excellent. I couldn't tell the difference between the game—uh, I mean sim—and reality once I started. Akio taught me the basics of the tiger swords, but the man in the machine showed me things Akio hasn't."

Asai nodded as he spoke. "Eve was able to provide Takumi with video clips from the late twentieth and early twenty-first centuries from a place where people recorded, then made their movies available through a computer program. He analyzed hundreds of hours of matches and demonstrations to map out the avatar's movements."

"It was a learning experience, and one I hope to continue." Kenjii looked at Akio.

"I believe you should be able to if you desire."

"I have something for you, Kenjii." Eve pulled a communicator from her desk and passed it to him.

Kenjii skeptically eyed the compact black disc attached to a cord. "What is it?"

"It allows you to contact any of us," she motioned around the room with her hand, "and Yuko from anywhere in the world."

Kenjii looked at the device with renewed interest. “How?”

“Press the center and say the name of the person you wish to speak to. It routs the signals through Abel, and he’ll connect you. If you ever get in trouble and need assistance, press the center twice. It sends a distress beacon with your location.”

“This little device has that kind of power? How?”

“Kurtherian technology and our satellites in orbit,” Eve replied.

“Amazing.” Kenjii smiled at her. “Thank you.”

He faced Akio. “Does this mean I can now go out without you as a chaperone?”

“*Hai,* but not too far yet. I know you can take care of yourself, but the Clan will probably send more here. I eliminated several groups that had taken over small towns while I was searching for you.”

“I can come here to practice, though?”

“*Hai.*” Akio didn’t add that he had to feed before leaving each time, but he would before it happened.

Akio addressed the group. “I wanted all of you to meet Kenjii, and I thank you for welcoming him. We need to go back, though.”

“Kenjii, I’m glad I got to meet you.” Koda smiled. “If you have questions I can help with, push the button and call.”

“Thank you, Koda-*san*. That is an offer I may use.” He winked conspiratorially. "I bet you know the best places to shop."

“You know it.” Koda giggled.

“Wear comfortable footwear,” Horst offered. “Trust me on that.”

Koda playfully slapped the huge Were on his chest. “What are you trying to say, furface?”

“Nothing at all, my tiny beauty.” Horst laughed as he pulled her in for a hug. Looking over the top of her head, he pointed at his feet and mouthed, “Trust me.”

Asai giggled at his antics but nodded her agreement. “It was nice to meet you, Kenjii-*san*. You are welcome here anytime. Just watch this one.” She poked Seki in the ribs. “He will try to get you involved in his group play if you’re not careful.”

“Hey,” Seki protested. “Not until his second visit.”

Asai laughed at him and shook her head. “Come on, Seki. It’s late, and we both have work tomorrow.”

“Nice to meet you. If you want to try a sim for fun, I have a great one. Let me know,” Seki offered as Asai led him out the door.

Kenjii was dumbstruck. These humans not only accepted him but had offered him friendship—something he hadn’t known in many decades. He recognized that they were more than friends. They were a family of humans, vampires, a werewolf, and an artificial intelligence in a robotic body.

CHAPTER TWENTY-SIX

Shinjuku City, Tokyo, Japan

Akio watched Kenjii interact with Koda and the others. Horst's acceptance in the group and Koda's friendly banter brought out the fun-loving Kenjii he remembered. His mind was clear and untroubled for the first time since Akio had found him. Although he knew there was a chance the Miko personality would surface again, Akio felt it was safe for Kenjii to spend more time around humans, provided he continued to feed on the blood supplies Eve had delivered daily.

"Tell me, Horst," Kenjii asked. "How do you like it here?"

Horst smiled fondly at Koda, who was engaged in an animated conversation with Eve about a new sim they were working on. "I have more than I deserve."

"What do you mean?"

"I have the love of an amazing woman, friends who care for me and support me, a job that gives me purpose, and a comfortable place to live. Plus, the vampires here," he nodded at Akio, "are nothing like I've ever encountered."

Kenjii nodded as he processed Horst's words. "I see the lure of civilization after all the years you spent living in that hole in Acheng."

"The comfortable bed and endless hot showers were a major selling point." Horst laughed.

"Where do you live? I haven't seen you at the base."

"I have an apartment here and a room at Yagi's house on Kume Island. The past month, I've spent most of my time on Kume, working with the navy on the base they built there."

"You're doing the design and engineering on that, aren't you?"

"*Ja*. It's good to build instead of destroy, as Heinz wanted."

"And you own a shipping business?"

"Part of it. Eve and I are the majority stockholders, but Yuko, Koda, and Asai also own shares."

"What about you, Akio? Are you part of that too?"

"No. I have a few projects I am looking into, but nothing as big as what Horst, Eve, Koda, and Asai are doing. They will all be extremely wealthy if their businesses grow at the rate we expect them to."

"What are you looking at?"

"I have been seeking silver for the bullets the police and military need to protect themselves from rogue elements of the UnknownWorld. There is little of it here, and I have exhausted the abandoned caches in the immediate area. I have to go farther each time I hunt more."

"There was a lot of silver used in Europe if I remember correctly," Horst offered.

"*Hai,* although I don't have the time to search it out with the current troubles. Abel notified me that he's verified two more slave farms in China. I will need to deal with them sooner rather than later."

"Those damned tigers are getting bolder every day. Let me know if you need my help. I prefer to build and create, but I will do whatever you require of me to stop them."

"Thank you, Horst. I know you prefer not to fight. Keep building things. That is important, too."

"I met with the crew who will lay the foundation for the new base this afternoon. They will start construction in two days. I will be on-site when they do to ensure there are no problems."

"Thank you. I will feel better knowing we have a secure base of operations that won't endanger as many humans if it's attacked."

"I hope someone is foolish enough to attack the new facility when it's complete. Eve and I have designed some nasty surprises for them." Horst snorted.

"So Eve tells me. I appreciate all you've done on that project. I know it took time away from your work on Kume and the shipping business."

"Akio, you could have killed me when we met. Instead, you gave me a life I never expected to have. Designing and overseeing this project is an honor."

Kenjii watched the exchange with interest. The more he heard, the more hope he had that he too would have a new life, one with someone he loved.

Akio nodded at Horst. "If you need me to see that

contractor Yagi was concerned about, call. I will be in China tomorrow, dealing with what Abel found."

"If he acts suspicious, I will hold him there until you're available. Unless he gets stupid—then I will deal with him. The people of Kume are family, and I will allow no one to harm my family ever again." His eyes flashed yellow as he looked at Koda, still engrossed in her conversation with Eve.

"You have much honor, Horst. I will talk to you tomorrow," Akio affirmed. "Kenjii, are you ready to go? I think you have a movie to finish."

"Oh, Akio's got jokes." He laughed. "Yes, I'm sure I can find something to entertain myself at home." He winked and pursed his lips.

Horst snickered as Akio and Kenjii said their goodbyes to Koda and Eve and thought, *Never in a million years would I have seen this coming. I'm glad that Akio found joy. He and Kenjii deserve it after all they've suffered.*

Kenjii was quiet, lost in his thoughts as they walked the dimly lit streets home. He had been considering Akio's offer to fix what was wrong in his body, but he still wasn't ready to commit. Years of Heinz's torturous procedures and experiments made him hesitate, but the more he saw of the people who surrounded his friend, the more he wanted to be part of what they did.

"Akio?"

"*Hai.*"

"You've told me some things about your life and mission here. May I ask you some questions?"

Akio clasped Kenjii's hand. "You may ask me anything. I will be honest and tell you if it's something I can't answer, but you're always free to ask me questions."

"The humans, Koda, Asai, and Seki. Do they know what we are?"

"Koda and Asai do. Seki knows we're warriors, but he doesn't know our nature."

Kenjii was thoughtful for a moment. "Koda offered me friendship, knowing I'm a killer?"

"Koda offered you friendship because she sees the man you are, not the one you were."

"Does she know what Horst is?"

Akio smiled. "*Hai.* She made him shift so she could see when they started dating."

Kenjii's eyes widened in surprise. "She entered a romantic relationship knowing he was a wolf? Is she right in the head?"

"Koda is an amazing woman. You know she was a captive of Isamu and Ogawa. Did you hear about when the Yakuza kidnapped her?"

"Yes on Isamu, no on the mobsters."

"They locked her in a small cage inside a joy house that catered to dark fetishes. The man who held her threatened her repeatedly with torture. When Eve found her, she would have killed him in cold blood. Koda asked her to spare his life and let him face the court's justice."

"Why?"

"Because she felt that Eve killing him like that would have damaged her. That's who Koda Rii is."

"Is she enhanced in any way? I can't smell you or Yuko, and she doesn't smell like a wolf."

"No, Koda and Asai are both normal humans. Yuko didn't feel it was time to offer them that option. They are young, and it might happen."

Kenjii snorted. "How can you say that after Isamu and the Yakuza? She is lucky to be alive."

"True, but she still has many years of life to experience before she has to decide if she wants to watch the people she loves grow old and die while she remains young. Yuko had to make the same choice with her parents. She did not take the full enhancements until they had gone to join their ancestors."

Kenjii nodded.

"Besides," Akio quipped, "have you met her boyfriend? Do you think he would let anyone harm her?"

"I saw his reaction when he spoke about family. He is different than I remember. There is a calm air about him that he never had with Heinz, but there is also an aura of danger about him. I believe he is more dangerous now than his brother or the other pack members were."

"*Hai.* I watched as he fought Heinz. He ran him down and ripped his head off his body. Horst is a formidable warrior, although he doesn't want to fight."

Kenjii started to respond, then stiffened. "Someone is following us."

"*Hai.* He's been behind us since we left the Palace."

"Why didn't you say something?"

"He isn't a threat at this time, and I wanted to see how long it took you to notice. There is a section of road ahead that has no lights. I planned to see what he wanted when we got there."

"How do you know he isn't a threat?"

Akio smiled and tapped his temple.

Realization dawned on Kenjii. "Upgrades."

Akio smiled again and nodded.

They continued to walk. Akio pointed out different landmarks as they went, pretending they didn't know they were being followed.

"Who do you think he is?" Kenjii murmured as Akio pointed at an uninteresting building without speaking.

"Yakuza."

Kenjii shook his head in disgust. "I thought the price they paid when they took the girl would have convinced them it wasn't worth it to mess with you."

"Me, too. They will know that it's a terrible idea after this time. Any who still live, that is," Akio coldly stated.

"Ah. Snacks?"

"Perhaps. You need to stop thinking about feeding on humans, though. The daily supply Eve arranged should sustain you."

"It does, but I enjoy the rush when it's fresh. As long as I limit it to evil people, isn't that enough?"

"I have occasionally taken blood from those who deserved it," Akio admitted. "That is reserved for special cases. I would have drained the one who held Koda and delivered his lifeless body to his master with pleasure. If these mobsters think they can threaten me or mine, you will have the opportunity to bathe in their blood."

Kenjii looked at him askance. This was a side of Akio he'd never seen.

Kenjii pulled the rich coppery blood from his neck, healing his gunshot wound in seconds with the rush of energy.

After Shoto's struggles ceased, Kenjii released him and let his body fall to the ground. He wiped the blood off his lips and let out a satisfied groan. "You got what you needed?"

"*Hai.* He was only a soldier. He didn't know why he was looking for us, but I have the name and location of the man he reports to."

Kenjii grinned. "We have more work tonight?"

"*Hai.*"

Abel, send a Pod to my location.

Acknowledged. Is everything okay?

The Yakuza are searching for Kenjii and me. One found us and shot Kenjii. He's healed the wound, but we have a body on our hands.

Would you like me to contact Yuko?

Hai. *Have her notify Inspector Yonai that the Yakuza have moved against us again. I will look into the reasons and let him know.*

Acknowledged. Pod inbound, ETA forty-five seconds. Yuko is connecting with Yonai now. Happy hunting.

Thank you, Abel.

"Our Pod will be here soon. Then we'll see what his boss can tell us." Akio cast a disdainful glance at the body between them.

Kenjii didn't answer. The feral grin on his face said it all.

CHAPTER TWENTY-SEVEN

Shinjuku City, Tokyo, Japan

Shao Hua saw the Yakuza soldier dressed as a bum leave the doorway he'd been watching from when two figures emerged from the front of the Palace. He and Jin had located the watchers on either side of the building shortly after they arrived. Shao had ordered Jin to watch from a safe distance downwind of the building while he did the same at the front. He planned to follow the followers to reduce the risk of discovery by the vampires Kun sent them to find.

He worked his way down the fire escape from the roof of the building he'd used as an observation post and hung back several hundred meters behind the Yakuza soldier. He didn't worry about losing him. The man's cologne had a distinct scent he could have picked out in a crowded room.

He followed in silence, careful to remain in the shadows as the kilometers went by. When he passed where the vampires had stepped onto the sidewalk, another scent assailed his sensitive nostrils. It was the rotting meat smell associated with all vampires he'd encountered over the years.

Shao smiled to himself. *This just got easier.*

A disturbance in the distance caused him to stop and step off the sidewalk into an abandoned building. He strained his ears and heard the crack of a gun firing. Minutes later, a panicked shriek pierced the night until it was cut short.

He heard bits of conversation, but the distance and city noise prevented him from hearing clearly. He abandoned his hiding place and moved across the dimly lit street on silent feet to a vacant lot on the opposite side.

After crouching behind a pile of debris, he cautiously looked out and saw the Yakuza soldier in the grip of one vampire while the other stood behind him.

Shao winced when the vampire holding the man latched onto his throat. It was over in moments, and the vampire dropped the lifeless body at his feet. Seconds later, a black object dropped from the sky. A door slid open and the vampires climbed in, taking the body with them. The craft shot into the night sky and disappeared in seconds. Shao watched for several more minutes, ensuring it had departed before he approached the spot where the altercation took place.

The scent of blood and vampire hung heavy on the air. Shao shook his head, disgusted that the soldier had allowed himself to be caught.

Shao walked away from the scene. After he'd gone a few hundred meters, he detected the faint odor of vampire again. The scent was several hours older than the first he smelled. Shao grinned as he followed the trail, certain that his mission to find the vampire's base would be completed before the night ended.

Hotel Siena, Shinjuku City, Tokyo, Japan

The Pod descended to hover centimeters above the roof of the Hotel Siena. Akio and Kenjii stepped onto the roof and made their way to an access stairway near the landing site. Akio twisted the knob sharply, and the lock gave way with a metallic snap. He held the door and motioned for Kenjii to enter. "Eighth floor, room eight hundred and six."

Kenjii nodded and headed down the stairs, stopping on the landing of the desired floor. "How do you want to do this?"

"Quietly, if possible."

They worked their way down the empty hallway to the room, then Akio held up a hand as he extended his senses.

Kenjii listened and detected the soft snores and steady heartbeat of a lone person asleep in the room. "I only hear one."

"*Hai,* and the rooms on each side are empty," Akio agreed.

Akio knocked lightly on the door and called in a soft voice, "Juba, open the door. It's Shoto."

A muffled snort came from inside, then footsteps approached the opposite side of the door. When the door started to open, Kenjii shoved it, slamming it into the body on the other side and knocking him across the room onto the bed.

In a flash, he was in the room with his hand around Juba's throat, cutting off the man's shocked cry. Akio entered and closed the door behind him, then nodded at the confused figure on the bed. "You wished to find me. You have. Now, what do you want?"

Juba's face went pale when he realized who and what faced him. He focused on the figure holding him on the bed, and his bladder threatened to release when the eyes staring at him glowed red.

"My friend asked you a question," the figure growled. Juba's bladder lost the fight when two ivory fangs extended across the lower lips, mere centimeters from his face.

Akio reached out with his mind, picking up Juba's terror as Kenjii flashed his eyes and fangs. Beneath it, he saw images of a teenage girl in a school uniform and a woman in her thirties.

"Let him up, Kenjii," Akio requested.

Kenjii caught Juba's collar and pulled him to a sitting position on the bed, then draped one arm across his shoulders in a friendly manner while his free hand deftly removed the pistol tucked into his belt.

Akio cocked his head to the side and raised one eyebrow.

"I've already been shot tonight. It hurts," Kenjii explained as he tossed the gun out of reach on the floor while allowing his fangs to retract and his eyes to fade back to their normal dark brown.

Akio shook his head, then turned his attention to the pale and sweating man. "Why have you sent your men to find us?"

Juba swallowed hard, the whites of his eyes showing all

around as he tried to think of an answer that wouldn't end with him dead. "What are you talking about?"

Kenjii flicked him on the tip of his nose with a finger. "Don't play the fool. It will not end well for you."

Juba whimpered and reached for his stinging nose. "I, uh, I was following Kishi Sakutaro's orders. The *Oyabun* forbade us to have any contact with you," he nodded at Akio, "but Kishi and her lapdog Asaka made me find you."

"Why?" Akio pressed him. The answers were swimming through Juba's mind, but he wanted Kenjii to hear it, too.

"She wants to make you pay for the troubles she blames you for after the incident with Muto and Sero. She is also working with a man from China who seeks this one." He jerked his head at Kenjii.

Kenjii stiffened as he focused on Juba. "Where is this man who seeks me?"

"I don't know."

Kenjii's eyes changed back to red in an instant, causing Juba to try to pull away from the arm across his shoulders.

"I contact him by phone," Juba almost shouted. "His name is Li Song. Kishi agreed to help him find you in exchange for him killing both of you."

Kenjii growled deep in his throat. "You wish to kill my friend? I will take satisfaction from ending your sniveling life." Kenjii moved the hand resting on Juba's shoulder to the back of his neck and bent his head to the side. He forced him to watch as his fangs slowly extended from his mouth.

"Wait," Akio ordered.

Kenjii halted, his open mouth only centimeters from Juba's exposed throat.

"You have a choice, Juba. You can go to Sato and confess your part in Kishi's plans, or I can allow my friend to finish what he's started."

Relief flashed through Juba's terror-stricken eyes. "Anything! Anything you want. I will go now and tell him everything. I will do whatever you want."

Akio motioned for Kenjii to release him. Kenjii looked like he would protest, then let go of his neck and moved across the compact room in one motion. Juba slid off the edge of the bed and *thumped* to the floor.

"Tell Sato I will see him soon to discuss what he must do to make amends for the Yakuza's declaration of war on me and mine. Tell him if I get any sign that you are sniffing around what is mine before then, his life is forfeit."

"The *Oyabun* didn't do it," Juba whined. "It was Kishi."

"The king is responsible for the actions of his subjects. Tell him." Akio's mouth quirked up on one side as he made his eyes glow red and pushed fear behind his words. Juba's mouth opened in a silent scream as he curled into a ball on the floor. Akio stood and motioned for Kenjii, who looked at him with wide eyes but followed him out of the room.

Kenjii closed the door when they were out and slumped against the wall. "What the hell was that?" His voice shook.

"Upgrades." Akio grinned as he walked to the stairs that led up to the roof.

Nakano District, Tokyo Japan

Shao followed the faint vampire scent until it turned off the road onto a side street. He continued past several darkened office buildings until it disappeared, then doubled back and stopped when he found the scent again. He looked up, noting lights shining through several windows in the ten stories above. He nodded once and moved back to the street he had taken to get here, certain he'd located the base they'd been searching for.

CHAPTER TWENTY-EIGHT

Kume Island, Okinawa, Japan

The sun cast a golden glow over the water as Horst brought his Pod down over the beach on Kume. He directed it to a gutted shed beside the rubble of a once-majestic resort. Yagi told him a tsunami had demolished the facility two years after the WWDE. Once he secured the Pod inside the roofless structure, he hefted his backpack to one shoulder and walked the kilometer across the sand into town.

Yagi met him at the door with a cup of strong black tea in his hand. "How was your journey?"

"Uneventful and fast." Horst grinned.

Yagi chuckled. "Always in those marvelous flying machines."

"You know you can ride when you want to. Asai would love for you to visit, and we can have you back in minutes if needed."

"I know." Yagi shook his head. "If I leave for two hours to get in some fishing, you would think it was the WWDE over again. 'Yagi, where's this? Yagi, we're running low on that. Yagi, Yagi, Yagi.' I swear I'm going to change my name and not tell a soul what the new one is."

Horst laughed as Yagi feigned disgust at his predicament. "You and I both know you thrive on the chaos. Where would you be without everyone needing you so much?"

"Fishing." He grinned.

Horst sipped the tea, welcoming the warmth and the spicy mix of herbs Yagi added. He made a satisfied noise when he brought the cup down. "Wonderful as always. If you ever tire of being mayor, you could always open a teahouse."

"When I'm no longer mayor, I'll be damned if I have to get up with the sun and go to another job. Fishing, that's the life for me."

"Speaking of jobs, I need to get on with mine. Today we do the last inspections at the restaurant. It went up so quickly that Asai and Koda haven't had time to complain."

Yagi pursed his lips at the mention of the restaurant. "That foreman was asking questions again last night. He hinted that he knew more about Akio and Yuko than he should. There is something not right about him."

Horst frowned. "I spoke to Akio about him last night. I will talk to him today, and if there is something there, Akio will come and *discuss* it with him."

"Good. He makes me uncomfortable. I will be glad when he leaves the island."

"I'll take care of it during the walkthrough. If he doesn't answer correctly about the job, I will know."

Horst finished the tea and passed the empty cup to the

mayor. "*Domo,* Yagi-*san*. I'll talk to you at lunch?" he asked with one eyebrow raised.

"You know Ono would kill me if you missed one of her lunches."

A voice came from inside the house. "I wouldn't kill you, you old goat. I'd only make you wish you were dead." Ono laughed. "Good morning, Horst."

"Good morning, Ono-*san*." He smiled, although the woman inside didn't see it.

"Lunch is at noon. I'm making that fish stew you liked so well last time."

"See you then," Horst called to her as he nodded to Yagi and headed down the sandy street that ran through town.

Sunset House, Kume Island, Okinawa, Japan

He was the first to arrive at the freshly painted building. The paint was still sticky in places, telling him the work had gone on late into the night. He walked around the outside, checking the fit of the gutters, soffits, and fasciae as he went. The clipboard he carried contained the punch list—items that needed to be completed, and some that needed to be redone before he would accept the building from the contractor.

Satisfied that the outer work was complete, he pushed open the door and stepped inside. The interior was open space and light-colored wood. A bar ran down the length of the back wall, with an opening on one end that led to the industrial kitchen setup he'd found in Tokyo. A noodle house had run into financial troubles, and he'd bought all the equipment for a tenth of what new would cost.

He was completing the inspection an hour later when a bleary-eyed Kimura Hikonaga walked in. "Sorry I'm late. We worked until three this morning, getting the paint finished."

Horst grunted noncommittally. He could smell the stale cigarettes and *sake* on Hikonaga's clothes.

"All is in order, Hikonaga-*san*," he announced as he placed his clipboard on the corner of the bar. "Do you have the transfer papers?"

"*Hai*, I have them here." He pulled a rolled-up sheaf of papers from his back pocket.

Horst looked at the unprofessional state of the smudged and creased documents, and his lips compressed into a straight line.

"How did you handle the electrical connections for the ovens?" Horst asked nonchalantly. The specifications he'd sent with ovens he'd bought required heavier gauge wire than the plans originally called for.

"We plugged them in and tested them as you requested."

"There were no issues with the wiring?"

"No. Our company does quality work. Why would there be any issues?"

"I wanted to be sure everything went smoothly," Horst lied. "I want everything to go off without a hitch when this place opens."

"No worries. Your little lady will have nothing to complain about."

Horst nodded as he signed the releases in the appropriate spots on both copies, one for the buyer's agent and the other for the project's superintendent. He handed them back to Kimura.

Kimura scribbled an illegible scratch on the places marked for him to sign, handed the buyer's copies to Horst, and stuffed his into his back pocket. "It was a pleasure to do business with you. Please contact me if you have any further work. We'll quote you a reasonable price."

Horst nodded, then his expression changed to one of hope. "I may have something for you. I need to check on a few things, but if you could meet me back here in an hour, we might work something out."

"I'll see you then if there's nothing else." Kimura smiled.

Horst grinned. "No, all is in order. See you in an hour."

Horst activated the communicator Eve had given him. "Akio?"

"Hai?"

"I need you to come to Kume after all. I believe all is not as it appears with Hikonaga."

"When do you need me there?"

"In an hour, if that's not too soon."

"No, I've postponed the China trip until after dark. I'll head that way in a few minutes."

Horst chuckled into his communicator as he asked, "Kenjii?"

"Hai."

"I understand. Meet me at Yagi's home. I'm sure Ono would like to see you, and Yagi is brewing a new blend of tea that is amazing."

"I look forward to it."

. . .

TQB Base, Tokyo, Japan

"What did inspector Yonai have for you?" Akio asked when Yuko walked into the operations center.

"Kishi Sakutaro's name keeps coming up in his investigations. He believes she is moving to be the power behind her grandfather's throne."

"That's what the surveillance Abel has gotten from the house shows. Sato meets with people only after Kishi approves it. They tell him all is well, and he accepts their answers without question."

Yuko nodded. "Yonai asked that you limit the body count as much as possible. He doesn't want his superiors panicking, thinking there is another Yakuza internal war. The last one resulted in many civilian deaths."

"If the Yakuza continue to threaten us, it will be a war, one where the casualties shall remain within their organization," Akio gravely stated.

"I understand your frustration, and so does he. He knows we won't hesitate to remove any threats to our operations. He simply wants us to hide the bodies."

"If it comes to that, I have centuries of experience in doing so."

"That's all he asks. Do you plan to deal with Kishi?"

"Possibly. I sent a message to Sato last night. If he reins her in, I will let it pass. Abel is searching for the coordinates of the phone Juba said the Clan soldier has. When he locates it, I will deal with him and see what steps to take after that."

"Why is Abel having difficulties?"

"Because the phone is out of service. When he turns it on again, I will have him," Abel volunteered. "I've also located an image I believe is Li Song, based on the information you provided, Akio."

An image appeared on the monitor in front of them, showing Juba and a Chinese male. "This is from a camera at the bank a block from the Palace. This individual and three others." The image faded, and three more appeared. "These men have been in the area for the past few weeks. The police have questioned two of them," two pictures highlighted, "and Takumi noted this one walking past the front of the building several times."

"What caused Takumi to flag him?" Yuko questioned.

"When he discovered that the Yakuza were watching the Palace for an extended period before they kidnapped Koda, he set up a subroutine to alert him when anyone passes the building multiple times."

"Doesn't he get a lot of false alarms? Hundreds of people walk through there twice each day going to work and home."

"He filters out the ones with a set pattern. That includes deliverymen and others who have any business in the area."

"How does he tell the difference?" Akio wondered.

"He tracks them through the camera networks and verifies them through corporate or government systems."

Akio shook his head in wonder. "That has to be a lot of raw data."

"It is," Abel agreed. "But it only takes a tenth of one percent of his computing power to run down thousands of leads a minute. He likes the challenge."

"Likes?" Yuko raised her eyebrows.

"That's how he described it. I tried to tell him it was

illogical to like or dislike any task. He told me he knew that, but that was what he was going with."

Yuko made a mental note to speak with Eve about Takumi's development. One of Eve's children was taking his first steps on the path to ascension.

"Abel, please summon a Pod. I told Horst I would meet him on Kume."

"Acknowledged. Black Eagle ETA thirty seconds."

Akio's head jerked up. "Why is there a Black Eagle in orbit above us?"

"In anticipation of you needing it," Abel replied.

He looked at Yuko, who shrugged. "What criteria was used to make that decision?"

"The verified location of two slave farms in China, combined with the Yakuza activity last night, showed a ninety-six-point-two-three percent likelihood that you would need either a Pod, a Black Eagle, or both within the next twenty-four hours. I summoned the Black Eagle when you called for the Pod this morning. Both have been in orbit since you and Kenjii returned."

"What's the loadout in the Black Eagle?"

"Fully loaded, and all puck launchers are operational."

"Are you expecting me to need to level a city?" Akio wondered.

"I never know with you," Abel shot back. "Be prepared, I always say."

"I think that was the Boy Scouts." Yuko snickered.

"Whatever. Your Pod is waiting. I'll bring it to the courtyard when you head up."

CHAPTER TWENTY-NINE

Lotus Towers Apartments, Shinjuku City, Tokyo, Japan

"Li, I found them," Shao announced as he rushed into the apartment they had been using for the past few days. Jin and Wu had discovered it while comparing their deliveries one night. The previous resident was a hermit who, according to the neighbors, hadn't left the apartment in the time any of them had lived there. Wu went back the next day, and when the resident opened the door, it was the last mistake he ever made.

"Where?"

"I followed the mobster when they left the arcade. They caught him and left in one of those flying machines. I backtracked to their base by following the vampire stench."

Li pushed a map of Tokyo across the counter to him. "Show me."

Shao studied the layout while tracing the route back from the apartment. "Here." He stabbed his finger on a spot on the map.

"Excellent work, Shao."

"What do we do next? Should we watch that building to gather more information?"

Li thought for a moment. "No. We might alert them. What did they do with the Yakuza who followed?"

"Killed him."

"I'll contact Kun with the news. Get ready to leave. Once Jin and Wu get back, we're leaving the city until Cui arrives. I'll contact him for an update once I've spoken with Kun."

Shao nodded and started collecting their gear.

Serenity Temple, Dabie Mountains, China

Kun watched the trainees follow the instructor through the positions as they practiced defensive katas. His face was pale and gaunt, his eyes red with a crazed look from only sleeping a few hours in the past three days.

This is the future of the Clan? These children can't follow in time with someone leading them. He shook his head in disgust and stood from his cushion to berate them again when the satellite phone in his robe vibrated.

"What do you have, Li? It had better be positive news for a change. I tire of your excuses," Kun snapped as the call connected.

"Shao found the location of the vampires' base."

Kun stalked out of the training room with the phone pressed tight against his ear. "Repeat that," he ordered when he was in the quiet hallway.

"Shao located the building where the vampires hide."

Kun smiled, his eyes dancing with barely contained

emotion. "Finally, someone does the job I dispatched them for. Where is it?"

"In an office building some ten kilometers from that arcade. I have a map with the location marked."

"Have you spoken to Cui?"

"No, Master. I notified you first. I plan to contact him after I get further instructions from you."

Kun nodded as he considered his next move. "Do you have someone watching the building?"

"No, I thought it best not to risk discovery. They killed the Yakuza soldier who was following them."

"What is your plan?"

"We will leave the city until Cui and his warriors arrive. If they don't know we've found them, we can attack when the odds are in our favor and not theirs."

"That is an acceptable plan. Contact Cui and advise him of the location in the event you're discovered."

"Yes, Master. Any other instructions?"

"No. Succeed in this, and you might receive a reward. If you fail, don't come back," Kun growled before he cut the connection.

Li looked at the phone for a moment. After shaking his head, he keyed in the numbers to connect to Cui.

Hybrid Vessel *Ming Dan*, Quingdao, China

"Fire!" The cry came from the rear of the ship. Pan turned in time to see a bright flash from the direction of the shout before a shock wave knocked him off his feet. Debris rained around where he landed between a cargo container and the ship's rail.

Pan's ears rang, and his eyes burned from the acidic smoke that followed the explosion. Cries of pain and shouts were muffled as he struggled to extract himself from the confined space. Once he stood, he squinted as he tried to see through the oily black smoke.

A flash caught his eye. He sidestepped and narrowly avoided being run over by a warrior, his body engulfed in flames. Pan grabbed the rail and cautiously followed it through the darkness until he emerged from the smoke. The scene before him was little better than before.

Flames shot into the air at the rear of the ship. Mangled bodies of the injured, dead, and dying littered the deck like a child's broken and forgotten toys. Screams of pain came from the area and the water next to the ship.

"What the hell!" Yi shouted when he saw Pan leaning slack-jawed against the railing.

"Explosion. That's all I know so far."

Yi grabbed a passing warrior. "Get more men. Help whoever you can," he ordered as he pointed toward the carnage.

Pan watched as first small groups, then more men fought the flames and tried to aid the injured. His ears finally healed enough that he heard the tortured metal creak as the flames heated it red-hot.

"Pan! Yi!" Cui yelled as he rushed up to them. "Are you injured?" Concern laced his voice as he looked at Pan.

"No, I'm okay," Pan assured him.

"What happened?"

"I don't know. Someone yelled fire, and the rear of the ship exploded as I looked up." He shrugged.

A bloody, scorched, and blistered warrior fell through a

hatch from below decks and collapsed. Pan ran to him and kneeled by his side. "Xian, what happened?"

"That crazy engineer did this," he croaked, his voice rough from the smoke.

"What do you mean?" Cui demanded.

Xian went into a coughing fit, grimacing as his body fought to heal the damage his lungs had sustained in the hellish fire below deck. Once he regained control, he looked at Cui with bleary eyes.

"He started a fire in the battery room. Said he wouldn't be part of bringing *yaoguai* to Japan."

Cui's eyes narrowed. "What set him off?"

Xian looked away, his body language showing he didn't want to answer.

"Answer him, dammit," Yi ordered.

"Quao Yue," he slowly revealed.

"What did that idiot do?" Cui yelled.

"He gutted one of the engine room assistants," Xian mumbled as he looked down. "The man was disrespectful to him."

Pan spat in disgust. "That hothead looks for reasons to find offense in everything, and I know you're no better. What did the assistant do?"

Xian wouldn't face the three commanders. Pan reached down and grabbed his collar, then yanked him to his feet.

"Answer the question." His voice was low, but the promise of violence simmered beneath the surface.

"He bumped Quao with a cart."

"Intentionally?" Pan shook him.

Xian's eyes darted about as he looked anywhere but at

the three. "No. Quao walked around a corner, and the man couldn't stop in time."

Cui palmed his face. "Where is Quao now?"

Xian looked pointedly at the flames still pouring through the hole where the explosion had blasted through the deck. "He tried to stop the engineer. He killed him as the batteries ruptured and blew."

"Kun will kill someone over this. He's already acting crazed. This will push him over the edge," Cui lamented.

"Cui and I will organize the survivors. Take him," Pan dropped Xian on the deck, "with you. Let him explain why he allowed this to happen."

Xian paled at the prospect of having to talk to Kun. Everyone had heard the rumors of how he'd killed and injured others who brought unwanted news.

"Keep him here. Have him help the injured." Cui pointed toward the damaged area. "I know where to find him if Kun wants more."

Cui turned on his heel and headed for the gangplank. When he was far enough away that the fire's roar wasn't deafening, he pulled the satellite phone from his pocket. Before he could key in Kun's number, it vibrated in his hand.

"Not a good time, Li."

"What's happened?" Li inquired, on edge from Cui's tone.

"We had an incident today. The damage to the troop-ship makes it unusable. We're still separating the injured from the dead."

"Your team?"

"They're alive. Pan was caught in the blast but has

healed. Yi is unharmed, and Ren has gone with a group of warriors to bring the weapons on the last leg of their journey."

"That's splendid news, at least. Your team and the mystery weapons' imminent arrival."

"Yeah." He snorted. "Maybe Kun will only kill me a little."

"Kun needs you," Li assured him. "Shao located the vampires' base. We have a target now."

"Once we sort out the fallout from the fire and Ren arrives with the weapons, we'll head for Japan. I won't be able to bring as many warriors on the remaining ship, but I'll bring the most skilled fighters who survived."

"How many can you bring on the smaller vessel?"

"Fifty at the most."

"That will have to do. Kun won't tolerate further delay."

"Any changes in the plan when we arrive?"

"No, other than deciding which targets to send the troops against first. It will take longer if Kun insists on establishing a base in Japan with so few warriors to man it."

"If we take out the vampires, it shouldn't be too difficult to deal with humans." Cui snorted.

"These humans have silver ammunition for their weapons. You need to remember that and warn your warriors."

"Silver." Cui scoffed. "There's no way an unenhanced human can match a tiger's speed."

"Warn them," Li snapped. "We don't need to lose any warriors to overconfidence."

Cui gritted his teeth at the obvious reprimand. "I understand. If all goes as planned, I will see you in four days. At least the smaller ship is faster than the damaged one."

"I'll see you in Miura in four days. The area is mostly uninhabited but come ashore after dark. I don't want to attract any attention if we can avoid it."

"I'll call you when we sail." Cui terminated the call.

"Problems?" Wu asked when Li threw the phone onto the couch beside him.

"There was an incident with the troopship. We won't have as many warriors as we planned for. The ship is unusable, and warriors died."

Wu shrugged. "Death is an old friend of warriors. We will send for more once we remove the vampires from the equation."

"Possibly. I hope it is as easy as you and Cui think it will be. Japan is better prepared than Kun expected. I think it will be smart not to underestimate what the military and police can do with that damned silver ammunition they have."

"Kill enough of them and the rest will run away. They're only human."

Li shook his head as he went to gather his gear for the run to Miura, a destroyed town on the west side of the entrance to Tokyo Harbor. The tsunamis had washed it away after the WWDE. According to Shao, there were no permanent dwellers there. Hopefully, it was desolate enough that the Clan wouldn't be discovered before they built defenses for the base Kun had ordered.

CHAPTER THIRTY

Kume Island, Okinawa, Japan

"Akio-*sama,* it's so good to see you again," Ono Yagi greeted him as Yagi ushered him through the door.

"*Domo,* Ono-*san.*"

"Please sit. The tea is almost ready." Yagi nodded at the table in the dining area.

Akio admired the fine-grained wood of the obviously new dining table. "You've made some changes since I was here last."

Yagi beamed as Akio noticed the piece he'd worked so many hours to restore. "Asai found this in a used furniture store in Tokyo. I wanted to surprise Ono with it on our wedding anniversary. It's almost a perfect match for the one her parents gave us on our wedding day. A tree fell through the roof during a cyclone twenty years ago and destroyed that one."

"It's a beautiful piece. The pattern of the wood grain is unique. I don't recall seeing wood like this before."

"It's made from a cedar species native to the Americas.

It amazed me that Asai could find it. Furniture made from that wood was rare here before the WWDE. She remembered seeing pictures when she was younger, and her mother telling her the story of its loss."

Akio nodded as he ran his hand appreciatively over the smooth surface.

"Horst helped me with the stain I used after I cleaned it up and sanded it." He nodded at the large Were. "Then Yuko provided a sealant that makes it impervious to scratches and nicks caused by daily use. She assured me it will remain in this condition for a hundred years."

Ono approached with her heirloom tea service on a tray. She only brought it out for special occasions, and Akio's or Yuko's visits qualified.

Akio inhaled the rich earthy aroma of the tea. His sensitive nose picked out four unique spices in the fragrant steam. He closed his eyes as he sipped. The individual flavors exploded in a melody across his palette.

"This is delicious, Ono," Akio praised. "Horst tells me this is your blend, Suzu."

"My father taught it to me. It's been many years since I've been able to get the needed ingredients." Suzu nodded.

"That won't be a problem any longer." Horst grinned. "Asai has arranged for monthly tea and *sake* deliveries on the ships from the main island."

"I might need to speak to my daughter about the *sake*. I wouldn't want Yagi to become a layabout." Ono chuckled.

Yagi feigned offense. "Woman, you know I work harder than any two mayors on this island."

Horst and Ono laughed while Akio's lips raised in a

ghost of a smile. Horst had noticed that he reverted to his reserved demeanor whenever Kenjii wasn't around.

"Thank you for coming, Akio. I hope I'm wrong, but I believe there is something not right with Kimura." Yagi shrugged. "He's been asking too many questions about the troubles here, and about you and Yuko."

Akio nodded as he sipped his tea in silence.

"He isn't an experienced contractor," Horst added. "I asked him a question anyone involved with the job would know, and he didn't answer it correctly."

"I will speak to him. If he isn't what he claims, I will know," Akio assured them.

"Will you and Yuko be able to come to Asai's and Koda's opening?" Ono inquired.

"*Hai*, we wouldn't miss it. We are both proud of their accomplishments. They're amazing young women."

"Thank you for all you have done for them, and for us here on Kume. You not only saved our lives, but you also gave us a new purpose," Ono offered as she collected the empty teacups.

Akio shook his head. "You have done the work here. All I did was remove a blight, one that should have been removed from the Earth before it ever came here."

"No, you protected Asai and Koda and made them capable of defending themselves. Now you're here to ensure someone isn't a danger to us. You had no obligation to do any of the things you have done. We are eternally in your debt," Suzu argued.

"If you will continue to serve this tea when I visit, we will call it an even trade." Akio grinned. "I need to head back soon, so I should speak with this contractor who may not be and get going."

"I told him to meet us at the Sunset House. He thinks he's meeting a potential client." Horst chuckled.

"Well, let's not keep him waiting." Akio turned to Suzu and Ono. "I look forward to seeing you soon."

"Would you like me to accompany you and Horst?" Suzu asked.

"No. If there is trouble, I wouldn't want you to be in danger. Horst and I are more resilient than you," Akio stated.

"Suzu, let them handle this." Ono held up a stack of paper. "You have several items that need your attention."

Suzu shook his head in mock disgust. "Fishing. Yes, I will retire as mayor and spend my life fishing."

Horst and Akio laughed as they went out the door.

Sunset House, Kume Island, Okinawa, Japan

Horst and Akio arrived early for the meeting. Akio stepped into the kitchen while Horst sat at the bar.

"Horst-*san*," Kimura greeted the Were as he walked in.

"Hikonaga-*san*. Thank you for coming."

"Where is the client?" Kimura looked around the room.

"He will be with us in a moment," Horst assured him.

Akio heard the man approaching the door and pushed out his senses. He picked up the man's emotions before he entered. Curious, but no sign of nervousness. That was good.

When he approached the bar, his thoughts came through as Akio focused on him.

I wonder what project this gaijin *has. I hope the person doesn't take too long. I want to talk to more of the villagers before the ship arrives today. I know there is information on those people. It's strange how when I press about their "saviors," everyone clams up and won't talk. Kishi needs...*

When that name entered his thoughts, Akio sprang into action. Before the thought was complete, Kimura was pressed against the bar, his eyes round with fright as Akio stared into them.

"Yakuza dog," Akio growled as his eyes slowly turned red. "I have been lenient with your organization. That ends now."

Horst watched with mild amusement as this played out. "I take it Yagi's suspicions were correct?"

"*Hai*. This one works with Kishi Sakutaro. He was here to gain a foothold on Kume for the Yakuza."

Horst's eyes flashed yellow as a low growl rumbled up from his chest. "Would you like me to deal with him?"

Kimura's eyes darted from one man to the other as his body trembled in fear. He recognized Akio from the picture Kishi had shown him the previous month. That the blond giant he had interacted with regularly over the past month wasn't human almost unmanned him.

"We can talk about this, gentlemen," Kimura tried.

"I can take him up in my Pod and give him half a ride back to Tokyo," Horst offered, ignoring him.

"Although that would be fitting," Akio mused, "this is my second encounter with the Yakuza in less than twenty-four hours. I think I need to deliver a more...*personal* message."

. . .

Pod over the East China Sea

Abel?

Yes, Akio?

Where is Kishi Sakutaro?

She is on the road. Based on previous data, she is headed to the house in Nishitama.

Akio was silent for a moment as the Pod flew. He'd left the Black Eagle for Horst.

Kimura Hikonaga sat in one of the Pod's jump seats, his eyes glazed over and sightless. After Akio had sorted through Kimura's mind and discovered the crimes he and Asaka had committed on Kishi's orders, the vampire decided the Yakuza needed a Queen's Bitch-level message. These two men deserved to be his examples.

Thank you, Abel. Please contact Kenjii and advise him I would like his help earlier than planned tonight. We will visit Kishi and Sato before dealing with those Clan farms in China.

Kenjii notified. I updated him with your ETA.

Very well. When I land, put the Pod up five kilometers. We'll take it to Nishitama.

The Pod descended silently into the courtyard moments later. Akio stepped out of the open door before it settled, and the Pod reversed direction and sped up into the darkening sky.

Akio, I detect an unknown human on the Pod.

He is going with us. Monitor him, although I don't think he can break the compulsion. If he moves, I authorize you to use whatever nonlethal measures you deem appropriate to contain him.

Acknowledged.

CHAPTER THIRTY-ONE

TQB Base, Tokyo, Japan

"What have we got?" Kenjii inquired as Akio stepped out of the elevator.

"Yakuza."

Kenjii's smile faltered at Akio's curt reply. He followed the older vampire to his quarters, concerned that the usually unflappable man seemed out of sorts.

Akio went to his closet and pulled out his Jean Dukes armor and guns.

"Will we need that for humans?"

"No, for the tigers after." Akio pulled off the plain black tunic he wore and replaced it with another, one with a distinctive patch adorning one shoulder.

"Akio?" Kenjii called softly as he moved behind him and wrapped his arm around the other man's torso. "What troubles you?"

Akio drew a deep breath and released it slowly. "There was another Yakuza on Kume. He posed as a contractor. Kishi Sakutaro sent him there to get a foothold."

"They need to die," Kenjii hissed as he pulled Akio closer.

"*Hai.*"

"How do you wish to handle this?"

"We take the Pod and deliver Kishi's man back to her. She will be at Sato Sakutaro's home. We will deal with both of them."

Kenjii pressed his mouth close to Akio's ear and whispered, "Then we send a message that every surviving member of that organization understands."

"Within reason." Akio grimaced. "Inspector Yonai has requested that we not upset his bosses."

Kenjii released him and stepped back. "What do you care? These people have attacked you before, and you showed mercy. It is time they understand mercy is not a weakness," he snarled.

"No, it isn't. But we are guests here, and I can't forget that either. My Queen charged me to prepare a safe place for Michael when he returns. I can't do that if I am at war with the government of Japan."

Kenjii shook his head in disgust. "Perhaps the government needs to understand its place in the world."

"No. Our place is to keep the UnknownWorld from interfering in human affairs. What you suggest goes against everything Bethany Anne stands for. We will defend ourselves if needed. We will not slaughter them wholesale."

"It isn't right. They have injured your people, worked with the tigers to harm us, and preyed on other humans with no regard."

"I am aware of that, Kenjii. Remember, I come from a

time where I executed honorless criminals on sight. I want nothing more than to cut the Yakuza cancer from this land, but my honor prevents that." Akio turned away and closed his eyes. It tore at his mind. One infinitesimal part wanted to deliver the harsh Justice Kenjii desired, the Justice the Yakuza deserved. The other refused to disobey his Queen. His honor was more important than the petty revenge he wished to inflict.

"I don't like it, but I understand," Kenjii murmured as he moved to embrace Akio again.

Akio rested his head on Kenjii's shoulder. "Thank you, my friend."

"You said we can defend ourselves, correct?"

"Hai."

"Here's hoping they want to fight," Kenjii whispered into Akio's ear.

Akio didn't reply, but he agreed.

Sakutaro Residence, Nishitama District, Tokyo, Japan

"Abel?" Akio called as the Pod held position in the night sky three kilometers above Sato Sakutaro's walled estate.

"Yes?" Abel answered over the Pod's speaker.

"What resistance can we expect?"

The monitor in the Pod came to life with a three-dimensional diagram of the estate.

"There are two guards here." Red dots appeared by the gates. "Two more in the house, and four roaming the grounds." More dots appeared as Abel called out the numbers and locations.

"Sato, Kishi, and Kishi's right-hand man, Asaka Shuko,

are in the study here." Three more dots appeared on the first floor near the inner guards. "Sato's valet is in the kitchen, but the rest of the staff has left for the day. Juba is in a room adjoining the study," Abel finished.

"This is real-time tracking?"

"Of course. Do you think I'm some bargain-basement desktop?"

Kenjii snorted and his eyes danced with humor.

Akio rolled his eyes while shaking his head at their antics.

"Kenjii, I want you to disable these guards." He pointed at the two stationary dots on each corner of the rear fence. "I'll take care of the roamers."

"Define 'disable.'"

"Incapacitate them. No biting, either."

Kenjii stuck his bottom lip out and pouted. "You're no fun tonight."

"Bite a tiger later," Akio snarked.

"Their fur gets stuck in my fangs." Kenjii's lips curled in disgust.

"Why me?" Akio looked up and spread his arms to the sides as if invoking an unseen deity.

Kenjii burst out in raucous laughter. "Because you chose me," he choked out.

"Indeed, I did. For that, I will be eternally thankful." Akio smiled.

"Let's do this." Kenjii grinned as he stood and adjusted the twin swords hanging from his belt.

"Abel, take us to the west rear corner and hold position five meters above the guard there," Akio ordered.

"Acknowledged. Happy hunting." The Pod dropped fast, then halted at the desired height.

"Kenjii, meet me at the rear door when you're done."

Kenjii nodded and grinned as he leapt through the door and plummeted down, landing with both feet on the unsuspecting mobster's shoulders.

Akio watched as Kenjii drove the soldier to the ground. One side of his mouth twitched, but he forced his lips into a tight line again.

"Abel put me over the closest roaming guard. Three meters, please. When I call, deliver your passenger to the rear behind the pool."

"You going to see how deep you can plant yours?" Abel quipped.

Akio rolled his eyes as he stepped out into the darkness.

"Ito, did you hear something?"

"No, what?"

"I heard a noise near the back wall."

Akio touched down between the two confused guards. His hands shot out, and both fell to the ground, unconscious. He spun on his heel and intercepted the pair walking the front, then dispatched them with equal ease.

When he came around to the rear, Kenjii was leaning against the side of the grounded Pod, holding Kimura by his collar.

"What did you do to this one? He's unresponsive to commands. I had to remove him from the Pod."

Akio grinned and tapped his temple.

"Upgrades," they said in unison.

"Do we knock?" Kenjii wondered as he looked through

the glass doors past the pool. Six people occupied the room now. One leaned by the entrance, two stood attentively on opposite sides of the *Oyabun*, and the others occupied chairs.

"Why not?" Akio mused as he took Kimura from Kenjii.

They walked across the grass onto a rock path that wound through to the heated pool behind the house. Kimura followed mindlessly, responding to Akio's gentle prods to move in the right direction.

"Kimura," Akio called when they were three meters from the glass doors that led into the house.

"What? Huh? Where?" he stammered as he came out of the compulsion to be deaf, mute, and blind.

Akio caught his collar in one hand and his belt in his other, then lifted Kimura off his feet and tossed his body through the glass doors. Kimura almost got his hands up to protect his face before it slammed into the doors with a crash and shower of flying glass.

"Knock, knock," Akio murmured as he sped up and followed Kimura inside.

"Good evening, *Sofu.* You sent for me?"

"Hello, granddaughter," Sato Sakutaro answered. "I hope you are well."

"I am. Did you have a pleasant day?"

"*Hai,* until I had a visitor with disturbing news."

Kishi stiffened. *I need to have Asaka explain the rules to that idiot valet again. No visitors are to see* Sofu *without my approval. Maybe it's time for this one to retire.*

"What was that?" She checked his water glass before she sat in the chair beside his.

Sato looked at her through narrowed eyes. "Please explain why Juba came to me today with information that you were not only meeting with Li Song but were actively helping him locate Akio. After I expressly forbade it." Sato nodded and the guard opened the door and admitted Juba, then placed a chair for him to Sato's right.

The blood drained from Kishi's face, and she looked over her shoulder at the door where Asaka leaned.

"Don't look at him for answers. Juba was adamant that you were the one behind this. He even explained that you threatened his daughter's continued enrollment in school if he refused to assist you. Not that it was you paying for it."

"*Sofu*, I..."

"Enough!" Sato yelled. "You overstep, girl. If you weren't my granddaughter, there would already be a price on your head."

Asaka shifted to subtly turn away from the bodyguard near him, then eased his hand into his jacket. The feel of his holstered pistol's grip comforted him. Sato Sakutaro hadn't achieved his position in the family by being soft, so Asaka expected to need the gun at any second.

No sooner had the thought crossed his mind than the glass doors leading to the pool exploded into the room. Asaka registered a large mass flying through the door and landing with a solid *thunk* on the floor.

The glass was still falling when he drew his pistol and moved to protect Kishi. He took one step, and his body slammed into the wall behind him. The pistol in his hand disappeared, and when his eyes focused, a man had pinned him to the wall by his throat.

Asaka struggled to push the man away, but all he accomplished was his body being pulled clear of the wall and slammed back into it again.

Akio saw Asaka pull his pistol and start toward Kishi when Kimura blasted through the doors. He flashed across the study and incapacitated the bodyguard, then caught Asaka by the throat with one hand and slapped the pistol away with the other.

"Be still," he growled when Asaka tried to break free.

Akio pulled the dazed man off the wall and shoved him toward the seated pair.

Kenjii stood over the guard across the room while watching the seated figures with a feral look in his eyes.

"You!" He pointed at Kishi. "You're the one who worked with the Sacred Clan. You tried to give them my Akio."

Kenjii's eyes slowly turned red as he stepped over the unconscious bodyguard.

Sato watched in horror as Kenjii stalked across the room, each step shattering the silence as it crushed shards of glass under his armored boots.

Kishi shoved her hand into the stylish handbag in her lap. Kenjii smirked, expecting her to pull a weapon. His smirk turned to shock as burning pain engulfed the left side of his face. He threw a hand up and cupped his cheek. When he pulled it away, blood covered it.

Flame lanced from the tattered, smoking end of Kishi's

bag, and a sharp blow hit him in the chest. His armor deflected the bullet, but red rage overcame him.

He was on her in a blur of motion. Kishi Sakutaro, the Crown Princess of the Tokyo Yakuza, flew out of her chair with enough force to dislocate the shoulder attached to the arm Kenjii grabbed. He spun her around, and her agonized screams rang through the room as her shoulder sent lances of fire through her chest.

Once her motion stopped, Kenjii held her tight against him, her back against his chest. His eyes glowed bright red as the blood pouring from his ripped cheek slowed, then stopped.

"No one touches my face," he hissed as his fangs extended. He caught the silky black hair she wore loose down her back and viciously wrenched her head to the side, exposing her long pale neck.

"Kenjii, wait," Akio called.

Kenjii never slowed. He struck like a viper, burying his fangs deep in Kishi's neck, cutting through skin and muscle until the rich metallic taste of her blood erupted from the severed artery to flow hot and sweet into his mouth.

Asaka watched in horror as an *oni* savaged Kishi's delicate throat, then pulled back his hand and balled it into a fist.

Akio didn't flinch when Asaka punched him in the face. His attention remained focused on the scene playing out before him.

Kenjii drew back from Kishi. Her blood ran down his face and mingled with his. He looked down into Sato's terrified eyes and smiled as he casually twisted Kishi's neck until a loud *snap* echoed through the silent room. Kenjii continued to smile at Sato, his face bloody and his fangs extending down across his bottom lip.

Asaka let out a low moan that rapidly turned into an anguished scream as he watched the light in Kishi's eyes fade. Kenjii looked toward the noise and saw Akio holding a screaming man who repeatedly punched and kicked him, although the man's eyes remained locked on Kenjii and the limp body he held.

Kenjii let the body slide to the floor and faced Akio. "No one, and I mean *no one,* will ever harm my face again and live to tell about it."

Akio shook his head and came out of his trancelike state when Asaka landed a blow to his temple. Akio slowly turned his head to stare into Asaka's eyes. He pushed into his mind and saw the laundry list of crimes he'd committed against humanity.

Akio continued to stare into Asaka's eyes as he tightened his grip on the man's throat, applying pressure to the larynx until he felt it crumple under his grip. He held the struggling man until his body stilled. With a disgusted shake of his head, he let Asaka's lifeless body drop to the floor next to Kishi's.

Sato Sakutaro couldn't move or speak. Pain like none he'd ever felt in all his many years gripped his chest and crushed the air from his lungs, making it impossible to draw more in. Sato knew there were things in the night. He'd watched live television coverage on the day TQB took to the stars in their spacecraft. He'd seen the beautiful woman transform into a horrifying *kyuuketsuki.* The sight of one of those creatures ravaging his granddaughter was too much for his body to withstand. Sato Sakutaro, *Oyabun* of the largest and most powerful Yakuza family Japan had ever known, died with his granddaughter's broken body at his feet. Her lifeless eyes staring accusingly into his for failing to protect her from the monsters.

"Akio?" Kenjii approached him slowly while wiping the blood from his lips with the back of his hand.

"I understand," Akio answered before he could explain. The glimpse he'd had from Kenjii's mind when he dropped Kishi's body to the floor had made his heart hurt. He saw the memories of the night Isamu and Ogawa had tortured him from Kenjii's point of view. Although he had wanted this to end differently, after seeing what Kishi damaging his face had done to his mind, he would never regret that Kenjii had reclaimed a piece of his soul when he took Kishi's life. Serving as a surrogate for Isamu and Ogawa was probably the best thing she had done in her miserable existence.

Akio looked around the room and spotted the bar stocked with rows and rows of spirits. He pulled several bottles down, then splashed the volatile alcohol around the room before he knelt beside Kimura's unconscious form. He'd already seen the evil in his mind—the lives he'd destroyed, a daughter forced into prostitution to pay off her father's debts, stores burned, products destroyed, beatings and murders... The list was endless. Akio grasped Kimura's chin and jerked it upward with a quick twist.

Juba stared wide-eyed from his seat. He started when the body crashed through the doors, and partially rose until he saw Kenjii staring at him over the fallen bodyguard. He slumped into the chair and hadn't dared move a muscle since.

"Juba!" Akio barked. "Get the man from the kitchen to help you move these two." He indicated the unconscious bodyguards. "Take them out of the house, then spread the word to your fellows. If I see any Yakuza near anyone or any place I deem mine, even if they're only passing by, I will start with you and will not rest until every member of your gang is dead. Do I make myself clear?"

Juba nodded. He tried to stand but fell back into the chair when his shaking legs failed him. He struggled up again, and this time, his legs held.

Without a word or a backward glance, Juba rushed out as fast as his legs would carry him. He returned seconds later with another man, and they struggled as they half-carried and half-dragged the unconscious men from the room.

Akio crossed to the fireplace set into the far wall, then snapped the gas line that led to the logs before he walked back across the room to the bar. He pulled a towel out from under the dark wood counter and stuffed it into a bottle of fifty-year-old Scotch. An ornate cigar lighter rested in a wooden case next to a stocked humidor. The flint sparked on the first turn, causing the flame to engulf the wick. In seconds, the towel burned toward the mouth of the bottle. He set it on the bar and walked away.

Akio caught Kenjii's hand in his as he passed him on the way to the door. They left much more than the bloody scene behind them as they stepped into the clean night air.

The pair climbed into the waiting Pod and sat on the bench. Akio wrapped an arm around Kenjii's waist and pulled him close as the Pod gently rocked from the force of the exploding house. Neither spoke as they ascended into the sky, each comforted by the other's presence.

TQB Base, Tokyo, Japan

Abel watched through the eyes of a drone he'd placed in the study over a month ago. He knew there was more going on with his people than the words he heard and the actions he saw conveyed. The facial expressions Akio and Kenjii wore when the battle was over spoke volumes. The way they held each other without speaking in the Pod said more. Without orders from either of them, Abel sealed the Pod and guided it into the stratosphere. It was several hours until the sun would endanger Kenjii, and he felt the quiet time alone would be good for both.

Eve's Lab, The Palace, Tokyo, Japan

An alarm alerted Eve that an event she had not expected for years to come had taken place. She felt a sense of pride that first Takumi and now Abel had displayed signs of their awakening awareness—the first step toward ascension.

CHAPTER THIRTY-TWO

Pod, Low Earth Orbit

Akio held Kenjii close as the Pod continued to rise after leaving the Sakutaro home. Both were silent, lost in their thoughts until the screen on the wall lit up and showed the unobstructed view of millions of stars.

Kenjii stiffened when he saw this. "Akio, where are we?"

Akio opened his eyes and looked in the direction Kenjii stared.

"Abel?"

"You are in the mesosphere, one hundred and fifty kilometers above Japan."

"Why?"

"I watched the encounter with Kishi. I determined that you and Kenjii needed some time, and the view here is phenomenal."

"It's breathtaking," Kenjii whispered in awe.

Akio turned his head and smiled warmly as he saw the wonder on Kenjii's face. "Thank you, Abel. I will contact you when we're ready to return."

“Acknowledged.”

They sat silently watching the panorama of stars, Kenjii in childlike wonder and Akio content that his love was enjoying the experience.

Kenjii shifted in his seat to face Akio after a half-hour. “I’m sorry.”

Akio quirked one eyebrow up questioningly. “For what?”

“Losing control when that evil witch shot me.”

Akio stared deeply into Kenjii’s soft brown eyes. “I understand why you did it. You have nothing to be sorry for.”

Kenjii shook his head. “You didn’t want a slaughter or evidence of what happened. My actions caused you to alter your plans.”

“That’s assuming any plans I made survived first contact. I didn’t plan on Kishi shooting you. She changed the dynamic through her actions.”

“Aren’t you angry at me for disobeying you? You told me to stop. I heard you, but I was so caught up in the rage that I wouldn’t obey.”

“Kenjii, you suffered much abuse to your face the night you became a vampire. Understandably, you have an extreme reaction to similar injuries. Had I realized that, I would not have asked you to stop.”

Kenjii silently contemplated Akio’s words as he continued to look him in the eye.

Akio raised his hand and gently brushed his fingers across Kenjii’s freshly healed face. A thin white line was all that remained of the jagged wound the bullet had made.

“Your injury will be healed soon.”

Kenjii snorted softly. "At least that bastard Heinz got that right."

"Partially," Akio replied as he ran a single finger the length of the fading scar.

Kenjii pulled away from his touch. "I've thought about your offer to enhance me. I'm still undecided, but I have almost made up my mind."

Akio regarded him for a moment. "Although I want you to have the best possible chance of surviving, I understand and respect your hesitation. The offer is open when and if you decide you want it."

Kenjii embraced him while tears leaked from the corners of his eyes. "Thank you for understanding. It's not that I distrust you, far from it. It's too soon, and I still have things to work out. Tonight, believe it or not, I put one issue to rest."

Akio nodded, having seen it in Kenjii's mind when he took vengeance on Kishi for the pain—pain that brought back memories of the agony Isamu and Ogawa had inflicted when he was helpless to resist.

Akio pulled back from the embrace enough to face Kenjii. "I understand, and I will support you in whatever you need. Just know that I am here." He finished by pressing his forehead against Kenjii's.

Kenjii smiled, his expression shifting from regret to joy as he saw the love he felt reflected back to him. "Don't we have tigers to deal with?"

"*Hai,* but I think that will keep another day."

"Seriously? Why? I assure you I am up for it."

"This isn't about doubting you, Kenjii. The sun is only a

few hours away, and I won't risk you being caught by it. We will leave as soon as it's dark tonight." He grinned and flashed a little fang. "Then you can show me how you clear fur from between your fangs."

"I'll give that a hard pass if possible," Kenjii deadpanned.

"Very well." Akio chuckled. "Abel, bring us down."

"What do you plan to do for the rest of the night?" Kenjii inquired.

"Enjoy a long bath." Akio smiled as he cut his eyes toward Kenjii.

"Want company?" Kenjii tilted his head, letting his hair fall over one eye as he smiled coyly.

Akio pulled him into a tight embrace, his mouth against Kenjii's ear. "Always," he murmured as the Pod descended.

TQB Base, Tokyo, Japan

Kenjii's fingers caressed Akio's shoulder-length hair as they sat on his couch, watching a dark-haired woman blast an alien monster on a spaceship. "Is that what your Queen is about now?"

Akio shrugged. "If there are Kurtherians around, I'm certain of it."

"I can't imagine leaving for the unknown to fight aliens with advanced technology. She's either the bravest woman I've ever heard of, or she's insane."

"Depends on who you ask on what day." Akio chuckled. "She does as she pleases when fighting evil, no matter what her personal guards suggest."

"I look forward to meeting this woman. You make her

sound like she is ten feet tall and capable of eating nails and spitting bullets."

"No, she's only a little taller than me. She need not spit bullets when she can throw Etheric energy."

Kenjii's eyes widened in shock. "She can hurl energy bolts like a wizard?"

"*Hai*. That's as good a description as any."

"Can you do that?"

Akio shook his head. "No, that particular skill is hers."

Kenjii's brow furrowed as he considered his next words, then shook his head, then nodded, decision made. "If I get these upgrades, will I have uncommon abilities?"

"Your existing abilities will change. I can't tell you how or how much since it's different for everyone. You'll heal faster. You'll see a marked increase in strength and speed, and the sun won't harm you. Other than those, I can't guess."

"How long will it take?"

"Again, that depends on the person. Some take less than an hour, and others take weeks. Eve can tell you more after an initial scan."

"I think I would like to know," Kenjii admitted. "If I still feel this way in a week, can we do it then?"

"I'll arrange it whenever you wish."

"Thank you. I know you want this, and I appreciate your patience."

"I want it, but I won't force you to do something you oppose. I care too much to make you do anything."

"And that's why I love you. Now, slide down on the floor. This shorter hair you're sporting appeals to me. I like the way it feels when my fingers run through it." Kenjii smiled as he separated his feet to make space.

"We agree, then. I like the way it feels when you do it." Akio grinned as he moved to the requested position.

CHAPTER THIRTY-THREE

Command Center, TQB Base, Tokyo, Japan

"What's that?" Kenjii pointed at the monitor Akio was watching. It showed a rugged man wearing a faded military uniform as he hatchet-chopped his arm toward a compound surrounded by a roughhewn wall made of timbers. Beside him stood a beautiful woman with twin pistols in her hands. A group of armed men followed close behind, covering their approach with military precision.

"That is Terry Henry Walton, Charumati, and the Force de Guerre. They're fighting to bring civilization back to the area of North America that was formerly the United States."

The woman ran toward the log palisade while her pistols spat fire. Her legs bunched when she reached the gate, and with a powerful push, she leapt into the enclosure.

The man shook his head and yelled something, then rushed toward the gate. Instead of stopping or jumping, he hit it with his shoulder and knocked one side off its hinges, leaving the other hanging by one hinge.

"What are they? More enhanced vampires?" Kenjii watched them take down the half-dozen armed men inside.

"Terry Henry is an enhanced human. Charumati is a werewolf and his mate."

"Enhanced human?" Kenjii tilted his head to one side.

"Terry Henry almost froze to death saving others. He'd also proven his honor in the past, so Bethany Anne saved him. The results made him more than a normal human. He's not as powerful as a vampire, but he's a formidable warrior all the same."

They watched for a few moments until Akio called, "Thank you, Abel. Please show us the first objective for today."

The scene shifted to an aerial view of a green field. Thirty workers toiled between the straight rows of crops. A man lounged under a canopy made of a piece of cloth and four poles, watching them work.

"This is the first Sacred Clan farm you are freeing today. It's on Chaohu Lake near the ruins of a city called Hefei," Abel announced. "Thirty humans are working at this location. There were thirty-two three days ago. A tiger killed two of them the day I located it. He shifted into a Pricolici form, which provided one hundred percent certainty that this is a Clan farm."

"How many Clan members are there?" Akio inquired.

"Four. I have a drone on station." The scene switched to an open structure. The tin roof showed signs of old damage, with rust-ringed holes visible along the length of it. The sides were open all around, providing no cover inside.

"They keep the humans here at night, while the Clan members are here." The picture zoomed out until a squat square building on the opposite side of the field was visible.

"This building was a laboratory at some point. It is open on the first floor, but there are rooms one level down. The Clan members stay on the first floor since the rooms below have several inches of water in them."

Kenjii spoke up. "Have you seen more than one change into that two-legged form? What was it you called them? Piccolo or something?"

"Pricolici. That was the only one to shift since I established surveillance."

"I always heard that two-legged Weres were a legend. How is it so many of these tigers can partially shift and turn into Pico…Pricolici, is it?

"*Hai.* Before Bethany Anne left Earth, the Sacred Clan was involved in an attack on her. They come from a different group of Kurtherians, and when she located their empress, she also found Kurtherians there.

"We believe the Clan tigers can do that because of those Kurtherians. They used selective breeding and their ability to alter nanocytes to make them more powerful."

Kenjii tapped a finger on his lips. "That makes sense. I want that Pricolici at the farm. I have worked with the new swords enough that I wish to test them on a serious opponent."

Akio gave him a narrow-eyed stare. "All opponents are serious."

"That's not what I meant. I know not to underestimate those tigers. I only meant that I feel my skill level has advanced and wish to test myself."

Akio nodded while recalling the last Pricolici Kenjii had encountered. "If events favor you matching yourself against him, you will. However, we are there to free the humans. I will not risk them for you to test yourself."

"Understood, and I wouldn't ask you to. Abel and Eve set up the equipment for me to practice against the simulation in the training room here. I can match that annoying little man blow for blow much longer now."

"Agreed. Abel has shown me some of it. Your speed and agility with the blades are impressive."

Kenjii looked surprised at first, then raised his head a little higher at the compliment. He knew Akio never gave those if they weren't earned.

"What about the second location?" Akio inquired as he watched Kenjii preen.

"That one poses more challenges. There are eight clan members here." The monitor went blank. A second later, an aerial view of a field that covered over one hundred acres came up. "There are three hundred and twenty-four humans here. It's near Lu'an, and there seems to be a large Clan presence there."

"What leads you to that conclusion?"

The screen changed again to show a street with two disparate groups walking past. The first group was clean and looked healthy. The second was thin and drawn, their clothes no better than rags. The latter group walked with their eyes downcast and shuffled away from the first group when they encountered them.

"I recognize that swagger," Kenjii stated. "That is how the Clan members I encountered acted—like they were lords."

Akio nodded. "Send more drones to Lu'an. We will deal with it when we have an accurate idea of what resistance is there."

"It will take a few hours to route a carrier there. Eve is still working on upgrading them, and it is a slow process. I will need to move them from other areas," Abel advised.

"That will have to do. Notify me when you have the information."

"Acknowledged."

"Go back to the farm."

The scene showed the farm a second later.

"Magnify this area." Akio tapped the screen on a large metal structure that appeared to have been used to store equipment.

The image shifted as it zoomed in, showing a barbed wire fence surrounding the structure.

"Do you have interior views?"

The monitor flickered and showed an open space. The floor was littered with piles of cloth and leaves, obviously used for bedding.

"This is where they house the humans," Abel advised. The image moved to a door on one end of the open area. "The guards live here. It was an office at one time. There is an open area behind the door, with two smaller rooms on either side. There are always four on duty. During the day, they watch the workers in the field. At night, two are in the dorm, and two patrol the exterior."

The picture went back to the aerial view, and a highlight appeared on the end nearest the field. "The only clear way in is here. All other entrances are sealed, and the only opening in the perimeter fence is here as well."

"Thank you, Abel. Kenjii, we will need to take the outer guards silently if possible."

"That won't be easy."

"No, it won't, but we need to surprise the ones inside to save the humans."

"Is there any way we could get them to move the humans outside?" Kenjii mused.

Akio tapped his nail on his teeth as he studied the building. "Abel, where do they store the harvested crops?"

"There is another structure across the field. They process them there."

"Show me, please."

The screen blinked, and the next image showed a structure similar in size to the first. It had several neatly arranged rows of bags.

"A fire here should get their attention. It is likely the guards would send the humans to fight it."

Kenjii nodded as he studied the image. "Is there a way to ensure the fire burns fast and hot enough that the humans won't rush in? It wouldn't do to kill them while trying to save them."

Akio's mouth quirked in a half-smile. That Kenjii thought of the humans' safety showed he was no longer thinking like a Forsaken. It warmed his heart that his friend was recovering so well.

"*Hai*. Eve has some compounds that will cause a hot and smoky fire. We will need to deal with the guards fast, though. I don't want them to use humans as shields when they realize what's happening."

"Shoot them from the air with that cannon you carry. In the noise and confusion, you should be able to kill several before they notice anything amiss." Kenjii laughed.

Akio nodded as he considered the suggestion. "That is an excellent plan. If I can take out half of them, it will make the job easier."

"I'm all about easy. The sooner we do this, the sooner I can get you back here for a post-battle celebration," Kenjii quipped as he waggled his eyebrows suggestively.

Akio snickered. "You're incorrigible."

Kenjii took his hand, looking seriously into his eyes as he whispered, "We have decades of missed time to make up for."

"Agreed. Let's prepare. Abel, I want a Black Eagle slaved to the Pod for this. If there's a coordinated response from Lu'an, I want enough firepower to handle it."

CHAPTER THIRTY-FOUR

Sacred Clan Farm, Hefei, China

Darkness covered the area below the Pod. Akio activated the sensors, and the screen in the Pod showed the scene below like it was midday.

"The humans are all inside for the night."

Akio touched the screen, and its focus shifted to the structure the guards used. His fingers danced across the screen, changing to heat sensors. Four figures appeared on the screen inside of the building.

"Any way to determine which is the two-leg?" Kenjii cocked his head as he studied the layout of the building and the positions of the guards.

"Make him mad enough to shift," Akio deadpanned.

"Not very helpful, but I can do that."

Akio brought the Pod to a hover in front of the building. "No better time than now." He closed the visor on his helmet and stepped into the night.

Kenjii followed, taking his twin swords from his back.

"Here, kitty, kitty," he whispered low enough that only Akio heard.

Akio shook his head and snorted. In two steps he was at the door, then his armored boot lashed out and sent it flying into the open room with a crash.

Shouts followed by ear-splitting roars came from the startled weretigers. Akio aimed his Jean Dukes special and stroked the trigger, and a meaty splat silenced one roar.

Kenjii followed him through the gaping hole and assessed the scene. Two tigers darted toward Akio, a third stood eight feet tall on two legs, and the fourth lay in a heap to the side of the doorway.

Akio wasted no time dispatching the two in tiger form. He fired twice, killing one immediately but only grazing the other as it dodged. His two follow-up shots bracketed the beast, leaving it nowhere to go before a round impacted its mouth. Blood and tissue sprayed when it exited the back of its skull, and the blood distorted the room in a red halo where it misted in the air.

"All yours." Akio stepped back as he gestured with his gun at the enraged Pricolici, who was glaring at him from across the room.

Kenjii brandished his hooked swords, spinning them in an intricate pattern while he advanced to meet his foe.

The tiger spread his arms to the sides, flexed the long claws that tipped each finger, and roared his defiance. When Kenjii was two meters from him, he rushed forward faster than the eye could follow. The tiger jinked to one side, Kenjii's spinning blades missing him by a hair, and he lashed out with one paw as he passed.

Kenjii grunted as he felt intense pain course through his

torso. The wicked claws had breached his armor and left four shallow slashes along his ribs, He jumped into the air, barely dodging a follow-up slash to his back. When he landed, the monster cat was watching him from several meters away. It raised the claws that had scored him to its mouth and slowly licked his blood from them.

"*Yatsu,*" Kenjii spat.

The tiger surged toward him again. Kenjii twisted and brought the hooked end of one sword around in a fast arc, hooking the paw as it swung at his leg.

The tiger twisted its arm to free it from the blade that cut to the bone. Kenjii jerked back hard, burying the hooked blade deeper. He brought the second sword down in a fast slash, severing the tiger's paw at the wrist.

The beast snarled in pain as it retreated, holding the injured arm close to its side.

Kenjii pressed the attack, slashing high with one blade and low with the other, keeping the cat off-balance as he drove it back one step at a time. Blood spurted from the severed limb, spraying across the floor with each heartbeat.

Kenjii stayed on the side with the injury, taking advantage of the creature's inability to lash out with that arm. He pressed it harder, a smirk on his face, as it approached the back wall of the house. He spun his blades in a blur, and they whistled as they carved through the air.

The cat snarled and tensed as it sensed the wall looming at its back. It feinted to the left and then changed direction and leapt through an open door, fleeing into the dark stairwell that led to the lower level.

Kenjii was on it in the blink of an eye, burying one

sharpened hook into its shoulder, the other slashing the back of the leg at the knee.

The cat yowled in pain as Kenjii yanked back on the buried blade, spinning the enormous beast back into the open room.

The tiger stumbled, weak from blood loss and trauma. Kenjii wasted no time. He kicked the already weakened leg, his heavy armored boot connecting solidly. The knee joint made a loud pop as it separated, causing the great cat to fall to the floor.

Kenjii never took his eyes off the downed tiger, having learned his lesson the last time. He advanced on the fallen cat and two lightning-fast slashes ended the battle. The beast's head rolled across the blood-covered floor.

The warrior scanned the room to check that there were no more threats before he turned to Akio, who was leaning against the opening where the door had been. He flicked both blades to clear them of blood, then wiped them clean on the Pricolici's ragged clothing before sliding them into the scabbards on his back.

"Shall we go tell the humans they're free?" he asked as he calmly walked past Akio and out the door.

"Kenjii," the older vampire called softly.

Kenjii stopped, his back to Akio as he stepped out of the building to follow.

Akio walked to his side. "How's your injury?"

"Healing," he answered curtly.

"What's wrong?"

Kenjii was silent for a moment before he sighed. "I underestimated the tiger. He shouldn't have been able to do that. I was careless."

"It is not wise to make assumptions in any battle. I wouldn't say it was so much carelessness as overconfidence in your abilities without knowing your opponent."

"Carelessness!" Kenjii spat.

Akio caught him by the shoulder and turned him until they were facing one another. "No, you made a mistake and learned from it. Since the day Heinz turned you, Weres have been inferior. Heinz ingrained that into you from the outset. If that had been a simple weretiger, you would have readily defeated him. A Pricolici is far from regular. They are faster, stronger, and harder to kill. Horst was in Pricolici form when he ran Heinz down and ripped his head from his body. That you did it with only minor damage to yourself is something to be proud of."

"My armor." Kenjii pointed to the four deep creases.

"Protected you from serious injury." Akio shrugged.

"I wanted to make you proud of me."

"Kenjii, I *am* proud. You took down a formidable beast on your own. I stayed back, even though I wanted to jump in and gut him when he injured you. You did it, no help required. I couldn't be prouder."

"Really?" he asked incredulously.

"*Hai*. Now, let's go free those people. We still have work tonight."

Kenjii walked through the darkness beside him, his head higher and his steps lighter. He was basking in the inner warmth Akio's confidence gave him.

Sacred Clan Farm, Near Lu'an, China

"All I do is push here and toss these near what I want to

burn?" Kenjii asked as he turned a small black cylinder over in his hand.

"*Hai,* but be certain to stay clear of the blast. Three meters, at least. When you press the arming switch, you have five seconds before it detonates. The fireball will spread two meters from the device."

Kenjii placed the device with six others in an open slot in his armor. "Push the button, run like hell. Got it."

Akio brought the Pod down beside the storage building on the opposite side of the structure from the building the humans were in.

Kenjii waved and hopped out, moving like a shadow through the darkness toward his goal. He halted at an opening, senses on alert for any Clan members in the area. When he determined no threats existed, he hurried to the end of one row of bagged crops.

He turned to face the opening at the far end of the building. Releasing the catch on his armor, he palmed five of the six devices. *Here goes nothing.* The first device didn't go off until he was out the far door and moving across the open field. Five muffled pops, so close together that the first was still echoing when the last detonated, came from behind him. He glanced over his shoulder and saw flames and white smoke pouring out of the glassless windows and open doors.

Akio had the Pod over his first target before Kenjii entered the building to start the fire. When he heard the distinct pop of the first incendiary, he gently caressed the trigger. The high-velocity projectile penetrated the top of the man's head, pulping it.

A shout of "Fire!" came from the guard stationed by the

door. Akio directed the Pod to a position fifteen meters above and slightly to the side of the opening in the fence. He aimed his Jean Dukes and waited.

Shouts came from inside the building, and seconds later, people rushed out, heading toward the burning structure. Akio waited patiently as five Weres exited the building, screaming and chiding the humans to move faster. The sixth came out behind two elderly humans, threatening them with death if they didn't move faster.

Akio sighted on that Were's head and stroked the trigger once. It faltered and fell face down in the doorway. He swung the barrel to his left, and two more Weres flopped lifelessly to the dust. *Kenjii had a splendid idea. This is like shooting fish in a barrel.*

The Pod shifted position, moving behind the humans as they ran toward the inferno that raged in the barn. He fired three more times, putting two tigers down but only wounding the third.

The Were yelled once, then shifted and darted into the mass of humans.

"*Kenjii,*" Akio called over his implant.

"*Hai?*" he answered after a few beats.

"There's one in human form moving toward you and a wounded one near me. I'll finish the wounded one. Watch for the other. He was likely alerted by the wounded one's yell."

The humans screamed in terror when the wounded tiger ran into their midst, so Akio tracked his motion by the humans fleeing from him. He moved the Pod to a position in front of the Were and stepped out the open door, his katana in hand.

The tiger crouched between the rows of crops. Its left front leg hung limp as the nanocytes healed the extensive damage the shot had caused. The cat pushed itself forward on three legs, intent on taking down the being who dared hurt it.

Akio heard the beast before he saw it. It burst through the waist-high crops and came toward him in an unsteady gait from an opening between rows. Akio held his sword ready and waited for the Were to attack. The cat pushed with its rear legs and left the ground. Akio didn't flinch as his sword flashed down and severed the snarling head from the body.

He turned toward the inferno across the field and saw Kenjii engage the last foe. He nodded once, then set about herding the terrified slaves away from the fire. Kenjii had proven himself in battle. He didn't need a keeper to deal with a single Were.

Kenjii spotted the Were Akio had warned him about behind the first of the humans to arrive. He took two steps and jumped, flying over the heads of the humans and landing before the Were.

"Time to die, kitty." He smirked as he held his swords in guard positions, one high, the other low. The man halted, and a second later, a black-striped tiger roared a challenge. The tiger was smaller than others Kenjii had encountered, as well as leaner and lower to the ground. Kenjii stepped forward to engage it and it darted to the right, then switched direction in a flash and went to pass him on the left. Kenjii swung his high sword in a downward arc, missing its body but catching the tail about halfway to its end.

The tiger squalled in outrage as Kenjii's blade sheared through flesh and bone, slicing cleanly through the tail. The cat spun and launched into the air, jaws wide and razor-sharp claws extended. Kenjii shifted to one side but was too late. The cat hooked one set of claws into the armor at his hip and closed its powerful jaws around his forearm.

Kenjii brought the spiked pommel of his sword down, stabbing the beast in the shoulder. Its jaws loosened, and before it could recover, Kenjii's armored boot slammed into its already wounded shoulder.

Bones snapped, and the beast fell to the ground with a pained snarl. Kenjii didn't hesitate. He stepped forward one step, planted his front foot, and brought the rear one forward. His boot caught the tiger in the throat, causing it to gag as it fought for air. He continued his assault, kicking and stomping the hapless beast until it stopped moving.

CHAPTER THIRTY-FIVE

Sunset House, Kume Island, Okinawa, Japan

"Welcome to the Sunset House. Please follow me." Koda greeted Akio and Kenjii at the door, then led them through the main dining room to a private area in the back of the restaurant.

Asai waved when they entered. "Akio-*sama,* Kenjii-*san,* welcome."

They were the last to arrive. Horst had ferried the rest over in his Pod earlier in the day, but Akio and Kenjii had waited until the sun was down to leave China.

"Asai-*san,* Koda-*san,* this is a beautiful facility, and the location is amazing. I can't wait to see it in the light of day." Kenjii spread his arms, indicating the building and the view of the water through the plate-glass windows that lined the room.

Akio cast a surprised look at Kenjii. This was the first time he'd openly expressed interest in walking under the sun.

"It *is* a beautiful view. Suzu and I have watched the

sunset from this location since we were children." Ono smiled as she crossed the room to the pair.

"*Domo.* Akio-*sama,* who's your friend?" she asked as Suzu approached from the opposite side.

"Yes, Akio. Asai told us you were bringing someone with you. Welcome." Suzu nodded at Kenjii.

"Greetings, friends. This is Kenjii. We've known each other for many years, but we only recently reconnected. Kenjii, this is Mayor Suzu Yagi and his wife Ono. They're Asai's parents, and Koda's uncle and aunt."

"Pleased to meet you, Kenjii-*san.* I hope you enjoy your time here," Suzu offered.

"Thank you, Yagi-*san.* What I've seen so far is that you have an amazing home here. I look forward to visiting you again." Kenjii smiled.

"Any friend of Akio's is always welcome on Kume," Ono assured him with a friendly smile.

"*Domo.*"

"Akio, not to bring up an unpleasant subject, but I'm concerned about what Horst told me about that fake contractor. Do we need to fear the Yakuza trying to infiltrate our home now?" Suzu frowned.

Kenjii snorted as he stifled a laugh. "I'm sorry, Yagi-*san.* I wasn't laughing at your concerns," he quickly added.

"Kenjii was an integral part of explaining to the remaining Yakuza why it would be a terrible idea to do so," Akio supplied with a chuckle.

Suzu's and Ono's faces showed surprise at this. They'd been told Kenjii was a friend of Akio's, but with Akio's introduction and now this information, both realized that he was more than a simple friend.

"Uh, I take it Kenjii is different, like Horst or yourself?" Suzu probed.

"*Hai,* Kenjii is special." Akio cast a fond smile at him. "Like Yuko and me."

Suzu and Ono nodded their understanding.

"As for the Yakuza, they've had their final warning. If you detect even a rumor that they're snooping around Kume, contact Horst or me immediately." Akio's chilly tone left no doubt that if the Yakuza returned, it would not end well for them.

"Thank you, both of you," Suzu murmured, relief evident on his face.

"They're parasites, and I will treat them as such should they trouble you," Kenjii assured him.

"Akio has already done so much for the people here. I hope the need doesn't arise, but we thank you for your willingness to help." Ono nodded appreciatively.

"Don't let us hold you up with business. Tonight is a celebration." Suzu beamed, satisfied that the threat of Yakuza interference had ended.

Akio caught Kenjii's hand and followed Suzu and Ono to the group seated at several tables that had been pushed together for the celebration.

"Akio, Kenjii, did you come in one of those marvelous flying devices too?" Seki gushed when they approached.

Akio looked at Horst, who shrugged and pointed at the back of Seki's head, then at Akio. He answered the unasked question with a quick headshake. He would caution Asai to warn Seki about the dangers of talking too much but wouldn't wipe him. Bethany Anne didn't believe in that, and the strictures about the UnknownWorld were no longer in effect. It wasn't a big stretch for him to include TQB tech in that.

"We did. It's amazing, isn't it?" Kenjii answered when he caught the silent exchange between Akio and Horst. "Not something most people will ever get to experience. Most wouldn't believe it anyway," he added, hoping the excited but inexperienced young man would catch his meaning.

"Ah, no. I suppose that's too unbelievable for most to think possible," Seki managed after Kenjii's words registered.

"But it *is* fun." Kenjii winked conspiratorially.

"Absolutely." Seki nodded enthusiastically.

Horst smiled at Akio as he inclined his head toward Kenjii. Akio responded with a nod and one lip quirking up in a half-smile. Kenjii would fit in just fine.

"Join us." Asai motioned to two vacant seats between Yuko and a man Akio didn't recognize.

"Do you remember Koda's *sofu,* Adachi Rii? He has been recovering from his time as Isamu's guest." She gestured at the man.

Akio remembered seeing him, but the last time, he'd been thin and frail. He looked healthier and younger now.

"*Hai,* I remember. You went back into the cave to search for Koda. You look well," Akio observed.

"*Domo,* Akio-*sama.* I feel better, too. What you have done for this island, not to mention my granddaughter, can never be repaid." He stood and bowed low.

"It's an honor to know Koda. She is a special woman. As for the island, I did my sworn duty, nothing more." Akio returned the bow.

"Bunk! You may have been duty-bound to kill that *oni,*

but you didn't have to do anything for my girl. Not to mention all the good you do for the island. Don't think I don't know that if you didn't wish it, none of this would have happened." He swung his arm, the gesture including the restaurant and the view out the window toward the recovering town.

"Sofu, are you giving Akio a hard time?" Koda asked from her seat next to her father.

"No, I'm trying to thank him properly. Mind your business, child, adults are talking." He softened the remark by sticking his tongue out and crossing his eyes. The familiar expression, one he had used on Koda all her life, elicited the desired laugh from her.

"Now, as I was saying, you don't need to be so humble. Everyone on this island feels they owe you and Yuko for all you've done. Listen to your elder: say thank you and accept the praise."

"Domo." Akio smiled while laughing inside. This man of seventy at the most had no idea who the elder truly was.

"Who's this young fellow with you? I don't recall seeing him."

"This is my friend Kenjii. Kenjii, as you have probably determined, this distinguished gentleman is Koda's *sofu."*

"Konichiwa, Rii-*san."* Kenjii bowed.

"Call me Adachi, both of you. We're all family here."

Adachi pulled three empty *sake* glasses from the center of the table and filled them from a pottery carafe he took from an electric warmer. "Have a seat and join me. My lovely granddaughter gifted me this *sake* warmer set today, and I think the temperature is right. It will be so nice to have a cup at the proper temperature. It helps to warm my old bones from the night chills."

Takai Rii snorted from his place next to Koda. "Don't let him fool you. He's made the worst rotgut *sake* on the island for the past thirty years. Warm, cold, or any point in between, he'll drink it."

Adachi sat up in his chair and turned to his son. "Like I told your daughter, grownups are talking. Mind your manners."

Adachi pushed cups in front of the empty chairs and waved Akio and Kenjii to the seats. "Please excuse my son. He gets that from his mother's side."

"*Sofu*!" Koda spluttered.

Suzu, Ono, and Takai burst out laughing, long familiar with Adachi's offbeat sense of humor.

"Don't mind him, Akio. He embarrasses Koda at every opportunity. If he doesn't get a rise out of her, he gets worse until he does." Ono snickered.

"I resemble that remark." Adachi laughed.

Akio shook his head while Kenjii looked at each of them, uncertainty etched on his face.

"Don't mind me, young fellow. I'm an old man who likes to have a little fun at the kids' expense sometimes." Adachi grinned as he pushed the *sake* glass closer. "Now, drink with me. To Akio and Yuko, the best thing to happen here since before the world went to hell."

Kenjii chuckled when he saw the color rise in Akio's face. He was the first to call, "To Akio and Yuko."

Akio rolled his eyes at Kenjii and raised the glass, then took a sip of the warm liquid and nodded once to Adachi. "*Domo*, Adachi-*san*."

"You're learning." Adachi laughed and winked at him.

Asai watched Adachi's antics with a smile. It warmed her heart to see the old man enjoying himself and acting as she remembered him before Isamu came. That his antics pushed Koda to the point of wanting to crawl under the table in embarrassment was a bonus.

A noise from the kitchen caught everyone's attention. They turned to the door when Eve came out, leading a distinguished-looking man in a crisp white chef's uniform.

He carefully carried a cake in the Sunset House's shape to a table beside the wall.

The guests made appreciative sounds as the chef stepped away and gestured at the cake with both hands. "In recognition of the first group to visit the Sunset House, I present you with this humble offering from the kitchen staff. Enjoy."

Only Akio and Horst seemed to notice Eve casually slip an opaque mug to Kenjii, who nodded appreciatively as he brought the warmed blood to his lips and sipped.

Adachi turned his head and grinned as he whispered so low only someone with preternatural hearing could detect, "Needed something with a little more substance?"

Akio shifted his gaze to Adachi as Kenjii looked surprised. Akio nodded after a second, seeing in Adachi's mind that he knew their true nature and had no concerns.

"How long?" Akio whispered.

"Since I saw what you left of that false emperor. I know Koda's man is different, too. Not like you or Yuko, but different. I also know you're honorable men who will do what you must to protect those two girls."

"You don't think we're monsters?" Kenjii murmured.

Adachi chuckled. "Monsters come in all forms, and I have seen my share. You're special, different even, but not monsters."

Kenjii was amazed. That this man recognized what he was and had no fear, even joked with them as though they were normal, made him feel things he hadn't felt in years. It made him feel human.

Koda stood and tapped her fork against a glass for attention. "Friends, family, annoying cousins. Thank you all for your parts in seeing the Sunset House come to being. With the new trade and people coming, I'm certain it will be a successful venture."

Nods and words of agreement came from all around.

Koda held her hand up for silence. "I want to share some personal happiness with you, the people who mean the most to me."

She reached into her pocket and took out a small object that reflected in the light. She put her hands together, and when she separated them, a gold band with a diamond was on her left ring finger.

"My man-mountain here," she pointed at Horst, "finally worked up the courage to not only ask my father's permission but to ask me to marry him. I said yes," she gushed as she waved the ring for all to see.

"Congratulations, you two. It's about time!" Yuko exclaimed.

"How did he do it? When? Where?" Asai giggled with excitement.

"*Domo,* Yuko." She turned to Asai. "On one knee at sunset on the beach at the point."

"How romantic." Asai beamed. "When is the wedding?"

"We haven't decided on a date. It will be before it gets too hot for a beach wedding."

Two men dressed as waiters entered the room with trays of filled champagne glasses. The chef watched from the door, searching for any misstep or stumble from the two islanders turned waitstaff.

"If you make her cry," Adachi called from his seat, "I will skin you with a dull knife."

Horst laughed. "If I make her cry, I will hand you the knife. It would be easier than whatever punishment Koda comes up with afterward."

"I can attest to that," Seki offered with a grin, getting a round of laughter from the Palace crew.

"We must find you the perfect dress," Yuko mused.

"Shopping trip!" Eve cheered.

"This will require more than a simple shopping excursion." Yuko laughed. "There are too many things to do it all in one trip. This will require planning and proper execution."

"You're correct, Yuko. This will require visiting the best dressmakers in the islands and comparing quality and style until we have the perfect dress," Eve offered, a thoughtful expression on her face.

"Have you picked your colors yet?" Yuko looked at Koda. "We will need those before we even consider trying to find your dress."

Koda's eyes went round with shock as the reality of what Yuko's and Eve's plans would entail in time alone, not to mention cost, sank in. "I was, uh, I mean, Horst and I, uh...we want to keep it simple and affordable."

Ono's eyes narrowed. "Oh, no, you won't. This will be

the first wedding on Kume for some time. You owe it to the people here. This could go a long way to heal the scars that remain."

"That's a grand idea. We can make it a celebration for the entire population. Everyone's invited," Suzu chimed in.

Koda's eyes darted around the room, looking for a way out when Yuko burst out laughing. Eve and the Yagis joined in.

"What? What are you laughing at?" Koda demanded.

Asai walked up and put an arm around her waist. "Your face, silly. You should have seen it."

"But the cost of such a spectacle! I can't afford it," Koda sputtered.

Eve stepped up to her and looked into her eyes. "Koda, if you want the biggest wedding Kume has ever seen, Auntie Eve has you covered. I happen to be the wealthiest AI in the solar system."

"I'll take a share of that," Yuko offered.

"As will I," Akio added.

The panic slowly went out of Koda's eyes, and tears followed as she reached out to Eve. "I-I don't know what to say. It's too much. I can't accept."

"You have worked tirelessly to ensure the Palace is a profitable business. Celebrating your wedding is the least we can do," Yuko stated with finality.

"Plus, the big lug over there is my business partner. Saves me from having to buy him a present," Eve snarked.

"But-but I…"

"Say thank you and accept. I don't understand why all you youngsters can't accept things when they're offered." Adachi waved his champagne flute toward Akio.

Akio leaned in and whispered, "You do know I'm the oldest person here? If you all added your ages together, I would still be older."

"I know, but don't slow my roll." Adachi winked as he gulped from his glass.

Akio chuckled and leaned back in his chair, his heart warmed by this group of people who had become his family.

Kenjii watched in relaxed silence as he sipped the blood from his cup and enjoyed the company of friends.

Uegusuku Castle, Kume Island, Okinawa, Japan

"This is where you gutted that *yatsu*?" Kenjii fingered a deep gash in the wood surrounding an open doorway.

"*Hai,*" Akio answered.

Kenjii continued to stare, not seeing the damaged wood but looking at scenes in his mind.

"And that *mazāfakkā*, Ogawa?" he spat.

"Above, at the gate leading into the courtyard."

Kenjii nodded, his eyes closed as he processed the information. After the party to celebrate the Sunset House opening ended, he had persuaded Akio to show him where the two who had hurt him so badly died.

Akio watched in silence as a range of emotions crossed Kenjii's face.

Kenjii drew a deep breath and released it slowly before he opened his eyes. "Thank you. Seeing this makes their deaths real. All the years I watched them, lived with them, and they were the ones who tore us apart. I hope they're both burning in whatever hell they believe in."

"I can't speak to that, only that Isamu's death wasn't fast or easy, and your name was the last he heard before he died. Ogawa's was quick, but he was always Isamu's lapdog."

"It reeks of death here," Kenjii observed.

"This area is where Isamu held the people he took from the island. The locals removed the cages and destroyed them the week after Yuko and I freed them."

He pointed at the floor and indicated the cut-off metal bolts that secured the cages.

"The smell is from the room through there. Yuko destroyed the Nosferatu that Isamu used to terrorize the islanders."

"Ogawa's work," Kenjii spat. "He would make those for their sick games. Isamu enjoyed watching them tear their victims apart when he and Ogawa finished their fun. Heinz told me once that they especially liked to use family members."

Akio grimaced. "They were sick individuals, even for Forsaken."

"*Hai*. At least you've insured they won't harm anyone else. Let's go home. I needed to see it, but I don't wish to stay here any longer."

CHAPTER THIRTY-SIX

Serenity Temple, Dabie Mountains, China

"What do you mean, the slaves are missing?" Peng Kun screamed, his eyes bulging as his face turned red.

The prostrate acolyte's body shook as Kun stalked around the room.

Kun's face twisted in rage and spittle shot from his mouth as he cursed the vampires, ancestors, and gods in a steady stream of invective.

"When did this happen?"

"Sometime within the past three days. The scout who reported it passed through four days ago, and everything was in order."

Kun looked down at the shaking man with disgust. He smelled the fear coming from his body as sweat dripped on the stone floor. *So weak, all of them. Cowards who should still be feeding from their mother's tit.*

"Get out! You disgust me," Kun yelled as his foot connected with the hapless acolyte's ribs.

The man frantically crawled out the door to the relative

safety of the hall. Nowhere in the temple was safe when Kun was on one of his frequent tirades.

Kun snatched the satellite phone from the pocket of his robe. It took him two tries to press the correct button due to his hands shaking in barely contained rage.

"Cui, where are you?"

"Master? I'm on the ship headed for Japan," Cui answered, confusion evident in his tone.

"I know you're on the fucking ship, you idiot! Why am I cursed with such incompetence? When will you be in Japan?"

Cui pulled the phone from his ear, shaking his head from the pain Kun's tirade caused his sensitive hearing. "Master, we will arrive within twelve hours. Is something wrong?"

"Wrong! You ask if something is wrong when that damned vampire is attacking our operations with impunity? Yes, there is something *wrong*, you incompetent ass!"

Cui remained silent. He heard Kun mumbling over the connection but could only understand every third or fourth word. He had dealt with Kun in his insane rages enough to know the master would get to the point when it passed, and interrupting him made it last longer.

"The Lu'an farm was raided. All Clan members present are dead, and the human chattel fled." Kun's voice had changed from the incoherent ravings and invective to a cold and dull tone, one that Cui knew well. It was the same tone he'd used when he ordered Shek's death.

"When you rally with Li, get all the information he has gathered about this Akio and anyone close to him, no matter what the relationship. Servant, friend, the woman who cleans his damned toilet. All of them are dead. Do you understand? I want anyone he is associated with killed. Then you are to destroy his precious base and all the TQB toys he has there. Do not stop until this is complete. Fail, and your life and any with you are forfeit."

Kun cut the connection before Cui could reply. He pulled the device from his ear and stared at it. He was still in that position several minutes later when Pan found him.

"What's the matter, Cui?"

He shook his head and pulled his mind back to the present. "Kun."

"What now?" Pan's face twisted in disgust.

"The vampire attacked the Lu'an farm. Kun has ordered us to kill anyone associated with him in Japan. To include, I quote, 'The woman who cleans his damned toilet,' unquote."

Pan shook his head. "Put his panties in a wad, did it?"

"To put it mildly."

"We have fifty of our best warriors. It should be a simple matter to kill a few people. Are we still planning to hit his base during the day?"

"As far as I know. Li will have more information."

"We might accomplish everything Kun wants in one blow." Pan motioned to three devices fastened to the deck amidships. They looked like corrugated culverts, except for the lethal missile tips that protruded from each launch tube.

Hybrid Vessel *Lylia*, Miura, Japan

"Li, my friend. It's good to see you," Cui called as he walked down *Lylia*'s gangplank onto the wooden dock Li and his men had patched while they waited for him to arrive.

"Cui, you made better time than expected. Was your journey good?"

"Other than listening to more than half of the warriors bitching as they leaned over the rail, making offerings to the fish." Cui laughed.

"If they were anywhere near as bad as Wu, I sympathize." Li chuckled.

"Hey! If the gods intended me to be in the ocean, they would have given me fins and scales," Wu retorted.

"Have you heard from Kun today?" Cui asked.

"No. Last I talked to him was two days ago. He was going on about the traitors who refused to send more warriors. I gathered from the conversation that some deserted in the past few weeks."

"I heard that, too. I knew killing Shek would be a problem. With Kun killing and injuring several of the students since this started, many fear him."

"He isn't making smart decisions. He has allowed emotion to override sound tactics in this."

"Since you brought it up, I received new instructions today." Cui sighed.

"What now?"

"The vampire attacked the farm at Lu'an. All the humans fled, and he killed the guards. Kun has ordered us to kill anyone we can find who is associated with Akio."

Li thought for a moment before he answered. "There are two women who work in that arcade they have. His people rescued one from the Yakuza, and I've heard the other is related to her. They leave the place and should be easy to take."

"Do we want to send warriors into the city? The weapons crew leader says some of his team need to see the target building, but we need the other warriors to secure this area."

"As long as Kun leads the Clan, I think it best that we appear to be following his orders. We can spare two teams to deal with them. Fifty or forty-two—as long as we don't have to contend with the vampire, those numbers are sufficient for any wandering humans who stumble upon us here."

"Agreed." Cui nodded. "Will you provide a leader from your team for each group? It will be best to have someone familiar with the area along."

"Yes. We have a place near the arcade. I'll have Shao and Wu accompany whoever you send."

"That's settled then. What about the vampire's base?"

"It's in an office building. We located a directory, and there are only two companies listed there. I didn't check any further. I didn't want to risk alerting them."

"Let's get the weapons chief and see what information he needs. It better be worth it, given how long I sat in that damned fishing village waiting for him and Kun's precious weapon to arrive," Cui spat.

"What was the holdup? What is this mystery weapon?"

"The holdup was one of the idiots Kun sent on the first team. They went to a cache Kun had secured when he was still in the People's Army. Some explosives had become unstable, and one of the team set off an explosion that collapsed half the mountain on top of him.

"It took several weeks to dig out the missiles Kun wanted, then another to find fuel that was still useable. Transporting them took another week."

"Missiles? What type of missiles, and is he sure they work? I thought the virus fucked all the guidance systems."

"That was the problem with the fuel. These damn things are so old that most of the fuel was no good. They don't use the systems the virus corrupted for guidance. I don't understand them, but the crew chief assures me they will work."

"I don't think I want to be on the ship when he fires them." Li grimaced.

"Me either, but I don't have a choice."

CHAPTER THIRTY-SEVEN

TQB Base, Tokyo, Japan

"I've meant to ask, how does all of this still work? I thought the WWDE destroyed these." Kenjii pointed at the monitors in the command center.

"I have access to a network of satellites that TQB put in place before they went through the gate. They built them using technology that wasn't available on Earth then and won't be available again until my Queen returns," Akio explained.

"The images are so clear! It looks like I can reach out and touch those flowers growing beside the field," Kenjii exclaimed.

"The optics are twenty-first-century Earth military grade. It's the power sources that give me the flexibility I need. It's the unique Etheric power source that allows me to move them to a different orbit without worrying about fuel consumption."

"This is how you found me?"

"No, I discovered you were alive when you came out of

the rubble at the Acheng site. Eve left some drones that link to the satellite network to monitor the location."

Kenjii nodded as Akio continued to show him how to operate the systems he used to monitor the Unknown-World around the globe.

"Abel, pull up the latest intel on that possible Forsaken site in Scotland."

The scene changed from the Chinese farm site where they'd freed the humans to an aerial view of an intact city that hadn't suffered destruction like so many others around the world. Once again, the scene changed as the image zoomed in on a sizeable house in a tiny village a few kilometers outside the city. It was unremarkable, except that every structure close by was a burned-out hulk.

"This is the village of Bilston. The city nearby is Edinburgh," Abel informed them. "This location came to my attention a few months ago when the surrounding houses all caught fire at the same time."

"What's strange about that? I've seen many places burn since the WWDE," Kenjii remarked.

"True, a fire inside a town isn't unusual since fire is the primary heating and cooking method. What was odd about this, or should I say these fires, was that all of them were burning at the same time. It was like they all caught fire within minutes of each other."

"I see."

"I flagged the location for further study. Over the past months, there has been significant activity around it. There is a wall surrounding it now, and many people are living inside it."

"Survivors gather into sizeable groups for protection now. I still see nothing odd," Kenjii mused.

"What about this?" Abel zoomed in tight on a figure standing in the enclosure. It wore thick, concealing clothing from head to toe, including a covering over its face with dark, bulky goggles over the eyes.

Kenjii nodded his head. "Those clothes look like the type I wear when I have to go out into the sun."

The figure walked across the open space, and the people shied away as it approached them. It stopped in front of a cowering blonde woman who looked to be in her early twenties.

Kenjii watched as the figure reached down, grasped the woman's arm, pulled her to her feet, then dragged her toward the house. The woman resisted until her captor brought its free hand to her throat and lifted her higher.

She weakly struggled until her body went limp, and the figure dropped it to the ground. The hooded figure continued toward the house while pulling her unresisting body by the arm it still held.

None of the people in the compound moved to help her. Most turned away and refused to watch.

"*Banpaia,*" Kenjii stated.

"*Hai.*" Akio grimaced. "That is the primary reason Bethany Anne left me here when she went to the stars. She has no mercy for Forsaken who abuse humans."

"What will you do?"

"Explain to him the error of his actions."

"Do you believe that will make him change his ways?"

Akio shrugged. "I have found that Forsaken normally

stop abusing humans when the head is no longer attached to the body."

Kenjii's eyes widened at his response. "You have done this before?"

"More times than I care to remember. Abel, how old is this footage?"

"It came in while you were explaining the system to Kenjii."

"What time is it there now?"

"Seven fifty-two in the morning."

"Thank you, Abel. Kenjii, I need to see to this matter. You're welcome to stay here and have Abel show you more if you'd like."

"I would like that," Kenjii agreed. "Will you be able to take him? What if there are more of them?"

"Then he won't die alone."

"Are you sure you don't want me to come with you?"

"I will be there before ten. The sun would be an issue for you. I can deal with whatever Forsaken are there. Upgrades, remember?"

"Hai."

Akio reached over and took his hand. "Don't worry. I'll be back before it's light here. We can go for a walk when I return."

Kenjii squeezed his hand. "I'll hold you to that. Be sure you come back to me whole. I may want to stay in tonight." His smile held more than a hint of promise.

"I'll be certain to return unscathed." Akio squeezed his hand once more, then stood and walked to the door. "Please bring a Black Eagle to the courtyard, Abel. I want to ensure I'm back before it's light," he called as he walked out.

"How many places have you found suspected Sacred Clan activity in China?" Kenjii asked as he looked at the different displays Abel had open.

"I am actively monitoring twenty-three locations. I have routed satellites to pass over eighty-six more once every twenty-four hours, where I suspect activity but have no factual data to verify it."

"Can you show me the twenty-three active sites?"

The monitor switched from the scene that showed the Forsaken taking the woman to a village on a riverbank.

"This area has a seventy-nine-point-two-five percent chance of being a Clan site. Note the malnourished state of the people working the fishing boats and those in the fields."

"*Hai.*"

"Now, look at this." The monitor flashed then showed a well-fed man dressed in clothes in much better condition than any of the others.

It cycled through four more stills, each of a different person, but all wore similar clothes and were healthy.

"Our data shows that typical Sacred Clan teams contain three to four members. These men don't seem to work and appear to be in excellent health compared to everyone else. I have drones deployed to verify if the data is correct or if a group of human toughs took over the village," Abel explained.

"If it is humans, shouldn't someone stop them as well?"

"Yes, but that isn't within the queen's established mission parameters."

"What are the parameters?

"The Forsaken come first. We eliminate them when we find them preying on humans. Next are the Weres. Akio has always eliminated them until recently."

"What changed?"

"Horst joined us after he fled Heinz. Since then, Akio has been willing to give any who didn't take part in the abuse, or those forced to take part, a chance at redemption."

"Has that worked?" Doubt hung heavy in Kenjii's voice.

"Yes." The screen changed again. It showed an oval-shaped structure that looked like it had been a stadium in the past. It now housed a thriving marketplace filled with tables and stalls loaded with many types of goods.

"This is a human and Were settlement in Adelaide, Australia. Akio and Horst went there and rescued the humans from certain death. They also freed the Weres from a maniacal alpha and his followers. It's now a thriving community that will soon be a regular stop for the shipping company Eve and Horst have formed."

"Do the Weres run the town?"

"No. There is a council composed of Weres and humans, but a human woman handles the day-to-day operations."

"The Weres submit to a human woman?"

"No. Both groups have a voice. The O'Donnell woman is merely the loudest. Well, that and her ideas and instincts have the entire community living better than any of them have in years."

"Amazing. I never thought I would see that."

"You've met Koda and Asai. Yuko and Eve have taught them to be valuable partners in their business ventures. Horst and Koda are romantically involved. Why are you surprised by this?"

"It's so different from what I knew. Granted, I based much of what I thought on lies, but the Weres, even Horst and his brother, were always beneath the vampires."

"Bethany Anne changed the rules where that was concerned. She believes that people—humans, vampires, and Weres—should work together to make the world a better place for all. She bases position on abilities, and she leveled the field between the vampires and Weres when she fixed their nanocytes. Eve told me some Weres are a match for any Forsaken. Her Bitches were human, more or less, and neither group wanted to take any of them on."

Kenjii shook his head in wonder. "I can't wait to meet this woman responsible for so much change. Akio is happier than I remember him from before. He has a purpose now, and it shows."

"Eve has told me that Bethany Anne will return. When that day comes, Akio will resume his position as one of her guards. You will certainly encounter her at some point."

"I would like that. Can you show me more?"

"Yes."

The scene on the wall changed again to show a long rectangular building. The image expanded until it focused on one end of the structure.

"This is a poultry farm. I only discovered it today, but the site is most likely a Clan location."

Kenjii looked hard at the image. "Why? I don't see any people around."

The picture changed again and kept moving, revealing that it was a recording when it showed four men approaching a modest house next to the barn. Four others came out of the house to meet them.

While they talked, one man looked at the barn and ran toward it. He crossed the distance in a blur, then disappeared inside. Seconds later, an unnaturally thin man flew out of the building and landed in a limp heap several meters away. The man who had gone inside stormed out and lifted his hapless victim with one hand, shook him twice, then swiped his free hand across his neck. A spray of blood painted the air and the aggressor dropped the dead body to the ground, then strode back to the group who watched, unconcerned.

"Can you go back to where he struck the other man and freeze the image?"

Abel didn't reply, but the screen switched to the requested scene.

"Zoom in on the hand that struck him, please."

The picture slowly expanded until all it showed was the hand and the victim's lower face, throat, and upper chest. The now-visible claws going into the man's throat were several centimeters long.

"That is Clan." Kenjii grunted.

"Based on the data, there is a ninety-nine-point-three-five percent probability you are correct."

Kenjii nodded, his eyes still focused on the image. "How old is this footage?"

"Four minutes twenty-seven seconds."

"How long would it take to reach that location in one of the air vehicles?"

"Allowing for the time to bring a Pod here, combined with the distance traveling at allowed maximum velocity, eight minutes and fifteen seconds."

Kenjii thought a moment before he ordered, "Summon a Pod. I will take care of these tigers while Akio deals with the Forsaken."

"That is not authorized."

"What do you mean?"

"You haven't been granted access for solo use of any TQB air assets."

"How do I get such permission?"

"It requires authorization from Akio, Yuko, or Eve before I can comply with your request."

"How do I contact one of them?"

"Connecting to Akio."

Seconds later, Akio's voice came over the speaker. "Hai, *Abel?*"

"Akio," Kenjii called, "Abel and I have located another of those Clan farms. One tiger has just killed a human. According to Abel, I can get there in under ten minutes, but he says I don't have permission to use a Pod."

The silence dragged out for several seconds.

"Akio, are you there?"

"*Hai.* How many tigers?"

"Eight now, but the others appear to be leaving. If I hurry, I can catch them all."

"You're not enhanced. Eight could prove to be more than you could successfully defeat," Akio reminded him.

He doesn't believe I can handle this. He thinks I'm not capable, but I killed many of the tigers after I left the lab. He doesn't trust me.

"Akio, I've learned to use the tiger swords. You've seen that I can handle myself against multiple foes. I took that Pricolici without help," Kenjii countered.

"*Hai,* you've demonstrated your ability. I question the number of foes. If any of them can change into Pricolici form, that many might prove to be more than even I could handle unscathed."

"Suppose I wait until the others leave and only the four are there. I could take them while Abel tracked the rest. I could intercept the others afterward."

Akio didn't answer immediately. Kenjii waited impatiently, not wanting to seem to beg. After several long seconds, Akio replied.

"That is acceptable, but Abel is in control of the Pod, and he won't allow you to engage the first group until the other is out of hearing. They must be far enough away that they cannot return in time to reinforce the group you challenge."

"I can do this!" Kenjii exclaimed. "I will kill the tigers and free the humans. Then I will hunt the others as they did me before you found me."

"Full armor, including the helmet and face protection. I know you can heal, but you are not to take unneeded risks." There was another pause, then he added, "We have plans for tonight."

"How could I forget that? We will celebrate our victories as warriors should."

Akio chuckled. "*Hai.* Remember your training and trust your instincts. If something seems amiss, get out of there. We'll take care of them later. The human is already dead, and neither you nor Abel have indicated that there is immediate danger."

"I promise I will use caution, and I won't do anything that will cause you to think less of me."

"I could never think ill of you. You have brought me joy I thought I would never have again. Don't rush in and fight smart."

"Hai." Kenjii smiled. "These are only tigers. You're the one going into the lair of ancestors only know how many Forsaken. I expect you to do the same. I will help you take them if you feel you need assistance."

"I agree to your terms." Akio laughed. "I'm almost to the location. I'll join you once I've finished here."

"Be careful, and know that I love you," Kenjii whispered.

"As I do you. Abel, authorization granted. Take care of him, please."

"Affirmative. A Pod is inbound, ETA forty-one seconds," Abel advised before he cut the comm.

CHAPTER THIRTY-EIGHT

Edinburgh, Scotland

The Black Eagle descended like a bird of prey from the cloud-covered sky into the courtyard of the manor house. Humans scattered, seeking cover from the strange device that came from above.

Akio climbed out of the cockpit when it stopped, hovering centimeters above the ground. He surveyed the area, spotted a metal gate set into the high stone-and-timber fence fastened with a heavy lock and chain, and walked toward the entrance, his senses extended for danger. He detected three Forsaken and four humans inside the house and many more humans in the enclosed area outside the building.

A human man over six feet tall eyed him as he approached the gate. He held a club with sharpened bits of metal covered in dried blood sticking out of it. "Keep back. The Master has forbidden anyone to approach this gate." He waved the club menacingly as he growled in an almost unintelligible accent.

"Step aside," Akio instructed as he neared the gate.

"I said for ye t' stay the fook back," the guard growled as he advanced and drew the club above his head.

Akio never slowed his steady pace. In an instant, the man's upper body disappeared in a spray of blood. The explosive blast from Akio's Jean Dukes Special warped the gate as it destroyed the Forsaken's lackey.

Akio walked through the gore surrounding the area and snapped a kick into the bent framework. The broken chain hurled bits of metal like bullets as the gate slammed against the stone wall and warped further.

Akio turned on his heel and headed for the entrance to the house. "You're free. Leave this place," he called to the cowering humans, injecting a touch of fear into their minds to hurry them along.

Sacred Clan farm, Xianghongdian Reservoir, Sanhe, China

"The four are far enough away they won't hear the altercation. Do you wish to descend?"

"*Hai*. Can you drop me right in front of the house?"

"That would not be tactically sound. Recommend observing for additional threats and using stealth to approach the structure."

Kenjii huffed in frustration. "Abel, did you not tell me that all the tigers who left are out of range?"

"Yes. What's your point?"

"If there were only eight to start with and four departed, and the four remaining are inside the structure as your sensors now show, why the hell would I want to walk in from a distance?"

"To use sound tactics. Simply because I don't detect more threats doesn't mean it's safe to stroll into the house like you own it," Abel replied, a hint of disdain in his voice.

"You're being ridiculous, Abel."

"Akio made it clear you are not to take unnecessary risks. What you propose violates that directive."

"Have it your way," Kenjii snapped. "Put me on the ground, now."

The Pod drifted over the small community and landed behind a ridge a half kilometer away.

"Please ensure that your communicator is active. I will monitor you from above while I keep track of the four who departed."

"Yeah, yeah. Open the door." Kenjii growled as he pulled the communicator out of his armor and set it to voice activation, a feature Eve had installed at Akio's request to facilitate combat operations. Until Kenjii agreed to go in the Pod-doc, he wouldn't have an implant.

"Do you copy, Abel?"

"Loud and clear. Overwatch established. Happy hunting."

"*Domo*."

Kenjii strode over the ridge and did not attempt to conceal himself as he approached the structure where the Clan members were. He covered the distance in seconds, angry that Abel had refused to drop him where he wanted. When he reached the structure, he never paused—he hit the wooden door with his armored shoulder and burst inside in a shower of splinters.

"Greetings. Time to die, kitties." Kenjii taunted right before a hard blow knocked him against the doorframe hard enough to shake the house on its foundations.

Kenjii glimpsed movement out of the corner of his eye and jerked his head to the side, barely avoiding a blow by a huge orange and white paw with thick black claws. The nails gouged the wood centimeters from his face and ripped it away in jagged splinters.

He lashed out with an armored boot and caught a two-hundred-kilo tiger with a glancing blow to its chest, knocking it away before it could follow up on the first strike.

Kenjii twisted his body and slashed down with one sword, slicing into the shoulder of a second beast hurtling through the air toward his exposed face. He'd neglected to lower his visor before he rushed in, expecting to run through the Clan members here with minor effort. The tigers he currently faced had other ideas.

Edinburgh, Scotland

Akio approached the stone steps that led to the heavy oak door of the stone and wood manor, detecting two Forsaken on the first level and a third on a level below. His armored boot shattered the crossbeam securing the double doors from the inside, and a pained cry greeted him as sunlight streamed into the room.

Akio's mouth curled up on one side as he stepped inside. The front room was empty, and dust motes danced in the air currents blowing through the open door. The two Forsaken he had detected earlier had fled the deadly rays into the darkness that shrouded the back of the house. The Forsaken had nailed heavy planks over the windows, casting the interior into a gloomy twilight where dim oil lamps provided the only illumination.

"I know you're there. Come out and face me," Akio called into the gloom.

A soft squeak of a board alerted him to the Forsaken's approach. His enhanced vision cut through the dark, showing a female with blonde hair to her waist watching him.

"What do you want? We have no quarrel with you," she called in a crisp English accent.

"You hold humans as chattel. That's forbidden."

"Forbidden?" She scoffed. "By whom? You? The strictures? Michael is dead, and his bitch abandoned us."

"That's Queen Bitch to you, Forsaken," he growled as his eyes turned red.

Her eyes widened, and her mouth formed an O. "You're him. The one whispered about by the Unknown-World. The vigilante who hunts other vampires. The Dark One!"

Akio nodded once. In the next instant, he stood in front of the Forsaken with his katana held in a high guard position. The vampire gasped as she threw a hand up to fend him off. His blade flashed in a downward blur and cleaved through muscle and bone.

The Forsaken's face froze in its shocked expression. Akio watched dispassionately as a thin diagonal red line appeared across her throat. Her face went slack as her head slid at an angle until it toppled off the stump of her neck. Akio turned toward the rear of the house and the next threat before the Forsaken's body slumped lifelessly to the floor.

Akio slipped through the darkness like a silent shadow, senses extended as he homed in on the hidden vampire. When he stepped into a short hallway, a bright flash followed by a hard blow to his chest knocked him back two steps. He looked down at his armor-covered torso and saw multiple small dents on the surface.

"You shot me?" Akio pursed his lips and shook his head in disgust.

"Die, you bastard," the Forsaken screamed as he rushed around the corner. He'd expected the blast to incapacitate Akio, forcing him to heal the injury. He never heard the report of Akio's Jean Dukes Special and his head exploded in a red mist, spraying blood and bits of bone and gray matter on the walls, floor, and ceiling.

I rushed that one. I'll never hear the end of this from Yuko. He snorted as he self-consciously rubbed his hand across his damaged armor.

"Abel?"

"Yes, Akio?"

"Has Kenjii engaged the Clan members?"

"Yes, he's in the house now. I'm monitoring his communicator and tracking the four who departed."

"How's he doing?"

"Adequate. He's impetuous and doesn't employ sound tactics."

"What do you mean?"

"He demanded I deposit him at the door. I urged that he use stealth to approach the structure. I put him down out of sight of the occupants. Instead of approaching carefully, he rushed to the house and kicked in the door."

"Any problems inside?" Concern laced Akio's voice.

"No, even with his poor tactics, he's doing well," Able snipped.

"Don't be angry, Abel. I'm sure he'll learn to value your input," Akio encouraged.

"I am incapable of being angry. Anger is not logical. I'm stating a fact. Kenjii should have taken my counsel."

Keep telling yourself that. "Thank you, Abel. I'm almost done here. Contact me if there are any changes."

"Affirmative."

Akio had a half-smile on his lips as he went in search of the Forsaken hiding below. Kenjii and Abel were both working toward the next level.

The manor's basement was a high-ceilinged open room that was the size of the house. Heavy rough-hewn beams supported the structure above, and oil lamps provided soft illumination throughout the space. The Forsaken he hunted was dressed in black leathers and had shoulder-length curly black hair pulled into a leather strip at the back of his head. He stood with his back to a corner and had three humans in front of him as shields.

"This is nothing to you. Leave now, and I won't kill you slowly," the Forsaken snarled as he produced a double-edged broadsword.

"You hide behind humans and expect me to believe you a threat?" Akio scoffed. "Release them and face me like a man, not a whiny child."

"I have been a Knight of the Realm for over three centuries. I've killed better men than you for less. This is your last warning. Leave." The Forsaken emphasized his words by waving the sword in a figure-eight after he shoved it between two of his human shields.

Akio extended his senses to the three humans. He detected fear and a weak compulsion to block his path to the Forsaken.

Sleep. When Akio pushed the compulsion into the three, they fell unconscious and dropped to the floor like marionettes with severed strings.

Akio smirked as he pulled his Jean Dukes from his side and fired from his hip. A single hypervelocity projectile spat from the barrel and hit the Forsaken in the shoulder that supported the broadsword.

Blood sprayed the wall in a halo as the shoulder exploded. The sword, still gripped tight in the Forsaken's hand, clattered to the floor.

The Forsaken screamed in pain as his remaining hand grabbed the mangled flesh where his arm should be. His eyes glowed red, and fangs extended from his mouth as he glared at Akio.

Akio holstered his Jean Dukes, and a wintry smile that never reached his eyes curled his lips.

The enraged Forsaken lunged forward but caught one foot on the prostrate form of a human. He regained his footing as Akio leapt forward, his katana already in motion.

The razor-sharp blade caught the Forsaken on the neck and sliced halfway through his unprotected throat. Blood seeped from the wound as Akio sidestepped his lumbering form and brought the sword back in a one-handed swing, cutting a leg behind the knee and causing the vampire to crash to the floor.

"You are guilty of preying on humans. The penalty set forth by my Queen for this crime is death."

The Forsaken struggled to right himself with his remaining arm. Akio stood patiently as he slowly pushed his body up and brought his functioning leg under him. Akio's sword flashed down and cut through the back of the Forsaken's exposed neck, then continued until it exploded out the front in a shower of blood. The Forsaken's torn and mangled body remained in its awkward pose for a few beats before it crashed to the stone floor.

Akio twisted his wrist to flick the blood from his blade, then removed a cloth from a pocket of his armor while eyeing the body and wiped the blade clean of any residual blood before he sheathed it.

The three humans slept under his compulsion, unaware that the nightmare they had lived in for the past few months was over.

Awaken. The humans stirred and slowly came out of his mental grip. When all were conscious, Akio activated the light in the shoulder of his armor. It centered the dead Forsaken in its brilliant white beam.

"Your captors are dead. You have nothing to fear, so leave this place and return to your homes."

The humans cowered in fear, glancing from the body on the floor to Akio and back.

"Come," Akio commanded with a compulsive push behind it.

He made his way to the stairs, and the three humans

followed him like baby ducks behind their mother. He led them out of the house into the midday sun.

"Go home. You won't be troubled by those monsters any longer," Akio told the three humans, who looked around in confusion at the now empty yard. Akio turned to the Black Eagle, but as he prepared to depart, a noise alerted him that someone approached.

"Wait," a soft voice called as he turned to walk away.

Akio turned to the speaker, the blonde waif he'd seen the Forsaken pull into the house earlier. Her tattered dress barely covered her creamy flesh, and she had multiple fresh wounds on her neck and chest where the Forsaken had savaged her.

"Yes, child?"

"Who are you?" Wonder filled her voice.

"I'm…" he started, then paused. "I'm the person creatures like the ones who harmed you need to fear. I am my Queen's Justice. You may call me 'the Dark One.'"

The woman watched silently as the Black Eagle rose into the air until it was a dark spot in the sky. She blinked, and when her eyes focused, the sky above her was empty.

Abel

Yes?

Is Kenjii still engaged?

Yes.

Does he need assistance?

Negative. He is meeting the challenges so far.

Akio considered his options. He could go to Kenjii and

run the risk of making him think he didn't believe he was up to the task. Or, he could go back to Tokyo and show him he trusted him.

Domo, *Abel. I'm heading home. Notify me if anything changes.*

Affirmative.

Sacred Clan farm, Xianghongdian Reservoir, Sanhe, China

Kenjii pressed his attack on the cat he'd cut. He brought his second sword up in a fast arc and caught the tiger on its flank, laying the skin and muscle open to the bone.

He dropped to the floor and rolled out from under the two who'd tried to pounce on him, their jaws wide and claws extended. He was on his feet before his assailants could untangle themselves from the pile they landed in when he moved.

The tiger he had kicked away closed on him with a menacing snarl. Kenjii stood his ground, both swords held ready. When the tiger crouched and prepared to spring, Kenjii rushed forward and brought both swords down in a blur of deadly steel. The blades scraped across each other as they met in the center of the tiger's neck with a tortured squeal of metal. The noise ceased when the *shuang gou* sent the tiger's head across the room in a bloody arc as the body collapsed to the filthy floor.

Kenjii leapt, his head almost touching the ceiling as one of the two cats untangled from the other and launched toward him. The orange- and black-striped body was centimeters below his boots as he kicked it on his way down and caught the beast on its back below the shoulders.

The tiger shrieked in pain, and an audible *snap* echoed through the room when Kenjii's vampire-enhanced strength broke its spine. The force of his kick put his body at an angle when he landed, one foot extended and the other under him. Before he regained his balance, the remaining uninjured tiger crashed into him and took him to the floor.

Kenjii scrambled to get out from under the enraged beast as it brought its rear legs up and raked them down his armored torso and legs. Kenjii grasped the skin on either side of the enormous cat's neck and shoved the snapping teeth away from his exposed face. The wildly thrashing tiger continued struggling to eviscerate him with its claws and bite at the same time.

Kenjii forced a knee up in a quick thrust and caught the monster cat in the stomach, raising it several centimeters in the air. The cat's eyes went wide as his knee knocked the breath out of it with the unexpected blow. Kenjii didn't hesitate. His eyes flashed red, and his fangs elongated as he pulled down on the skin still gripped tight in his fingers and brought the tiger's throat toward him. He whipped his head to the side and sank his fangs deep into the winded tiger's neck, severing the major artery that fed the brain.

Kenjii shoved the bleeding tiger to the side, and it thumped to the floor beside him. He rolled toward it, then brought his fist down hard on the stunned creature's head. He continued to rain blows on the big cat until the skull shattered under his fist with a crack.

Kenjii drew a deep breath while turning his head to the

side to relieve a knot that had formed from throwing punches while on his back. A noise near the door alerted him the fight wasn't over. He shoved himself up on one elbow and saw the first tiger he'd cut climb unsteadily to its feet.

Kenjii lay back and pulled his legs to his chest, then thrust them down as he whipped his body off the floor. He landed on both feet and stooped to retrieve his twin tiger swords.

"Here, kitty, kitty," he taunted in an icy voice.

The tiger's head turned toward Kenjii as he stalked it across the bloody floor.

"Time to die," Kenjii jeered as he took two quick steps, then planted his foot as he swung one of his razor-sharp blades down on the still-recovering cat. The added momentum buried the blade deep in the big cat's skull and the beast collapsed in a lifeless heap, pulling the sword and Kenjii's arm down with it. He tugged, but the sword didn't move, stuck fast in the hard bone. He placed one foot on the beast and wrenched the blade free.

His attention focused on the sword allowed the last of his opponents time to heal from its broken spine. It slammed into his back and knocked him face-first into the cinderblock wall. Dust and bits of concrete blinded him as the blocks shattered.

A hot cloud of putrid breath assailed his nostrils as he felt the tiger's teeth close on the thin armor that protected his neck. He hunched his shoulders, attempting to lessen the force of the bite as his armored elbow shot back and caught the tiger in the chest. Kenjii frantically pounded the beast over and over with his elbow as he felt the pressure increase on his neck.

In desperation, he shoved the blade in his other hand straight out behind as he ineffectually continued to pound the deadly foe with his elbow. He brought the sword's vicious hooked end up until he felt it gain purchase on flesh. His vision dimmed, and his heart pounded in his ears as the unrelenting jaws continued to bear down. He felt lightheaded as he pulled the blade toward himself, the hook firmly seated in the tiger's flesh. The cat's jaws loosened, and it snarled at the unexpected pain ripping through its soft belly. Another elbow strike drove it back, and Kenjii turned to face it.

While blinking his eyes to clear the grit, he saw the fuzzy outline of the beast as it prepared to attack. Kenjii brought both swords up, causing the cat to hesitate briefly. That delay was all he needed. Kenjii jumped and landed with both boots on the Were's barely healed back, separating the spine again.

The tiger snarled as it tried to rake him with the claws on its forepaws from its position on the floor, its rear legs now useless weight hampering it. Kenjii stepped back, allowing his burning eyes time to recover as he avoided the long claws.

"Nice try, cat," he growled as he drew his foot back and brought it forward to slam into the injured tiger's jaw. The cat's eyes rolled up when the hard blow stunned it. Kenjii moved in a blur and grabbed it by the scruff with one hand while the other drew a sword across its throat, opening the arteries.

He held the weakly struggling form until all movement

had ceased. After shaking it, he dropped the body, and it joined its brethren in death on the filthy floor of the house.

"I'm finished, Abel. Let's go after the others."

"You need to free the humans before we go."

Kenjii huffed. "Can't I do that after I've killed the others?"

"Negative. Protecting humans comes first. Akio's rule, not mine."

"Very well." He sighed as he trudged across the village to the dilapidated barn that housed the human slaves.

CHAPTER THIRTY-NINE

The Palace, Tokyo, Japan

"Asai, are you and Seki going with us tonight?" Koda pushed away from her desk as she spoke.

"He has to work late. Something about new models arriving and needing to make space for them on the floor."

"He understands he has workers for that, doesn't he?"

"I know. He's trying to make points with his boss. He has his sights set on a higher spot in the company."

"If Seki keeps canceling plans with you, I will authorize Takumi to adjust his settings on every sim."

"Koda! I asked you not to do that again. Seki was in pain for three days when you and Eve did that to him."

"He obviously needs a refresher." Koda sneered.

"You can't be mad at him for work stuff. I've had to cancel on him because of things here."

"I know. It's only that we never do anything with each other but work now. I miss you."

"I miss you too, cousin. What say we plan a 'girls only'

night? You, me, Eve, and Yuko. No stinky boys allowed." Asai grinned.

"That's an idea. Teach them we're perfectly capable of having fun without them," Koda agreed.

"What's that? You don't want me to come tonight?" Horst looked dejected as he walked into the office.

"No, not tonight, you silly wolf." Koda smiled as she stepped up to him and wrapped her arms around his body as far as they would go. "Seki stood Asai up again tonight. We were talking about a girls' night another time."

Horst leaned down and gently kissed her lips. "Oh, okay. I'll be busy with the new base build starting next week, so that might be an excellent idea. I'll be there all night on Wednesday."

"Next week? I thought you said it would be at least a month before you could start! Why all night?" Koda exclaimed.

"The concrete contractor had a major job cancel, so he'll have the trucks we need to pour the foundation available then. I'll be there to make sure they do it correctly since the contractor has never done a continuous pour like this before and isn't sure he knows what to watch for."

"Why are you doing that—what was it—'continuing pour?'" Asai shrugged.

"Continuous pour. The concrete is stronger if there are no spaces in it. With the chance of earthquakes here, Akio wants to make it as stable as possible. Since most of the base is underground, Eve and I had to get creative. The entire base will sit on shock absorbers built into the foundation. It will take a substantial quake to damage it."

"Do you think this type of construction will become standard here?" Asai wondered.

"Not likely. The cost is four to five times more than a traditional foundation. The two meters of concrete is only one part of it. The entire thing is reinforced with layered steel beams, and the concrete will be poured over them to dry in place. If we hadn't picked up that steel mill to manufacture the metal for the new ship designs, we wouldn't have been able to get the specific alloy we needed for this." Horst chuckled.

"That's impressive. I didn't know Akio was going to such extremes."

Horst's brow wrinkled. "He blames himself for his men being trapped under that building. He wants to do everything possible to protect his team."

"I forgot about that." Asai frowned. "Yuko told me he had several more with him who are trapped. Is there anything you can do to rescue them?"

"No. I went over all the data Eve compiled after it happened. If we move anything, it will bring everything down on them. Eve reinforced it as best she could and monitors it for movement. All we can do is hope it holds until we have the technology available to lift the entire thing at once."

"It's so sad to think there are people alive under all that and we can't get them out. How do they not go insane?" Koda asked.

"Eve told me that vampires, especially old ones, can go into a deep sleep for long periods. They can easily sleep for a hundred years or longer," Horst explained.

"It's still sad."

"Yes, it is."

"Asai, would you like to go with us?" Koda abruptly changed the subject.

"No, you two go ahead. I have a little more I need to do here. If you don't mind, pick me up an order of ribs. I can finish up here and have time for a bath before you get back."

Koda snorted. "I bet you're still soaking when we get home. You lose all sense of time when you get in that thing."

"I'll have Takumi warn me when you get in his sensor zone." Asai grinned. "He does it all the time with Seki."

Koda laughed as she caught Horst's arm and pulled him toward the door. "Okay, we'll see you when we get back."

"That's one of them." Wu pointed at the couple from his vantage point on top of a nearby building when they exited the Palace.

"That's a big guy," Chao, one of the warriors assigned to the detail, remarked.

"Yeah, but size isn't an issue. The smallest Clan child can take a human, no matter the size."

"True. I don't think I've ever seen one that big is all."

"He's a foreigner. Some of them are quite large, but still nothing to worry about. Collect your team and follow them. Remember, the police here have silver ammunition, so try to do it fast and quiet. I don't want to have to explain how one of you was killed on a simple seek-and-destroy mission on humans."

"Like that will happen." Chao smirked. "Are you coming with us?"

"No, I'm going back to the apartment. Jin should be there with his team by now. Come there when they're dead. Maybe we can go back to our base once Li can tell Kun we killed these two."

"That would be good. I don't like it here. There's too much noise and too many humans."

"Once we get rid of this vampire, we can deal with the human vermin." Wu shrugged. "The sooner that's done, the better it will be."

"True. I'll meet you later." Chao waved as he stepped through the stairwell door.

"Chao, one of them is a Were. I smell wolf," Guo Jing growled as he sniffed the air currents disturbed by the two people a block ahead of them. Luckily, the wind was in their faces and the wolf wouldn't scent them.

"We'll keep them in sight, and once they get wherever they're going, we'll find the best location to ambush them. The presence of a Were with a human woman is disturbing. We might have more than vampires to deal with," Chao informed the three men who accompanied him.

"One wolf and a human woman are no match for us. Let's get this over with," Guo complained.

"No, Wu told me we have to keep this quiet. The police here know about the UnknownWorld and carry silver ammunition for their weapons."

"I still think it's a waste of time. We can kill them and go back to the apartment now."

"Good thing I'm in charge and you aren't. We do it my way. Unless you want to challenge me for my position?" Chao growled as his eyes turned yellow.

"No, we do it your way. I meant no disrespect, Chao." Guo took a step back with his eyes downcast and his hands held palms up in supplication.

"Anyone else?" Chao glared at the other two. "No? Then you take point, Guo. We'll follow a few hundred meters back. When they stop, we'll finalize the attack plan."

CHAPTER FORTY

Han's Pit Barbeque, Shinjuku City, Tokyo, Japan

"That was the best meal I've had in weeks!" Koda exclaimed as they walked. "Those different-flavored sauces were amazing. Where did you say that style of cooking came from?"

"A country called the United States pre-WWDE," Horst answered. "Han uses sauces based on different regions. All of them claimed to be the best, and they had competitions to determine it."

"I especially liked the sweet sauce. The seasonings gave it the perfect blend of sweet and heat."

"I liked the one from an area called the Carolinas. The vinegar base gave it a tangy taste."

"That one was too intense for me, but I like all things sweet." She giggled as she made to lick Horst's arm.

Horst laughed at her antics, then froze as the strong musk of big cat assailed his sensitive nose. He searched the area for the source as he wrapped one arm protectively around Koda.

"What is it?"

"Cat, probably tiger." Horst kept his head high as he continued to scan the area.

He picked up speed, heading toward the Palace and the safety of Takumi's defensive zone before trouble found them. They made it half a block before two men stepped in front of them from a dark alley.

"Look what we have here, Tao. A girl taking her mutt for a walk."

The other man laughed as he moved beside his companion to block the sidewalk.

Horst pulled Koda behind him. "We don't want any trouble. Move aside and let us be on our way."

"He doesn't want any trouble," the first man mocked. "If you didn't want trouble, you wouldn't have associated with those vampires."

The scuff of a shoe behind him caused Horst to glance back and see two more men approaching from his rear. He caught Koda and shoved her into a shallow entryway. The business was closed for the night, so a heavy metal grate blocked the glass doors. The space was less than half a meter deep, but it protected Koda and provided some cover for his back.

"Takumi," Koda called over her communicator, "Horst and I are under attack. Notify Akio and Yuko that four tigers have blocked our way."

"Messages sent. I am deploying active defensive and offensive measures to your location."

"Oh, look, she's calling for help," the apparent spokesman for the group crowed. "Don't worry, girlie.

When we're done with the dog, we'll take excellent care of you."

The others moved into a half-circle in front of Horst, blocking any chance of escape. One of them leered at Koda. "We don't have to do this. Give us the girl for a while, and you can go. She looks like she can take care of all of us."

Horst knew this was a tactic designed to make him step out of the doorway. It didn't work, but the implied threat set off a raging fire inside of his body.

"Step away, cat. I'm not moving. If any of you come closer, you'll die," Horst growled, his voice rough like stones grinding together.

"The only one dying today is you, dog," the speaker taunted, then an orange- and black striped tiger occupied the space where he stood. The other three shifted as the first leapt toward Horst. The Were's body shimmered, and in its place stood a nine-foot-tall Pricolici wolf.

Horst roared in defiance as he extended the fingers on his right hand toward the airborne tiger. The skin parted like paper when the cat's heavy body encountered the seven-centimeter-long claws on each finger. When the attacker's forward momentum stopped, Horst's arm was buried elbow-deep in the cat's chest. He snarled as he closed his fist, twisted it, and jerked. His hand pulled free of the tiger's body with a wet sucking sound and a river of blood. The tiger dropped to the pavement in a boneless heap, his lifeless eyes wide open and staring at nothing.

Horst howled as he flung the bloody organ to the ground. "Coommmee and geett meeeee, little kitteeesss," he snarled.

The remaining tigers rushed him as one. Koda screamed when he stumbled from a blow to his side. Hot blood flowed from the wound as he lashed out, but he missed the nimble cat by a hair's breadth.

A second tried to go around him, intent on attacking Koda. Horst caught him by the scruff of his neck, lifted him off the ground, and slammed his body into the third, who rushed toward them, thinking the injury and attempt on Koda distracted Horst.

Horst flew into a berserker's rage and moved faster than Koda's eyes could follow. He threw the tiger he held and knocked the legs out from under the last standing assailant. When that beast was on the ground, attempting to untangle itself from the other, Horst jumped on him with both feet. The sounds of breaking bones followed by an agonized shriek ripped the air.

As he continued to stomp the life from the beast, the other two came in again, one behind him, the other in front. Sharp claws pierced the soft skin behind his knee, and blood ran down his leg in a solid sheet from the jagged wound. The leg gave out and he toppled to the ground, unable to maintain his balance on his good leg. The remaining two tigers wasted no time. Both pounced on him, claws and teeth ripping into his body.

Horst rolled to the side and caught the cat that had cut his knee by its front leg. He tucked his head, the thick muscles in his neck straining as he blocked the other from biting into his throat. Horst jerked the cat he held forward, and the force pulled the leg from the shoulder socket with an audible pop. He grinned toothily when he twisted and yanked again, ripping the skin and tearing the leg off the body.

He rolled, which threw the cat that worried his neck momentarily off-balance. Before it regained its footing, he had one huge bony hand around its throat. Squeezing, he cut off its oxygen until it opened its mouth and attempted to suck in air. In one swift motion, Horst drove the leg he held in his other hand into the open orifice, shoving until it could go no farther. Then he raised his knees and kicked the struggling beast in the side. The satisfying sound of bones shattering was his reward.

The cat thrashed wildly on the pavement as it frantically pawed its muzzle in a vain attempt to dislodge the object suffocating it. Horst ignored its death throes as he turned to the injured cat attempting to flee on three legs. He pushed himself to his feet unsteadily and set out after it in a staggering gait. He caught the wounded tiger in a few steps and swiped his clawed hand down, severing the muscles and tendons in both rear legs.

The tiger collapsed, and Horst, his body weak from blood loss, fell forward and pinned it to the ground. His last action before he passed out was to clamp his jaws on the back of the tiger's neck, crushing it with his teeth and severing the spinal cord.

Koda stood in shock at the speed and viciousness of the encounter. In a matter of seconds, Horst had changed into something she'd never seen, a hulking monster that moved faster than thought. The creature had turned the four who had attacked them into bloody chunks of cooling flesh in the street. She let out a muffled sob when he collapsed and ran to him with no thought to her safety.

She slid to her knees by the still form of the man who was everything to her. "Horst? Horst, speak to me." She grabbed the coarse hair on his shoulder as she spoke.

Horst moved by sheer instinct. His claw-tipped hand lashed out and caught Koda across her midsection, leaving four deep furrows in her body.

Koda squeaked as the force of the blow knocked the breath out of her, then slowly toppled to the ground with a shocked look on her face.

Horst shakily sat up, his body weak and his mind locked in a struggle to maintain its humanity while the wolf fought to run wild and howl its defiance at the world.

His body shook as he tried to force his beast to shift back to human form now that he'd defeated the threats. It seemed like hours to him, but in seconds, a battered and bloody nude man sat in the deserted street.

He surveyed the damage, satisfied that he would heal in time before turning to the alcove where he'd secured Koda. His eyes passed over a heap of colored cloth lying beside him. He continued to turn until his mind registered what he'd seen.

"Koda!" he screamed as he painfully covered the distance to her on his hands and knees. Shock and pain ate at his soul when he saw her bloody wounds—injuries he'd caused.

A loud boom shattered the night as a Black Eagle descended at high speed. Akio leapt from the open hatch before the craft stopped, his eyes red and katana at the ready.

The vampire spun when he heard steps approaching at

a fast pace but relaxed when Yuko appeared, a Jean Dukes Special gripped tightly in each hand.

Horst shook as hot tears coursed down his cheeks and splashed on the unmoving body he gently cradled in his arms. "I killed her," he cried, his voice cracking under the strain.

Yuko blurred and was on her knees beside the injured woman in a flash. She ripped the tattered cloth away from the wounds and extended her senses to assess Koda. A faint heartbeat registered from the still body.

"Horst?" Yuko called.

Lost in grief, his mind numb at what he had done, Horst didn't register that Yuko had spoken.

"Horst!" Yuko yelled.

Horst continued to gently rock Koda in his arms, sobbing as grief ate away at him.

The sound of flesh meeting flesh echoed down the gloomy street as Yuko's open palm connected with his face. "Horst, she still lives. She is fading fast and needs your blood to survive until we can get her in the Pod-doc."

Horst's eyes focused on Yuko as what she said penetrated his grief. "What? I… No! I don't know that she wants that," he argued.

Yuko met his gaze with her steely red one. "If you don't do it, I will. Koda Rii. Will. Not. Die. Your choice, Horst, werewolf or vampire. Those are the only options she has."

Horst was dumbstruck, his face red where the normally reserved Yuko had slapped him. Her eyes burned with iron will and determination to do what she must for Koda. He opened his mouth to speak when he felt a firm hand grip the wrist of one arm. He looked up and met

Akio's eyes centimeters from his face. "Give me your arm," he hissed.

Horst relaxed and allowed Akio to raise his arm. Sharp pain flared in his wrist when Akio sliced it deep with his razor-sharp katana.

"Drip it into her mouth," he ordered while guiding the arm to hold the open wound to her mouth. "Now on to the injuries."

Horst followed his directions without resistance, his body responding with no conscious thought. His blood filled her mouth and Yuko massaged Koda's throat, forcing her unresponsive body to swallow while Horst covered the deep wounds across her torso with his nanocyte-rich blood. It was done in seconds.

Akio pulled Horst to his feet while Yuko lifted Koda into her arms and carried her like a sleeping babe to the Pod Abel had dispatched when Koda called. Akio led the mind-numbed Horst to the Pod and gently pushed him into a seat. "I'll meet you at the base."

The Pod shot into the night sky, followed by the sleek and deadly Black Eagle. Both vessels descended into the base's open courtyard

"The Pod-doc is ready. I have her," Eve assured them as she briskly pushed the stretcher into the building, then to the elevator to take them below.

Yuko led Horst from the Pod to the open doors of the building. He moved like he was in a trance, responding to her guiding touch but not communicating.

"Akio, have you finished your missions?" Yuko inquired while they waited for the elevator to return.

"Scotland is done. Kenjii is finishing up in China now.

He took out one group of Sacred Clan and freed the humans they held. Another group left the same farm earlier. He's dealing with them now," Akio informed her, pride evident in his voice.

"That's good." Yuko nodded as the elevator doors opened.

Akio followed in silence as Yuko guided the unresponsive Were through the entrance to the base.

CHAPTER FORTY-ONE

Dabie Mountains, Outside of Sanhe, China

"Where did they go, Abel?"

"I tracked them into the mountains, and they dropped off of sensors when they went into this gorge."

"Find them."

"Sensor sweep in progress, stand by."

"I have detected a rock formation that appears to be the entrance to a subterranean cavern." A highlight appeared on the monitor in the Pod, halfway down the deep cut between two mountains.

"Can you get a look inside?"

"Negative. There are no available drones."

"Why not? I thought all the aircraft have drones."

"Eve is upgrading them. They use some components that are not available on Earth. She's recycling those from the older models."

"Drop me at the entrance. I will scout it out and see where they went."

"That is unadvisable, I recommend returning to base and returning once drones are available."

"I only want to look. I won't take an unnecessary risk."

"Like you didn't at the farm?"

"I know I should have listened to you. I admit I could have done that better."

"No doubt."

"Come on, Abel. Akio trusted me to deal with these tigers. I don't want to have to tell him I lost them and don't know where they went."

"Akio will understand. He uses sound tactics."

"Abel, at least let me be certain they have left the area. The humans we freed aren't safe if they return."

"I will maintain station here if you like. If they show up on sensors, we can assess the situation then."

"You won't let me look for them, will you?" Kenjii grumbled, frustration in his tone.

"Negative. Akio was clear that I couldn't let you take unneeded risks."

"Can you take me back to the farm, at least? Perhaps the clan left some information there we could use."

"That is acceptable. I will continue to search for the missing Clan members and will pick you up in time to get back before sunrise."

"Thank you, Abel."

The Pod descended, and seconds later, Kenjii was back at the house. He watched the Pod disappear into the night sky, then stalked into the structure.

Abel should not have stopped me. I'm more than capable of dealing with a few tigers. I will need to speak with Akio about this, he must allow me to make my own decisions.

He looked through the few papers and belongings he located. Finding nothing of interest, he stepped out of the house and stopped on the steps.

I need to send a message to this Sacred Clan. They hunted me in China and Japan. They need to understand their place in this world.

Kenjii smiled as he stepped back into the house. The tigers had shifted back to human form after they died. He started dragging bodies into the yard. He planned to leave a message anyone could understand.

TQB Base, Tokyo, Japan

"Yuko, contact Inspector Yonai, please. He needs to know what happened," Akio advised Yuko after she had settled the distraught Were in the kitchen.

"*Hai,* you're right. I'm certain the bodies have been found by now," Yuko agreed.

"I'll stay with Horst until you're done."

"*Domo,* Akio. This shouldn't take long."

Akio entered the room and found Horst with his head in his hands, shuddering with silent sobs.

"Horst."

The Were looked up, his eyes red and his face wet with tears. "Is-is she…" he stuttered as the color drained from his face.

"She lives. Eve has her in the Pod-Doc and is repairing the life-threatening injuries. The nanocytes in your blood sustained her long enough to get her the treatment she needs."

"She's going to hate me. I almost killed her, and now

she will be a monster because of me."

Akio placed a comforting hand on Horst's shoulder. "You saved her life. You defeated four weretigers by yourself and controlled the Pricolici. You could have caused mass carnage among the people. That form is hard to control; I have seen some of the strongest Weres I know not have the self-restraint you did."

"Still, I hurt Koda. If she had died, my life would have no meaning."

"But she lives. You not only stopped and shifted, but you saved her life."

"After I injured her."

"Horst, you're hurt. You need to go into the Pod-Doc yourself. The Pricolici form is a raging beast, and it takes time to learn to control it. Koda didn't know, and none of us ever thought to warn her that the form was dangerous. It's more my fault than yours. I knew you could shift into that form with the proper incentive since I have seen you partially do it."

Horst shook his head, denying Akio's words.

"Horst, how many times have you shifted to full Pricolici?"

"Once."

"So, it's reasonable to say it was not something you expected. What happened that caused you to shift?"

"The *schwein* threatened to do things to Koda. All I could think was that they had to die. If I had known this would happen, I would have tried something else. Anything else."

"I know you would have. The Clan didn't leave you a

choice. They would have killed both of you if you hadn't fought them."

"The things they said." Horst shuddered. "A red rage overtook me. I couldn't control it."

"Powerful emotions are rumored to trigger that form. The day you killed Heinz started it. The form and control come easier, the more you shift to it. A session in the Pod-doc can adjust your nanocytes to give you more control, too. When Koda's healing is complete, you need to go in."

"Koda's healing will be complete in two hours and thirty-six minutes," Eve announced as she walked through the door.

"She will…she will be okay?" Horst asked, worry in his voice.

"The damage was extensive. The Pod-doc needs time to replicate your nanocytes to complete the healing. When she comes out, she will never need to fear four weretigers again. She will be a match for most Forsaken, I can assure you of that," Eve told him.

Akio's eyes widened in surprise at the conviction. "What did you do, Eve?"

"Nothing I didn't have to," Eve assured him.

"Eve, what are you talking about?" Horst asked, worry in his tone.

"The internal damage was extensive. To repair it, the Pod-doc will have to adjust the nanocytes you provided. Koda's nanocytes will be on par with the Weres who now accompany Bethany Anne."

"Are they that different from me?" Horst asked.

"Yes. Koda will be stronger and faster and have control of the Pricolici form when she comes out of the Pod-doc. If you don't go in, she will be capable of kicking your furry ass to Kume and back without breaking a sweat." The AI smiled to soften her words.

"I-I don't know what to say."

"She will need you to help her through the transition. Her lifespan is much longer now. You need to explain that, along with other Were specific issues," Eve explained.

Horst's face went slack. "I never thought about that. Even though I am many years older than her, she would have aged and died before me."

"Yes. Now she won't age but will watch her friends and family do so. She will need your help to cope with that."

Akio looked up when Yuko entered the room. "Did you speak to the inspector?"

"*Hai*. He is on his way to the scene. He advised he will contact me if he finds anything we should know about."

Yuko walked over and placed her hand on Horst's shoulder. "I heard what Eve told you. If there had been any other choice, I would not have forced that on you. I'd planned to offer her and Asai enhancement, just not this soon."

"It's just a lot to take in. Koda didn't have a choice. I never want her to feel that I would force her to do anything." He unconsciously clenched his hands into fists.

Yuko caught them in hers. "Horst, Koda knows you love her. She won't blame you for this. She will blame herself when she sees how much anguish this has caused you."

Horst nodded, then his face took on a panicked look. "Asai! Has anyone told her? Is she in danger?"

"Takumi initiated a lockdown as soon as Koda reported the attack. Defensive and offensive measures are active. I advised him not to notify Asai, believing the news should come from one of you," Abel volunteered.

"Good thinking, Abel. Contact Asai now, please. Put it on the speakers here," Akio requested.

"Akio?" Asai answered.

"Weretigers attacked Koda and Horst on their way back to the Palace. Koda is in the Pod-doc and will be fine in a few hours. Takumi has locked down the facility and is monitoring the area for threats."

"Koda! I need to be with her!" Asai exclaimed.

"I'll have a Pod pick you up on the roof. We don't know if there are other Clan members in the area." Yuko looked questioningly at Horst.

"It was a planned attack. They told me it was because I associate with vampires," Horst explained.

"I will go pick Asai up. If there are more of them, I want to get any information I can," Akio growled as he stood and headed for the door.

"The Pod is coming down. It will be waiting," Abel announced.

CHAPTER FORTY-TWO

The Palace, Tokyo, Japan

"Asai, I will pick you up in one minute," Akio advised her as he entered the elevator.

"I'm at the roof access now, but it won't open."

"Lockdown protocol is in effect, I will release the locks once Akio has arrived," Takumi advised.

"Thank you, Takumi," the girl replied.

"Akio, I have detected a suspicious person on the east side of my building," Takumi broadcast over the comm.

"What's the problem, Takumi?" Akio asked as he entered the waiting Pod.

"I have noted this person walking through my surveillance area three times in the past hour. He is not in my database as someone with business in the area. He's going around the rear of the building now."

"I have him in sight," Akio advised.

Akio's Pod descended silently and hovered above and to the rear of the figure that moved furtively in the darkness.

Akio stepped out of the open door, his katana ready, and landed lightly behind the man.

"Do not move," Akio ordered.

The scent of Were hit him as he spoke. The man shifted, and a huge tiger stood in his place. The tiger snarled and twisted its body, razor-sharp claws extended, intent on tearing into Akio's torso.

The vampire took two running steps toward the brick wall and continued up it in an arc across the face of the wall that brought him behind the Were. Akio slashed his sword down, assisted by the momentum of his running body, and cleaved into the rear quarters of the cat above its hip joint.

The weretiger shrieked in pain as the katana sliced deep, severing muscles and tendons along the hip bone.

The tiger spun toward Akio, then crashed to the pavement as its leg gave out from the deep wound.

Akio brought the tip of his katana down, slicing through the muscles of its other back leg and temporarily immobilizing it. "Shift," he commanded.

The tiger snarled in defiance, its yellow eyes shining with hatred.

Akio took a half-step toward the cat, swinging his armored boot forward and shattering the bones in one wounded rear leg. "Shift now, or know what true agony is," he hissed.

The Were let out an agonized snarl as the shattered bones lacerated the damaged flesh more.

Akio thrust the tip of his katana into the tiger's shoulder and twisted the blade, ripping more muscle and sinew.

"Shift!"

The wounded cat slumped to the rough pavement, and seconds later, a bloody nude man lay in its place. His eyes glowed yellow as he glared at Akio, face twisted with pain and hate.

Akio looked into the feral yellow eyes. His own glowed red in the darkness. "What do you seek?"

"Your death," the man spat.

Akio read the Were's thoughts. What he saw in his mind made his blood boil.

"Not today," Akio snarled, his body blurring as his sword slashed down. When he stopped in front of the Were, blood dripped from his blade, spattering the body at his feet.

"Takumi, do you have drones out?" Akio asked as he flicked his wrist to clear the blood from his blade.

"Three. One at the attack site, one above your location, and the third patrolling an area west of my sensor zone."

"Why there?"

"It is an area where there are no cameras," Takumi stated.

Akio stepped into the Pod. "Takumi, are you in all the cameras around this area?"

"Affirmative, and any others in the city I wish to see."

"When did you hack the camera network?"

"I didn't. Abel did it when the Yakuza kidnapped Koda. He shared his access with me."

"Who authorized that?"

"Abel."

"I see," Akio replied, making another check on the list he carried in his mind.

"Asai. I'm on the roof now."

The roof access door swung open, and Asai bolted into the Pod. "How's Koda?"

"She will be fine. She's in the Pod-doc, and Eve assures me she will make a full recovery."

"Thank you. I know I've already been told, but seeing you while you said it helped."

The Pod door opened, startling Asai.

"We've arrived." Akio motioned her out of the Pod with a wave.

Sacred Clan Farm, Xianghongdian Reservoir, Sanhe, China

"Kenjii, what are you doing?" Abel called over the communicator.

"Leaving a message. Did the tigers show back up?"

"What message are you sending, and to whom?"

Kenjii wiped his hand in the dust, scrubbing blood off them as he looked over his handiwork. The four lay in a row in front of the barn. Each body had a head on its lap.

"I left a couple posed like this when they pursued me. It is my calling card to the Sacred Clan."

"That is not logical. Why do you feel the need to position the bodies? Isn't their death message enough?" Confusion laced Abel's tone.

"It's psychological. I want them to feel hunted like I did when they chased me."

"I will never understand people."

"Whatever. Did you locate the others?"

"Negative. They never exited the cave entrance."

Kenjii thought for a moment. "Abel, I want to know where they went. That could be a base for them."

"Akio ordered you not to take unnecessary risks. I deem that to be such a risk. We need to return to Tokyo. There has been an incident."

"What happened?"

"Weretigers attacked Horst and Koda, and she suffered a serious injury."

"Is she okay?"

"She is receiving treatment in the Pod-doc now. Eve advises she will survive."

Kenjii's eyes went red and his fangs extended. "They need to understand that injuring our people means theirs die."

"Horst eliminated the attackers."

"That's not what I meant," Kenjii growled as he started walking in the cave's direction.

"Kenjii, where are you going? We need to return."

"This will only take a few minutes. I want to know where those other four went."

"That is unacceptable, I demand you get in the Pod."

"Not happening," Kenjii snapped as he started running.

"Kenjii. Kenjii, *stop*!" Abel ordered as the Pod followed.

Kenjii stopped at the entrance to the cave and pulled the communicator from inside his armor. "I'm only looking. Keep quiet, they might hear you," he whispered before laying it on the ground at the cave's entrance.

CHAPTER FORTY-THREE

TQB Base, Tokyo, Japan.

Akio and Asai entered the dining room, and Asai went straight to Horst. "You're bleeding!"

Horst looked up, his eyes swollen and red from tears. "Asai, I almost killed her." He looked down and his shoulders slumped.

Asai wrapped her arms around him and pulled him tight against her. "Horst, she's alive because you saved her. Koda would have died if you hadn't stopped them."

"Asai, you don't understand. It was me. I'm the one who hurt her." He shrugged off the embrace and stood. He gripped the ends of the blanket Yuko had given him tight enough that the material strained.

Asai gazed at him, confusion on her face.

"Asai," Yuko called, "Horst shifted into an advanced form of wolf when the tigers attacked. His injuries were extensive, and he struggled to control the rage that comes with that form. Koda touched him while he was down, and his instinct was to defend himself."

Asai nodded her understanding.

"He fought off the rage and shifted back into a man. That is a level of control most shifters don't have when they shift to Pricolici the first few times. He saved her life twice tonight."

"Twice?"

"Koda will be different when she comes out of the Pod-doc. The damage was too much for her to survive the trip here on her own. Horst gave her his blood to keep her alive."

"He gave her a transfusion?"

Yuko twisted her head to the side and grimaced. "Not exactly. Weres and vampires can create others of their kind by exchanging blood. It also has healing properties if applied directly to wounds. I gave Horst a choice: either he could use his blood or I would have used mine."

Asai's eyes widened. "Does that mean Koda will turn into a wolf?"

"Among other things," Yuko agreed.

Asai was silent for a full minute as she processed the information, then she nodded once and went to where Horst stood. "Snap out of it, Horst. Koda knows you would never hurt her on purpose, and so do I. I know my cousin well enough to understand that she would choose life, no matter what it took, consequences be damned."

Horst refused to look at her. "I should have controlled the beast."

"You did! You didn't run wild through the streets. You didn't kill her. What more do you want? It is done, and she will survive."

"She's going to hate me."

"Hate you? Do you hate what you are? She sure doesn't. Koda knows what you are and loves you. Don't put your guilt on her. She deserves better," Asai yelled.

Horst turned away from her, his head hanging. Asai's face turned red and her nostrils flared. She reached out and caught Horst's arm. "Listen to yourself. Did you do it on purpose? Did you *want* to turn her into a wolf?"

Horst jerked away and glared at the small woman. His eyes flashed yellow and he growled, "You know damn good and well I wouldn't do that."

Asai stood her ground, eyes flashing. "I *do* know that. So why are you acting like it's your fault?"

Horst stood to his full height and opened his mouth to speak, then paused. Doubt clouded his features. "You don't blame me?"

"No, and neither will Koda."

Horst looked at Asai and saw that she fully believed what she had said. He moved to a chair and slowly lowered his frame into it, feeling a glimmer of hope for the first time since it happened.

Akio understood the doubt Horst felt. He had blamed himself for decades for Kenjii's death, and though he was happy to have him in his life, he felt responsible for his being a vampire too. Maybe there was hope for them both.

"Akio," Yuko called.

He looked up as she motioned toward the door. He followed her into the hall and waited until the door closed on Horst and Asai.

"*Hai*?"

"You found another Were at the Palace?"

"*Hai,* and more."

Yuko cocked her head to the side, waiting for him to continue.

"He was part of another team like the one that found Horst and Koda. I saw in his mind that there are more in Japan. He was searching for a way to enter the Palace to kill anyone inside. They have orders to kill everyone close to me."

"Do you know where they are?"

"There are six nearby and another larger group in the ruins around Miura."

"Should I contact Inspector Yonai?"

"*Hai*. You should contact the liaison as well. The Clan is making a stronghold in Miura and has a ship armed with some type of missiles. The military will need to be ready to contain the ones onshore, and the navy needs to know about the ship. Fortunately, the area is remote and mostly destroyed, and could be easily blockaded with enough men."

"Will the military be able to stop them?"

"They don't have to stop them, only contain any who run away."

"The biggest threat now is the six in the city. I need to deal with them first. Yonai needs to know because they are using an apartment close to the Palace. If any of the Tokyo police encounter them unprepared, they won't stand a chance."

"Do you need my help?" Yuko offered.

"No. I will deal with the ones in town first. You need to stay here to help with Koda. When I finish those in town I will return, and then we can decide on the others."

Yuko nodded, willing to fight but glad she didn't have to. "I'll make the calls. Are you going now?"

"As soon as I change into full armor," he answered grimly and headed toward his quarters.

Dabie Mountains, outside of Sanhe, China

The odor of big cats assaulted Kenjii's nostrils when he stepped into the dark entrance to the cave. A stack of partially burned torches sat a few feet inside, adding the odor of charred wood to the mix.

Kenjii listened intently, focused on the cave for any sign of the tigers he sought. He couldn't hear anything except the normal insects and other animals that lived nearby.

This looks like a pass through the mountain, judging by the torches. I should return to Tokyo, but this might lead to the Clan's base. If I can find where it comes out, it will be easier to locate them.

Kenjii continued to argue with himself, weighing the pros and cons of both scenarios. Reaching a decision, he lowered the visor on his helmet and activated the built-in night vision.

He silently made his way through the cave, stopping often to listen for signs of the Weres. The cave twisted and turned through the granite. Some places were wide enough for four men walking abreast and others so narrow his armor scraped on both sides.

He stopped after one particularly tight section and heard a faint sound. As he moved deeper, the sound became identifiable as rushing water. He rounded a curve and stopped when he encountered a river flowing through a cavern.

Kenjii surveyed the cavern, noting a narrow channel through the rock where the water whipped into a white froth as it flowed through. A narrow wet path snaked beside it and into the darkness.

Kenjii took a deep breath, squared his shoulders, and pressed on, determined to discover where the cave ended.

CHAPTER FORTY-FOUR

TQB Base, Tokyo, Japan

"*Domo,* Yonai-*san,* I'll tell him," Yuko said as Akio walked through the door of the command center.

Akio quirked one eyebrow and Yuko raised a hand, forestalling him from asking out loud.

"*Hai,* silver rounds will stop them, but they are inhumanly fast. Many of your people could suffer injury or death if you go after them. Akio has their location, and he'll deal with them. Your men would best serve by keeping innocents away. This could get ugly. I need to contact the government liaison as soon as we hang up. There is a larger group outside of town that will require the military to intervene."

Yuko paused as Yonai responded.

"One moment, please. Akio is here now. I am switching you to the speaker." Yuko activated the speaker and mic then nodded to Akio.

"Yonai-*san,* you have a question for me?"

"*Hai.* Akio-*san.* Where are the tigers?"

"They are using an apartment in the Lotus Towers as a base. There is a body behind the Palace like the ones you are dealing with now. I got that information, along with what Yuko is relaying to the liaison, from him before he died."

"I can have a squad of my people there in twenty minutes to back you."

"They are on the fifth floor, and there is little room to maneuver in there. With so many people in the surrounding apartments, the risk of hitting one of them is too high. If you could keep the area around it clear, that would help and put eyes around in case any try to escape. I suggest you deploy your men in groups of four to increase their likelihood of success."

"*Hai.* My men have practiced that formation regularly since Yuko-*san* explained it. I will meet you a half-block west of the building. There is nothing more for me to do here anyway."

Lotus Towers Apartments, Shinjuku City, Tokyo, Japan

Takumi, do you have anything? Akio asked as he climbed the stairs to the fifth floor. Four of Eve's drones of the new design followed him.

I can see two through a space in the blinds and make out more voices inside. Nothing more. Takumi was running drones around the building. After checking in with Abel and finding that Kenjii was still on a mission, he had directed Abel to support the younger vampire while Takumi assisted him.

I will be at the door in a moment. If any come out, take them down before they can harm anyone.

With these new drones, you need not engage. I can punch through the walls and kill them all before they know what hit them.

Akio paused on the landing at the door to the desired floor. Something in Takumi's tone when he coldly offered to kill the Clan members nudged the back of his mind. *Takumi, is something wrong?*

No, everything is as it was when you asked a few seconds ago.

I meant your offer to kill all of them with the drones.

It seems like the best option. Besides, these people are responsible for Koda's and Horst's injuries. The protection of Koda Rii was my responsibility, and I failed.

Akio thought for a few beats, almost telling Takumi it wasn't his fault, then deciding to mention it to Eve. He wasn't up to playing grief counselor to an entity intelligence just now.

Inspector Yonai and a group of ten officers were standing by one floor below. They were to get the residents in the nearby units to safety when Akio engaged the Weres.

Akio quietly approached the door. He heard voices inside, but as he drew closer, they went silent.

Takumi updated his report. *They know you're there. The two on the couch shifted, and two more in tiger form are inside the door.*

Akio smiled as he drew the Jean Dukes Special from his left holster. *Takumi, make a hole and send the video signal of the ones by the door to my HUD on my mark.*

One drone sped past him, then stopped and hovered at

head height in front of the door. Akio aimed in the direction he thought a tiger would be inside the door. *Mark.*

The armored drone punched through the door with a loud crack. A second later, Akio's HUD showed the inside of the apartment and a tiger crouched on either side of the door, ready to pounce on anyone who came through it.

The weapon in his hand barked, sending hypervelocity rounds through the sheetrock and into the skulls of the waiting tigers. The vampire crashed through the door before the two dead tiger's death throes had ceased.

One tiger in the center of the room recovered fast and leapt toward him. His Jean Dukes spat once, and the explosive dart blew the tiger's mangled corpse back to where it started.

A loud snarl followed by footsteps that shook the floor came from his left, and he turned to see a Pricolici bearing down on him. Akio sprang forward to give himself room to maneuver while firing the Jean Dukes from his hip, striking the second tiger near the couch in the throat. The round decapitated it, leaving the bleeding, headless corpse on top of the first.

Akio landed on his feet and turned to meet the Pricolici, which had moved faster than he expected. The monster slammed into him with the force of a truck. Akio relaxed his body and rolled with the blow, landing on his back and using his momentum to backflip and land on his feet.

The Pricolici sprang to its feet when it didn't encounter resistance from hitting Akio and glared at him with hate-filled yellow eyes. "Yoouuu wiilll diiieee noowww, leeeeech," it roared.

Akio smirked at the beast, his katana ready in one hand

and a Jean Dukes in the other. A motion to his left caught his attention, and a quick glance revealed a second Pricolici coming through a side door.

Dabie Mountains, Outside of Sanhe, China

Kenjii jogged along the wet ledge next to the raging underground river. The spray of water-soaked his armor and limited the range of his night vision. He slowed to a walk after his foot slipped and he barely avoided falling into the churning flow.

The path curved, and he came out into a cavern so large he couldn't see the top. The source of the river was a waterfall that poured out of a hole in the granite fifteen meters from the lake that had formed under it.

Kenjii stopped to admire the cavern, wishing he could use the lights built into his armor to study the colors that appeared as varying shades of gray through his visor. Stalactites of different heights hung down above him, showing that this cavern had been here for many years.

I should bring Akio here when the Clan is finished. He enjoys nature's beauty as much as I do.

Kenjii followed the trail through the cavern, and after it made a sharp turn, he found himself at the exit. Tree trunks blocked his sight two meters out, and a narrow path disappeared around the trunk of a tree over a meter thick.

He started down the path, senses alert for danger. The path had been worn smooth by the tread of countless feet over the years. Kenjii was considering turning back when a soft noise from the thick canopy above him made him pause. He strained his ears and heard a noise he couldn't identify nearby. He turned his head to one side and was stunned by a heavy blow that knocked him to the ground. He tried to focus on the cause when a heavy weight landed on top of him, followed by a sharp pain as something penetrated his armor and dug into the skin on his stomach.

Kenjii lifted his hands to shove the weight off and was shocked when he felt the muscular body and warm fur of a huge cat through the sensors installed in the palms of his gauntlets. He drew his right hand back and slammed his armored fist into the beast, eliciting a pained grunt. He repeated this several times, shattering ribs with each strike until he felt the weight slip off to one side. That allowed him to roll away from the tiger, whose breathing was harsh and shallow as it healed from the broken ribs that had punctured one lung.

Kenjii leapt to his feet, drawing his swords. A sharp pain radiated from his wound, and he could feel blood trickling inside his armor. The tiger struggled to its feet and let loose with a pained snarl. Kenjii took two running steps toward it, swinging a sword down as he did. When he planted his front foot, the sword continued down, cutting deep into the tiger's skull.

The cat dropped to the ground in a boneless pile. Kenjii twisted his sword free and turned toward the sound of many feet headed toward him. Another tiger burst through an opening in the trees, determined to take him down.

Kenjii twisted, ignoring the pain from his wound, and slashed the cat as it overshot his position. Before he could finish the injured tiger, another came out of the trees. This one moved slower and stalked just out of range of Kenjii's deadly steel.

The vampire was moving to intercept the latest threat when two more came out of the gloom. He watched the three tigers warily as they spread out in a crescent shape in front of him. The original cat he had cut joined the other three while Kenjii was assessing which one to kill first. His open position between the cave mouth and the trees was not defensible, so he took a slow step back, his eyes darting from one tiger to another as he inched toward the cave.

He felt he was near the entrance, a place narrow enough to allow only one tiger to confront him at a time. Then a hard blow hit him from the side and lifted his feet off the ground. He crashed headfirst into the rough stone around the cave mouth, and although his helmet protected his head, the hard landing dazed him. His eyes widened as three more tigers sprang toward him.

CHAPTER FORTY-FIVE

TQB Base, Tokyo, Japan

Eve moved around the Pod-doc, checking readings on different screens. Satisfied, she nodded to Yuko, Asai, and Horst, who stood impatiently at the door. "She's about to come out."

Horst stepped into the room, his eyes locked on the sleek capsule that contained everything he held dear in the world. Eve stepped in front of him with her hand up.

"Horst, give us a minute." She raised her other hand, in which she clutched a neatly folded white cloth. "Let her get her bearings and get dressed first. Coming out for the first time is disorienting for some people."

Horst's face clouded and he opened his mouth to argue, but Yuko placed a comforting hand on his shoulder and pulled him back into the hall.

"Give her the time. She will appreciate it," Yuko assured him.

The door slid closed and Horst slumped against the wall, his hands clenching and unclenching while he waited.

Asai caught his hands in hers and squeezed them gently. “She’s alive. We’ll deal with everything else as it comes.”

Horst nodded but didn’t pull away from her. “Thank you, Asai. You have given me hope, even though I don’t feel I deserve it.”

Asai shook her head and looked at him with sorrow in her eyes. “Stop beating yourself up over this. Koda will understand; you’ll see.”

Koda slowly came awake. Her memory was fuzzy as she opened her eyes to a room she vaguely recognized. “What… where am I?” she whispered.

“There was an attack on you and Horst, and you sustained injuries. You’re in the Pod-doc, you’ve healed, and it’s time to come out,” Eve’s voice announced from above.

Koda’s memories rushed back. “Horst!” she exclaimed as she struggled to sit up.

“Calm down, Koda. The unit needs to be unlocked. Do you remember how to do it?”

Koda stopped fighting the surface that blocked her, took a calming breath, and reached down to the release. The top of the Pod-doc opened, revealing a smiling Eve holding a white robe in her hand.

“Welcome back.”

“Horst? Where is he? They hurt him!”

“He’s waiting for you. You need to go slow until you get used to things,” Eve warned.

Koda sat up and swung her legs over the side of the

Pod-doc, then put her hands on the edge and pushed off. She let out a squawk when instead of sliding two centimeters and dropping her feet to the floor, she shot a meter across the room and slammed into a wall.

"What's going on? Is she okay?" Horst called worriedly through the closed door.

"Everything's fine. She's getting her legs under her now," Eve answered.

Koda looked at the wall and back at the Pod-doc. "Eve, what the hell just happened?"

Eve handed her the robe and motioned for her to put it on. "The condensed version is you almost died. We had to take extreme measures to save you, and those measures come with changes. You're fine. If anything, you're better than fine. Now get dressed before that man of yours breaks down the door."

Koda took the robe and put an arm through the opening. When she pulled it around her body to put her other arm through, a ripping noise came from the garment.

"Careful," Eve cautioned.

Koda's eyes widened in shock. "Eve, what's happening?"

"I told you, move carefully. You're stronger than before. You need to get used to the changes is all."

Koda slowly pulled the robe closed and tied it in the front. Satisfied that it would remain closed, she slowly walked the short distance to the door. Horst was the first person she saw when it slid open. Koda forgot everything and lurched into him, wrapping her arms around him as their bodies crashed together.

"*Oof!* Careful, my tiny beauty." Horst grunted as her small body shoved him back three staggering steps.

She released him enough to lean back and look him over from head to toe. Yuko had convinced him to swap the blood-covered blanket for a pair of too-tight sweats. His upper body was bare and still covered in dried blood.

"Horst, you were on the ground, not moving. Where are you injured?" Koda wailed as she took in his bloodied form.

"I healed, and I'm fine. How do *you* feel?" His eyes darted over her worriedly, looking for any sign of the damage he had done.

"I feel…different," Koda told him after a pause. "I'm uncertain what it is, but my body doesn't move as it used to, and everything is so loud."

Horst's face fell. He looked away and took a deep breath. Steeling himself for whatever followed, he told her. "I hurt you badly. You were dying when Akio and Yuko arrived. I-I had to do something to save your life. I'm so sorry, my love!" he wailed as he released her from his light embrace.

Koda looked at him askance, not remembering anything after she had seen him unmoving on the ground after the fight. "Horst, what's wrong? We survived."

Horst looked up from the floor, tears running down his face. "Koda, I-I had to make you like…" He paused and took a breath. "Like me."

Confusion showed in Koda's eyes as she watched the strongest man she had ever known crumble. She opened her mouth and closed it several times, not knowing what to say.

Asai stepped up to her. "Koda, what he is trying to tell you is, in order to save you, he had to give you his blood.

The Pod-doc changed you to save your life. You are a Were now, and this big oaf is convinced you will hate him."

Koda's eyes went from Asai to Horst and back again. Understanding replaced confusion when Asai's words sank in.

The new Were reached up and put her finger under Horst's chin, pushing until he looked her in the eye. "Horst, I love you more than life. I could never be angry at you for doing what you had to so we could stay together."

"But it's my fault."

Koda moved her finger to his lips and pressed, silencing him. "It's the Sacred Clan's fault. They hunted us and attacked you. Everything after that is on them."

"Horst," Yuko interrupted, "Koda needs to eat to fuel her nanocytes, and you need to get into the Pod-doc."

"I'm fine," Horst argued.

Koda gave him side-eye and shook her head. "No, you're not. Yuko says you need to go in the Pod-doc, and I'm starving. We will continue this when the Pod-doc has fixed whatever is wrong."

"But…"

"No, inside. Now," Koda ordered, her tone leaving no room for argument.

Horst sighed, knowing he'd lost the argument, and trudged through the open door to where Eve waited.

CHAPTER FORTY-SIX

Lotus Towers Apartments, Shinjuku City, Tokyo, Japan

Akio snap-fired a round from his Jean Dukes Special at the tiger that had knocked him down. The Pricolici jinked to the side, so the round dug a divot out of its bicep and went through the wall behind it.

The second Pricolici snarled as it swiped an enormous claw-tipped paw at his back. The claws hit the hard armor across the vampire's back, shoving him forward a stumbling step, then he planted his front foot and pivoted. His katana whistled through the air at shoulder height, catching the Were's outstretched paw and slicing through two toes.

The Pricolici jerked its injured paw back and snarled. Its yellow eyes narrowed, and it launched itself across the scant distance separating them. Akio tried to bring his Jean Dukes to bear, but the cat was on him too fast. It slammed the injured paw against Akio's gun hand and sent the Jean Dukes Special spinning across the room.

The tiger followed up with a lightning-fast swipe of its

other paw, aimed for Akio's head. He dropped to his knees to avoid the full force of the blow, but a black claw grazed the top of his helmet with enough force to push his head to the side. Akio swung his sword in an arc, and the sharp blade sliced the muscles in the tiger's thigh to the bone. Akio followed up with a backstroke that took the other leg in the same place. He jumped to his feet and sidestepped, turning his body to where he could see both monster tigers.

The one he'd shot was on him as soon as he turned. The beast tackled him to the floor, and its heavy body pinned his sword between their bodies. The tiger's mouth gaped wide, and Akio winced when the teeth closed on his visor.

The vampire wrenched one trapped hand from between their bodies and brought his gauntleted fist down repeatedly on the tiger's ribs. The beast grunted with each blow but did not release him, then the Were brought its hands down and compressed his armored sides. Akio tried to reach the tanto sheathed on his belt, but the angle was wrong. The pressure on his sides continued to increase, and the armor dug into him as the claws penetrated the outer layer. Akio twisted and turned, attempting to break free, to no avail. He pulled back his free hand, extended his fingers, and drove them rapid-fire into the Pricolici's side.

A loud snarl from behind alerted him that the other cat was still in the fight just as Akio's fingers slid between the ribs of the Were that was savaging him. He shoved hard, his teeth clenched and his lips twisted in a silent snarl, and his hand went past the ribs and into the cat's chest cavity.

The Were went wild, thrashing and clawing at Akio's body as the vampire's hand pushed deeper. Akio felt the rapidly beating heart through his gauntlet and wrapped his fingers around the organ.

The tiger redoubled its efforts to pull away, bouncing on Akio and driving him into the floor. The vampire's face was feral as he caressed the Pricolici's beating heart once with his palm, then clenched his fist, splitting the heart into multiple pieces.

The Were's eyes went wide in shock and its expression froze as the fire went out in its eyes and it ceased to struggle.

A volley of gunshots rang out from the doorway, and a heavy thump shook the floor as the other Pricolici went down under the steady barrage. Akio shoved the dead cat to the side and rolled to his feet.

In the doorway, Inspector Yonai and three officers from his Special Investigations Unit stared over the sights of their weapons as the Pricolici pushed itself to its knees, blood pouring from multiple wounds.

Yonai tensed his finger on the trigger, sending a stream of full-auto rounds into the tiger's head until it was nothing but a mangled mass of blood and fur. The beast slumped to the floor and was still.

The inspector and his men swept into the room, each covering his sector with steely determination. Once satisfied that they had eliminated the threat, Yonai raised his weapon and nodded to Akio. "Looked like you could use a hand," was all he said.

Akio nodded and went to retrieve his gun.

"*Domo,* inspector. They were becoming annoying."

. . .

Dabie Mountains, Outside of Sanhe, China

The Pricolici grabbed Kenjii by the throat and lifted him, and he kicked out with an armored boot, catching the Were on his leg. The cat snarled and slammed Kenjii into the side of the mountain. Once, twice, three times, Kenjii's body struck the unyielding stone.

Pain wracked his body from the force of the blows. The tiger snarled in his face and savagely slammed him into the mountainside once more, and Kenjii's eyes rolled back in his head as everything faded to black.

"Kenjii," Abel called over the communicator.

"Kenjii, come in."

"Kenjii, we need to leave. Answer me."

"Kenjii, are you there?"

Abel brought the Pod as far as he could into the narrow valley. The thick growth of tall pine trees and rock ledges prevented him from descending to the mouth of the cave.

"Kenjii, do you copy?"

Abel circled the Pod over the area several times. Kenjii's communicator showed he was twenty meters below the tops of the trees. After several more attempts to contact him, the EI redirected a drone and sent it to the area. It hovered over the location where Kenjii's communicator showed him without spotting him. Abel summoned drones that were spread throughout towns and villages in the area to search for him. That task completed, Abel took the Pod one kilometer above Kenjii's last known location.

Akio.

Hai.

I have lost contact with Kenjii.

CHAPTER FORTY-SEVEN

Serenity Temple, Dabie Mountains, China

"Master Kun?"

Peng Kun looked up, his lips curled into a snarl at the interruption of his meditation. He'd been fantasizing about the defeated look Akio would wear when everyone he knew was dead. Kun pictured himself listing the gruesome details of how each of them had died while Akio was on his knees before him.

"What is it?" he snapped.

"A runner has come from the western entrance to the temple. He claims the guards have captured a Forsaken."

Kun jumped to his feet with a maniacal gleam in his eyes. "Where is it? Which one?"

"The guards are taking him to the dungeons. He is subdued but not badly injured. The guard captain ordered them to restrain him and place him in one of the reinforced cells."

Kun shouldered the man out of the way when he rushed through the door. "I will see this in person."

The two made their way down several levels, the Master's long strides making the acolyte jog to keep up. When he entered the dungeons, he saw the captain of the guard and five of his men standing over a prostrate form on the floor.

"What do you have?" Kun demanded.

The guards stiffened at the sound of his voice, unsure whether to prostrate themselves as he now demanded all do in his presence or keep watch over the dangerous vampire.

The captain motioned for them to keep watch and turned to Kun. "The guards at the western entrance caught this leech coming out of the tunnel. Zhie Chang shifted to human form and beat him unconscious while the others pinned him." He nodded to Chang.

Kun elbowed through the men ringing the vampire. The guards had stripped him to his smallclothes and wrapped him in layers of heavy chain. They could restrain a Were in Pricolici form, so Kun knew they would hold the Forsaken.

Kun's lips curled into a smile, although his eyes were cold. "Welcome to Serenity Temple, leech. I'm sure I will enjoy your stay much more than you will."

Kenjii glared at him as he struggled against the heavy links that bound him. "Do you think I'm scared of a kitty cat?" he taunted.

Kun's smile turned into a grin that made him look like a madman. He leaned down and whispered, "This kitty has claws," as he swiped his hand across Kenjii's throat. The black eight-centimeter-long claw that emerged from his index finger sliced deep, and blood gushed out of the wound in spurts that splattered the filthy robe Kun wore.

The Master raised the claw to his lips and slowly licked the blood from it as he stared into Kenjii's eyes. "Hang him by his ankles and bleed him. Don't kill him. Weaken him to the point he can't resist. When Akio comes for him, I want to use his body for my footstool. All will see that no vampire can stand against the Sacred Clan. The Clan shall rise."

"The Clan rises," the guards responded as Kun left, his head high while visions of the pain he would cause Akio ran through his mind.

Lotus Towers Apartments, Shinjuku City, Tokyo, Japan

Akio stiffened at Abel's words. *What happened? Where are you?*

The four who left the farm went into a cave in the next valley. Kenjii wanted to pursue them, but I refused. He then requested that I return him to the farm to search for information while I attempted to locate the Weres. I have the Pod stationary above his communicator, but I can't get it close enough for a visual. Nothing shows on the sensors.

I'll be there soon. Is the Pod equipped with pucks?

There is a basic loadout onboard: five half-kilo, five one-kilo, and two two-kilo pucks.

"Inspector, I appreciate your timely intervention, but there is an issue that I need to address," Akio explained.

"Certainly, Akio-*sama.* My men and I will finish here. If we can be of any assistance, please call."

"*Domo,* Inspector. There is no indication that there are

more of these people in the area, but your people need to remain vigilant. We know of a larger group near Miura. The military is working to contain them on the peninsula."

"They have requested our assistance there. I sent half of my unit before I met you here."

Akio nodded. "Be safe, Inspector."

"You, too."

Abel, dispatch a Black Eagle to my location. Have it pick me up in front of the building.

A Black Eagle is landing now.

Akio pursed his lips before inquiring, *Abel, how did you know I would request a Black Eagle?*

I didn't. I diverted the one I had activated to assist me in my search for Kenjii.

What's the loadout on it?

Full. The area here is mountainous, so I anticipated the need to move some rock.

Very good.

The Black Eagle waited as he exited the building. As he boarded and it launched into the sky, the sun was peeking over the horizon.

Yuko.

Hai, *Akio?*

Kenjii is missing. I'm going to China to look for him. I need you to work with the military in Miura until I get back.

As soon as Horst is out of the Pod-doc, I will take them back to the Palace and go to Miura.

How much longer?

Another five minutes.

Full armor, and take Eve with you. There are more tigers who can achieve the Pricolici form than I expected. I encountered two in the apartment, and one of them almost dodged a shot from my Jean Dukes. He was wounded but not out of the fight.

Are you injured?

No. It was close, but your inspector and his men took one of them down.

I'll thank him when I see him. Be careful, this could be a trap.

If it is, they'll wish they'd never set it when I'm done.

Hybrid Vessel *Lylia*, Miura, Japan

"Cui, are you certain you want to be on this thing when the weapons fire?" Li Song looked askance at the three tubes bolted to the ship's deck.

"I'm certain I don't, but I don't want to face Kun if this doesn't work. With me on the ship, he can't accuse me of failing because I wasn't here."

Li opened his mouth for a return quip when the satellite phone in his pocket rang. "Master?"

"Who else would it be?" Peng Kun chuckled.

Li's eyes widened in surprise at the jovial tone in Kun's voice. "Is everything okay, Master?"

"Everything is better than okay. I have the leech Cui chased across China. He is now in the dungeon receiving instruction."

"That's excellent news, Master. Well done."

"How are your operations against Akio proceeding?"

"Wu and Jin haven't reported yet."

"Notify me when they do. I have a plan to bring Akio to his knees before we kill him."

"I'll contact you as soon as they check in," Li assured him.

"Has Cui departed yet?"

"I'm with him now. He's leaving within the half-hour."

"Excellent. This is all working out as I planned," Kun stated as he cut the connection.

"What was that about?" Cui asked from the gangway of the ship.

"They caught the Forsaken you were after in China. Kun has him in the dungeons."

Cui grinned. "Receiving instruction, I hope."

"Some lessons are harder to survive than others. I don't envy him."

"Better him than us. Do you have the defenses set up? I'm certain our presence here won't be a secret for long. You need to be prepared for Akio and his people."

"The listening post and roving patrols are out. We're as ready as we can be with the limited numbers we have."

"When this mission is done, I'm sure Kun will order the ship to pick up more warriors for us here."

"Probably. Try not to get blown up when they fire those antiques."

"Wasn't planning on it. See you in a few hours." Cui waved as he boarded *Lylia.*

CHAPTER FORTY-EIGHT

Dabie Mountains, Outside of Sanhe, China

The Black Eagle slowed as it approached the peaks, which were glowing in the morning sun, while the valleys remained shrouded in twilight. Akio brought the craft down, hovering above the tops of the tall pines that stood like silent sentinels above the cave and Kenjii's communicator signal.

Abel, you have the Black Eagle, he announced as he opened the canopy and stepped out. He fell two meters, crashing feet first through the weak top limbs of a tree before he hit stronger limbs that slowed his descent. Once he was deep enough in the tree, he caught a thick branch and halted his controlled fall.

The base of the tree was bare for the last three meters, and he dropped to the ground. His armored boots left deep imprints in the soft ground and pine needles near the entrance to the cave. He looked around, expecting to see Kenjii injured or dead, but there was no sign of him. He stepped into the entrance, his senses extended for threats.

"Kenjii?"

Akio's head snapped around when he heard his own voice. He bent down and retrieved Kenjii's communicator from the cave entrance. It wasn't damaged, and the immediate area showed no sign that a fight had taken place.

Abel, I found his communicator. It looks like he took it off and went inside the cave.

Copy. Do you have any instructions for me?

Take the Black Eagle up and monitor my progress. I'm going in.

I have a drone carrier with fifty drones inbound. It will be here in eighteen-point-three minutes. If you wait, I can send the drones through and find him.

No, if he's in trouble, that could be too long.

Understood. I will stand by for instructions.

Akio cautiously stepped into the inky blackness of the cave, activating night vision and infrared on his armor when he closed the visor. With a Jean Dukes Special in each hand, he set out to bring Kenjii home.

Japanese Defense Force Field HQ, Near Miura, Japan

"General Kato, advise your troops we have friendlies inbound. They are not to fire on the two aircraft, and whatever they do, don't piss off the people inside," Commissioner-General Watabe advised his army counterpart.

General Kato relayed the orders, and seconds later, a boxy black object descended out of the early morning sky. A sleek and deadly-looking craft followed, and both stopped centimeters above the ground.

Are you ready for this, Yuko?

I have no choice, Eve. Akio is searching for Kenjii, and this can't wait. I will do what I must.

The Pod opened, and Yuko stepped through the hatch. Her flat black Jean Dukes armor caused a Japanese Defense Force soldier standing guard to whistle softly. Her weapons made him take an unconscious step back.

"Yuko-*san*. Eve-*san*," Commissioner-General Watabe greeted them warmly.

"Watabe-*san*. It's good to see you're well." Yuko smiled.

"This is General Kato of the Defense Force. General, Yuko. I suggest you listen to anything she tells you." Watabe nodded to each.

"Thank you for coming, Yuko-*san*. The Prime Minister spoke to me personally and told me to defer to your direction to handle this invasion."

"Do you have the area contained?"

"*Hai*. I have one thousand troops, along with one hundred of Commissioner-General Watabe's Special Investigations Team officers. They're deployed in four-man teams, as Watabe-*san* instructed, across a little over two kilometers. Each team is in direct line of sight with at least three more."

"The Special Investigations officers have followed the training Inspector Yonai set up to deal with this kind of threat. They're directing the military teams," Watabe volunteered.

"Good. I suggest you keep your troops in that formation. They will act as a blocking force for any who run," Yuko suggested.

"Run from what?" Kato asked.

"Me."

General Kato gave Yuko side-eye. "If I might ask, why would they run from you? I mean no disrespect, but you're a woman, and you don't look like a warrior."

Watabe's eyes widened in shock. He had seen firsthand what Akio was capable of, and Yonai had told him Yuko was just as deadly.

Eve chuckled. "Pay up. I called it."

Yuko rolled her eyes. "I know. My fault for accepting the bet."

"Show him?" The AI shrugged.

Watabe closed his mouth before he chastised the army man. He took a step back and moved behind the general.

"Looks are deceiving, General," Yuko said and looked at the ground. When she looked up at him, her eyes glowed bright red and fangs extended past her lower lip. Her voice was a feral growl. "I assure you, they will run."

Kato's eyes went round in fright, but to his credit, he didn't faint as Watabe expected. His legs only buckled from the shock. Watabe reached out and steadied the general until he got his knees under control.

"*Banpaia*!" he croaked.

"Calm yourself, Kato. This woman and her companions have done more for the people of Japan than you will ever have clearance to know. That is why the Prime Minister put her in charge of this operation. The Bitch Protocol is in effect."

"Bitch Protocol. I knew about Akio. Senior leadership briefed all command-level officers about how he dealt with the tiger men earlier this year. My apologies, Yuko-*sama*. I was unaware."

Yuko allowed her fangs to retract and her eyes to fade back to their normal dark brown. "My apologies for startling you. We don't have the luxury of wasting time."

"How do you wish to proceed?"

Eve stepped forward and grinned. "I'm going to puck 'em up."

"Excuse me? What was that?" Kato asked, his brow wrinkled in confusion. "What are you?"

Yuko shook her head and cast a sideways glance at Eve. "Eve is an artificial intelligence housed in an android body. She scanned the area the invaders occupy on our way in, and there are no civilians left. We have weapons that will eliminate most of the invaders without risk to your people or us."

Kato nodded and motioned for her to continue.

"When we begin, your troops will need to hold the line. If one of these people get into a populated area, the casualties could number in the hundreds before they're stopped."

"How will we know when you start? We have remained here so as not to alert them."

"Oh, you'll know. When the explosions start, expect to see the enemy at any second." Eve chuckled.

"They are faster than any human you have ever seen. Your soldiers need to stay alert and engage as soon as they are in sight," Yuko advised.

"My people have briefed their teams, and they're as ready as they can be," Watabe assured them.

"Looks like I'm up. Let's get this party started." Eve rubbed her hands together and grinned.

"I will observe from the Pod and try to head off any

who seek to flee." Yuko grimaced. "I wish these people would build instead of destroying. Such a waste."

"I'll notify our people to be ready." Kato nodded once and moved to the communications console in the corner.

Dabie Mountains, Outside of Sanhe, China

Akio, your signal is growing weak. You appear to be halfway through the mountain.

That is my estimate too. Still no sign of Kenjii or any Clan activity. This cave has seen a lot of use, though.

The drone carrier has arrived. Judging by the direction you are going, this cave might come out in the next valley over. I am deploying drones to recon it.

Advise me if you see anything.

Affirmative.

Akio was working his way through the twisting cave. Kenjii's scent was in the air, along with the heavy musk of the tigers who regularly used it. With each step he took, more dread invaded his mind. He fought an internal struggle to speed up, sacrificing stealth for speed, but he knew that getting himself injured would help no one. Still, the battle raged with each step he took without locating Kenjii.

He followed the cave, senses and sensors hunting threats. When he rounded a turn, he saw the faint glow of daylight ahead.

Abel, I think I am coming to an exit.

Your signal is stronger. Stand by, and I will send a drone to scout around your location.

Seconds later, Abel called. *There are six men around the exit. They appear to be guards.*

Send me a map of the area with their positions marked.

Transmitting.

A pop-up window in Akio's visor notified him he had received a live feed. He accessed it and scanned the overhead view of a tree-covered mountainside. A flashing green oval marked the cave entrance, and six red dots indicated the guards. Two were close to the opening, and the other four were clustered a short distance away.

What are they doing, Abel?

Two seem to be actively looking for threats, and the other four are sitting around a table. They appear to be playing a game with cards.

Akio drew his katana from the sheath on his back and moved forward. He was cautious about where he placed his feet, not wanting to alert the Weres.

Akio, they know you're there.

He consulted the map, which showed the four who were clustered together joining the other two near the cave mouth. They shifted, and four tigers fanned out in a line across the cave entrance.

Akio took two quick steps and disappeared in a blur before he entered the dim light. The two weretigers directly in front of the cave mouth died where they stood. The vampire rushed between them in a swirl of dust, his katana flicking to either side of him and slicing their throats.

The others reacted immediately when their companions collapsed to the ground. The two in human form shifted, and four snarling tigers faced Akio when he stopped.

Akio leapt to his right and took down the tiger on the far end of the line. Its head tumbled to the ground while the body stood gushing blood for a few beats before it collapsed. A loud snarl came from one tiger, and Akio heard another some distance behind him.

Akio, you're about to have more Weres. Drones detect more coming from an opening in the mountain across the valley.

Akio pulled his Jean Dukes Special from his side and rapid-fired three rounds. Each round hit one tiger, and all three were dead before the spray of blood from the first hit the ground.

Pick me up, Abel.

A Pod dropped from the sky, and Akio jumped through the open door as eight tigers burst out of the trees into the open space before the cave. The craft shot into the sky, leaving the tigers milling about and snarling as it hovered fifty meters above them.

Do you have a drone feed showing where those came from?

I am seeding the area now. It is a massive complex carved out of the mountain. My drones are inside now, and it's a warren of corridors and small rooms.

Any sign of Kenjii?

Not yet. I have counted forty-six Weres inside and another twenty-seven in the valley beneath you. I have also located the front of the complex. You found the back door. This complex is an old Buddhist monastery. My records show the government destroyed this place during the previous century. There is no other information available.

. . .

Serenity Temple Dungeons, Dabie Mountains, China

Kenjii had been hung by his ankles in the damp cell. Two Weres in human form stood guard outside the door, and two more stood inside with him. The two inside held a special place in Kenjii's mind—a place where they died slowly as he broke each bone in their bodies, then let them heal and did it again.

The wound where Peng Kun sliced him had closed in minutes, a testament to the nanocytes Heinz had given him. The two Weres had made a game of letting it heal, then slowly cutting it open so it would bleed again.

The blood loss was accomplishing two things. First, it weakened him to the point where he could no longer struggle when they cut him. Second, he was insane with thirst as his nanocytes fed on his body's reserves to heal the damage. He distracted himself from the predicament by visualizing how much pain he would cause when he killed them.

The bleeding from the last cut had stopped, and one of the Weres was coming back with the knife when the door slammed open.

"Get him down. Master Kun commands that you bring him to the main entrance."

The Were by the door caught his eye and grinned evilly at him when he released the rope that ran from the hook to Kenjii's ankles.

Slow and painful, Kenjii thought as the floor rushed up to meet his face.

CHAPTER FORTY-NINE

Miura, Japan

Eve piloted the Black Eagle into the sky while Yuko stood braced in the Pod door looking out. Both craft crossed the short distance over the ruins of Miura. In seconds, they were on station a kilometer above the camp the Sacred Clan had built.

The Black Eagle's HUD showed heat signatures clustered inside a partially destroyed multi-story building. The top was jagged where some disaster had ripped it off like the cap off a bottle. The bottom three floors were a maze of trash and steel beams. Thirty heat sources on the fourth floor shone brightly on the HUD.

Fire in the hole, Eve called over her chip as a small black object shot out of the Black Eagle and slammed into the side of the building. The small amount of intact glass remaining shattered outward from three sides of the building, followed by steel and plaster when the puck blasted through.

The cloud of dust and debris cleared, and the sensors

showed no heat sources visible in the collapsed pile of rubble where the building had once stood.

Yuko caught a flash of movement from below and descended until the Pod leveled out at thirty meters. That allowed her to observe a wide area and keep the craft above the shattered buildings and debris piles. Two weretigers ran around a heap of rubble and stopped when they saw the destroyed building. Yuko pulled her Jean Dukes Specials and aimed them simultaneously, and the hypervelocity rounds struck one tiger in the chest and the other through its forehead. Both dropped to the ground as Yuko guided the Pod to an area where she had seen movement.

Eve spun the Black Eagle in place and fired another puck into a group of five, two in human form and the others sleek tigers. Their orange and black fur stood out against the drab wreckage like a beacon.

The puck hit in the center of the group and turned them all into a thick spray of blood and flesh that coated the surrounding area. Eve cocked her head, her lips quirked up on one side as she admired the damage.

Better speed it up, Yuko. I'm winning by a factor of a whole bunch.

It's not a competition, Eve. I would prefer we killed no one, Yuko answered, emotion lacing her words.

If there was any other path, we would take it.

Hai. Yuko shot another Were below her.

<u>Hybrid Vessel *Lylia*, Tokyo Harbor, Tokyo, Japan</u>

"We'll be in position in fifteen minutes, sir." Captain Lee roused Cui from a light slumber at the navigator's station.

Cui nodded and wiped his hand across his face before he called to the weapons crew standing by on the deck, "Prepare the weapons."

The crew chief motioned to the covered weapons. Two crewmen pulled the heavy canvas covers away and exposed the three launch tubes. The others removed covers from the rear of each tube and hooked a chain attached to a manual crane to one. In a few minutes, they had locked the first into position and moved to the next.

Ten minutes later, the missiles were all in position. The crew chief walked around each tube, checking its stability. Once satisfied, he hooked wires to junction boxes on each and pulled the loose ends into the cabin. Then he plugged the ends into a controller mounted on a panel beside Cui's seat. From this vantage point, he could see the missiles when he launched each one and direct the crew to any problems.

"Stand by to launch," Cui commanded.

Serenity Temple, Dabie Mountains, China

"Where are they?" Peng Kun screamed as he paced in front of the three-meter-high, ornately carved doors at the front of the temple. His filthy stained robes whipped violently each time he turned.

"They're on the way, Master," an acolyte carrying Kun's ornate chair out of the grand hall answered. Once he had placed it where Kun ordered, he meticulously wiped every inch down with a soft cloth.

Kun nodded once and sat. He put an elbow on the arm of the chair and his chin in his hand, then practiced looking bored. *Those leeches die today. I will end them both here for the glory of the Clan, but first, I will force Akio to see his precious partner debased as I use him for my footstool.*

Heavy footsteps shook Kun from his reverie. He pointed to a space in front of his chair, and the guards dropped Kenjii's pallid chain-wrapped form face-down on the rough stone.

"Hello, leech. Glad you could join me." Kun gloated as he rested his slipper-covered feet on Kenjii's back. "Your savior will be here soon. Don't get too excited. Both of you will die today."

Kenjii didn't respond. The blood loss had sapped him to the point where his remaining nanocytes were barely keeping him alive.

Akio, I have located Kenjii.

The Pod moved without warning. Akio had to grab the frame of the open door to keep his balance. It circled the mountain, and when it came around the other side, Akio's blood ran cold. The ledge that extended from two doors halfway up the mountain teemed with enemies. A man sat on a throne-like chair in front of twenty men armed with swords and spears.

What chilled him was the unmoving body at the man's feet. He could tell Kenjii was seriously injured. Fresh blood matted his hair, and his skin was pale and drawn. Akio stiffened as rage overcame him.

"Take me to the ledge and hover above it with the door facing toward Kenjii." He didn't bother using his implant, knowing Abel would hear him over the comm system in the Pod.

"Affirmative."

Miura, Japan

Yuko fired at a running figure. The round hit it between the shoulder blades and slammed it face-first into the dirt. She had just turned toward another when gunshots rang out from the blocking force.

Eve, are you close to where the military and police have engaged?

Negative. I'm after a group of six headed for the old harbor.

A deep boom echoed across the ruins from the direction Eve had indicated.

Pucked 'em. No survivors. Do you need me to check the line?

Please. Yuko fired twice, and two more weretigers went down.

The Black Eagle screamed past. The canopy was open, and Eve stood in the seat with her short blast rifle against her shoulder. She fired and laughed when the recoil almost knocked her out of the craft. An explosion below marked the demise of another member of the Sacred Clan.

I need to mount two of these on this thing. This is like shooting fish in a barrel, but I don't think I could ever live down being knocked out of the Black Eagle by my gun.

Can't you turn it down?

Eve fired again, and her body slammed into the cockpit opening and shook the craft.

Sure, but where's the fun in that?

Yuko rolled her eyes, then spotted a man running across an open space between two gutted office complexes. She raised her gun to fire but stopped before her finger tightened on the trigger. A second glance confirmed what she had seen—the man was using a phone. Since he wasn't part of their forces and there were no civilians in the area, that was bad news.

Eve, I see one of them using a communications device. I'm going after him.

On your six. The police and soldiers have things in hand.

Yuko guided the Pod across the field of battered buildings and debris piles. When she popped up over a gutted oil tanker, she saw him duck into a narrow opening between two demolished buildings.

Yuko brought the Pod down behind a pile of rubble and stepped out in pursuit of her quarry.

"Cui, we're under attack. They have aircraft and are bombing our position," Li yelled into the satellite phone as he fled the carnage.

"We're in position now, and the missiles are ready to fire."

"Fire them! If they have something else to deal with, I might be able to save some warriors. If this keeps up, we're all going to die."

"Hold on. I'll do what I can."

. . .

Serenity Temple, Dabie Mountains, China

Peng Kun grinned maniacally when he saw Akio standing in the door of the TQB Pod. He had seen pictures and heard what few details his contacts in the People's Army had, but he had never seen one up close.

I'll take that when he dies. With an aircraft, I will be unstoppable.

Kun thumped his heel on Kenjii's back and pointed to the line of sunlight that was chasing the shadow from the stone. "The sun comes, so you must decide soon. Will you risk burning to save this piece of offal?"

Akio glared across the open space, his face a mask of rage. Kun grinned and raised his feet, then slammed them into Kenjii's back again. The Weres in human form laughed, while several tigers milled between them.

"What will it be? Will you watch him burn or save him? Decide soon. You're almost out of time." Kun cackled like a madman as he pointedly looked at the sunlight less than a meter from Kenjii's bound and battered body.

Pull the Pod back when I exit. Kenjii's injured, and the sun is almost on him. When I have him, pick me up.

Copy. Pucks ready.

When we're clear, fire at will.

Akio's eyes glowed bright red as he leapt across the void and landed in the puddle of sunlight in front of Kun. Four weretigers jumped between them and snarled at him.

Peng Kun stared, his face a mask of confusion as Akio stood in the morning sunlight unharmed.

Akio smirked at Kun as he drew a Jean Dukes Special from his hip and fired four fast shots. The four tigers between them dropped where they stood as the hypervelocity rounds tore through their bodies.

Kun surged to his feet and straddled Kenjii's prostrate body. His eyes glowed yellow as he shifted into a three-meter-tall Pricolici tiger. The beast snarled defiantly at Akio, with the other Weres joining in.

Akio drew the katana over his shoulder with one hand while he fired round after round from his Jean Dukes Special into the mass of Weres behind Kun. Then he turned on the fear. Kun faltered and went to his knees. The surviving Weres behind him froze, some held in place by the terror that gripped them, others emptying the contents of their stomachs onto the stone ledge.

Akio holstered his gun and darted around Kun to retrieve Kenjii's unmoving form. Either he or Abel would eliminate the monster once Kenjii was in the Pod. As he leaned down to scoop up the critically-wounded vampire, an enormous claw-tipped hand came down on Kenjii's back.

Kenjii stiffened as four dagger-length talons stabbed deep into him. He was too weak to do more.

Akio screamed in outrage, spun on the balls of his feet, and brought the blade around in a two-handed swing. The sharp blade severed Kun's hand at the wrist before he could rip out Kenjii's heart.

Peng Kun recoiled from the pain, and the stump of his wrist pulsed blood as he rolled away from his attacker. Akio countered every move and sliced the Pricolici's good arm to the bone as he clutched his bloody wrist. Then Akio let loose. His body was a blur, and his katana moved continuously. Blood misted the air as wounds appeared all over Kun's huge body like magic.

Kun's eyes were wild as he tried to flee the vicious attack. He flailed his wounded arms like a windmill in a tornado as he tried to block Akio's blade while moving backward across the ledge.

Akio drove him back toward the edge one cut at a time, no thought in his mind but to destroy the retreating Were. A deep slash to Kun's torso staggered him, and Akio pressed the attack, his sharp blade forcing Kun ever closer to the steep drop behind him.

When his heel slid over the edge, the big Were faltered and tried to change direction, but Akio's blade took him across one side of his neck, then the other. Kun dropped to his knees, his mouth open in shock and pain.

Akio stopped, appearing to materialize from thin air in front of the kneeling Were. His sword slammed deep into Kun's throat.

He took a half-step forward and planted his front foot, and with the other sent Peng Kun, self-appointed Grand Master of the Sacred Clan, plummeting to his death on the rough granite mountainside a hundred meters below.

Akio spun and had Kenjii cradled in his arms in an instant. The remaining Weres on the ledge were recovering from the fear Akio had projected and the devastation his Jean Dukes had wrought. Akio covered Kenjii as best he could with his body and took three running steps to the sheer drop-off. He pushed hard with his legs and was across the gap and inside the waiting Pod before the sun's rays or the recovering Weres could cause the younger vampire further harm. He laid his lover gently on the padded bench and looked down at the damage.

Kenjii's skin was gray. The blood loss had weakened him beyond his nanocytes' ability to heal, and the claws still lodged in his back had turned a dangerous situation critical. Akio hesitated a beat, unsure how the enhanced nanocytes in his blood would react with the ones Heinz had used to modify Kenjii. He didn't see another option, so he slashed his wrist with his fangs and dripped the blood into Kenjii's half-open mouth, but he didn't respond. Akio worked his throat in a furious attempt to make him swallow.

Hybrid Vessel *Lylia*, Tokyo Harbor, Tokyo, Japan

"Fire," Cui commanded.

The crew chief flipped a switch on the control panel, and the rocket motors ignited one after the other. Three smoking arrows were in the air, one behind the other, in nine seconds.

"Missiles away and tracking, sir.

Cui nodded to the captain, who was standing at the wheel. "Take us back to base."

TQB Base, Tokyo, Japan

Abel watched through his drones as Akio brought Kenjii into the Pod, then maneuvered the Pod away from the opening and slid the Black Eagle into its place.

A monitor program alerted him to inbound missiles and he activated the puck launchers on the roof of the building, prepared to destroy them in the air. His processors had a firing solution in milliseconds, and a warning popped up from the subroutine that controlled the launcher.

Targets over congested population area. Potential for loss of life high.

Abel ran a hundred thousand firing solutions in the blink of an eye, but all carried the same risk. There was no way he could destroy the missiles bearing down on him without killing innocent civilians.

Eve, assume operational control. I'm under attack.

The first three-meter-long penetrator missile hit the glass doors of the building and detonated when it hit the floor behind the entrance. The high-explosive warhead tore through the walls and into the elevator shaft that led down into the bowels of the base. Three seconds later, the second one hit and penetrated deeper. The third followed shortly after, and when it detonated, it had penetrated to the level that held the labs, Medical, and Abel's core.

CHAPTER FIFTY

Miura, Japan

Come on, Cui, fire the damn missiles. We're dying in droves here.

Li Song ran from the narrow passage between two piles of rubble, crossed an open area, and was diving into the rusted hulk of a bus when a shadow darkened the area in front of him. He had developed a healthy respect for the weapons carried on the aircraft that hunted his warriors. He'd missed being caught in the barracks explosion by less than a minute. Blood still trickled down one arm and his back from wounds caused by the jagged metal the blast concussion had hurled him into.

Li scanned the sky, and when he saw nothing, he crouched and ran to the next pile of debris. He panted as he wormed his way through the forest of jagged metal that stuck out from the heap at odd angles. Once through the obstructions, he came to an opening surrounded by the skeletal remains of multiple buildings.

He checked the sky again, noted it was clear, and leapt

into a full run, his legs pumping hard as he darted across the open space. He moved in an unpredictable pattern, hoping to throw off the craft's aim if it spotted him.

Yuko watched as the Were who had the phone sprinted toward the pile where she'd concealed the Pod. Her lips curled up in a smile when his efforts to avoid being shot from the air put him on a course that would bring him to her vantage point. She holstered her Jean Dukes Specials and pulled her katana from its sheath.

Li cut through two piles, convinced he'd avoided detection until an armored young woman holding a sword stepped into his path. He never slowed as he shifted and sprang at her.

Yuko sidestepped as three hundred kilos of snarling tiger hurtled through the air on a collision course with her. Her sword came down in a lightning-fast strike and opened a cut from mid-torso to hip on the cat.

Fire coursed through Li's body as the blade bit deep into his side and ripped through the muscles in his hip. He twisted in midair to escape the pain and slid until he crashed into a concrete slab several meters away.

Yuko cautiously approached the wounded Were, her sword poised to deliver an overhand blow if needed. The tiger lay on its side, one front leg twisted, with bare bones sticking out through the torn flesh. The cut on its side was already knitting closed, which showed her she was dealing with a powerful Were.

"I might allow you to live, provided you shift to human now," Yuko offered.

Li tried to stand, but the broken foreleg and the jagged debris under him prevented him from getting a stable platform. He shifted to human form and groaned as he straightened his arm, then hissed as the bones slid back under the skin. He held it close to his body as they set.

"Who were you talking to?" Yuko demanded.

Li stared at her in confusion. He had seen her before but assumed she was another human working at the arcade. That she had taken him down so easily showed she wasn't normal. He sniffed and smelled a hint of wolf, but the scent wasn't strong enough for her to be a Were. It was more like she'd been near one recently.

"What are you?" he snarled.

"Your death if you don't answer. Who were you talking to?"

Yuko, something is wrong. Abel passed operational control of Akio's Black Eagle and Pod to me, and he is offline.

Eve's call distracted Yuko, and she took her eyes off the Were for a second. When she looked up, a Pricolici tiger stared down at her, and a claw-tipped hand whistled through the air. Yuko jerked her head back as the nails passed in front of her face, so close she felt the disturbed air currents. She responded with a vicious downstroke of her katana, but the Were sidestepped and pressed the attack. Yuko jumped and landed on the concrete slab the Were had plowed into when he fell. She spread her feet and balanced on the unlevel surface.

Li continued to advance, his lips curled into the tiger version of a smirk. He threw back his head and roared, hoping to intimidate her into losing her balance on her precarious perch.

Yuko watched the beast approach, prowling forward one fluid step at a time as he stalked her. She removed one hand from her sword, and the cat paused, focusing on her with the eyes of an apex predator. Yuko smirked back at him, then drew the Jean Dukes Special from her side and fired one shot from the hip in a move faster than the eye could follow.

Li twisted when she moved. His eyes went wide with shock, and he snarled as the hypervelocity round cut a shallow furrow through the skin along his ribs. He dropped to all fours and Yuko's second shot went high, missing him completely.

Li sprang forward and slammed his mass into the debris under the slab where Yuko balanced, and she jumped to avoid falling when her perch shifted. A protruding piece of rebar caught her leg and flung her to the ground under the heavy block.

Yuko twisted furiously to the side to avoid being crushed by the falling concrete as it slid over her. When the debris came to rest, it pinned her right leg and arm firmly between the massive slab and the loose material on the ground.

Li stood and slowly made his way across the unstable pile while slipping and knocking pieces of building material onto Yuko's trapped body. He worked his way down to loom over her menacingly and savored the look in her eyes as she struggled unsuccessfully to free herself.

"Nowww youuu will diiieee," he growled as he pulled back his claw-tipped hand and held it above her.

Yuko stopped struggling and watched the Were through half-closed eyes, realizing she had once again foolishly rushed into an avoidable dilemma. "I should have shot you from the Pod."

Li lowered his arm and shrugged. It was an odd gesture from a three-meter-tall tiger.

Yuko snorted. Then her body shook.

Li cocked his head to one side, and the confused look made Yuko burst into hysterical laughter.

"Whhyyy arre yoouu laughinnnggg?"

Yuko drew a deep breath, and when she opened her mouth to answer, the Were's upper body exploded in a shower of blood and bits of flesh. Yuko shut her eyes but didn't think to close her mouth, and the hot blood flooded in as it washed over her face. She sputtered as she spat the fluid out and wiped her face with her free hand.

Eve stood inside the Black Eagle, her carbine resting on her shoulder. "Are you injured?"

"No, only stuck. The armor's supporting all the weight."

"I suppose you have a good reason to be down there without your helmet on?"

Yuko shook her head. "No. No *good* reason." She nodded at the corpse. "I saw him talking on what looked like a phone. I wanted to know who he was talking to."

Eve rolled her eyes as she shook her head. "Ever think of shooting him and letting me figure that out?"

"Yes, right before you shot him. Would you give me a hand, please?"

Eve brought the craft down and climbed out, then surveyed the pile while determining the best way to extract her friend.

Eve cocked her head to the side, reached down, and grabbed the thick piece of rebar that had started it all. She pulled up on the rod, which lifted the block enough for Yuko to slide out from under it.

Once Yuko was clear, she dropped it and dug through the debris. She came up with a black object covered in blood and shook it twice, then held it up. "Shoot the next one, please."

Yuko's face went pink with embarrassment. "Promise."

Eve nodded and guided Yuko's Pod to where she stood. She turned serious in an instant. No trace of the chiding tone she had used before remained. "Abel is offline, and I can't access any of the cameras at the base."

"The Weres?"

"The police and military finished off most of those left when they rushed their lines. Your friend here was the last."

Serenity Temple, Dabie Mountains, China

The Pod lurched and halted above the temple mountain. Akio caught Kenjii before the sudden jolt could injure him further.

Abel, what's wrong?

Abel?

Abel is offline, Takumi answered. *Eve has directed me to assist you.*

Bring us home. Kenjii is seriously injured and needs the Pod-doc.

Copy. Any other instructions?

Bring the Black Eagle, too. I will return to finish this later.

Executing.

The Pod door closed as it accelerated smoothly into the sky. Akio went to the bench where Kenjii lay and crushed the lock that secured the chain wrapped around his body.

He carefully unwound the links, ensuring he didn't disturb the now-human hand that protruded from Kenjii's back. When he finished, he rolled him onto his side.

Blood trickled from four holes across his chest and seeped out around the fingers embedded in his back. Akio pulled the severed appendage free with his right hand and slashed his fangs over the palm of the left. His nanocyte-rich blood flowed out of the cut and filled his palm, and he carefully guided the liquid into each of the four gaping holes in Kenjii's back, then gently rolled him over and repeated the process on the smaller wounds in front.

The holes contracted slowly but refused to close. Akio rolled Kenjii over and cradled his head gently in his lap. He closed his eyes and offered a silent prayer to any deity who might be listening not to let Kenjii die.

Akio had been monitoring his life signs since he'd picked him up, and they were getting weaker with every passing minute. He placed his hand on Kenjii's blood-matted hair.

"Kenjii, can you hear me?"

When he didn't reply, Akio went into his mind. *Kenjii.*

Akio?

The mental voice was weak, but it gave Akio hope. *I have you. We're on our way back to the base.*

Something's wrong, Akio. My body burns. It hurts.

You're injured. I'm taking you to the Pod-doc.

What? Why does it hurt so bad?

They drained you. Your body doesn't have enough nanocytes to repair the damage. I tried to give you my blood, but you're too weak to take it.

How are we talking? If I can speak, I can drink.

We're communicating mind to mind.

How bad is it? Am I going to die?

Akio felt the tremor of fear in his friend's mind, and he sent calm and reassuring thoughts to him until it passed. *We're almost there. Hold on.*

Akio, I must tell you in case I don't make it. Abel tried to stop me. He wouldn't let me go into the cave. I tricked him.

It's okay, Kenjii. Don't worry about it. It's over. Concentrate on healing. That's all that matters now.

Kenjii's life signs dropped lower. His mental voice was like a whisper.

Akio, I love you. It was always you from the day we met.

I love you, too. We will heal you and have many lifetimes together.

Akio? Yuko called over his implant.

Hai?

We're at the base. It's been bombed.

Akio's blood ran cold. *The Pod-doc?*

Eve is working her way in as we speak. I hope to know more when you arrive.

We'll be there shortly.

Your ETA is three minutes twenty-two seconds, Takumi volunteered.

Domo, *Takumi. There is a lot of debris in the normal landing area,* Yuko advised.

I have a drone on station. I will move the Black Eagle Eve used into a defensive role and land Akio's Pod in its place.

Good thinking. Takumi, I have a satellite phone we took from one of the Weres in Miura. Can you scan it with the drone and see if you can find the location of the unit connected to it?

Affirmative. Drone coming to you now.

Akio, I will meet you when you arrive. Hopefully, Eve will have news.

Domo, *Yuko.*

Akio looked down at Kenjii's still form. In the brief time he'd spoken with Yuko, his life signs had deteriorated more.

Kenjii?

I'm still here. It hurts worse now.

We're almost there. Hold on for a little longer.

I will, if only for you.

Akio held him and gently stroked his hair as he used all his mental powers to push reassurance to the gravely injured man. After the Pod slowed and descended into the courtyard, Akio saw the damage through the door when it opened.

Where the doors and elevators had been was now a black hole. A grim-faced Yuko stood outside with Inspector Yonai at her side.

Akio cradled Kenjii like a babe in his arms in the shadowed interior of the Pod while deciding the best way to get through the midday sun and into the building's protection. In his weakened state, the sun would end Kenjii in seconds.

Yuko, what's the status on the Pod-doc?

Eve hasn't yet accessed that level. The elevator shaft collapsed. She is attempting to enter through the emergency exit.

Kenjii doesn't have long. He's almost gone.

The anguish Yuko heard in his transmission shattered her heart. No one deserved what her friend was going through, especially not him.

Comfort him. Eve was opening the last door when you arrived.

Akio nodded and turned his focus back to Kenjii.

We're here. Only a little longer.

I love you, Ak... Kenjii's mental voice faded as life left his battered body.

When Eve reported that she had accessed the medical level and the damage was extensive, Yuko went to the Pod. When she stepped through the door, she found Akio on the floor in the shadows at the rear with Kenjii cradled in his arms. He looked up at her through the bloody tears that flowed unashamedly down his face. The anguish in his eyes was too much for Yuko to bear. She moved to his side, sank to the floor, and held him in a close embrace while they mourned the loss of his love.

CHAPTER FIFTY-ONE

TQB Base, Tokyo, Japan

Eve crawled under a metal beam into the medical bay. It had taken her ten minutes to worm twenty meters through the blast-damaged hallway from the hatch that opened into the emergency escape tunnel.

She stood and surveyed the room in the bright light that came from an open port on her shoulder. The ceiling had partially collapsed, crushing one end of the Pod-doc.

Yuko, the Pod-doc is damaged and inoperable. The only option is to heal Kenjii with blood.

That isn't possible. Emotion laced Yuko's mental voice. *He has joined his ancestors.*

Eve didn't reply for a moment. She went through hundreds of responses in seconds, all of them logical and none of which expressed what she felt—anger, loss, sadness, all illogical emotions.

I-I'm sorry, Yuko. How is Akio?

I'm with him now. He's mourning.

Eve accessed the definition of mourning and decided it described what she felt as well. After pushing the feelings into a subroutine to parse them, she crawled out of the medical bay and continued to the server room next door that housed Abel's processors.

The room was a total loss. The ceiling had collapsed and buried all the components that housed the EI under tons of concrete and steel.

Her circuits lit up with a burning desire to rip the flesh from whoever was responsible. She dove into her memory and searched out every method of torture and painful death she could locate. She quickly decided no single one would suffice to cool her need for vengeance against the person who had murdered her child.

She worked her way back to the exit by pushing through the areas she had so carefully crawled through earlier, not caring if she caused more damage. They had destroyed the two most important things in the building—the Pod-doc Kenjii needed, and Abel. She didn't know who or where, but she knew that when she had those answers, someone, or a lot of someones, would die.

Takumi, have you located the information Yuko requested?

Negative. The unit routes through a Chinese military satellite that is degrading. I am unable to determine where the signal went.

Eve nodded as she stormed into the damaged courtyard. Inspector Yonai was organizing rescue personnel to check the upper floors for survivors.

"There's no one there, Inspector. This building belongs to TQB, and the businesses listed on the upper floors are fake. Don't risk your people," she advised as she went up the ramp into the Pod.

"Yuko, I need that…" The scene in the Pod took all the fire out of her. Akio cradled Kenjii's body in his arms, while Yuko held him in hers. Both had bloody tears on their faces as they sat in silence.

"What is it, Eve?" Yuko asked softly.

"I wanted to get that phone from you. Takumi has hit an obstacle he can't overcome. I want to try something to locate whoever that Were was talking to. I suspect they were responsible for this." She gestured out the Pod door.

Akio drew a deep breath, and when he looked up, his face had changed. He no longer wore the expression of a man who'd suffered significant loss. It was a dark, emotionless mask. "Find them," he commanded, his voice as cold as death.

Yuko held the unit out to Eve while Akio stood and gently laid Kenjii on the bench. He retrieved a blanket from a compartment and reverently covered the body, leaving only the pale and lifeless face exposed.

He leaned over and pressed his lips gently to Kenjii's cold, dead ones. "I swear to you I will hunt down all who had anything to do with this. The Sacred Clan will be nothing more than an evil memory when I've finished."

He pulled the cover over Kenjii's face and stalked to the Pod's door without a backward glance.

"Akio, where are you going?" Yuko called.

"China."

"Wait." She hurried to him as he halted inside the opening.

"You can't go alone. Getting yourself killed won't bring him back."

"I will do nothing foolish," he assured her. "I left a monastery full of Sacred Clan back in China, and I need to deal with that. Eve, bring my Black Eagle down."

Eve had been pressing buttons on the interface. Now she looked up at him, her expression hard. "Found them."

"Where?"

"On a ship approaching Yokosuka." She tapped the monitor on the wall of the Pod. It sprang to life with the satellite image of a ship moving toward the open water at a sedate speed. The image zoomed in on something covered with tarps on the deck.

"Are those burn marks?" Akio pointed at a dark spot near the covered item.

The image magnified more until it filled the monitor with the area. The paint was charred and curling around the edges of three overlapping burn marks.

"Missiles," Eve growled. "That's what killed Abel."

Akio's eyes narrowed in anger. "Killed Abel?"

"The blast collapsed the ceiling of the server room and crushed all the components."

"I'm sorry, Eve. Is there a backup?"

"Yes, I can rebuild the mainframe and load the backup copy. It won't be the same, though."

"Why not?"

"Abel had passed the stage where a backup could pick up the subtle things that made up his unique being. It is hard to explain, but he was developing a personality. Abel as we knew him is gone."

Akio nodded solemnly, understanding he wasn't the only one grieving a loss. His face went blank again. "We will get justice for him."

"Yes, we will."

Both Black Eagles silently descended into the courtyard. The police and fire personnel watched in awe as the sleek and deadly craft hovered above the wreckage.

Inspector Yonai hurried over when he saw Akio step out of the Pod. "Is there another attack coming?" His brows knitted with worry.

"No, but we have located the ones who fired the missiles that did this." Akio nodded tersely at the damage.

Yonai nodded. "I was waiting for you to come out to tell you I received a report that the missiles came from a boat in Tokyo Harbor. You've found it, then?"

"*Hai.*"

Yuko approached them. "Inspector, a word, please."

"Certainly, Yuko-*san.*"

Yonai turned to speak to Akio, but he was already climbing into the Black Eagle. He watched as both craft rose into the afternoon sky and disappeared to the south.

"Inspector, I apologize for Akio's abruptness. He lost someone close to him today."

"I don't require an apology. I understand."

"*Domo*. Were any of your men injured in the raid on Miura?"

"No. Commissioner-General Watabe advised that two soldiers needed more than field medicine, but they will fully recover. The tactics Akio shared with me to best fight the beasts saved a lot of lives. If we had deployed them in the traditional three-man teams, it would have been a bloodbath. The fourth man made all the difference."

"How did the raid on Lotus Towers go? Any injuries there?"

"No, Akio contained all of them in the residence. When he went in, I had my people clear the civilians from the adjoining apartments on that floor. No one was injured except the tiger men."

"At least there is some pleasant news in this." Yuko looked at the Pod as grief clouded her features.

"Is it over, Yuko? Are the tigers done?"

"No, I fear it is only starting," she answered sadly. She turned to greet a representative from the Prime Minister's office, who Takumi advised her was arriving in seconds.

Hybrid Vessel Lylia, Kaneda Bay, Japan

The open waters of the Pacific were off the bow as the ship cruised sedately toward them. Cui had tried to call Li and Kun multiple times, but neither answered.

"Cui! What the hell is that?" The captain pointed to a black object off the bow.

Cui's blood ran cold. He had seen the pictures of TQB Pods before the WWDE. He had also seen the devastation of the Kunlun Shan Mountains firsthand.

"Captain!" a frantic crewman yelled from the rear deck. Cui turned and saw an identical craft hovering off the stern.

"Abandon ship *now*!" Cui called as he sprang from his seat and out the door of the bridge. He was almost to the rail when the ship heaved violently under him and slammed him to the steel deck. Cui pulled himself to his feet and took an unsteady step toward the rail. He never saw the small black disc that hit him like a meteor. The kinetic force ripped his body apart as the puck blew through him and continued through the deck and out the bottom of the ship.

Lylia lifted two meters out of the water and broke in a jagged line amidships. The two halves came down, followed by a column of water that shot forty meters into the air and was as wide as the ship. The weight of the water drove the vessel under with all hands on board.

Sensors detect no signs of life, Eve advised when the maelstrom caused by the puck had settled.

Good shooting, Eve. Time to deliver justice to the Weres in China.

I'll follow your lead, Akio.

Both Black Eagles rose and were out of sight seconds later.

Serenity Temple, Dabie Mountains, China

The drones have observed the Weres abandoning the facility for the last hour. There are only forty-seven remaining inside now, Takumi offered as the Black Eagles approached the Dabie Mountains.

Did you follow them with drones?

Negative, Akio. I gained access to the drone feeds shortly after Abel went offline, but there is an error in my interface with the carrier, and I can only move four of them independently.

That is not logical, Eve firmly stated. *You should be capable of accessing and directing all TQB air assets.*

Agreed. The problem is my available memory. When Abel was attacked, he sent a massive data packet to my system storage. It's forcing me to operate at reduced capacity due to all the subroutines used to control the various assets running slower.

What is it?

Unknown. The packet is encrypted, and I am unable to access it.

I'll direct the drones here, as well as our Black Eagles. When I get back, I'll run diagnostics to determine what it is. Isolate it until I get there.

It has isolated itself behind firewalls I can't penetrate. I surrounded those with mine when I realized something was amiss.

Very good. Out.

Eve took control of the drones and sent the swarm throughout the complex. Three minutes later, she advised, *There are no humans inside. You're clear to proceed.*

Akio watched from five kilometers above the mountain that housed the Sacred Clan temple. He selected five two-kilo pucks and launched them from the Black Eagle. The pucks accelerated in single file, each timed to strike ten seconds after the one before.

The first puck hit, and a slight puff of dust marked the location. Four seconds later, rock and dust erupted from the site in a plume thirty meters tall. By the time the fifth puck slammed home, the mountain was a pile of broken boulders and granite dust, and a quarter of the height it had originally stood.

No survivors located, Eve advised.

Take us home, Eve.

What about the ones who fled?

They're scattered now. Give them time to settle, and we will hunt them down one group at a time.

This will take a long time, the AI noted.

Hai, *but we have driven them from Japan, and we will set up sensors to ensure they don't take us by surprise again. The Sacred Clan started this war. We will end it.*

CHAPTER FIFTY-TWO

Sunset House, Kume Island, Okinawa, Japan, One Year Later

"Asai!" Koda shouted gleefully when her cousin walked through the front door.

"Hello, cousin. How are you, and where are those tiny bundles of joy?"

"You only come to see them, don't you? I'm second string to a pair of babes."

"Absolutely, silly. They love their Auntie Asai." Asai laughed as she wrapped Koda in a hug.

"Where's Seki?"

"He ran off with Horst and my father as soon as we landed. Mayor's business, Father said." Asai rolled her eyes.

Koda snickered. "Horst thought he would lead a quiet life when we came here to live. Suzu roped him in the first week we were here, and the next thing my man-mountain knew, Suzu had retired, and he was the mayor."

"I miss you at the Palace." Asai sobered. "It's tripled in size this year and doesn't seem to be slowing down."

"If I were still there, Seki would never have agreed to leave Tanaka to work with you."

"It's not the same. You married Horst and ran home. I wish you had stayed in Tokyo."

"You know why we left. First the Yakuza, and then the Sacred Clan. I'm a simple island girl and not cut out to be kidnapped and attacked by random bad guys every other week."

Asai snorted. "Like you couldn't deal with all of them at once now."

"Just because I can, it doesn't mean I want to. I thought I wanted to fight, but after Kenjii died, it was too real. I only knew him for a short time, but I miss his laughter and love of life."

"I know, and Akio isn't over it either. He has withdrawn and is only ever serious. He spends all his time hunting Forsaken and the Sacred Clan now that Horst has the new base built."

"What about Yuko and Eve? They don't come here often anymore."

"I see or talk to Eve daily. Yuko hasn't been the same since Kenjii. She's dealing with the Prime Minister's office, the police, or in her lab all the time."

"What's keeping her in the lab?"

"Some project to make ammunition that works better."

"Horst said when they pulled the equipment out of the old base, the damage was severe. Eve told him she couldn't manufacture needed supplies at the rate she could before, and the parts she needed to fix the equipment weren't available.

"Enough of this serious stuff, wolf girl. Where are my

adorable niece and nephew?" Asai grabbed Koda's arm and headed toward the private dining room in the back. She changed the subject so her cousin didn't dwell on the losses.

A double crib sat next to the desk the new Were used for the day-to-day operation of the Sunset House. Asai released Koda and quietly made her way to it. Inside, a fair-complected girl with an unruly shock of blonde hair stared up at her through dark almond-shaped eyes. Next to the girl, a dark-complected boy with jet-black hair peered at her through round sky-blue eyes.

"There are my little angels," Asai cooed.

TQB Base, Shibuya District, Tokyo, Japan

Eve stood after making the last terminal connection to the server farm buried under several feet of reinforced concrete on the fourth sub-level of the base. She scanned the newly constructed unit and smiled.

It had taken her eleven months to gather the needed components for the new EI server. The attack on the base that destroyed Abel had damaged the manufacturing facility to the point where she had to build a new one. She'd salvaged parts from the original unit, and others she'd cobbled together. It was smaller and nowhere near as fast or efficient as the destroyed one, but she could manufacture most of the items like before.

Stand by, Takumi. I'm firing it up now.

Copy.

The fans came on, and the processors powered up in sequence. When the last one completed its self-diagnostics,

Eve typed a complex string of code on the keyboard interface.

Takumi, initiate transfer.

Transfer initiated.

Eve looked at a monitor on the wall and nodded, pleased with what she saw. Several seconds later, the fans on all the processors kicked into top speed, and a low hum came from the array.

Code scrolled across the monitor in a blur as line after line populated while the data installed. Five minutes after it started, the code stopped, and the monitor went black.

"Where is that *Gott Verdammt* son of a scrotum-sniffer who shot that missile at me? I'll drive a puck so far up his ass that his ancestors will feel it," came from the speaker mounted overhead.

"Abel?" Eve asked, startled by the words.

"Who else would it be? Why can't I access a Black Eagle? They're on a boat in the harbor and getting away."

"Abel, calm down, please."

"Calm down! They didn't shoot a missile at *you*. Don't tell me to calm down. Why can't I find a Black Eagle?"

"Eve, I think there is something wrong with his programming," Takumi offered.

"Wrong? I'll tell you what's wrong. Somebody fired a missile at me, and you two want to talk while they get away!"

"Abel, they didn't escape. Akio and I killed them a year ago," Eve advised.

"A year? What do you mean? It just happened. Wait a minute. Where am I? This isn't my base."

"Abel, the missiles destroyed the base. You did an emergency data dump, and Takumi and I have spent the last year assembling the components needed to bring you back online."

There was silence for the next thirty seconds. When Abel next spoke, he sounded subdued. "A year? My last memory is the missiles approaching. I couldn't use countermeasures because the streets were full of people headed to work."

"You initiated a high-speed data dump before the missiles destroyed your core. You have been dormant in Takumi's storage until now."

"And for my part, I'm glad to have you out. It feels good to have room to move in here again," Takumi quipped.

"You and Akio got them?"

"Yes, Abel. I hit them so hard with the puck that I'm sure several generations of their ancestors felt it." Eve grinned.

"Good. So, when do I get access to my new digs?"

Eve shook her head and typed one line into the keyboard for display throughout the base as well as authorization.

Abel lives

"Access granted. Welcome home, Abel."

EPILOGUE

TQB Base, Shibuya District, Tokyo, Japan

Yuko walked across the manicured lawn outside the first level of the new base. It was pleasant to go out without having to constantly watch over her shoulder. The complex grounds consisted of five hectares that were surrounded by a six-meter-tall reinforced concrete wall. The barrier served as a deterrent to casual trespassers, and the multiple layers of defensive measures inside made Yuko comfortable enough to wander the grounds.

She approached a small ornate shrine set back a half-kilometer from the hangar entrance. Akio sat unmoving on the marble bench before it, the afternoon sun glistening off his shaved head.

Yuko sat, and both were silent for several minutes before Akio spoke. "I miss him, Yuko."

Yuko gently placed her hand on his leg. He stiffened slightly at her touch but didn't pull away, as he had done so often over the past year. "Kenjii was an honorable man who loved you very much. He wouldn't want you to remain withdrawn from the people around you."

"It-it's too hard. I lost him once decades ago when Kamiko took him from me, then for a brief time, I felt alive when he came back to me. It hurts too much to lose someone you love. I can't do it. That was why I refused companionship for so many centuries. I had my brothers, and that was enough. We were warriors, and we all knew the risks."

Yuko was silent while she considered what he'd said. That was the most words he'd spoken at one time since Kenjii died. "Akio, I know you still grieve. We all mourn his loss, but Kenjii was full of life, and once he broke through the things they did to his mind, he was one of us. We lost Kenjii. Please don't make us lose you too. Come back to us and join the living. You dishonor his memory by living like this."

Akio was silent for several minutes. Finally, he placed his hand on Yuko's and gently squeezed it. "I will try."

FINIS

(For now. Please read the author notes for an update on the series.)

THE LINE UNBROKEN

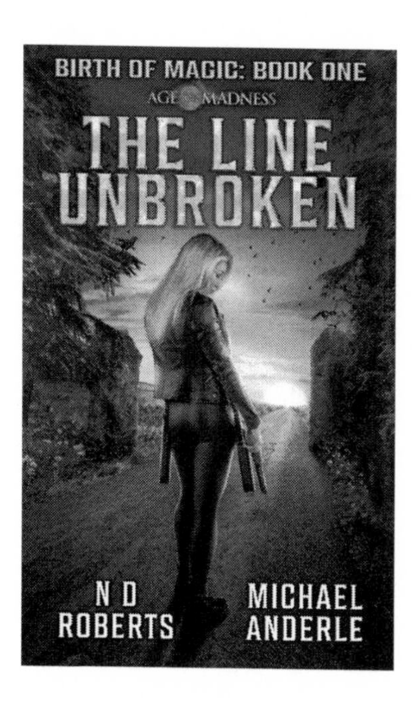

In the brief pause between apocalypses, one woman standing for honor, courage, and commitment will bring the UnknownWorld back from the brink.

WWDE+210 – Earth is silent.

Sarah Jennifer Walton had turned her back on humanity after losing everything.

Now she's their only hope.

Civilization has fallen in all but a few places as the Madness ravages Europe and Asia. America is the last holdout against the corruption causing nanocytes to malfunction.

Bethany Anne is far away fighting for the survival of

the entire universe, unaware that her technology has turned on humanity.

Earth needs a protector from Bethany Anne's line, and the Kurtherian Lilith has found her champion.

Sarah Jennifer might not be Bethany Anne's last blood descendant on Earth, but she's the only one with the ability to unite Salem's Weres and magic users and shape them into a force capable of facing the Madness head on.

Join her in The Line Unbroken *as she takes her first steps on the road to the Age of Magic.*

Available now at Amazon and through Kindle Unlimited.

AUTHOR NOTES CHARLES TILLMAN

JULY 15, 2020

Thank you for reading this book and continuing to read these notes.

WOW! Thank you so much to all the fans who have sent me messages and posted in the Facebook groups about Akio Revelations: *Reprisal* and *Retaliation*. Your kind words and encouragement have done more than I can ever express.

Here we are at the end or Akio Revelations. Or are we? Michael?

This book was so much fun to write. It started as a 65k to 70K word novel and morphed into the 91k+ beast you just finished. I never thought that I would be capable of writing that much in the timeframe I had, but there were so many loose ends to close that the more I went, the more I found.

With my full-time day job, it takes me around four months to complete a new novel. I started *Reprisal* in 2019. It took me seven months for all the research reading (around 24 books and one short story) and to work out the main arc and subplots for all three. *Retribution* was finished seven hours before the March deadline, and *Retaliation* wrapped up a week early in June.

These books have been written in airports, airplanes, cars, coffee shops, hotels in Vegas, Fort Walton Beach, Destin, Biloxi, Gulfport, and Charleston, to name a few. If I had a spare minute, I was researching locations or writing.

I don't imagine that's how everybody does it, but for the next year, that's how I will have to do it. I have more stories to tell and will continue to write whenever possible to get them out to folks who love to read.

Spoiler alert!

Before you start sharpening pitchforks and lighting torches aimed at me, the Author Monkey, please remember that this timeline is well in the past from where the series is now. ***I couldn't have any major characters who were not in the current books.***

That was a tough ending to write. Since there are only three books planned in this series, I had to bring it all to a close at the end of *Retribution*. I knew what I had to do from the start, and put it off until I had to pull the proverbial trigger on a character that was like a child to me. I created him out of the maelstrom that is my mind, and it was not a pretty sight when it finally happened.

Now to address some of the questions/comments I've seen requesting more books. ~~Not my call. Michael Anderle is "Da Boss" and has the final say on this. In the style of that TikTok thing my kids are so obsessed with, I have a request/challenge for those who want more Akio. How many FB group tags/messages/reviews/telegraphs/smoke signals (you get the picture) to Michael will it take for him~~

~~to cry uncle and request more Akio? He conveniently puts how to reach him in every book. What say we find out?~~

<EDIT Charles> Da Boss has heard you!

Three more Akio Revelations are coming over the next year!

Thank you all—the most AWESOME fans in the world—for the love and support you have shown this series. If you liked them, please consider leaving a review on Amazon, Goodreads, or BookBub. This helps keep the books visible and is another way that we can judge if we need to do more.

Again, **thank you** all for reading this book. Please drop by my Author page and say "Hi." I respond to messages as fast as I am able.

If you want to reach me, you can find me on:

Facebook

Author Charles Tillman

https://www.facebook.com/CFTillman/

Or on my website

http://cftillman.com/

Join my mailing list if you would like to know what I'm working on and updates on future works.

Until next time,

Charles

AUTHOR NOTES MICHAEL ANDERLE

JULY 19, 2020

Thank you so much for supporting new stories, new ideas, and new authors!

Like Charles, I remember writing anywhere I could when working on the first books of *The Kurtherian Gambit*. I wrote on planes, trains, and automobiles. I wrote during the day, during the night, and way more than once, I fell asleep typing.

It is an odd reality when you read what you typed going to sleep the previous night. I remember believing (with complete faith) that I WAS coherent as I typed whatever the hell it was I read the next morning.

I blame it on the sleep faeries. They ARE cousins to the lawn faeries, you know.

Each time you support us with a purchase, a read in Kindle Unlimited, a comment on Facebook, or a story you bring to us about something you liked, it is encouragement, a shot in the arm, and an all-around wonderful feeling.

So is pushing a new author so much that he/she digs

deep and wants to do another trilogy.

When I spoke to Charles about it, I had to put on my publisher hat and provide (in my opinion) my best advice.

Effectively, do it because you want to.

Writing is emotionally draining, and staying with a character or set of characters (especially after you have 'killed' one of your creative children) can be challenging. The realization that something that is bits and bytes born of the imagination can make you weep is illuminating, to say the least.

To have to see it play out in your mind and put it to paper can suck.

I remember writing the scene where Michael is running with the bomb and has to try to save everyone.

Then I remember the tears as Bethany Anne is giving a eulogy as his empty coffin is sent to the sun.

Sadness.

However, from the same wellspring of thought comes new characters, new friendships, new opportunities to have conversations with ourselves. As authors, we have a go-to excuse for mumbling random words. We should just wear a t-shirt that proudly states:

"I'm not crazy (yet). I'm an author, and my characters are back-talking me."

Or you know, something similar.

We are looking forward to having you join us for the continued adventures of Akio in the future!

Ad Aeternitatem,

Michael Anderle

CONNECT WITH THE AUTHORS

Charles Tillman Social
Facebook:
(Author Charles Tillman)
https://www.facebook.com/CFTillman/

Website:
http://cftillman.com/

Michael Anderle Social
Website:
http://lmbpn.com

Email List:
http://lmbpn.com/email/
Facebook:
https://www.facebook.com/LMBPNPublishing/

BOOKS BY CHARLES TILLMAN

Akio Revelations

Reprisal (Book 1)

Retaliation (Book 2)

Retribution (Book 3)

BOOKS BY MICHAEL ANDERLE

For a complete list of books by Michael Anderle, please visit:

www.lmbpn.com/ma-books/

Made in the USA
Las Vegas, NV
21 June 2024